SPARE HEIR

THE ROCHESTERS

RACHEL HENKE

RED BALLOON PRESS

This novel is dedicated to those who fear they are not enough.

CHAPTER 1

Sebastian

I'm at my London hotel office in Mayfair, ready for an early morning meeting. My eyes drift to the silver-framed photographs on my desk. Daisy, my five-year-old daughter, takes pride of place, and I feel my heart expand as I gaze at her mischievous grin. She's the light of my life and keeps me going when life throws me curveballs.

When my ex-wife left, the collapse of our marriage stunned me. I just presumed we'd be together forever, and for some reason, I didn't see the end coming. I didn't know she'd been busy falling out of love with me whilst I was absorbed in the workings of the hotel division of Rochesters & Co.

I blamed myself for not being more attentive to her and not noticing what was going on at home. Daisy coming into our lives when we hadn't planned on a child so early in our marriage was the best thing that ever happened to me. But Madeleine found motherhood stressful and restrictive.

She adores Daisy, but she's not keen on the daily demands of parenthood. She prefers the glitz and glamour of society life, which I suppose was part of the initial attraction of marrying into the Rochesters. I think she imagined married life with me would be far more glamorous than it is when you pull back the curtain.

I work hard and take the family legacy seriously. Grandfather has seen to that. If I or any of my siblings step out of line and it comes to his attention, we soon receive a warning to correct the error of our ways.

I prefer to stay behind the scenes and out of the spotlight whenever possible, but I'm the first to admit I do let myself get consumed by the business. I'm no different from the rest of the family in that respect. We were raised to be competitive and to strive for excellence whilst developing the Rochester dynasty.

There's no doubt we are privileged to be born into an ultra-high-net-worth family with a global business empire. We didn't have to build it ourselves from the ground up like Grandfather, but the expectations that come with the privilege can be a heavy weight on our inexperienced shoulders.

Understanding why things happen and how they unfold is easier when you look back, but when you're in the thick of it, you don't always see what's coming.

At least, I don't…

The car weaves slowly through the congested London roads until we reach the brow of Richmond Hill. I raise my head and catch a glimpse of the view of the sparkling Thames, nestled in the patchwork web of meadows. The late afternoon sun dances across the hedgerows. Spring is merging into summer, and I let out a contented sigh and lean back and stretch. It's good to be home in daylight.

In all my travels, I've not found anywhere to beat British summertime when the sky is a glorious azure blue and the countryside glows in shades of lush green. It's so beautiful, it's difficult to believe it's real life and not an oil painting. The famous artist, Turner, painted the panoramic Richmond scene of the Thames, and it's obvious why. It's the only English landscape view to be protected by an Act of Parliament, and it never disappoints.

We take a sharp turn and within a few minutes; the car pulls up in front of the house, and I thank my driver and tell him I'll see him in the morning. I left the office earlier than usual. The new nanny started work today and although I trust my assistant to have hired the best, I want to meet her as soon as possible, and check my daughter is happy with the new arrangement.

I can just as easily tie up loose ends from the office whilst sitting in the garden. Summer or not, I don't take the sunshine for granted. British weather is notoriously unpredictable, and it might rain tomorrow, and the blue sky will be washed away and replaced by a dull grey, as though it never was.

'Daddy,' shouts Daisy, barrelling towards me as soon as the door clicks shut. I stride into the hall and sweep her up into my arms, holding her small wiry body high in the air before kissing her and gently lowering her back down to the marble floor. 'Daddy, Nathalie, the new nanny is here,' she exclaims. 'We've been swimming, and it was amazing. She's amazzzing.'

Amazing is her current favourite word. She fixes her big

brown eyes on me. I know immediately I'm about to be suckered into something. 'Please, please, will you come out to the pool and swim with me?'

Daisy's wearing a damp robe and her hair is messy and tangled from swimming.

'Don't you want to dry off and warm up a bit?' I ask. 'And where is Nathalie, by the way? I want to meet her.'

A tall, stunning blonde wearing only a wet swimming costume appears near the bi-fold doors that lead into the garden, and my breath snags. I didn't expect to find a sexy Bond girl emerging from my swimming pool when I got home. She is most definitely not the nanny I envisaged.

Isn't it an unwritten law that nannies are elderly frumpy figures?

I've obviously made a stupid assumption. I didn't give my assistant any age criteria for the candidate, which is only fair, but presumed she'd be much older and now I feel like a fool.

She couldn't look more different from our previous nanny, and I'm awestruck. I just stare at her and gulp as I search for something to say.

The nanny shifts from one tanned bare foot to the other and clears her throat. 'Good afternoon, Mr Rochester. I hope it's okay we went for a swim, right away. Your assistant said you wouldn't be back until this evening. It's such a beautiful day and Daisy wanted to use the pool—'

Her words tail off and I can tell she's embarrassed by my unexpected arrival and meeting me when she's wearing just her costume.

Smiling and trying to put her at ease, I say, 'I'm sorry to appear out of the blue like this on your first day. I should have called and let you know I was on my way.'

The new nanny smiles, and it lights up her face. Something strange is going on in my chest. There's an unsettling flutter that I haven't felt in a long, long time.

I stretch out my hand towards her. 'As you can probably guess, I'm Sebastian Rochester, Daisy's dad.'

We shake hands. 'I'm Nathalie,' she says, with a trace of an alluring French accent. Her cool fingers feel delicate in my warm hand.

'Thank you so much for starting at such short notice. I'd hoped to interview you myself, but my schedule's been a little crazy.'

'Good to meet you. Sorry about this,' she says, signalling to her wet swimming costume.

I want to say: *Oh, don't be sorry. You're the most gorgeous sight I've ever seen,* but I bite my tongue. That would be a wholly inappropriate way to greet the new nanny, and so instead I say, 'No problem at all. Daisy adores swimming, which is one reason we chose this house. Thank you for being such a good sport and swimming with her on your first day.'

She's obviously cold—her nipples are standing to attention and poking against the wet fabric, which has an instant effect on me. I feel myself harden. Now it's my turn to shift on the spot.

In a breathy voice, she asks if it's okay to go and get changed quickly.

I nod and tell her, of course it is, and that we want her to feel at home.

'Can I go with you?' Daisy beseeches her.

I'd go with her like a shot if she invited me...

But I command my cock to calm the fuck down. I resume my role as sensible single dad and tell Daisy to give Nathalie a chance to settle in, and I want to hear all about her day at school. Sufficiently distracted, Daisy reaches for my hand and swings on my arm, so I pick her up and she giggles when I smother her face in kisses.

Nathalie throws me a shy smile and thanks me before she darts across the room, out the door, and up the stairs.

I breathe deeply several times, desperately trying to calm my wildly beating heart and act normal for Daisy.

The knock-out nanny is another twist I didn't see coming...

CHAPTER 2

Sebastian

Daisy and I wander outside to the large rambling garden, and I drop into a poolside chair while Daisy dangles her feet in the pool and fills me in on random events of her day.

I brace myself before the irresistible nanny returns. I don't know why I'm having such an intense reaction to her, but I can't deny it.

'We're breaking up for summer holidays soon, and I can't wait,' Daisy chatters. 'I'm going to ask Nathalie if we can swim *every* day in the holidays.'

'I hope Nathalie enjoys swimming as much as you or she's in for a long, old summer,' I tease.

'Nathalie is lovvvvvely, Daddy. And she said her name is spelt with an h, which is the French way. She likes swimming a lot more than my old nanny. Thank you for finding her.'

Her face glows and seeing her so overjoyed makes my

heart twist, and I'm grateful to my assistant for hiring someone young and energetic. On reflection, Nathalie is probably exactly what Daisy needs. My ex-wife, Maddy, is so often unavailable, our daughter misses out on having her mother in her life in any dependable pattern.

I'm relieved Daisy and Nathalie have hit it off immediately. It's only the first day, but one of the most difficult things about parenting, especially as a single parent without a partner to share the daily load, is trusting a stranger with your child. I'm used to having a small staff at home, but we've never had a live-in nanny for Daisy before, so I was unsure if it was the right decision.

Of course, we have lots of live-in staff at Greystone Manor, the Rochester family home, so it's not an unfamiliar concept to me, but it's been some years since I moved to London, and I hire live-out staff whenever possible to protect our privacy.

My mind wanders back to knock-out Nathalie, and I try to remember what my assistant said about her. I recall she is from Paris and has a degree in childcare. I can't remember anything else, and I kick myself. Despite the breathy French accent, her English is almost perfect, which intrigues me further.

Daisy's still chatting a mile a minute when Nathalie reappears. This time, much to my disappointment—although after my reaction to her I know I should be relieved—she's no longer wearing her wet swimwear but looks beautiful in a summer dress.

If I'd met Nathalie at the interview stage, I might have thought twice about hiring her. I'm a red-blooded male, when all is said and done, and she is a feast to the eyes. It's never going to be a sensible idea to find yourself lusting after your daughter's nanny, so I have a stern word with myself and try to get a grip.

She is strictly off-limits, Rochester. No matter how fucking gorgeous she is.

That trace of a sultry French accent is so damn sexy. It makes my blood tingle, and I feel lightheaded, but I pull myself together and have no problem projecting a confident exterior under pressure. I'm a Rochester, after all.

'Come and join us, Nathalie. I'll ask Mrs Johnson to bring us tea.'

'May I have apple juice?' Daisy asks.

Nathalie crosses her long legs as she settles in a chair nearby. I ask what brings her to London from Paris, desperate to get my mind on safer topics.

'My mother was a huge fan of all things English,' she says, flicking her tawny blonde hair out of her face. 'I've wanted to visit since I was a kid, but never had a chance.'

Willing her to say more, I search her cornflower blue eyes. I yearn to know all about her, but don't want to interrogate her. She might think me rude and invasive.

She returns my gaze but falls silent.

She's hot as hell without trying to be. I'm aroused by her proximity and reposition myself in my chair. The image of her stiff nips protruding through the wet fabric consumes my mind. It wasn't a particularly revealing costume, but I couldn't fail to notice her long shapely legs and tiny waist. And if that's not enough to drive me wild, she has an air of vulnerability and innocence that makes me long to touch her.

Daisy has wandered further into the garden and is rocking gently on her swing.

My eyes seek Nathalie's again, and I hope she doesn't see how she's affecting me. She's like a magnet and I can't stop looking at her. I get the sense she has no clue how attractive she is, and that she has thrown me completely off-guard.

We talk, and she tells me about her last nanny job in Paris

and soon I forget all about the loose ends I was supposed to tie up from work. The golden sun hangs low in the pink sky, and when the conversation reaches a natural pause, I rise and call Daisy. 'It's time to get ready for bed, sweetie.'

'Please, Daddy, may I stay up late for dinner with you and Nathalie?'

I roll my eyes in mock despair, and Nathalie smiles indulgently.

'I gave Daisy an early dinner in accordance with the instructions your assistant left.'

'Thank you. This little girl always likes to try and stay up late for a second dinner,' I say, tickling Daisy, who giggles hysterically and gasps as she begs me to stop. 'I'm afraid it's time for bed,' I say, falling far short of being stern, but doing my best to set a good example for Nathalie. I don't want her to think I'm a complete pushover, although I'm not far off it where Daisy's concerned. 'You've got school tomorrow. Let's take you up.'

Daisy moans and groans. Nathalie rises as if to accompany her, but I signal for her to stay seated. I like to put Daisy to bed when I'm home. 'It's your first day. Help yourself to a drink and enjoy this lovely evening.'

Once Daisy is tucked up in bed after story time, I come back down and see dinner is about to be served. It's usually just me if Daisy hasn't managed to wrangle me into allowing her to stay up for a late supper, but I invite Nathalie to join me.

It's the least I can do to make her feel at home on her first day...

That's what I tell myself, anyway.

I'm pouring a glass of wine and looking forward to resuming our conversation when I glimpse her in the hallway, slipping a blue denim jacket over her dress.

'I thought you might want to join me for dinner,' I call out.

She pokes her head into the room and says, 'How kind of you, Mr Rochester. I would love to another time, but I've already arranged to meet a friend this evening. I hope it's okay. I checked with your assistant, and she said it shouldn't be a problem.'

A wave of disappointment slithers through me as I say that, of course, it's fine, and she slips out the door. A car engine roars to life and the wheels crunch on the driveway.

I settle down for a solo dinner. I rarely mind eating alone, and even relish the solitude after a busy day at the hotel, but today I'm curiously bereft, and my chest feels hollow after the door closes behind her.

What the hell is going on with me? I don't think I've ever been so instantly affected by any woman in this way. And certainly not a member of staff.

After the heartache of my marriage fiasco, followed by the divorce, I've played it ultra-safe and thought I was immune to this kind of all-consuming attraction.

Throughout the meal, I wonder who she's having dinner with. Is she on a date? She said she only just arrived in London. Against my better judgement, I find myself longing with every fibre of my being that she's single.

This is the last thing I expected when I hired a new nanny, and I chastise myself for allowing my romantic nature to tempt me into such dangerous waters. My heart beats erratically as I think about Nathalie with an h sleeping in my house for an entire year.

One thing is certain. This is going to be tricky...

CHAPTER 3

Nathalie

I didn't expect my new boss to be so impossibly handsome. In truth, I didn't pay that much attention to the details about him when I took the job. I knew he was divorced and is a member of the wealthy Rochester family. There's a Rochester hotel in Paris, so I'm familiar with the name.

When considering the position, I paid more attention to what I saw as the most important criteria. Daisy sounded like a sweetheart and at five years old, she is an age I adore. Their house is in Richmond upon Thames, which is a town I discovered in my research. It was described as an affluent area in South West London and one of the top places to live, offering the best of town and country. And the nanny gets a self-contained suite at the top of the house, which sounded perfect.

Nice homes come with the job, so I've grown accustomed

to a higher standard of living than I had growing up in a poky two-bedroom apartment in the suburbs of Paris. Having some privacy is important to me. So far, the new job ticked all the boxes.

Then, I was approved for a volunteering role at an underprivileged children's centre just a few miles away, and it all fell into place, so when Mr Rochester's assistant offered me the position, I snapped it up without another thought.

But now my dreamy billionaire boss is standing staring at me and I'm wearing only my wet swimming costume and feeling exposed and unprofessional. If there is a more embarrassing way to meet your new boss, I can't think what it might be.

Heat rushes to my face. I don't look down, but I feel my nipples thrusting against the thin fabric of my costume and I want the ground to gobble me up. There's no way he won't notice.

I think he's undressing me with his eyes, but after his gaze skims over me, he looks up and behaves like the perfect gentleman. It might be appreciation I glimpse in his expression, but I can't be sure.

He seems like a decent guy, and I release a measured sigh of relief. Committing to a live in position in a house with a family you've never met is nerve-wracking, even if the house is big, and they are out a lot. Kids are easy for me, but adults typically present an unpredictable set of thorny challenges.

I hadn't bargained on sharing a house with this single dad hottie. I realise now I presumed he'd be a staid business type with spectacles and thinning hair like the other fathers I've worked for. The agency vets their clients thoroughly, so I didn't even think to look him up.

I can't help noticing his blue-grey eyes and lush dark lashes, and I have to stop myself gawping at him. He's as beautiful as a Parisian male model. His pale blue shirt skims his broad shoulders and tapers down neatly into the slim waist of his immaculately tailored trousers. He picks up Daisy and smothers her face in kisses, making her giggle and snort.

My heart glows at the sight of him with his daughter. They obviously have a wonderful relationship, which is rarer than one might think. Nothing pleases me more than seeing happy children. That's why I do this job. There are too many neglected, sad kids in this world, and I want to do my bit to make it better in my own small way. First impressions tell me Daisy isn't one of them.

I chastise myself for not going to get a towel after emerging from the heated outdoor pool instead of parading around the garden half-naked in my costume for our first meeting. It's a baking hot day and not the weather I'd been warned to expect in London. The house is so comfortable that I made myself at home without giving it much thought. The assistant said Mr Rochester wouldn't be back until early evening, so I was making the most of the pool with Daisy.

As soon as I can, I excuse myself and rush upstairs into the rain shower in my ensuite bathroom to cool down. And it's not just the temperature of the sunshine that's got me hot and bothered.

I hope I haven't blown it. Mr Rochester seemed pretty easy going and was so friendly that I think it'll be okay, but I feel on edge. I debate changing into a different outfit for dinner and then decide to slip back into my pretty summer dress. I brush my hair and apply a touch of make-up. All the while, my mind tangles with thoughts of my new boss—thoughts I know I shouldn't be entertaining.

My eyes sparkle in the mirror, and I look a little feverish. I tell myself I'm just nervous and excited to have a new job and to be meeting my best friend for dinner. My heart pitter patters in time with my feet as I return downstairs and go in search of Daisy and her handsome daddy. I smile at the housekeeper before stepping out into the garden and taking another deep breath to steady my nerves.

What have I got myself into?

I needn't have worried because Sebastian—as he asks me to call him—puts me at ease immediately.

'Please make yourself at home. If there's anything you need, just ask Mrs Johnson, our wonderful housekeeper, and she'll be happy to arrange it. Or you can ask Daisy. She doesn't miss a trick, and knows where everything is, don't you Daisy chain?'

Daisy crinkles up her adorable, freckled nose and smiles to reveal gaps where her baby teeth have fallen out. She reaches for my hand and squeezes it. 'Don't worry, Nathalie,' she says solemnly. 'I will show you where everything is.'

Sebastian winks at me. 'You're in expert hands,' he says, and I feel a blush creeping up my cheeks and struggle to banish it before he notices. Even at twenty-eight, I still blush sometimes, and I hate that about myself.

When I was a teenager, I blushed like a tomato, but it doesn't get the better of me as often now.

My mother died when I was twelve, and my father fell apart. He died a few years later and my sister and I had to go into foster care. Some say he died of alcoholism, but my theory is he died of a broken heart. So, it's been just me and my sister clinging to each other since then.

Sabine has a lovely long-term boyfriend, and a great new job she's thrilled about. Now she's all grown up and settled, I finally gave myself permission to follow my dreams. I feel like it's the right time to have an adventure of my own after years of being the responsible older sister.

Our mother was an English teacher before she got sick, and she used to love telling us stories in English. She was a passionate anglophile and spent time in England before she married. My memories of her have faded and are blurred around the edges, but I can still see her sitting on the edge of our bed lulling me and Sabine to sleep with her fascinating tales. I know it would please my mother that I've made it to London.

But I'm going to have to be careful around my new boss if I'm to make it through a year of living with him.

CHAPTER 4

Nathalie

I scan the faces in the restaurant, searching for my best friend. She waves and stands up as I walk towards her. We kiss and hug and then kiss again before I sit down opposite her at the small table.

'You're glowing,' Juliette says, beaming at me.

'As are you! You look exactly the same,' I say.

'And there was me thinking I look like a glamorous Parisian in London,' she says, laughing.

'And you do. You look *très chic, ma chérie*,' I say. 'Just as beautiful as always.'

I decline the offer of a glass of wine from the bottle on the table. 'I hired a car for a few days so I can explore the area a bit.'

'That's brave of you,' she says, taking a sip of wine. 'You won't need a car here,' she declares in a dramatic whisper.

'The traffic in London is an absolute nightmare—even worse than Paris—if that's possible.'

'Well, that might be just as well because so far I'm finding driving on the opposite side of the road quite tricky.'

Juliette touches my arm and gushes, 'I couldn't believe it when you told me you're coming to London for a whole year. You can pop on the train and come to town to hang out whenever we're free. We'll be able to see so much of each other. Remember when we were at university, we used to fantasise about living here?'

I smile, relishing her enthusiasm. 'That's so cool. I don't know how packed my schedule will be yet, though. I won't know until I settle in and see how much the father is away and I need to be available. Honestly, I may not have much free time.'

She rolls her eyes and tears a corner of bread violently from a chunky roll in the basket. 'Don't let these people take advantage of you. Everyone is entitled to at least one day off a week, you know. Anyway, tell me all about the new job.'

'Well, the father is a single dad of an adorable little girl called Daisy, and he's the CEO of a big company, so his schedule could be quite demanding. Remember the Rochester Hotel in the centre of Paris?'

She nods and her eyes widen when I tell her it belongs to his family and that as far as I can make out, he's the CEO of the hotel chain.

I chew my lip as I consider whether to tell her how gorgeous Sebastian is and about my nipple faux pas. 'I only just arrived here this morning, so I don't know much about him.' I decide to keep it to myself for now and feel a tingle in my chest at the knowledge we'll be living in the same house for the next year.

But she knows me too well. 'Come on. What are you

keeping from me? I can tell you've got something up your sleeve.'

I shake my head and laugh. 'No, no. Nothing at all,' I say. 'Just that my new boss isn't quite what I expected, that's all.'

She leans forward conspiratorially, clutching the menu in both hands. 'I knew it! Tell me more.'

The server arrives and rescues me from having to explain how blown away I was by my new boss. We order spaghetti and chat about all sorts over dinner. It's like old times in Paris when we were at university. I carefully steer the conversation away from Sebastian and to what's going on with Juliette. She tells me she's loving life in London and her job as a translator is going well.

I've been in a whirlwind since arriving in London, and hearing what's new with her is refreshing and a welcome respite.

'The mother is not in the picture, then?' She asks suddenly in between mouthfuls of creamy mushroom spaghetti.

I might have guessed she wouldn't let it go. She's like a dog with a bone when she wants to know something.

After eating my last forkful of spaghetti, I dab my mouth with a napkin. 'That was quite good,' I say, hoping to divert her again, but she's not letting me off the hook so easily.

'Come on, don't change the subject,' she says.

I laugh. 'I'm not sure how much the mother sees their daughter, but I got the impression from the interview that it might not be often. The little girl lives with her father, anyway. That's why they hired me as a live-in nanny. I'm their first one.'

'Hmm. And what about this CEO boss? What did you mean he isn't what you expected?' She quizzes me and I falter—never one to hide my innermost thoughts and feelings well.

I look downwards and focus on moving our plates to distract her from how flustered she's making me with her questions.

'You're blushing! Oh my God, he is a hottie, isn't he? I knew it when you were all coy about him earlier.'

I shake my head but can't help smiling at her teasing. She's always had a knack for making me laugh when I get too serious. We met in our first year at university and we've been besties ever since. When she moved to London for work a few years ago, I missed her terribly and it seemed like a perfect opportunity to find a position in London while she's here. I won't feel totally alone with her just a train journey away.

'He's a good-looking guy,' I say. 'I promise I'll tell you more when I've got to know him better. We only met for a moment. I spent time with the daughter, though, and she's an absolute sweetheart.'

Once more, I steer the conversation away from how hot my new boss is. It feels like a dangerous secret I should guard closely, and I don't want to talk about him. Our meeting seems sacred somehow and I don't want to break the spell by dissecting it.

The rest of the evening flies by in a rowdy discussion of old memories and catching Juliette up on what our friends are doing at home.

Her eyes mist over as she says, 'I can't tell you how happy I am that you're here. I have a good life in London and have some nice friends, but I've missed you so much.'

I squeeze her hand. 'It seems like fate is at work, doesn't it? Bringing us together again, like this…'

We order coffee before settling the bill and strolling outside into the cool evening air.

'Where are you parked?' she asks.

'I squeezed into a spot just up the street. I hadn't realised the restaurant was so close to the house or I would have walked. Thank you for coming here and making it easy for me.'

'Have you time for a quick walk before I head back to the station?'

'Sure,' I say, and we cross the flag-stoned street, arm-in-arm.

'Richmond Bridge and the River Thames are just a few minutes' walk away. I studied the map on the train as I've never been here before but had heard it's a beautiful old town,' Juliette says.

'I came to the same conclusion when I researched what part of London to apply for a job in,' I say.

'Isn't it lovely? You've really landed on your feet,' she says.

'What's it like in Knightsbridge?' I ask. 'You've landed on your feet too, by the sounds of it.'

'Come and visit as soon as you can. The embassy is in a busy part of town, but it's next to Hyde Park, which is a heavenly green oasis in the middle of the madness. One perk of the job is they allocated me an embassy flat, which is just a short walk from work and the park. It's a beautiful apartment which would cost an absolute fortune to rent if I wasn't embassy staff.'

We take a stroll along the riverbank, and I clutch my jacket around me as the evening breeze whips up a chill and the trees shiver and shake. We admire the river, and it feels like old times, walking along the banks of the Seine.

Juliette says she has an early start at the embassy and had better catch her train soon. We hug and kiss and I promise I'll come and visit her in Knightsbridge just as soon as I have a day off.

I feel validated in choosing to come to London. It was so lovely to see Juliette and, knowing I can visit her anytime, reassures me.

My mind ticks over as I drive back to the house using my phone to make sure I don't take a wrong turn in the unfamiliar neighbourhood. I tuck the rental car into the little spot at the side of the house that the housekeeper directed me to when I arrived earlier, and I inhale the fresh evening air as I approach the front door.

It's still quite early, but I don't want to disturb anyone, so I scramble about for the keys Mrs Johnson gave me. My head's bent over my handbag and my heart's beating fast as I search for them amongst the many belongings crammed into the small space. I know they're in here somewhere, but I'm panicking and can't find them. I'm nervous about letting myself in for the first time. What if there's an alarm system, and I set it off on my first night?

Just as my fingers close over the set of keys, which I find in the zipped side pocket, I hear a noise. I raise my head to see Sebastian standing in the doorway. He doesn't just stand in it—he fills it with his height and presence, and my heartbeat revs as I look up at him. I'm reasonably tall, but he's much taller.

He looks weary but pleased to see me and flashes me a charming smile. 'Good dinner?' he asks, and he stands aside for me to enter as though I belong inside, and I've come home.

And this is how I find myself sharing a luxurious house in one of the most exclusive neighbourhoods in London, with the grandson of one of the richest men in the world.

I'm reminded that you never know how life is going to surprise you...

CHAPTER 5

Sebastian

My assistant tells me my grandfather wants to see me. He rarely comes into London these days, so I'll need to carve out time to visit him at Greystone. It's not a bad thing, and I can see my mother at the same time.

It sounds important and I wonder what he wants to talk to me about. He's not one for casual messages, and he doesn't usually summon me like this via my assistant, except for scheduling family events. This is a one-on-one, and I guess he wants to talk about my progress as CEO of the hotel division.

Occasionally, I drive over on the spur of the moment to check in on him and my mother when she's home. It's been five years since my father died and she hasn't truly recovered from losing him. She tends to become melancholy if left on her own a lot. I think that's why she travels to the US so much. She says New York HQ needs her on site for our mutual charity foundation projects, but my theory is she prefers flitting about, so she doesn't have to stay at Greystone for long periods and dwell on the fact that her beloved husband isn't there.

Losing Dad, when he should have still had years ahead of him, was a tragic blow for us all, and it affected each of us in different ways. But eventually we got on with our lives and threw ourselves into our work or studies. That's the Rochester way.

It hit Damian, my elder brother, the hardest of all my siblings. He and Dad were particularly close because Dad was mentoring him to step into his shoes. When he died suddenly in a car crash, Damian had to assume the role of primary heir much earlier than he anticipated.

He split with his girlfriend around that time too. And we used to be very close but grew apart when he spiralled into a wild playboy lifestyle. It was his way of dealing with his grief; I guess. Since then, he's pulled himself together and seems to be getting back on track now. But he's not the Damian he used to be. He's closed himself off and I find it hard to get through to him these days, although we still go out occasionally with our younger brother, Caspian, another of the 'ians', as Damian dubbed us when we were kids.

There was a period where things got so out of control and Damian was splashed over every tabloid, that Grandfather spoke to me about the possibility of replacing him as official heir to the British branch of Rochesters & Co. I've always known I'm 'the spare' because I'm second-in-line to Damian. I already inherited a considerable fortune through my trust fund, and the chances of me becoming number one in the Rochester empire were always minuscule, so it was shocking, to say the least. My dad was still a relatively young man, in good health, and then Damian was in the wings, so I hadn't ever considered the reality of stepping into that role.

I didn't take grandfather seriously. Don't get me wrong—I'm ambitious—but I have no desire to topple Damian from his position as future head of the family and make an enemy of him. Our parents always taught us that family comes first, and I try to live by that. Besides, I have a great life and don't crave the glory, or the pressure, of being the top dog.

Grandfather playing us off against each other created tension between us, and I'm doing my best to repair the damage and get us back to where we used to be. Damian is a complete workaholic and as far as I can make out, doesn't have any relationships or interests beyond work since Dad died and his girlfriend broke his heart. He went into a meltdown, and I worry about him.

Like I said, my dad's death affected us all differently, and we're still reeling.

I've always been more lighthearted and less intense than Damian, which has helped me through my own dark times. I seek to find the humour in situations whenever possible, which isn't usually that hard when you look for it.

Soon I saw the humour in me arriving home to find the gorgeous nanny emerging from the pool, wearing only a wet swimming costume. I'd expected a sensible Mrs Doubtfire type and after I recovered from the shock, I had to laugh.

Nathalie has already won Daisy's heart, and they've settled into a routine. I don't remember seeing Daisy so content, which is a tremendous relief. The nanny has a knack for putting her at ease, and I see why she works with kids, because she's a natural. When she spoke about her choice of career, it sounded more like a passion than a job she does purely for money, and that eased my lingering fears.

I'm sitting at the table in the sunny breakfast room overlooking the terrace and flicking through the business section of today's newspaper as I sip my morning coffee. Daisy's little feet hammer the stairs, and she flies into the room with Nathalie on her heels. I hear her caution Daisy to slow down. Her tone is kind but firm as Daisy clambers onto her favourite chair next to me.

'Good morning, my sweetie,' I say, pulling my eyes away from the article I was immersed in to give her my full attention. I ask her how she slept, and Mrs Johnson serves breakfast as Daisy tells me all about her dream.

'You and Nathalie were in it, Daddy. We went away on holiday together,' she says.

'Well, that sounds like fun. Where did we go?' I ask as I spread a generous layer of strawberry jam on my wholemeal toast, and my eyes meet Nathalie's across the table. I notice she seems a little embarrassed by Daisy's dream and looks away quickly.

Daisy takes a bite of her toast and continues talking about the amazing holiday we took together, oblivious to the embarrassment she's causing poor Nathalie.

I can't help smiling at the scenario.

'We were at the beach, and it was a hot, sunny day and we were all swimming in the sea,' she gabbles on relentlessly.

'Don't talk with your mouth full,' I remind her.

'Sorry Daddy,' she says, pausing for a second before she crunches through the rest of her toast and guzzles her glass of freshly squeezed orange juice.

'I like your new dress, but what about your normal school uniform?' I ask.

Nathalie raises her head and meets my eyes. Eating breakfast together every day is something I look forward to. It's remarkable how quickly we've fallen into our breakfast routine, and it almost feels like we're a family.

'This is the summer uniform,' Nathalie explains. Her eyes are a dazzling blue, like this morning's summer sky, and I have to pull myself back from drinking her in. She's even more attractive than the first day we met when it was all I could do to drag my eyes away from her body.

'The kids don't wear school uniforms in France,' she continues.

'Can we move to France?' Daisy asks. 'I'd like to not wear a school uniform, too. This dress is itchy, and I love wearing shorts.'

I snort with laughter. 'We're not moving to France just so you can wear shorts, pumpkin.'

'You can change into your favourite shorts when you get home,' Nathalie promises Daisy, her tone soothing.

Life is much calmer since Nathalie arrived. She's so good with Daisy that I feel confident she's in excellent hands when I leave for the office most mornings, and no longer suffer from the nagging guilt I felt before. Our previous nanny was great, but there's something special about the way Nathalie handles Daisy, who responds to her effortlessly.

Not for the first time, I thank my lucky stars for bringing Nathalie to us. She's only been here a short while, but already I can't imagine how we'd get along without her now.

The thought that she won't be with us forever floats into my mind like an ugly cloud, but I push it away. No point worrying about that now. Besides, perhaps she'll agree to extend her contract when the year is over. I'm doing my best to make sure she has a good time, and her duties aren't too arduous.

Daisy resumes her holiday talk in between mouthfuls of boiled egg.

'Maybe a holiday would do us all good,' I say, getting carried away before I consider the wisdom of my suggestion.

Daisy jumps up from her chair and flings her arms around me, shuffling onto my lap as I help her up. 'Yes! May we really go on holiday together, Daddy? Can we go to the beach and stay in a house overlooking the sea like in my dream?'

I kick myself. What the hell am I thinking? Everyone knows it's parenting rule number one not to make promises to kids that you probably won't keep.

I muss Daisy's hair. 'Come on, kiddo. You'd better finish getting ready for school. It's time to leave soon.'

She turns her big brown eyes on me like search lamps and beseeches me again. 'But you said we can go on holiday together. Can we go in the summer holidays? My friend at school says she goes on a family holiday every summer. Can we do it too? Pleeeeease—'

Nathalie glances at me and then quickly looks away. I notice she does that a lot. For a second, I swear she looks as disappointed as Daisy when I don't immediately respond. Me and my big foot. I must be more careful not to get Daisy's hopes up—or Nathalie's—or mine. Although I'm probably imagining Nathalie's disappointment. I'm sure the last thing she'd want to do is take a family holiday with her boss!

'Have you any plans for this summer?' I ask as she stands to help Mrs Johnson clear the plates.

She looks at me with her cornflower blue eyes and my heart twists.

She shakes her head. 'No, I don't have any plans. I'm available for whatever you need. I would like to explore London when I get a chance, though,' she adds.

'Of course, forgive me for not asking about your holiday plans before. Please reach out to my assistant and she will let you know when you can take time off.'

Her smile is genuine and knocks the breath out of me, making me long to earn more of them.

'Have you anything particular in mind to see in London?' I ask.

Daisy slips her hand into Nathalie's as she waits, bobbing about, for us to finish talking.

'My friend from Paris lives in London,' she says with a hint of shyness.

'Is that who you went to dinner with on the day you arrived?' I ask, knowing I'm out of line and shouldn't be probing for personal details in this manner, but unable to resist.

'Yes,' she says. But to my frustration, she doesn't clarify who the friend is, and I'm none the wiser.

I chastise myself. It's none of my business if she's dating someone in London.

Nathalie looks down at Daisy. 'Come on, we'd better hurry, *ma chérie.* We must get your bag ready for school,' she says.

'Have a good day, Daddy.' Daisy reaches up to kiss me, and my eyes meet Nathalie's again briefly before they both hurry away from the table.

'I'll see you this evening,' I call after Daisy, who turns back to grin at me and blows me another kiss. Nathalie smiles and then they're gone.

I always look forward to spending time with my daughter, but now I can't wait to see Nathalie each evening, too.

I tell myself it's just because she's living in our house and is becoming like one of the family. It's nice to have an adult of a similar age around to talk to at home again.

Even if I do fancy her, it can never be more than that. I must keep it a secret for all our sakes.

I get ready for work and wonder again what the meeting with my grandfather is about.

CHAPTER 6

Sebastian

I decide to drive myself to Greystone today and give my driver a well-deserved day off. I fancy giving the Porsche a good run and having some time alone.

What's the point in buying flash cars if you never drive them yourself? The Porsche sits unused in my garage and my driver takes it out from time to time, so it doesn't seize up. It's dirty work, but someone's got to do it…

The Range Rover is more comfortable for trips to the office, and it's productive for me to work in the backseat, while my driver plods through the never-ending roadworks and temporary traffic lights.

Today, I've skipped rush hour and the route to Hampshire shouldn't be slow like driving to the hotel. Grandfather is expecting me around 11 a.m. so I took Daisy to school this morning and told Nathalie she could give the morning school run a miss. We agreed she'll pick Daisy up because I won't be back in time, which is a shame because I love turning up at school and surprising Daisy.

On the rare occasion I'm back in time to collect her from school, we sometimes take a detour and drive through Richmond Park and stop for ice-cream. If the weather's warm enough, we sit and watch the deer graze in the park. We haven't done it this summer, and I think Nathalie would appreciate the wild deer roaming about the royal park. It's not the sort of sight you see in Paris, and I imagine she hasn't seen anything quite like it. I decide to surprise them both with a visit to the park as soon as I can get off work early.

Nathalie. Nathalie. Nathalie. She's in my thoughts all the time, and I can't get her out. The thought of her in bed at the top of the house drives me wild with desire. As I wait for the traffic lights to change, a vision of her long legs tangled in the sheets, and her golden hair spread across the pillow, does something to me. Images of making love to her haunt me before I drift off to sleep and I wake in the morning, rock hard, after she dominates my dreams.

I groan as my cock strains against my crotch, and I shift my position in the low leather seat, trying to ease the dull ache.

I've wanted her since the first moment I saw her, and the fact that she's forbidden fruit makes the thought of touching her even more tempting.

It's a phase and it will pass.

The lights finally change, and I push my foot down on the accelerator, hoping speed will give me relief from the all-consuming thoughts of her, and the intense yearning in every cell of my body.

It's a given that you want something you can't have more than if it was freely available. *Right?*

These thoughts featuring Nathalie plague me night and day, and I'm growing used to my obsession.

I console myself that I only want her so much because I can't have her. That must be it. I simply can't fall in love with the nanny, no matter how hot she is, so I put it down to pure lust, and I almost believe it. I know I can't have a relationship with her, so I must stop torturing myself like this.

When I look at her, I feel like a schoolboy in love for the first time. She's so magnetic I can't take my eyes off her when she's in the room. And when she's not in the room—like now—she may just as well be.

I keep wondering whether she feels the same way, which is so juvenile. I'm her boss, for Christ's sake. Knowing it's stupid doesn't stop me from obsessing, though. And if she does like me in any way other than as her boss, she doesn't show it. She's wonderfully warm with Daisy but with me she's polite and 100% professional, to the point where I don't know what to make of it. It's like she has her guard up, which is only to be expected in her line of work. I bet she's had some real creeps come on to her, and I feel the urge to protect her, which I realise sounds ridiculously incongruent with my intense sexual fantasies.

I put my foot down on the open stretch of road and flick on the radio to take my mind off my predicament. Not that there is a predicament, as such. Even if she does secretly like me, it can't go anywhere, anyway. If I make a move, it can only end in disaster and put us both in an awkward spot. We're out of options before we even begin.

Grandfather would have a fit if he so much as got a whiff of me lusting after the nanny. He has strict behavioural codes for how we all must interact with our household staff.

Even worse—if a worse scenario is possible—would be me messing things up for Daisy. She's the happiest I've seen her—she's loving school, and she adores Nathalie. We've both fallen for the nanny in a big way, so we have that in common. Our house is like a proper home for the first time in years, and I must not fuck with that. More's the pity, but I must try not to fuck with her. *Literally.*

I shake my head and sigh.

Rochester, you're being a complete and utter dick.

The truth is, I know women think I'm a charming smooth talker, not to mention I hold the attraction of being a high-net-worth divorced guy from a famous family, but underneath the bravado, I'm terrified of rejection.

It's probably just as well, because it means I won't make a move on Nathalie unless I'm certain she likes me, too. And we can barely steal a moment alone, what with the household staff and darling Daisy attached to her like superglue.

So that's that.

I haven't heard a word of the news, so I give up all pretence of listening and switch to a music channel as I abandon myself to the comforting growl of the Porsche and the engine gobbles up the miles to my childhood home.

Maddy, my ex-wife, was my only long-term relationship, and I've had just the occasional hook up since we split. I was faithful all the years we were together, which made me feel even more cheated when she walked out and married someone else.

Damian and Caspian like to play the field and I go out with them to a private club in town if I'm in the mood, but more often than not, I don't. I must be missing an essential gene in my chemistry, as I can't turn off my feelings like they do. There was one encounter after a night out with them, but that's ages ago now. I was too uptight to relax, and then I felt so guilty about not wanting to see her again, that the experience left a sour taste in my mouth, and I vowed not to repeat it.

It's not my style and the callousness of it made me feel

shit. I just don't operate that way any longer. Call me old-fashioned, but the thought of pretending I'm going to call when I know I won't, ties my emotions in knots. And I can't bring myself to say it's just a one-off, so I've stopped doing it.

Caspian told me his fake girlfriend dating arrangement with a girl he's known since university morphed into a sexual benefits scenario, so I think even he's stopped hooking up for the time being.

Playing the field isn't as much fun as people think.

Dating is a complex business for the Rochester heirs, and most of us keep our activities well under the radar, but even that's difficult. The reporters are all over us like a rash at every opportunity. I hope Damian's face hasn't been flashed across the tabloids again, and the meeting with my grandfather isn't anything to do with him.

As I don't avail myself of random hook-ups, and don't fancy a friends with benefits arrangement, sadly, I'm reduced to relieving the stress with my right hand. And I get stressed *a lot*, but never more than since the golden-haired Nathalie appeared in my front room with her stiff nips standing to attention.

Just visualising our first meeting has me bone hard again and like I'm going to bust out of my trousers. I curse. I must stop doing this to myself. But picturing her like that has become my favourite fantasy and turns me on every time. I imagine we're alone, and I peel her costume off her body and suck on those tantalising nipples.

I think about what else I'd like to do to her with my tongue.

She seems like such an innocent and I'm sure she doesn't suspect I fantasise about her in this crude manner.

Really, Rochester, you deserve a very hard slap.

The sign for Greystone Village looms before me and I

dart off at the turning as my thoughts move to my grandfather and what he has to say that's so important, he couldn't tell me over the phone, and couldn't wait until the next family get-together. I must calm down and focus.

What does the wily old fox have on his mind?

CHAPTER 7

Nathalie

I appreciate the luxury of staying in bed this morning and stretch like a sleepy cat. My suite is fabulous and the kingsize bed is the most comfortable I've ever slept in. I've stayed in some beautiful houses in Paris, but Sebastian takes lifestyle to another level. Not that he is tacky or unduly ostentatious. It's just that every feature in the house is obviously top of the range.

And why not? If I was from a multi-billionaire family, I'd buy the most elegant furniture and have the best of everything, too.

For Sabine and I it was a stretch to make ends meet, and I struggled to make sure we both got through university, even with all the subsidies we qualified for. Once we were out of foster care, we were free to do as we pleased, and I'm proud of both of us for completing our studies. Circumstance forced us to grow up quicker than our contemporaries did. I think we're stronger and better women for it, but it's nice not to worry about money or have money be the first thought on my mind when I wake up in the morning. We're both much more financially stable now, and I breathe a sigh of relief at the realisation.

My employment package is more than generous and because I live in, I barely have any outgoings, so I plan to save the extra cash as a safety net for the future.

I lie in bed, relishing the rare lazy start, and my boss's familiar face looms in my mind, stealing the show as usual. My heart flutters and I wonder if this crush I've had on him since the first second our eyes met is going to pass before my year in London is up.

It doesn't help that he's not only mouth-wateringly delicious to look at—and he has the *whole* package—if you know what I mean, but he's also considerate, funny, smart, and a wonderful father. Being a dedicated single dad, especially with his business responsibilities, can't be easy. It feels impossible not to fall under the spell of such a man, and it amazes me he hasn't been snapped up in a heartbeat already.

His financial position would be alluring enough for many women, but even without millions in the bank, he's the most charming guy I've ever met.

Occasionally, I wonder what's wrong with him. Is he too good to be true?

He's single—at least as far as I know. I've not seen him go on a date since I've been here, and it's been quite a while already. Of course, I have no idea what he's up to when he's in London all day, so perhaps he does have a girlfriend but doesn't want to complicate home life for Daisy.

Maybe he stays single because he's a dad, and not only that, but Daisy lives with him full time too. I suppose that would put many women off who might want to start their own family, and not take on someone else's child.

It's just as well they don't know what an amazing girl Daisy is, or they'd be queuing up around the block. I realise I'm biased and not everyone loves children like me. Even so, little knots of jealousy tie up my stomach when I think he is bound to remarry soon.

Either way, he's ranking remarkably high on the perfection scale in my book, so my crush is raging, and I think about him pretty much all the time. He's in every thought, somewhere, and I'm not proud of my obsession. I thought I was a strong, independent woman who didn't need a man.

Okay, so I don't *need* a man—or should I say—*this man,* but boy, how I want him. I yearn for him. And in those seconds between dreams and lucid thought in the early hours of the night, I imagine him touching me with his big, smooth hands and making me scream with pleasure.

I fantasise about running my hands over his broad chest and wide shoulders. His body is hard and muscular—I've seen him swimming with Daisy and getting out the pool dripping.

My face grows hot, and I'm embarrassed at the thought of him finding out how I feel about him. I'm wet just picturing him in his bed all alone. I wonder if he sleeps naked or if he wears shorts.

He's out of my league and strictly off-limits to me, but that doesn't stop me from longing for him.

Not only is he my boss, he's also from one of the wealthiest families in the world. Even if he likes me as more than a member of his household staff, I would be the last girl he would choose for anything serious. I'm not naïve enough to think it could go anywhere. If, or I suppose *when,* he remarries, it will be to some lucky woman from a family like his. That's how the rich operate. From what I've observed, working in wealthy elite households, they like to keep their money in the family, and the best way to do that is to marry someone who also has lots of it.

I don't suppose five thousand euros in a savings account in Paris would qualify… I've got some money in my new London account too, but I want to make sure there is some cash in Paris as a back-up for Sabine just in case she needs it. In many ways, I behave like her mother, and she teases me for it, but I know she appreciates the way I look out for her. And she has my back too. That's what sisters do. My mother taught me that before she died. She made me promise to look after my little sister.

My mind circles back to Sebastian. It was thoughtful of him last night to let me know in advance that he would get Daisy ready for school and take her this morning. That way I could sleep in. I heard Daisy on the stairs but resisted the urge to join them for breakfast and make sure she had everything she needed. I figured Sebastian wanted some 1:1 time with his daughter, so I rolled over and drifted into a luxurious sleep, that was all the sweeter because it was stolen.

Mrs Johnson isn't here this morning and unusually I have the place all to myself. I mooch about making the most of the quiet time before I leave to collect Daisy from school later.

It's a perfect, blisteringly hot summer's day with only a few puffy white clouds floating across the cerulean blue sky, so I slip into my costume and swim several lengths before flopping onto a sun lounger to dry off. I've been careful to be fully dressed when Sebastian comes home from work, and not repeat the scenario from the first time we met. But now I've got the place to myself, it's wonderful to laze in the sun. I nip back into the kitchen and make myself a latte with the extravagant coffee machine and take a sandwich and book out to the pool.

Bliss!

As I turn the pages of my latest romantic suspense novel, I find Sebastian wandering into my thoughts again, and it's difficult to concentrate on the story.

Stop it, Nat. Stop thinking about him all the time.

I tell myself that a man like him won't look at a woman like me. I've come a long way since I was a penniless orphan in an institution in a poor Paris neighbourhood, praying for someone kind to take me and my sister in. But I'm still just a nanny. I'm his employee and he's my unattainable boss. He's a good guy, but there's no point in fooling myself. Where marriage is concerned, the class divide is still alive and well despite the French Revolution.

A sly voice whispers in my head—but he does look at you, Nathalie. He looks at you rather a lot, in fact…

CHAPTER 8

Sebastian

It feels good being back in Hampshire and I inhale a blast of fresh country air as I roll the window down and race up the drive that cuts through the acres of vivid green parklands in the estate. No matter how much I love Richmond, Greystone Manor will always be my childhood home, and I enjoy visiting.

My mother rushes out the door to greet me before I've even reached the big old house. When we were kids, our friends used to say the grey turrets reminded them of a fairy-tale castle, and the gothic-style manor has lost none of its magic all these years later.

Mother waves enthusiastically as she waits for me. There's no point parking in the old stables because I won't be staying overnight, so I pull up on the circular drive near the entrance to the ivy-covered house. Reaching across the seat, I grab the bunch of multi-coloured tulips I bought for her on impulse, on the way out of London.

Tulips are her favourite flower, and I know she'll appreciate the surprise.

'Oh darling, how cheerful they are. You are always so thoughtful,' she says, hugging me like she hasn't seen me in years as I climb out of the low-slung Porsche and unfurl my cramped legs. 'Thank you so much. I'll ask Alice to put them in water.'

Mum is thrilled to see me, and it warms my heart. It's always worth making the effort to come over, even when it's crazy at work.

'I understand the chief has summoned you,' she says with a mischievous glint in her green eyes as she flashes me a sparkling white smile.

I nod and ask if she knows what it's all about, but she shakes her head, and her bottom lip juts out slightly as she tries to think what it could be. 'No, he didn't mention. Hotel business, no doubt. I'm just so happy you're here. I'll let you two have your meeting in peace and then I thought we might all have lunch together afterwards, if you have time?'

I say that sounds perfect and after dropping a quick kiss onto her forehead, I stride off in search of my legendary grandfather, Arthur Rochester.

Albert, the butler, who is as much a part of the Greystone furniture as my grandfather, stands holding the front door open. 'Good morning, sir,' he says in his characteristic formal manner even though he's known me since I was born.

'Morning Albert. Good to see you. You well?'

Albert tells me that Bessie—his wife and head cook—has made Daisy's favourite cake for me to take home, so I promise to stop by the kitchens before I leave.

'In the library, is he?' I ask.

I tap on the door and hear Grandfather's deep voice. 'Enter.'

And I'm met with a swirl of apricot loveliness as Honey the cockapoo, Grandfather's most loyal companion flies across the room and hurls herself at me, yelping and jumping up to lick my face frantically.

'There you are my sweet girl.' I bend down and make a fuss of her, stroking her silky ears and tickling her soft warm tummy until gradually she calms down. I raise my eyes and see my grandfather is on his feet, a smile on his face.

'Morning Grandfather.' I cross the room swiftly and we embrace before he sits back down in his chair, and I face him from the comfort of the Chesterfield.

He thanks me for coming so soon and asks after his great-granddaughter. I tell him about how well Daisy has settled in at school and promise to bring her to visit in the summer holidays. He asks me about our new hotel that has been delayed but is due to open in the next couple of weeks.

After a few minutes of business chitchat, I relax and assume he must have just wanted to talk to me in person about the Cannes hotel opening. He's old school and likes to see people face-to-face, when possible. I must have read more into the purpose of the visit, and my stomach grumbles and idly I wonder what Bessie has made us to eat.

'Mother wants us to lunch together, so I'll shoot off after that, if that's okay. I want to be back in time to see Daisy when she gets home from school.'

Grandfather nods amiably and I'm relieved to be off the hook. We'll have a leisurely lunch, and then I'll head back to Richmond before rush hour. It'll be a perfect day away from the office.

Nathalie's face reappears in my mind, and I imagine her and Daisy sitting at the table in the breakfast room where Daisy has taken to doing her homework under Nathalie's supervision. She's even started teaching her a bit of French and Daisy's picking it up quickly.

But then I notice a shadow cross Grandfather's face. 'There's something I've been meaning to talk to you about,' he says, and his voice is sombre.

My heartbeat speeds up. Oh-oh, here we go. Grandfather, although a kind man, has a reputation for being single-minded when he decides on a course of action. For this reason, my siblings and I do all we can to avoid being in his firing line. We keep our heads down, so he doesn't feel the need to interfere in our lives. We have to report to him and the board on business matters, which is fair enough, but we try to keep him away from our private affairs and personal lives.

And some of my brothers have more affairs than others… Personally, I've not had anything of this nature to discuss with him since the divorce was signed and sealed, and that's how I like it.

Just as I think he's about to bring up Damian, and I'm wondering how to sidestep being wedged back into an awkward spot between Grandfather and my brother, he says something completely unexpected.

His words knock the wind out of me. Immediately, I sense he's not talking about Damian.

'I won't beat around the bush. I'm sure you've been expecting this,' he says.

What? This sounds ominous, and now my heart thuds hard and fast.

I sit up straight and prepare myself for what's coming my way, clearing my throat as my eyes meet his. 'I don't know what you're referring to.'

He raises an eyebrow and studies my face, and then sighs.

'I was hoping not to have to bring this up, but as you're showing no signs of dating someone suitable, never mind remarrying, I'm afraid it's time for me to help matters along.'

Oh fuck. Arranged marriage alert!

I remain silent because honestly, I'm lost for words and fear I will only make it worse if I tell him how I really feel about the prospect of an arranged marriage. It's a *fait accompli* that my siblings and I must marry and do our best to continue the Rochester line. That might sound simple enough, but that's not all there is to it, unfortunately. Grandfather must approve of our marriages, and if he doesn't give the stamp of approval to our chosen match, we stand to lose our seat on the board and the shares in the company that we should inherit upon his death.

We receive access to our trust funds when we reach the age of twenty-one, so we're already wealthy in our own right by most people's standards. But after the divorce, my grandfather alluded to the fact that he expects me to remarry and next time, he will be more involved in helping me choose a suitable wife.

The implication was I fucked up in a major way with my former wife, and he won't let me do the same again. All this time, I've been thinking it was a vague threat to keep me in line, not something he was waiting to spring on me.

Finally, I manage to construct a sentence and hear the words come out of my mouth and I know he won't like them. 'But I already have a child and am fine as I am. I have no wish to remarry.'

Grandfather draws himself up to his full height in his chair and steeples his fingers against his chin, pondering as he studies me. Sadness is etched into his rugged features as he speaks.

'Sebastian, my dear boy. I know you've been through the mill, and I have no wish to push you into doing something you don't want to do, but you are aware of the terms of receiving your full inheritance. I can't make an exception just for you. It's not fair to the others. And your New York cousins also abide by the same inheritance terms with your uncle.'

Honey whines as if she picks up on my discomfort, and she licks my hand to comfort me and leans against my legs like a warm wall.

Grandfather didn't take the news of my divorce well, but once he understood it was inevitable, he advised me accordingly and we handled it in the business-like manner he's taught us to approach all obstacles.

'I thought you were okay with how things are, seeing as I've already been married and given you a grandchild,' I say, my chest tight.

Grandfather sighs and shakes his head. 'There's a clause in the terms that covers what happens in the event of divorce. You are required to remarry, and I must approve of the marriage. It's not as lenient as the first marriage, for obvious reasons.'

'I see,' I say, bowing my head. I feel sick. All I can see is Daisy and Nathalie sitting next to each other doing homework or eating breakfast before school. The thought of bringing a wife into our home and destroying this newfound harmony turns me over.

'What's on your mind?' Grandfather probes. 'I can see there's more going on than I realised. Are you seeing someone?'

I shift in my seat. Nathalie's face dominates my thoughts. It's not that I've thought of marrying her. That is out of the question, given her status. If the truth be known, my thoughts have been a whole lot more feral.

But now he's ambushing me with this arranged marriage thing, all I can see is an image of Nathalie in a wedding dress.

I'm losing it. We haven't even kissed.

And so, with a sharp tug, I pull myself back to reality and say, 'No. I'm not seeing anyone. There's been no one serious since Maddy.'

Grandfather nods. I see sympathy in his eyes. 'Just as I thought. That girl has a lot to answer for,' he says, tutting. 'She broke your heart and ruined your life.'

I shake my head vigorously. Whilst I want him to be understanding, I don't want his sympathy at the price of painting my ex as the villain. It's important to me that lines of communication remain open between Daisy's mother and my family. We must nurture goodwill or Daisy will have a hell of a time and I'm willing to do anything to stop that happening.

'No,' I say. 'It wasn't all her fault. I should have been at home more. I was too obsessed with the business, and she was struggling as a new mother.'

'That's no excuse for her walking out on you and Daisy and marrying another man before the ink was dry on the divorce settlement.'

I know I'm fighting a losing battle, so I let him say his piece.

'But I'm not ready to remarry,' I say, raising my chin and looking him in the eyes. I feel the fire of defiance raging within me.

He sighs again. 'A man needs a wife and even more so in our business. I'm growing old and more responsibility is coming your way. It's time for you to step up.'

'But Damian is the primary heir. I'm only the spare,' I remind him.

'Maybe so, but you are bound to a legacy. Many thousands of people depend upon our family for their livelihoods. Damian can't shoulder it all alone, and besides, the way he's going, who knows if a suitable wife will even agree to marry him?'

I snort. 'He may have a reputation as a bit of a playboy, but you know he's a great catch. He could have a wife by bedtime today if he wanted one.'

Grandfather ignores my comment and continues with his diatribe, while I wish silently that he would focus his energies on marrying Damian off.

'As second-in-line to the British Rochesters & Co. I need you married and properly settled. It's time, Sebastian. Daisy needs stability at home, and from what I see in the papers, she doesn't get it from her mother gallivanting around the football circuit.'

I can't argue with that point. 'We've got a new live-in nanny,' I offer. 'She's brilliant and Daisy is the happiest and most settled she's ever been.'

There's a hard gleam in his eyes and I see he will not back down now. He's not moved by my mention of a nanny. Mind you, he hasn't met Nathalie yet…

But I know when I've been dealt a losing hand and I sense I'm not going to win today. And I can't afford to lose. The stakes are too high. There is my seat on the board, and shares in the company to secure. If I don't want to piss him off again, I realise I'm going to have to make some kind of a nod toward seeking remarriage.

'So how does this arranged-marriage business work?' I ask.

He assesses me for a minute, and then he wields his blade and slices my tender underbelly. 'I have the perfect girl in mind for you. She's the granddaughter of my dear old friend and business colleague.'

My stomach churns violently, and I sink back on the sofa.

How long has he been plotting my marriage to the daughter of one of his cronies?

CHAPTER 9

Sebastian

Lunch passes in a blur, and I process little that is said. I'm grateful when the conversation revolves around anything but me and my apparent urgent need to secure a new wife.

Mother mentions the ghostwriter who is staying in the cottage whilst she writes the family biography that Grandfather has been talking about for quite some time. This piques my interest, and I welcome the distraction from the tension streaming through my body.

'How is she getting on?' I ask.

'Did you meet Jamie? She's a rather fabulous fiery redhead,' says Grandfather, in-between bites of Bessie's mouth-watering home-cooked cod and chips. 'Got Damian on his toes, I can tell you.' There's a wicked sparkle in his eye and I guess he's having fun pitting them against each other.

My mother says Jamie is working closely with Damian

and, although they had something of a bumpy start, they seem to have settled into a productive routine.

'Yes, I've met her. She's great.' I laugh, imagining what a nightmare it must be to extract any personal information from between Damian's tight lips. He's notoriously closed off and keeps his thoughts to himself.

'Poor woman,' I say. 'I bet she had no clue what she was signing up for.'

'She didn't.' Grandfather lets out a sudden loud burst of laughter, like a cracking machine gun. 'She thought she would be working with me, but I decided I'm far too old for all that, so I passed the baton to Damian.'

'I bet he didn't thank you for it.'

When lunch is over, I say goodbye to Grandfather, and he reminds me that his assistant will be in touch to set up a date for me with my *perfect* future wife. Those aren't his exact words, but they're the words running through my brain.

I feel like he's just handed me a death sentence.

'Great!' I don't want to upset him, and I don't know what else to say.

I promise to follow through, even though every fibre of my being is urging me to run.

Daisy leaps from the chair where she's leaning over her schoolbook as soon as I poke my head into the room.

'Bessie baked your favourite cake, pumpkin,' I say.

Nathalie smiles at me, her blue eyes as deep as the Aegean Sea, and I swear the angels break into song.

'How was your trip?' she asks, her voice soft.

'Pretty good,' I reply, over the top of Daisy's head as she scrambles up and wraps her arms around my neck. I don't tell her that things are about to change dramatically if my grandfather has his way, and I'll be engaged just as soon as he can arrange it. I don't tell her there's a heavy weight, that is not Daisy, bearing down on my chest, and I can barely breathe.

In true Sebastian style, I push those ugly thoughts right out of my head and say to the girls, 'Who wants to go deer watching and eat ice cream?'

Nathalie looks confused.

I suppose it does sound like an odd combination.

Daisy shouts and almost pierces my ear drum. 'Yes, please, Daddy. Me! Me!'

On the drive home, I decided that today's the day to take Nathalie to Richmond Park for the first time.

'I would love to,' Nathalie says in her breathy voice that sends shivers down my spine and other places.

'Do you like ice cream?' I ask her.

She nods enthusiastically.

I realise how little I know about her, and it saddens me. It's like I've known her all my life, but I don't know her at all.

'Then grab your shoes, you two, and let's go. It's too hot to be stuck indoors on a day like today.'

They rush off to get organised and then we pile into the Range Rover. It's only a short drive to the park, even in the afternoon traffic, and I can taste freedom. My driver is brilliant and saves me hours on the roads. Without him, I'd be circling around London trying to find parking spots and not able to work in the car. But after the sobering conversation with my grandfather, I realise how much I take my freedom for granted.

So, this afternoon—more than ever—I relish driving myself. And with Nathalie at my side, exclaiming at the beauty all around us as I point out the sights, and Daisy in the back seat buzzing about going to the park, my world feels complete.

I don't need anyone or anything else.

I definitely don't need a date with the granddaughter of an illustrious banker, and I grow cold at the prospect of what's to come.

But I thrust that thought deep into the recesses of my mind, determined to enjoy this precious afternoon. I ease the car into a parking spot near the café before turning to Nathalie. 'Are you a chocolate or strawberry girl?'

Nathalie's eyes sparkle as she says, '*Chocolat, s'il vous plaît!*'

Daisy unbuckles her seatbelt and jumps up and down in her seat. '*Chocolat, s'il vous plaît,*' she repeats, giggling.

'That settles it then.' We jump out of the car, and I order three big waffle cones with double scoops of Italian chocolate ice cream.

'Yummy,' says Daisy, licking the cone. 'My favourite!'

Nathalie's eyes meet mine and my heart explodes like a firework.

We wander away from the café and sit on a low wall overlooking the park, and Daisy points to the red deer grazing nearby, in between giant licks of ice cream.

Nathalie says, 'You're so lucky. It's almost like the deer are in your back garden. I didn't realise it was this easy to enter the park.'

Richmond Park never fails to inspire awe in its visitors. One minute you're in town and with just a few steps, you're plunged into the heart of a glorious nature reserve.

'It's the largest of the Royal Parks,' I tell Nathalie. 'It was created during the reign of Charles I in the seventeenth century, as a deer park.'

Her eyes shine and I can tell she's moved by the sight of the wild deer in our midst.

'It's hard to believe this is so close to the centre of London, isn't it?'

She nods and falls quiet as she takes it all in.

I love how she doesn't feel the need to fill every space

with words. It's enough that we are here together, and I feel her presence all around me.

These feelings I have for her are spiralling out of control and I don't know how much longer I can pretend I'm just her boss and she's just Daisy's nanny. I can deny my feelings all I want, but deep down, I know I'm in serious trouble.

And I'm beginning to think she likes me too. The way I catch her looking at me sometimes gives me hope she sees me as more than her boss.

But if I'm to secure my future inheritance and retain my seat on the board, an arranged marriage is on the cards for me. For that reason, it would be unfair to give Nathalie any inkling of how much I want her, so I hold myself back on a tight leash.

I can't do that to her.

I can't do it to either of us.

One taste of her and I fear I'll be lost.

CHAPTER 10

N**athalie**

Sebastian asked whether I'd like to attend the Rochester Charity Ball. Initially, I declined. I don't want to stick out like a sore thumb amongst all the rich and famous I imagine will be attending.

But he tries to talk me around in that charming way he has. I don't know how he does it exactly, but I'm beginning to suspect he could talk me into pretty much anything that's legal.

He must guess I'm nervous about meeting the family and he immediately puts my mind at rest.

Long dark lashes frame his blue-grey eyes, and my heart cracks open a tiny bit more. Each time we are close, I feel him infiltrating my fragile heart. A man shouldn't even be allowed to have such long eyelashes. It seems grossly unfair. I have to coat my fair lashes with expensive black mascara to get them anywhere near that length and thickness.

'Nathalie?' he says, smiling. 'Earth to Nathalie.'

My stomach churns and crashes like a drunken roller-coaster.

What the hell is he doing to me? Sebastian clearly has no idea of the effect he has on me when he lavishes me with this kind of personal attention and makes me feel like I'm the only woman in the world. He lights me up and I radiate with an inner glow whenever he's near me.

Charming but dangerous. He should come with a health warning.

Do not come near if you don't want to get burnt.

'It'll do you good to get out,' he says, flicking on the coffee machine and throwing an appealing glance in my direction. 'You said you want to see more of London, so here's your chance. Mayfair is in the heart of the West End.'

'But won't we just be in a hotel?' I ask, spreading butter on bread to make Daisy's sandwiches, just how she likes them.

He raises one eyebrow. 'Well, yes, but not just *any* hotel—it's at our London Rochester Hotel.'

He's next to me again now and his masculine scent is like a drug, pervading all my senses, and my thinking grows fuzzy.

'Why are you making sandwiches now, by the way?' he asks, peering curiously over my shoulder and brushing lightly against my arm.

The heat of his body surges right through me.

'Mrs Johnson isn't coming in tomorrow. She has a family event, remember?'

'Oh yes,' he says, clapping his hand to his forehead. 'Forgot about that.'

The house is unusually quiet. The staff has gone home,

and Daisy's tucked up in bed after a bath and a bedtime story. It's rare for us to have a moment alone like this, and it feels dangerous. Or more accurately, I feel reckless.

'They look fantastic. May I have one?' he says, eyeing up the tuna and mayonnaise triangles.

I nod. 'Okay. I can make more if you want. Thought I'd make them now to get a head start for the morning.'

He leans nonchalantly against the kitchen island, devouring one of the freshly cut sandwiches.

'I bet you were the kind of kid who ate your school sandwiches before lunch time.' I focus on keeping my hands steady, as though I've been hanging out with smoking hot billionaire-heirs in the kitchen for most of my life.

'I'm sure I would have been, if I had taken a packed lunch, but I went to boarding school.'

Of course.

'How was it?' I ask, neatly cutting more sandwiches and popping them into a lunch bag for Daisy.

'It was alright, most of the time. But I missed home.'

'I meant the sandwich!'

He laughs. 'Oh! Tasty.'

'I can't even imagine sending my kid to boarding school,' I blurt out without thinking. I don't mean to offend him and sound judgemental about his parents' choices and I wish I could take the words back. But it's too late now, so I raise my eyes tentatively to his.

'Ahh, it wasn't too bad,' he sighs. 'Toughened me up, I guess. Although, I wouldn't choose it for Daisy, that's for certain. But it's a different world now. All my siblings went to boarding school and seem to have come out of it alright.'

'Was it like in the British movies?' I ask.

He smirks and rolls his eyes. 'Well, it wasn't like Hogwarts! In what way do you mean?'

'You know, the British upper-class school system where you get bullied and humiliated by the other boys.'

'Oh, I see. Well, yes, there were some first-rate arseholes, but fortunately, my brother Damian was there to keep an eye on me for much of it. No one likes getting on his wrong side.'

I can't bear the thought of little Sebastian being bullied, so I release a jagged breath when he assures me he didn't have to go through that.

'I did cry myself to sleep every night, though,' he says. His tone is heavy and serious, as if he's reliving the childhood trauma.

My eyes grow moist, and I feel the emotion building. If there's one thing that really gets to me, it's the thought of traumatised kids.

And the vision of a miserable, lonely Sebastian who I have no doubt was an adorable kid, tugs at my heart and I choke back the tears.

I look the other way and busy myself adding some stuff to Daisy's lunchbox in the fridge. The chilled air hits my hot skin and I breathe it in to calm myself. I don't want him to see his childhood memory upset me. He'll think I'm pathetic.

'Hey,' he says. 'Look at me.'

I blink away the tears and raise my head and look at him.

'What's the matter?'

'Nothing,' I say, trying to smile, but failing horribly.

'I was *joking*,' he says. A wicked grin lights up his handsome face, and my heart flip-flops as I search his eyes.

'Oh, you were teasing me,' I say, shaking my head. If he wasn't my boss, I would call him a rude name, or throw something at him, but I'm constantly aware that I must be professional. It wouldn't be right to call your boss a bastard. But I feel silly and can't help muttering, '*Merde*' under my breath, as I return to my spot at the kitchen island and start clearing the surface.

'That's the first time since you've been here that I've heard you lose your cool. Well, except for our first meeting, perhaps,' he chuckles.

I feel anything but cool.

I feel hot. Blisteringly hot.

He hasn't moved and is still standing close to me, leaning against the counter. The sex appeal oozes from his every pore, but I don't think he realises how attractive he is. I'm drowning in him. The air surrounding us is scalding and I struggle to draw a breath and worry I will pant if I even try.

It feels like I've been craving him forever and the pulse between my legs hammers manically, making me faint with longing. My need for him is urgent, but simultaneously a warning voice in my head shouts that it must not happen.

Billionaires don't fall for nannies. And if they do, it will end in tears. There's no other way for it to go.

But he's staring at me in a decidedly un-boss-like way. I can tell he's feeling the chemistry between us too, and I stand there next to him, suspended in time, unable to touch him but unable to move away.

Our eyes lock and the world disappears as his lips draw closer to mine and before I can remind myself this is forbidden, he's kissing me, and I'm kissing him back.

Our kiss isn't gentle and romantic like kisses in the movies. It's frantic, like we're both going to die if our lips don't touch.

He moves into me, closing the remaining space between our bodies and I'm flush against him, my back leaning on the island and his body covering mine. His arms come around me as our feverish kissing continues, and he wraps his hands in my hair and I surrender to the bliss of being in his muscular arms.

It feels right even though it's so wrong.

Isn't it?

And then the sensual haze guzzles me up whole, and it is perfect. It's all perfect as he sweeps the sandwich board out of the way and lifts me effortlessly, so my feet leave the ground and my bottom perches on the cool marble. I'm wearing the dress I wore on my first day, and as he leans into me, I feel his hard length pushing through the fine material.

He's breathing fast and heavy, and I feel his heart pounding as we kiss and explore each other's bodies for the first time. I touch him through his jeans, and he groans. It's the most erotic groan I've ever heard, and something about him makes me want to surrender all of myself to him. I don't know why he has this power over me, but I don't hold back. A distant cavern of my brain tells me I *should* hold back. But I don't. I stroke his bulging mound and it grows harder, and he groans more until he begs, 'Have mercy. You're killing me. I'm going to explode if you carry on touching me like that.'

I'm so hot for him I feel the urge to drop to my knees, unzip his jeans, and take him in my mouth. I want to see him lose control. Like I've been losing control in the early hours of the morning just before first light seeps through the shutters, when I've yearned for him and imagined him making love to me.

I can see he's losing it as I press my hand against his groin, but before I can ease myself off the island, he pulls away slightly and his blue-grey eyes search mine. 'I want you,' he says. 'If you don't want this to happen, we should stop now.'

He's breathless, and I'm out of my mind with lust. I can't stop now, so I say, 'I want you, too.'

And then he lifts the skirt of my dress. I'm wearing little white cotton panties and he sucks in his breath when he sees them.

'You're so beautiful,' he says. And he lowers his head and moves my panties aside with his warm hands. His fingers dip slowly into the folds of my flesh, and I gasp. His breath is on me and then his tongue opens me up like a flower budding in spring. I clutch his dark hair with one hand and hold myself up with the other as my legs grow tense and he makes me forget my name.

His tongue teases me—in and out—in and out until I'm on the edge of oblivion. I'm almost through the gates of paradise when he expertly withdraws his tongue again and I cry out his name and beg for him to make me come.

'Please, don't stop,' I plead.

'You don't want me to stop?' he says playfully. His voice is deep and melodic, like music, and I know I love him. I love him like I've loved no man before. I don't even know him, but paradoxically, I know him better than I know myself.

He takes me by surprise and slips his fingers back inside me. I cry out louder, and grip onto the edge of the marble. I fall apart the second he does it, and a wave of exquisite pleasure floods through me—over me—consuming me. Then his tender mouth is back on my pussy, and he sucks my clit until I can barely stand the bliss. It's sweet torture and I never want it to end.

'*Mon Dieu. Mon Dieu.*' I hear my words, but I have no control over them or over myself. It's like someone else is speaking.

I can't even think. I only feel his tongue on the most sensitive part of me. And I want more of him. I want to feel him deep inside me. I want to give him this same pleasure he's giving me.

I open my eyes and smile at him. I must look like the cat who got the cream, but I'm past caring. This is not the time to be coy.

Straightening, I reach my hand out to touch his cock and he makes the delicious groan that drives me wild. My legs are dangling off the kitchen island and I feel weightless, like

I'm floating in a bubble of pleasure where nothing else matters.

I ping open the top button of his straining jeans and tug at his zip. I can feel him looking at me as I do it, and the air between us sizzles.

When the zip opens, I place my hand on his bulging shorts and pull at them until his throbbing shaft springs out, standing to attention. It's thick and long and desperate for my attention. His eyes meet mine and I see the hunger in them.

I hold his shoulder, and he catches me and lifts me down with one fluid movement. I'm just about to touch him again when a sweet voice echoes down the stairs and into the kitchen.

'Daddy. I can't sleep. I had a nightmare.'

I stare at him, transfixed, and dishevelled.

'Fuck!' he says.

He shakes his head and leans over to kiss my lips, before hastily rearranging himself in his shorts and zipping up his jeans with an effort.

'I'll go,' he says.

There's a wild hammering ache between my legs, and a sharper ache in my chest as I watch him exit the kitchen, barefoot, and his hair tousled.

What have we done?

CHAPTER 11

Sebastian

The conversation with my grandfather keeps spinning around my brain and I can't stop thinking about it.

What made this so urgent now? I think of Nathalie and wonder if he has some strange spidery sense about my feelings for her.

I shake my head. *Don't be silly.*

He's obviously been biding his time and has grown tired of waiting for me to remarry.

My thoughts drift back to the club. Now I think of it, Caspian didn't seem all that into it either, which is unusual for him. He's got a reputation as a bit of a player and has never had a committed relationship. But the press always picks on Damian, presumably because he's the next in line to be custodian of a huge portion of the Rochester empire. Damian asked Caspian to arrange a night out. Knowing him, he is seeking distraction after being cooped up at Greystone with grandfather and the ghostwriter.

My guess is she's got right under Damian's skin. Grandfather intimated as much, and when I met her, I could tell she is dedicated to her work which will naturally involve Damian's worst nightmare—talking about himself and sharing personal information about the family…

Some time with Jamie will do him good. I got the impression she's strong enough to push back when he gets too forceful, but gentle enough to nurture him. He's had a tough time and although he drives me mad with his arrogant attitude and big brother dominance, I love him and want him to be happy again like the old days.

I excused myself at the first opportunity. Who wants to be in a heaving club full of husband-hunting women and rich men wanting their inflated egos—and other things—stroked?

I've never been much of a one for clubbing. I enjoy being at home or at work and am a family-oriented person at heart, which makes it even more ridiculous that I'm single again. I had lots of casual girlfriends before my ex, but I've lost interest in picking up random women. I'm a romantic and as my romantic dreams have been blasted to hell, I've given up on the idea of marrying at all.

Me and Daisy get along just fine, thank you.

Until Nathalie came along. And now, more often than not, it's: *Daisy, Nathalie, and I get along just fine.* But I'm aware I've lost the plot, and it's not realistic to allow myself to think like that. She'll be with us until her year is up, and then she'll return to Paris and probably find a good husband. She loves children, so will no doubt want some of her own.

I wonder what type of man she'll marry and try to picture her with a French truck driver. *No.* Perhaps a middle-class banker or lawyer?

The vision triggers a painful stab in my chest for which I'm unprepared, and I inhale sharply.

As my driver manoeuvres the car smoothly through the streets of late-night London, onto the road to Richmond, my head falls back against the seat, and I drift into a light doze for a few seconds. Thoughts of Nathalie touching me and me touching her consume me, and then my eyelids peel open and I'm wide awake. And uncomfortably stiff.

Since that night, I crave her even more desperately than before.

We haven't spoken about our erotic interlude in the kitchen. By the time Daisy settled down to sleep, it was late, and when I went back downstairs, Nathalie had gone to bed.

I didn't want to be pushy by going to her room, in case she had second thoughts, so I sat up for a while hoping she'd reappear, but the house was silent.

The next day brought a hectic breakfast routine without Mrs Johnson to organise things and the usual getting ready for school shenanigans. I tried to draw Nathalie's eyes to mine, to gauge her reaction, but she kept busy with Daisy and didn't look me in the eye once. She seemed distant and I guess she regrets compromising her position, which I can understand.

I sigh as we enter Richmond. I know I must broach the subject to clear the air, but I don't know what to say or how to say it, which is not a problem I typically encounter. Words come easily to me, but with her, I struggle to find the right ones.

I want her desperately, but I can't have her.

It was a fatal mistake to make a move on her like that, no matter how much I crave her. I curse my impetuous action and regret putting us both in this awkward spot. Daisy must always be my top priority, and I can't risk messing things up for her. *Again.* But it looks like I already did, and I hope

Nathalie can forgive me and we can move past this and be friends.

I like her a lot and if we can't be lovers, then I hope we can at least be good friends. The thing is, although I fancy her madly, I also *really* like spending time with her. She has an easy way about her, and when we're together with Daisy, we all just click effortlessly. It's magical and I don't want to lose it. I don't want to lose her.

I consider apologising for the other night and proposing a friendship, and I try to imagine how she'll react. Honestly, other than mutual physical attraction, which can't be denied after the red-hot session in the kitchen, I don't know how she feels about me. When you're the boss, you never know if people's reactions to you are genuine, or if they're just being polite and professional.

I know I could fall for her completely, but I also know I can't let myself do it, so I try to lock down these intense feelings and fortify myself to protect Daisy. And my battered heart.

My personal assistant forwarded me some potential days for a date with the banking magnate's granddaughter. The email is sitting in my inbox, and I've ignored it for two days. But I can't ignore it forever. I mustn't kid myself—this is like any other business merger. She's the heir to a powerful family who own an international banking empire that spreads all the way to Asia. I don't need Grandfather or Damian to explain to me why this would make sense for Rochesters & Co. It's obvious that on paper it would be a fortuitous match for both our families.

But what about for me? And Daisy?

And what about the woman being offered for sacrifice to unite Rochesters and Archer Banking?

I'm not ruthless, and the prospect of marrying someone I don't love turns me cold. It's unfair to both of us, not to mention to Daisy, because if it doesn't work out there'll be another divorce which will be more upheaval for her.

'No more divorces.' I hear Grandfather's sharp words ringing in my head. 'You've had one failed marriage. We cannot afford another divorce scandal.'

The car pulls into its spot, and I thank my driver and wish him goodnight as he gets into his own car to go home. He'll be back first thing to drive me to Mayfair.

The irony isn't lost on me. All this supreme privilege, but I'm like a caged bird with clipped wings. All the money in the world to buy whatever toys I want, but my life is about to be auctioned off to the highest bidder and I can do nothing to stop it.

I feel powerless and trapped as I enter the house in a sombre mood. It's quiet and no one's around. When I say no one, I mean Nathalie, of course. She has to be up early to get Daisy ready for school, so she's probably been in bed for hours.

I think she may have overheard my conversation with Daisy when I took her up to bed, and Daisy noticed I was dressed for going out. I told her I was meeting Uncle Damian and Caspian.

When I came back down, shortly after, Nathalie was nowhere to be seen.

A couple of times a week she volunteers at a children's centre and doesn't return until quite late, so I called up to her to check she would be at home for Daisy and there was no clash in our schedules.

'Have a good night,' she replied.

Her usually bubbly voice sounded flat, and her words were devoid of emotion.

I can't say I'm surprised.

What a supreme nob I am. I've completely fucked everything up.

CHAPTER 12

Sebastian

We're at the Rochester Annual Charity Ball and the only way I could face attending was if Nathalie came too. She didn't want to come as my date. Not that I asked her specifically. I was too scared of rejection after what happened between us.

First, she declined, but later she agreed to come when I mentioned the event raises money for disadvantaged children. I swear her cornflower blue eyes lit up, and suddenly she was all in. I paired her up with my assistant, and they worked together to increase the number of guests and sponsors.

Of course, it thrilled my mother to have an enthusiastic volunteer on the team because these days she spends most of her time working with our charity foundation, which is very much her baby.

It's a shame mother can't attend the ball this year. I would have liked her to meet Nathalie in person, and this would have been a natural way to arrange it. A glow permeates my chest when I think of her meeting my mum. I think they'd take to each other.

Things have been weird at home since we kissed—well, we did *a lot* more than kiss—I grow hot under the collar of my dress shirt, just at the memory. We've still not talked about it.

Nathalie looks so beautiful tonight. *Who am I kidding?* She looks beautiful *every* night.

If only things were different.

Damian's sitting opposite me, being his naturally dashing self in a tuxedo. He looks like he's enjoying the evening, which is a rare thing. Jamie is radiant in an emerald-green dress and I notice Damian's eyes keep straying towards her.

I wonder if something's going on between them. The press captured them driving into Greystone together and they've been all over the media recently. They've dubbed Jamie as his mystery redheaded girlfriend, so Damian is back in the press with a bang. I smile wryly. Perhaps that's an unfortunate choice of words, considering the girl from the club dished the dirt on him, stirring up all the old playboy stuff.

But he is a free agent and so is Jamie. We all thought she was engaged, but it turns out that ended before she came to Greystone, and she'd been embarrassed to tell us her situation.

If something is going on, the poor lovestruck fools will be in for a shock when Grandfather learns of it. I imagine he's got a marriage candidate lined up for Damian, too. He'll be giving him a chance to find someone himself, but if it doesn't happen soon, he'll push him along like he is doing with me.

I think Grandfather has gone easier on him because he knows he's been in such a state since our father died, and his ex-girlfriend cut his heart into tiny pieces and stamped on them.

Grandfather doesn't seem to realise that I went through the same traumatic experiences, losing my father and my wife.

My optimistic, sunny nature often works against me. People think I can handle anything, so they throw it all at me without a second thought, and I bounce back, smiling like a pop-up clown. What they don't see is my bleeding heart and the tears behind the smile. I suppose I only have myself to blame, but I detest appearing weak.

Grandfather isn't showing the same leniency to me as he is to Damian, and I can't deny it irks me. Damian is the eldest, and he will inherit Greystone and be the majority shareholder of our company and so I wonder why he doesn't force him to marry before he pressures me.

Not much I can do about it, and I don't hold it against Damian. We're just cogs in the Rochester wheel, and our fate was decided by the year we were born.

I take a swig of champagne and exchange a few words with Jamie between courses. She really is lovely, and when she tells me she is helping Damian out by being his fake date for the evening, and going along with the mystery girlfriend rumour, I say I wish she would be my fake date for an upcoming event, too.

Damian is so possessive, and his blazing eyes tell me all I need to know. He is so into her. Bit naughty of me to wind him up, but we always have an edge of sibling rivalry going on and I can't resist.

Damian remarked on me not bringing a date. Grandfather likes us to bring a date to official events, and it's Damian's way of reminding me of my duty. He already acts like he's the head of the clan. I remind him I'm just the spare. It's him everyone's watching.

My eyes seek out Nathalie, but she must still be helping behind the scenes. She was weird about not wanting to join me for dinner, as if she wants to draw a strict border around our boss-employee relationship.

Hopefully she will be finished soon, and we can have a dance before I take her home. We both have an early start, but I want her to have a good time and not only work every second she gets.

I haven't raised the subject of us being just friends, but I hope when I buck up the courage and get the right moment, she will understand it's for the best. The thought of losing her from my life is unbearable, but she might be offended.

I don't know if she'll care all that much. Maybe our making out in the kitchen was just a bit of fun for her. She certainly has not tried to be alone with me since. Even on the journey to the hotel this evening, she insisted on sitting next to the driver, so we haven't been alone for a second since we kissed, when she lost control and came under my tongue.

My ex said I was a bit dense when it came to picking up on her signals, and there's no point in denying it. I must have been, or she wouldn't have left me for someone else…

Anyway, I'm aware I'm not always the most attuned to what a woman wants, and I have a lot to learn. I'm doing my best not to put my foot in it with Nathalie, so I don't make our situation any more awkward.

But I feel like I'm treading cautiously around a landmine that could explode at any second. If she won't be alone with me, I can't talk to her. And if I don't talk to her about what happened, she might think I just take it for granted and treat all my nannies this way.

A smile crosses my lips as I remember the previous elderly nanny.

No, I most definitely don't treat all the nannies this way. In fact, I've treated no nanny this way, and never even had a thing with any of the Rochester staff before. It's an unwritten law that we don't mess with the help. But she doesn't know that, and I fear she thinks the worst of me.

My eyes stray back to Damian, and I watch him studying Jamie again.

The music blares and the dancing begins. I can't hear what they're saying, but Jamie turns to ask if I dance.

Damian has obviously declined to dance, even though he's clearly mad about her.

Nob.

I rescue the poor girl and we dance for a while and have a laugh. I keep wondering when Nathalie will come and find me, but she's nowhere to be seen. When the music turns slow, Damian appears over Jamie's shoulder and glowers at me to allow him to cut in.

I do so with good grace, trying not to show I'm amused by his ridiculous behaviour. Just as I'm heading back to the table, Nathalie crosses the room towards me and if I didn't know it couldn't be the case, I'd think my heart stops beating at the sight of her.

Her blonde hair is swept into an elaborate updo, and she looks effortlessly elegant in her black evening dress, which hugs her tall slim frame in all the right places. She is Parisian, so I suppose I shouldn't be surprised that she has buckets of style.

I offer her my arm, and she accepts it. She smiles and agrees to one dance with me when I whisper the invitation in her ear.

I can't help noticing she attracts more than her fair share of envious looks and my heart swells with pride that she's on *my* arm.

Pulling her gently into my embrace, we dance slowly to a crooning ballad about lost love. She moves with me in perfect time, and it feels so right.

How the hell am I going to agree to an arranged marriage, when I'd rather dance with Nathalie than anyone else, anywhere?

This situation isn't fair to either of us. But what am I supposed to do?

My mind wanders back to my inheritance dilemma as Nathalie sways in my arms. I'd like to pull her in closer and hold her flush against me, but I stop myself. The second her body touched mine, I felt myself hardening, and she will feel it too. And given that I'm going to propose friendship, rather than sex, this would be in poor taste. So, I hold her lightly, one hand on her shoulder and one on her waist and pretend I'm not desperate to be inside her and that there isn't an ache in my groin that has been my ever-present tormentor since she came into my life and blew the breath out of my lungs.

After the one dance which I wish wasn't over so quickly, she pulls away, and I see she's still avoiding meeting my eyes. She says she must be up early with Daisy.

I don't feel like I can leave just yet. Damian has disappeared, and Jamie is sitting like a lost soul at the table. I introduce her to Nathalie, and they chat briefly. Then I notice several of my mother's friends hovering nearby, wanting to have a word with me. It's my duty to do the rounds before calling it a night. This event is being held in our flagship hotel, so I mustn't shirk my responsibilities.

Nathalie asks if it's okay to leave soon. Her words tickle my neck as she leans into me so I can hear her over the music. I feel her warm breath on me, and her familiar scent wafts up my nose. The dangerous proximity of her makes me stiffen again in my tuxedo trousers. I wish she would stay by my side, but I call my driver to bring the car round and take her home.

She is clearly concerned about being alone with me, and there's absolutely nothing I can do about it.

Soon, I'm going to have to deal with the email in my inbox about organising a date with Elizabeth Archer of Archer International Banking.

I stare after Nathalie's back as she walks out of the ballroom, wishing I was going with her. I'm angry I allowed myself to get so attached to her.

I must get a handle on my emotions and attend to the lingering guests, and then I can go home.

My eyes follow Jamie's to where Damian stands at the bar in deep conversation with a brunette. She turns her head and I realise it's Stephanie De Winter, the ex who left him for his best friend. One of my best friends too.

What the hell is she doing here?

If the haunted look in Jamie's eyes is anything to go by, it looks like mine isn't the only bleeding heart in the ballroom tonight.

Oh, the tangled webs we weave.

CHAPTER 13

Nathalie

I've barely been able to meet his eyes since it happened. What was I thinking? I berate myself for losing it like that and getting carried away in the heat of the moment.

One minute I was being a dutiful nanny and making sandwiches for Daisy, and the next he was driving me wild with his tongue.

I feel myself blush at the memory. I'm no prude but he's my boss for God's sake. It was bad enough I was crushing on him in secret, but now he knows I'm crazy about him, I don't know how I'm going to stand the humiliation.

If the agency finds out, I will be instantly dismissed, and my career ruined. I beat myself up for being such a cliché—nanny falls for billionaire CEO boss.

It's a gorgeous day so we left early this morning and walked to school. There's a car I can use whenever I want, but it's a shame to drive on a day like this and it's not far on foot. Also, I wanted the fresh air and headspace to try and calm my whirling thoughts. I'm finding it difficult to sleep and am restless and overtired.

There's no rush, so I meander back, admiring the Georgian buildings along the way. I love living in Richmond and after spending a day in the centre of London with Juliette, I appreciate it even more. It's like being in a little cocoon with all the amenities of city life whilst surrounded by the peaceful beauty of the countryside. At the brow of the hill, I pause and catch sight of the shimmering Thames in the valley below.

There's no point in keeping on beating myself up about what happened. Sebastian is always the perfect gentleman, so I don't really think I have anything to fear from him. He's not going to tell anyone and if he does it will reflect just as badly on him. Not that I think he will, anyway.

It's my own feelings I fear the most and I've got myself riled up into a terrible state.

It's unusual for us to be alone in the house because Mrs Johnson stays late to clear up and prepare for the next morning. I think she lives by herself and enjoys our company.

My thoughts veer back to that night when it was just him and me.

I waited in the kitchen for a few minutes to see if he would come back down after checking on Daisy, but when he didn't, I panicked. I was desperate for more of him and would have resumed right where we left off, if he'd come back then. But as the minutes ticked by, the reality of what we had done, hit me and I was filled with doubt.

What if I lose my job? Even worse, what if I can't get another one because they exclude me for unprofessional behaviour?

What if he regrets it and doesn't come back down

tonight? I'll be waiting here like a fool, and I'll never get over the shame of it.

Heart beating like a manic drum, and the blood pounding in my head, I ran for the stairs. I didn't stop running until I reached the top floor and the safety of my suite. Then I sank onto the bed and tried to calm myself down. My breathing was shallow, and I couldn't think straight. Any minute, I expected a tap at the door from Sebastian.

I wanted him to come and find me, but a conflicting part of me was terrified by the prospect. If he came to my room, it would become real. We wouldn't be able to classify it as a wild moment when we forgot ourselves. If he came to my room and I let him in, there wasn't a flicker of doubt in my mind that we would make love.

I know desire when I see it and he desired me. My resolve was weak from craving him for so long, so if he came in, I knew I wouldn't be able to resist him. In fact, I was desperate to feel him against me again—to feel him inside me.

A harsh voice in my head, reminded me that I'm just an employee and this is a dangerous situation. I crossed the red flag danger line and was about to be swept into treacherous waters if we slept together.

It would become a thing.

It would be unbearable. And so, I didn't make any noise, and I didn't open my door. I resisted the primal urge to go back downstairs in search of him and seek his lips with mine. I resisted the pull of the memory of his confident hands touching my body and making me moan for more.

The voice in my head whispered, 'He doesn't want you for more than a bit of fun. How could he? You're just the nanny. His family would be appalled and forbid him from having a proper relationship with you, even if he wanted to.'

I heard a movement and footsteps on the stairs.

The erratic beat of my heart increased again as I sat there

not knowing whether to pray for him to come up or pray for him to leave me alone.

The sound of the footsteps grew distant until the noise faded, and I guessed he went downstairs. Did he wish I had waited for him, or was he relieved I had gone to my suite?

In a robotic stupor I took off my makeup and cleaned my teeth, before pulling back the duvet and sinking into bed. I pulled the cover over my head to try and block out reality, but it didn't. I lay there for hours thinking of him and yearning for him. His bedroom is only one floor below mine and I could easily go and find him. The thrill of the temptation was overwhelming. I could knock at the door and talk to him about what happened. I could go to him and see if he wanted me as much as I wanted him.

But I didn't. My limbs froze and I lay there for hours replaying how he kissed me and made me cry out for him, like the rerun of an old movie.

I enter the house, and for just a second, I imagine what it would be like if this was my real home. What would it be like to be Sebastian's wife? My heart stirs at the feelings it evokes deep within me. Daisy would be my stepdaughter. I think she'd be happy about it because we spend so much time together and get on well. Since I've been here, her mother has barely seen her. Daisy goes to her place for the occasional weekend but that's about it.

Her mother often cancels at the last minute, and it makes me so sad for Daisy. I try not to let it get to me because it's none of my business. But I know it bothers Sebastian too. His blue-grey eyes usually sparkle with good humour, but last time she called to say she couldn't make it, they darkened, and he cursed.

The first couple of times she cancelled, he didn't display

any emotion, and I thought he took it remarkably well. It's not like he had plans and couldn't go because of her letting him down. He has me here and I'm always available when needed, so even if he did, he could have gone anyway.

But when it happened last time, his carefully constructed, always-happy mask slipped, and briefly I saw how upset he was. He left the room and when he returned; he confided in me that his ex-wife does this repeatedly, and whilst he's happy to have Daisy all the time, he worries about the long-term effect it will have on her. He said he thinks she needs her mother, at least occasionally, and he asked for my professional opinion. The pain on his face stabbed at my emotions, and I chose my reply carefully.

I said that of course it's ideal if a child gets lots of time and attention from both parents. But there are plenty of well-balanced kids who thrive in the care of one loving parent. He exhaled and smiled at me, before briefly touching my hand.

'Thank you,' he said.

I could feel the sincerity in his words, and my heart danced.

'What for?' I said, and my voice sounded more business-like than I intended.

'For being so caring and diligent in your duties. Daisy has flourished since you've been with us. Now her mother seems to have become even more unreliable, and I want you to know how much we appreciate you.'

I lowered my eyes to shield my feelings. As a professional, his words should encourage me. But as a woman in love, his words cut me. They showed so clearly how he thinks of me only as Daisy's nanny. Important for the job, yes. Important to him in any other capacity, no.

But he picked up on my energy, and asked, 'What's the matter?'

My chest was tight, and I blinked back the tears. How stupid of me to think I could mean more to him than that. I was determined he wouldn't see how his words affected me, because I know it was unfair of me to expect anything more from him.

At that point, he had given me no reason to think he wanted anything more from me, so why did I jump to the conclusion that he might like me too?

Something about his teasing, light-hearted banter reaches into my soul, as if it's designed especially for me. I couldn't help but fall in love with him. He's unlike any man I've been involved with before. When I look back on the few serious boyfriends I had in Paris, they pale in comparison.

He's eloquent, funny, and kind. He's sexy in an effortless way, and he's such a brilliant dad to Daisy, it seems impossible for me not to fall for him.

He's smart and sophisticated and I could talk to him for hours.

We did talk for hours sometimes. We talked about Daisy, and he asked what it was like growing up in Paris. When I told him about my mother dying, his eyes glistened.

'I'm so sorry you had to go through that,' he said. 'I know how painful it is to lose a parent, but I can't even imagine how awful it must have been for you to lose your mother at such a young age.'

In truth, I find it difficult to believe that his charms don't bewitch every woman he meets.

I wonder if that's the definition of romantic love.

Loving someone so much that you can't imagine anyone not loving them. He's a single guy, and to me he seems like the best kept secret in London. I can't believe how lucky I am to have such a fabulous boss.

I also can't believe how *unlucky* I am to have such a fabulous boss.

Juliette said if I'm not careful, this is going to end in heartbreak. And I didn't disagree.

But I don't know how to stop this torrent of feelings I have for him. He's charming with everyone, so I guess I'm reading a lot more into our relationship than there is. He's an upper-class gentleman who has been raised to be charming and polite.

The sensible thing would be to stop dreaming about being with him and keep a discreet distance. I'm here for Daisy, after all. She's delightful, so that's a pleasure, too. This is the best nanny position I've ever had. And here I am risking screwing it all up.

But I don't know how to stop.

And then what happened in the kitchen gave me hope that he does have feelings for me.

How do I stop his face from filling my every waking moment and taking over my dreams?

CHAPTER 14

Nathalie

I can tell he has something to get off his chest about what happened between us, and I'm avoiding being alone with him. I'm terrified by what he's going to say, so I keep running away. Whenever his eyes search mine, I busy myself with some activity.

My biggest fear is he's going to say it's not a good idea for me to stay on, because it's too awkward. And I can't deny it is awkward. Even when he persuaded me to attend the ball, I made it clear I didn't want there to be any chance of anyone thinking we were there as a couple. I spent most of the evening behind the scenes. A charity event like that is so much work, so it was easy for me to hide. I'm a member of the Rochester household staff and I made sure everyone I met knew it. I'm trying to be professional, and not risk getting into a compromising situation again.

But then he asked me to dance, and I melted. The air crackled, and I felt dizzy with longing for him. I couldn't think of a reason to say no, and it would have been rude, so I nodded and moved tentatively into his embrace. His touch was gentle but firm, and I loved every second of being in his arms. The tension between us was tangible, and I wanted him to pull me in closer, even though I knew it was a terrible idea and would just make me want him more.

He's so handsome, and in his tux, he looked like a movie star. On the way to the ball, I was about to get into the back-seat of the car, but at the last second, I panicked and jumped in next to the driver.

He must think me strange. All the way into London I regretted it and wished I'd sat next to him, but it was too late. On the drive, I found myself wondering why he didn't bring a date to the ball. How is it he's still single, or at least not dating casually?

I don't get it. I'm relieved he's not seeing anyone as that would destroy me, after having him and Daisy to myself all this time, but if he'd been seeing someone when I turned up, it would have stopped us getting into this awkward situation in the first place.

He would be taken, and I wouldn't have started thinking of him as mine. I don't know when that happened, but it was soon after I moved in. It's presumptuous and naïve of me to fantasise that a billionaire CEO belongs to me, and I can win his heart.

I am a silly, silly girl.

Nothing about my love for him is sensible or logical. It's like a fierce, untameable creature and I don't recognise the sensible, do-the-right-thing Nathalie anymore.

Where did she go?

In the past, when I've been smitten, I've always kept some perspective. When we were released from foster care, my sister and I shared a flat and I wasn't tempted to move in with a man.

Never have I chosen someone forbidden to me. I guess it's not appealed to me before. But perhaps it's simply not something that came my way, and I'm just as susceptible as anyone who gets thrown into the clutches of an irresistible love affair.

My brain says no, but my heart keeps saying yes.

One thing is certain. Sebastian Rochester is forbidden to me. He is off-limits. He is not going to marry the nanny, no matter how much electricity rages between us.

But now I realise he is *everything* I want in a man.

One morning he asks me to come to his home office after I've dropped Daisy at school. I'm nervous as he's never done that before, and I wonder if this is the day when he's going to terminate my employment.

He's usually in London at this time, so it's an unusual set up all round, which puts me even more on edge. Did he stay at home to fire me when Daisy's not around?

I know Daisy loves me, and I think he knows it too, but I mustn't kid myself into thinking I'm the only good nanny he could hire. There are thousands of nannies with similar credentials, and I'm sure Daisy would soon settle down with a different one. She's sweet natured, probably much like Sebastian as a child. She's especially well-adjusted considering the divorce and absence of her mother.

The truth is I've fallen in love with Daisy and her father. The thought of her quickly growing used to a new nanny physically hurts my heart.

My legs are like liquid, barely holding me up, as I move towards his office door.

The room is all clean modern lines, perfect lighting and

photos of family and hotel industry events on the walls. It's elegant, warm, and unfussy, like him.

'Please sit down, Nathalie,' he says, as I buck up the courage to look at him. It seems I can't avoid him any longer.

His beloved face flickers into a smile and he asks lightly, 'How are you doing?'

I straighten my back in the seat and square my shoulders as I say I'm doing fine. I hope my lip doesn't quiver, and I don't betray the many conflicting emotions passing through my body right now.

He talks a bit about how well Daisy is doing and how grateful he is to me for the effort I have made to connect with her.

This doesn't sound like he's about to fire me.

But I stay tense and ready for whatever he is about to say.

He coughs, and I shuffle in my seat. I can feel the heat on my neck and my cheeks grow warm. My shirt sticks to me, and I wish I was wearing something looser.

Sitting here like this is too embarrassing and my heart is slamming into my chest. Being around Sebastian involves many heart pounding moments.

His thick dark lashes flutter briefly, and his blue-grey eyes meet mine dead-on. 'I've wanted to speak to you privately for a while now, but there never seems to be a good time. So sorry for taking this long to get around to it.'

I'm barely breathing now. I'm barely alive. Is this the moment he's going to fire me?

He says, 'I'll just get to the point. I want to apologise for what happened between us.'

I search his eyes for a deeper meaning. All I see is kindness and a hint of shyness.

'It was selfish of me, and I lost control and let the fact that I'm attracted to you, blur my good judgement. I seem to be doing a lot of apologising.' He lets out a short round of his staccato shotgun laughs and pulls a wry face and shrugs his broad shoulders.

He is attracted to me.

My cheeks are burning up. My whole body feels like it's on fire. I wish I could disappear into the floor or merge into the air.

'It's important to me that you know, I have never taken liberties with a member of staff before,' he says.

His eyes are piercing my soul now and I feel hopeless. I feel useless. His words confirm that it was all a mistake. It was just a moment of crazy abandon that he regrets.

I take a quick shaky breath and pray I don't look as gauche as I feel. Thank God I didn't wait for him downstairs after he went to check on Daisy. It would have been mortifying when he came back down and apologised because he wished it hadn't happened.

I've never felt so awkward with a man as I do now. But it's not over yet—his punishing words continue as he slays me with kindness.

'You are by far the best nanny we've had, and I want to do all I can to make sure you are happy here and will stay as long as we can possibly have you.' He smiles at me as if he's just awarded me a prize. He has no awareness of the fact that his polite words are like sharp blades twisting in my gut, confirming that he has no feelings for me beyond fancying me momentarily.

He's obviously trying to put the situation right to make sure I won't leave, for Daisy's sake. At least he's not firing me, I console myself.

But I'm not consoled. My heart has shrivelled into a blackened raisin, and I feel dead. Briefly, I consider resigning. I could make up an excuse about having to return to Paris earlier than expected. I could say there's been a family emergency, or my sister needs me. There's not much point saying a family emergency as he knows I don't have a family. My sister and I only have each other. A sister emergency, then.

The thoughts flash into my head but my heart refuses to follow through on the idea, and my lips won't form the words. The idea of leaving him and Daisy fills me with dread. I can't bear it, and the more I realise how deeply I've fallen in love with him, the worse I feel.

And then just as I think it can't possibly hurt any more, and I'm experiencing a crescendo of pain, he says, 'I've been thinking about us a lot.'

What?

My heart is bashing so hard I fear I might actually faint. It would be a welcome relief from his relentless blue eyes boring into mine.

He continues. He appears confident and smooth and not at all awkward like me. 'Despite coming from such different backgrounds—and countries—' He smiles his charming smile again, the one that makes me lose myself in his eyes, and then with a final flourish of his sword, he thrusts his blade into my heart and lands the lethal blow. 'I'd appreciate it if we can forget that little faux-pax—which was wholly my fault—and just be good friends.' He studies my face, waiting for my answer. There's a pause and then he adds, 'Daisy needs you, and you and I get on so well, it's a perfect arrangement.'

I can't bring myself to speak. I don't know what I want but I know it's not this. I don't want to be good friends with him. It will be like bittersweet torture, and I will only fall harder for him if that's even possible.

But what am I supposed to do? I can't tell him the truth—that I want him more than life itself and I've been in love with him since the second we met. And I don't want to resign because I can't bear the thought of never seeing him again which is undoubtedly what will happen if I return to Paris.

My throat is dry, but I force down the lump stopping me from swallowing.

His eyes are still on me, and they are hopeful. One of the things I love about him is he sees the good in every situation. But how can this be good? It is like a death sentence to our budding romance. Doesn't he feel the bond between us and sense there is more to us than him being my boss and us being good friends?

The tears are building behind my eyes, and I have to get out of there. He's waiting for a response, but I am frozen like an ice statue.

'Nathalie,' he says. 'Are you okay?'

I force myself to speak and barely recognise my croaking voice. 'Yes, I'm fine. Thank you for being straight with me. It's good to know where I stand.'

Now the tears are spilling into my eyes, and I must get away, so I untangle my clasped hands and bounce out of the chair. 'I'm late for an appointment. I have to go now.'

And just like that, I flee his office. And I flee him. I grab my keys and rush out the front door and throw myself into my car. The engine revs and I blast out of the driveway and don't look back.

The tears roll down my face and I'm shaking as I grip the steering wheel.

I feel like I'm in hell and it has just iced over.

CHAPTER 15

Sebastian

Well, that didn't go as I envisioned. I thought Nathalie might be hesitant about my 'just friends' proposition, but I didn't expect her to run out of my office in floods of tears.

I think back to my ex-wife telling me I'm a natural with women, but sometimes I don't know when to be quiet. Looks like she was right. Instead of healing the rift between Nathalie and me, I seem to have turned it into a chasm.

That was not my intention, and I had no hidden agenda. All I tried to do was smooth things over between us so we can go back to an uncomplicated home life. I love having her around, so the friend suggestion seemed like the perfect solution.

I'm not a complete idiot. My feelings for her are way stronger than just friends, but my attraction to her is dangerous, so I must nip it in the bud. I lost control once and if it wasn't for Daisy's bad dream, we would have gone all the way. It would be even harder to come back from that. As it was, I had a sweet taste of her and she's in my veins, but I know I can't have her, and it has to stop.

So, right or wrong, I made the decision for both of us, and was hoping she would see the sense in it, and not react like that.

I fear she is going to get badly hurt if we carry on fooling around, because it can't ever be any more than that. I daren't examine too closely to what extent I may get hurt if we sleep together, but I know I've fallen hard.

The connection between us is profound, and it terrifies me. But the reality is I'm not free to marry whoever I want. The last thing I want is for her to get hurt and to end up hating me. She's too precious for that, and I would rather sacrifice the possibilities of a love affair with her and cherish our friendship. But it doesn't stop me craving her…

Daisy adores her, and it would be irresponsible of me to let things go any further. I kick myself for making a move on her in the kitchen and fucking everything up.

When I make a decision, it's hard to change my mind, and I still think telling her we can't repeat what happened was the right thing to do. But now I feel like I just poked my own eyes out.

I shake my head and click on my inbox. I have a ton to do and need to get on with work.

But her face rises in my thoughts again and I see her blue eyes turn dark and fill with tears. She did her best to hold them back and not let me see how upset she was by my words, but by the time she rose from her chair and left the room, she was sobbing.

I considered going after her, but what would be the point? It would just make not being able to have her, worse. As much as her pride must be wounded and she feels rejected, she'll get over it and then hopefully we can salvage a good working relationship, and perhaps even a proper friendship.

Real friends are scarce when you come from a wealthy family like mine. I try not to be jaded, but many people want to exploit us as a meal ticket. It's no coincidence that Damian and Caspian are struggling just as much as me with the immense challenge of finding the right woman to marry so they can fulfil grandfather's inheritance clause in the will.

There was an obvious attraction between Damian and Jamie. But I can't see Grandfather approving of the match, even if by some miracle she has managed to pierce my brother's impenetrable veil. She's clearly an independent businessperson, but I didn't get any sign she comes from money.

Grandfather was born into a working-class Yorkshire family and founded the company in an astonishing rags-to-riches phenomenon, but he solidified his place amongst the wealthy in society through a combination of his father-in-law's elite position and by making buckets of his own money. And we are long considered a part of the establishment, and he's got the expectations to match. Grandfather expects us to make collaborative marriages that strengthen the family.

The thought of my inevitable impending date with Elizabeth Archer flashes into my head and I push it forcefully away. I don't want to think about that now. I'm too upset by Nathalie's reaction, no matter how much I tell myself it's for the best. We've only known each other a short time, and she's the nanny, for God's sake. What is this feeling between us?

One thing is certain—I'm not rushing down the aisle with Elizabeth Archer or any other 'suitable' bride selected by Grandfather. The whole arranged marriage business is archaic, so I will play along with the dating and let him see I'm trying. But that's it for now. I'll drag it out as long as I can and tell him I haven't found the right woman yet. That will buy me some time.

Nathalie's face hovers at the back of my mind and she springs into my thoughts again and I hope she's okay. Clearly, she doesn't want to be just friends, and judging by her emotional reaction, she has feelings for me, too.

If I'm to keep her on as staff, I must tread carefully and not give her hope that anything can happen between us. On reflection, it was selfish of me to think we can be friends, just because I don't want to lose her. I see that now, and I decide to back off from that idea.

My thoughts slide to my siblings. I'm close with Caspian and I know he is rebellious about the prospect of an arranged or even an approved marriage. Caspian knows that if he doesn't get engaged to someone suitable soon, Grandfather will insist on helping things along. He is more vigilant about it since my divorce, and Damian's relationship ended in such a spectacular fashion. All Damian has done since is party like a wild thing and then take it to the other extreme and hide away from the world and become a workaholic.

Like I say, the oldest three Rochester brothers are not doing too well in the realm of romantic relationships. Our sister Marian is slightly younger than Caspian and shows no signs of settling down either, so I understand why my grandfather is on edge. She's obsessed with her career and spends most of her time at the London flagship store, which she uses as HQ for the home of her Marian Rochester label. As far as I'm aware, she's still single and keeps her private life a secret.

Years ago, she had a crush on one of my best friends when we all still lived at Greystone. He would visit and stay over, and we'd all hang out. She used to turn blood red whenever he came into the room, and I teased her terribly. But other than that, I've not heard a whisper of her going on a date, never mind having a long-term relationship. After university, my friend joined the army and was posted overseas. I haven't heard from him in ages, and briefly I wonder how he's doing and make a mental note to look him up and try to reconnect.

We seem to do a stellar job of disappointing Grandfather. Aside from the strict terms of his will, there's nothing he wants more than a load of great-grandchildren piling in and out of Greystone. My mother's keen to see babies in the nursery too, but she doesn't badger us, fortunately. I've contributed my beautiful Daisy, but no one else looks remotely near the point of having a child. Our New York cousins are slightly younger than us and as far as I'm aware, there are no American great-grandchildren on the horizon either.

Then we have our brothers, Christian, and Max or Maximillian. They are too busy getting laid to worry about marriage yet, and a part of me envies them. Bringing up the rear is dear, sweet Lillian, who we call Lily. She's the baby of the family, and we all spoil her. She's at university, so I hope it's going to be a long, long time before she produces a baby for the Rochester clan. The thought of a guy messing with my baby sister is not something I wish to contemplate.

No one escaped the dreaded *ian* at the end of their name. Mum and dad must have used up all the suitable names, so it's just as well they didn't have more kids.

I must stop wasting my morning. There's a ton of stuff to do, and I click onto my calendar and check the latest updates from my assistant.

My mood darkens as I see the entry for Friday evening: Dinner with Elizabeth Archer.

I let out a long, heavy sigh. *Dinner. Really? Fuck.* I don't know how I'm going to get through an intimate dinner with a woman I don't even want to date. It seems like a death sentence.

Pull yourself together. You're a Rochester and you knew this day was coming.

I sigh again, and then click 'accept' on my calendar. Looks like I'm going to dinner with Elizabeth Archer on Friday evening.

My heart sinks at the prospect of Nathalie finding out. Maybe I'll avoid mentioning it. She doesn't have to know where I'm going. It's not like we're in a relationship—I mean, we kissed for a few minutes, and yes, I kissed her in places I most definitely shouldn't have—but that's it. I've apologised and told her it can't go any further. We're both free agents, and I won't disappoint my grandfather again.

So why do I feel this heavy gloom descending on me and enveloping me like a shroud? My feelings for Nathalie torment me. I can't stop my sexual urges for her.

Even at the end of my marriage, I didn't feel this solid bleakness. Now, looking back, I knew we weren't right for each other, but I didn't want to accept it. I was so wrapped up in work I avoided thinking about my personal life. And when my wife left, I dealt with it reasonably well. I was hurt, yes. But I didn't have the luxury of brooding for long.

Daisy was the focus of my attention, and I channelled my energy into making sure she was okay and keeping the business moving forward. The separation and divorce happened relatively quickly and although I felt like she'd kicked me in the nuts, I knew I'd get over it. I didn't get close to a woman again because I didn't want to risk the heartache. Then Nathalie infiltrated my barriers because I didn't expect her…

Everyone who knows me will tell you I'm an upbeat, sunny-natured kind of guy. I don't do gloomy.

So why do I feel like I'm suffocating in a dark pit?

CHAPTER 16

Nathalie

Just friends?

After we almost had full-blown sex in the kitchen, he now wants us to be friends? I'm struggling to get my head around it and was so embarrassed that I couldn't keep my cool when he called me into his office. I'm avoiding him even more than before now, but I know this can't go on. He is my boss. Avoiding him is on the brink of being negligent in my job. And unless I'm getting paranoid, I think he is avoiding me too, so we are in a terrible spot.

The memory of how I started crying and ran out of his office makes me burn with humiliation and I feel the tingle on my cheeks as I relive it.

He's been leaving earlier and returning home later than usual all week. This is the first time we've had breakfast together in ages. We've only interacted briefly when discussing Daisy's summer schedule and we have her as our chaperone. It's less dangerous this way. Daisy seems oblivious to the weird atmosphere and asks if we can visit Richmond Park again. I told her I'll take her, but she insists she wants us to go with her daddy, and she badgers him about it now.

I'm buttering a slice of toast for her before sitting down for breakfast. His eyes are on me, and I muster the courage to look at him. One look is all it takes, and the spark runs between us like a city power line.

'Would you like to go to the park again, Nathalie?' he asks.

His sensitive blue-grey eyes appear guarded, and I wonder if he's shielding himself from me like I'm shielding myself from him.

The question triggers a mix of emotions in me, and the adrenalin rushes through my body as hope flutters in my chest.

Is that an invitation?

Before I can stop myself, I reply, 'That sounds good. It was such fun last time.' I can't maintain eye contact with him as his eyes burn into me and I worry he can see into my soul. I look at Daisy and see her happy, eager expression.

'Today! May we go today?' she pleads.

'Not today, darling,' Sebastian tells her.

Her bottom lip protrudes slightly, and she clutches her half-eaten piece of toast in a sticky little hand. 'Please, Daddy. Why not today?'

'If your daddy says he can't do it today, then we must accept that with good grace,' I tell Daisy, kicking into my nanny role on autopilot.

But the hope that fluttered in my breast shrivels, and I chastise myself for reading too much into his question. He was just being polite and making conversation. It wasn't an invitation.

I'm cross. I got my hopes up, even though I promised myself not to fall any deeper. He's effortlessly charming and I fall for it every time, but I must accept that there's nothing special between us beyond sexual attraction. He told me so, and I should believe him. I'm allowing myself to get carried away with fantasising about him again, and it's fatal.

'I can't today,' he says, 'but tomorrow we can go if you like.' He moves his plate to one side and picks up his phone. 'Let's check the weather and see if it's nice enough to go tomorrow morning.'

My heart skips faster as he checks the weather app. How pathetic am I that I let my happiness depend on tomorrow's weather?

If it's dry and sunny, I'll get to spend some stolen moments with him. If it's raining, the park visit won't go ahead. I pray for a dry forecast.

He raises his eyes to mine again and now they are warm and full of light. 'Sunny and dry tomorrow. Should be quite warm. We could go about 10 a.m. before it gets too hot if that suits you?'

Daisy bounces off her chair, jumps up and down, and starts dancing. 'Yay! Yay! Yay!'

Joy floods through me and I laugh at her antics, even though it's not proper table etiquette. 'Daisy, you'll get indigestion like that,' I say.

I feel his eyes still on me. He's waiting for my reply. I turn to him. 'Perfect,' I say. 'We'll be ready at 10.'

Daisy's enthusiasm is infectious, and we both laugh. The fog of pain lifts, and I'm optimistic for the first time in days. He still wants to spend time with me. Then I realise this may be part of his plan for us to be friends.

And it's your job, you fool. He's just spending time with his daughter, and you're tagging along as her nanny. Don't read more into it than that.

But all day, my treacherous heart glows, and all I can think about is we're going to glorious Richmond Park tomorrow morning. We'll get to hang out and chat about nonsense, eat ice cream and Daisy will ask me to take more photos of the graceful red deer. They are her favourite.

I feel my resistance slipping, almost like the removal of a physical barrier. Maybe being friends isn't such a terrible idea, after all? At least I'd get to enjoy his company.

Later that afternoon, I hear the Range Rover pull up. I'm only just back from collecting Daisy from a play date and she is changing in her bedroom. I peer out the window and there is Seb, taking long strides towards the front door. My heart taps faster, knowing I'll see him any second.

Briefly I wonder why he's home now. It's Friday, and he usually gets home later. He said we couldn't take Daisy to the park today, so I presumed he would work late.

His phone rings as he enters the house and I hear the echo of his deep voice reverberate through the large entrance hall. My mind's racing and I sense something is going on, but I tell myself I'm just getting in a panic. We go downstairs and he sweeps Daisy into his arms, and she gabbles in his ear about her day. He places her back on her feet and says he must go and get changed. It's unusual for him to change when he comes in, and I wonder what his plans are. Maybe he's going out this evening. He hasn't been out in the evening since we went to the ball, and only on one occasion I recall before that when he said he was meeting his brothers.

But who's counting?

I shouldn't be, but I am. I've grown used to the idea of him either being in London at work or at home with us. I suppose that's odd for a single guy of his status and you'd think he'd be out more. It kills me not being able to ask him what he's doing, but he's my boss, not my boyfriend. I must remember that.

Sebastian says we should go ahead and give Daisy dinner. He likes to sit with her when he's home usually. Today, I eat with her and try to give her my full attention, but my mind's spinning and I've no appetite. My stomach churns, but I tell myself to relax. It's none of my business where he's going, and besides, he's probably going to some dull business event and I'm overreacting.

Then he walks into the room, and his familiar aftershave teases my senses. Memories of us kissing and him touching me in all the right places flood back. His smell drives me insane, and I focus on moving broccoli around my plate as he leans down and kisses Daisy on the cheek. 'Goodnight, sweetheart,' he says. 'Be good for Nathalie and go to sleep when she tells you, so you've got plenty of energy for the park tomorrow. I'll check on you when I get home.'

Daisy is fine about him going out, but the food is lodged in my throat.

'Have a good evening, Nat,' he says. 'See you in the morning.'

He winks at me, and my insides turn to liquid. He's dressed in navy trousers and a beautiful crisp white shirt accentuates his broad shoulders. His hair is still damp and shining from the shower and his masculine scent surrounds and torments me. I look at him and do my best to smile, but it's fake and doesn't reach my eyes.

'You okay?' he says, lingering near Daisy's shoulder as he gazes at me.

I nod. 'Of course. I'm great. Have a wonderful evening.'

Daisy pipes up. 'Where are you going, Daddy? Are you going to see Uncle Damian?'

He pats her shoulder. 'Not tonight, sweetie.'

She says, 'Have you got a girlfriend?' Daisy then

bombards him with questions and doesn't give him a chance to answer any of them.

My heart is hurtling around inside my chest, and feels like it might burst out, as I hold my breath and wait for him to answer.

'My friend says her daddy doesn't live with her and her mummy anymore, and he has a new girlfriend now,' she continues.

Sebastian strokes her head and says, 'There are all sorts of families, pumpkin.'

Daisy thrusts her chin out and looks sad. 'But Suzie said his girlfriend is mean to her. She pretends to be nice, but when they're alone, she's horrible. Promise me you'll only have nice girlfriends, Daddy.'

I glance at Sebastian and see a muscle twitch in his jaw. His discomfort is palpable.

'Of course, I will only have nice girlfriends,' he says to Daisy, avoiding looking at me. 'Same as you only choose nice friends.'

He ruffles her hair and turns to leave, but Daisy is oblivious to the tension she's causing and isn't finished with her questions yet.

'Daddy. Can Nathalie be your girlfriend?' she says, her eyes gleaming. 'Then we can go everywhere together like a family, and you won't need a mean girlfriend. We could go on holiday to the seaside like you promised.'

He winces slightly, and there's a cautious note in his tone. 'I don't want you to worry about things like that. I promise you there will be no mean girlfriends and you've got me and Nathalie right here with you.' He glides over the holiday comment.

I can't resist looking at him. I want to see his reaction even though my cheeks are hot, and I'm embarrassed as hell by Daisy's request.

He avoids looking at me as he plants another kiss on Daisy's head and makes his escape. At the doorway, he glances back, and his eyes sweep over both of us, and he throws me a mischievous smile. 'Be good and keep the noise down. Remember, we're going to the park in the morning.'

And then I hear the door click shut, and he's gone.

Daisy chatters on about mean girlfriends and I can't eat any more of my dinner. My emotions are all over the place and I feel nauseous. Clearly, he's going on a date. I'm not mad at him. How can I be? I have absolutely no right to be because he promised me nothing beyond a job. Zero. But I can't help being disappointed and my heart feels as though it's withering more each day, like a dying flower in a drought.

I'm mad at myself. What kind of fool am I to let myself fall for a guy like him? He's completely out of my reach, and Daisy's outburst must have mortified him.

Daisy and I watch a feel-good film together after I help her get ready for bed. It's summer holidays and we don't have to be up that early. She snuggles against me on the big, cosy sofa. Towards the end of the film, she fights to stay awake, but her eyelids droop and her head follows as she succumbs to sleep and slumps against my arm. I carry her upstairs and lay her in bed.

She's a little angel and such a joy to care for. I stroke her mussed hair and bend down to kiss her warm cheek.

She shifts and opens her eyes a slit. 'I love you, Nathalie,' she mumbles. 'Don't ever leave.'

My heart is full of tenderness. 'I love you too,' I whisper, pulling the blanket over her bare arms and tucking her in. 'I'm right here.'

Downstairs, I watch TV for a while, flicking from one channel to another. Mrs Johnson pops her head in to say goodnight and then the house falls silent. I try to get into a popular show my friend Juliette recommended, but all I can see is Sebastian's face.

I've not been jealous over a guy before, but the thought of him dating someone wounds me deeply. Poisonous darts ricochet through me and pierce my delicate heart. It doesn't matter how much I tell myself I have no right to be jealous. I am. Now I regret not being receptive to his offer of friendship, but part of me hates myself for being weak. Perhaps if I hadn't been so weird about it, he wouldn't have even gone on a date.

The thought crosses my exhausted mind that maybe he's doing it to draw the line and show me there can be nothing romantic between us. I'm obsessing again, and he probably hasn't given me a second thought since he left the house. He's a single man in his prime, and it was only a matter of time before he started dating.

I should leave and get a new position before this grows any more painful. If he's seeing someone seriously, he will want to bring her home. If I stay on, I will have to pretend I don't care, and judging by my performance today, I won't be able to pull it off.

Juliette texts me to ask if I want to come into London tomorrow. It's my day off and as much as I'd like to stay and hang out with Sebastian and Daisy after the park, I must create distance between us. If he is dating, I need to get some perspective.

I don't have the resolve to resign now, but I need a break from thinking about him. Getting away will do me good and so I agree to meet Juliette at her flat the following afternoon.

She teases me a bit when I say we're going to the park together. Juliette knows I have a crush on my boss and that we had a bit of a thing. What she doesn't know is how deeply I've fallen, but I intend to tell her because I need to talk about my horrible dilemma.

I go to bed and sleep intermittently until I hear him come in. I squint at my phone and see it's not that late—not even eleven yet. My ears strain for noises, as I listen for whether he's brought someone home with him. He could do, and I need to be prepared. But the house remains quiet apart from one set of familiar footsteps on the stairs. There's a pause and I imagine him creeping into Daisy's room to kiss her goodnight without waking her. And then I hear his footsteps again as he walks towards his bedroom. My heart is sore, but I'm relieved he's home, and I fall into a restless sleep.

CHAPTER 17

Sebastian

My date wished to meet for dinner, so I told my assistant to book whatever restaurant Elizabeth Archer requested.

I arrive ten minutes early and the host shows me to our table in a prominent part of the restaurant.

I don't know if it's a coincidence, but she chose a swanky restaurant that is just a few minutes' walk from my hotel.

I come here occasionally for business lunches but have never been here on a date before. Her restaurant choice says a lot about her. She must like to be seen in the coolest spots. I'm told this place has a long waiting list, but my assistant always gets a table when she drops my name.

They would know my date's name, too. Archer is one of the most prominent international banking families, and the more high-net-worth people dine here, the better for the restaurant's publicity. It's a match made in heaven for everyone but me. Well, possibly not for her either. For all I know, she's being dragged here kicking and screaming.

I wish I could say I had pre-date nerves because that would mean I was excited. But the reality is I don't feel anything about this date, other than dead inside.

I understand my responsibilities as a Rochester, but must I really be forced into an arranged marriage and have to pick my future wife like I'm at a cattle market?

It all seems so old-fashioned to me. Damian gave me a pep talk when I vented to him. He said he understands it's tough, and to just take it as it comes. He suggested maybe I'll like her, and that marrying a woman with a similar background could be the best thing. Be open-minded, he said.

It's alright for him, spouting off about what's *best.*

I feel like a sacrificial lamb. My theory is Grandfather is putting all the pressure on me to remarry because I'm the spare, so he has a backup heir in case Damian goes completely off the rails again.

I try to shake off the frustration, and remind myself, it's not my date's fault, so it's not fair to blame her. She's probably just as irritated by this scenario as me and may not want to date me at all. It's my grandfather who's insisting on me meeting her. Bubbles of resentment rise in my chest as I think about our recent conversations.

She's his number one candidate for me to marry.

No pressure.

It's Friday evening, and I'd rather be at home, relaxing in the garden watching the sun go down in the bright summer sky, glass of Chablis in one hand. Daisy is most likely tucked up in bed by now.

Before things got complicated, Nathalie would join me for a glass of wine in the garden before dinner, and I loved those evenings most. There's nothing better after a hectic week at the hotel than chilling at home with your favourite people. And I realise that Nathalie has quickly become one of my favourite people. It was difficult to tear myself away from her this evening, and I saw the pain in her eyes when Daisy asked about girlfriends.

I glance at the Rolex my mother bought me. Elizabeth Archer isn't late yet, but if she doesn't arrive in the next few minutes, she will be.

I abhor lateness. There's no excuse for it, but I realise she may want to be fashionably late and is leaving it to the last minute to make an appearance, so she doesn't seem too keen.

I sigh. I've never enjoyed playing power games, which is another reason I haven't dated since my marriage ended. In my experience, the best people come into your life organically. I've not used a dating app, not that it would be a good idea as a member of the Rochester family. We need to be discreet, which is why I find myself in this situation, about to meet my potential future wife.

Tension grips my chest as I face the reality of what I have to do. If I go with the flow and marry a suitable woman so grandfather gives me his blessing, I will keep my shares and seat on the board and secure my full inheritance. That will make me a billionaire in my own right. Or I could disregard his wishes and take my chances—see where the chips fall.

The host heads my way, and I glimpse a dark-haired woman walking towards me. She's not a complete surprise—I looked her up online before agreeing to the date, just to be on the safe side. Lucrative collaboration of assets or not, I won't consider marrying someone I'm not remotely attracted to.

I rise from my seat and welcome her as the host pulls the chair out for her to sit opposite me.

She's pretty, and if I wasn't crazy about Nathalie, I might be pleased about having dinner with her. As it is, I just need to get through this evening and make it as painless as possible for both of us.

I tell myself it's just another business deal.

I ask her what she'd like to drink, and we order, and the host leaves us. We're alone. There's an awkward pause, but she rushes to fill it and chatters about the traffic on the way over and how she's sorry she's a few minutes late.

She is obviously nervous, and I do my best to put her at ease. 'No problem,' I say. 'You weren't late at all.'

'So,' she says, raising one eyebrow slightly. 'This is weird, isn't it?'

I smile, relieved she's not acting like this is a regular date where we are excited to get to know each other.

I agree it's weird and tell her that my grandfather is keen for us to get together.

'Your grandfather is lovely,' she says, a hint of shyness in her eyes. 'I'm very close with my grandfather, and as you probably know, they have been good friends for years.'

I nod. 'Yes, they go way back, since they were both expanding their empires. I suppose we should be flattered they selected us for each other.'

She grimaces. 'Can I be straight with you?'

'Of course,' I reply, curious about what she's going to tell me.

'I didn't want to date you.' She swallows and looks sheepish. 'No, that's not what I meant. It's nothing to do with you. I mean, I didn't want to date *anyone*.'

'Ah,' I say, pleased she's not pretending we could be a great love match. 'So, why are you here?'

She spins her diamond bracelet around one delicate wrist and looks flustered. Her long pink nails are perfectly manicured, and the rings on her fingers sparkle.

I wait for her response. If I'm going to have to date until I find a woman, I can eventually force myself to marry, I'd better learn how to do this with grace, or it will be a shit-show. It's hard enough I haven't dated in years, never mind dating someone I've never met before.

She looks into my eyes, and I see sadness lurking in hers. 'Grandfather says it's time for me to marry and he's let me have long enough to find someone suitable.'

I roll my eyes. 'Sounds like our grandfathers are singing from the same hymn sheet.'

'What about you, then? It's embarrassing, but I'd rather know where I stand. Did you want to date me or were you pushed into it too?'

'I don't wish to be ungallant, but yes, the latter.' I pause and sip my wine, then flash her a quick smile to soften my words. She seems lovely, and this date might not be as awful as I feared. 'It's nothing to do with you. Dating just isn't my thing, really. My marriage ended badly and I'm in no rush for a repeat.'

She smiles back at me and nods.

'So, you have a young daughter, I understand,' she says.

This is safe territory, and I could talk about Daisy all day, so I tell her an amusing story and top it off with how she's worried I'll get a mean girlfriend. To her credit, she laughs, and listens patiently, and asks all the right questions.

Of course, she's been raised to behave impeccably in society and I'm under no illusion that it means she's as interested in my daughter as she makes out. Why would she be?

The date passes quickly enough as we eat, and I notice several curious pairs of eyes on us.

Our forthright approach seems to have taken the pressure off and we chat naturally over dinner, and it's not altogether unpleasant.

We skip dessert and order coffee, and she catches me checking my watch.

'Somewhere to be?' she asks, her eyes shrewd.

'No, nowhere, in particular,' I say, wondering what Nathalie is doing and if she'll still be awake if I leave soon.

When can I leave without appearing rude?

I'm not remotely interested in Elizabeth Archer as a future wife, and I don't think she's remotely interested in me as a husband.

'It's okay,' she says. 'It's not going to work, is it?'

'What do you mean?' I ask, circling around her comment and unsure what to say.

'I mean, you clearly have something else you'd rather be doing—*or someone*—perhaps?' She laughs in a conspiratorial manner.

I shake my head and meet her eyes. 'Is it that obvious?'

She nods and pulls a wry expression. 'Yes, I recognise the symptoms. I'm in the same boat. I've been seeing someone, but my family will never give their blessing for me to marry him. *Not suitable*.'

I sigh. 'Sorry to hear that, Elizabeth.'

'Please call me Lizzy. We can be friends. We both need an ally, given this awkward situation we find ourselves in.'

She's not wrong, and I'm grateful for her pragmatic attitude.

'What are we going to tell our grandfathers when they ask how our date went?' I ask her.

We agree on a mutual course of action, and I thank her for her honesty.

She laughs when we emerge and see our drivers parked next to each other, waiting outside the restaurant.

'Thanks for a lovely evening, Sebastian. It was good getting to know you. I will tell my grandfather you were the perfect gentleman.'

How will I ever find a suitable wife when all I could think about was Nathalie?

CHAPTER 18

Nathalie

My alarm rings and I ease myself out of bed and open the shutters. It's as bright and sunny as the forecast, and I wonder what the day will bring.

The excitement I felt about spending the morning with Sebastian and Daisy at the park has waned since I realised he went on a date.

I'm still on edge about what happened yesterday and, to make it even worse, I'm beating myself up about being on edge. It's not my place to judge him, and now I'm making myself wrong for how I feel, so it's double heartache.

My head throbs as conflicting thoughts crucify me. Daisy's excited about our outing, and I pull myself together and paste a smile on my face as her small hand slips inside mine on the way downstairs.

When she sees Sebastian, she flies into his arms. 'Sugar

plum,' he says, pushing the open newspaper aside and pulling her onto his knee.

I can't help genuinely smiling at all the pet names he has for her. Many of them are new to me. I've not worked for a British family before, so I'm learning lots of new words.

The sun is high in the azure blue sky, and I can feel the heat on my face as we jump out of the car and walk across the carpark to a play area near a small café. It's mid-morning and promises to be a scorcher. The deer are already seeking shade beneath the ancient oak trees.

Daisy sees one of her friends from school and asks if she can play with her. They run around on the grass playing tag and giggling. Sebastian and I sit on a café bench watching them. A tense silence descends over us, and I fumble for something to say. Last time we were here, there was an easy camaraderie between us, and I miss it. The future was full of the thrill of the unknown, but now I see only no-entry signs.

I chastise myself for being over-dramatic. This is just one job and I'll move on when the time is right, and I'll meet a man who loves me like I love him.

Won't I?

I don't understand why, but falling for Sebastian seems like a much bigger deal than that. We've not even slept together, so why does it feel like he's taken a piece of my heart and I'll never get it back? I muse whether he is *the one,* and I will not get over him.

His phone buzzes, and out of the corner of my eye I see him send a quick text. Fleetingly, I wonder if he's replying to his date from last night. He returns his phone to his pocket and says, 'You're very quiet this morning, Nathalie. Are you still mad at me?'

I fight back the blush that threatens to creep over my cheeks, and I turn to him. 'I wasn't mad at you,' I say.

'Upset then?' He pauses. His deep, gravelly voice sends goosebumps over my skin. 'I'm sorry I upset you. That was the last thing I intended to do.'

I shake my head and swallow. I feel stupid.

'No, it was my fault,' I say, turning to him. 'You tried to make things right, and it took me off guard, that's all. I'm fine.'

His eyes emanate kindness as they bore into mine. I do my best to hold myself together and not let him see the emotion that's rippling through me. The kindness just makes it harder.

'You sure?' He presses. 'I don't want you to be uncomfortable in any way.'

'I'm okay,' I say, tight-lipped, even though I feel anything but.

'Can things go back to how they were between us, before, you know—' His words tail off and he runs a large hand through his dark hair. He seems sad too, and it gives me courage.

'Before we kissed?' I say, suddenly bold, pushing my nervousness aside.

He nods and looks downcast. 'I've said I'm sorry about that. Will you please forgive me?'

Clearly, he doesn't realise his polite apologies destroy me. His apologising repeatedly just makes me feel worthless—like I'm a mistake he made and is desperate to tidy away as though that incredible time between us never happened.

The familiar vein of unworthiness rushes through me and I poke at my insecurities like a sore tooth. I thought I'd worked through my 'not enough' pattern with a therapist, but this dynamic with Sebastian brings it all flooding back to the surface.

I was a confident, happy child until my mother fell ill, and when she died, my father, sister and I fell into a despondent state. He started drinking even more heavily than he did during her illness. When she was alive, even from her sickbed, she somehow kept him from self-destructing, but after her death, he lapsed into a dark space and drank himself steadily into oblivion. I still remember the feelings of despair and hopelessness. I wanted to help him, but he was beyond my reach and whatever I said didn't seem to make any difference. He was no longer the same adoring father he had been when we were younger.

Sabine and I didn't just lose our mother. When she died, we lost our father too. He couldn't bear life without her and was never the same again. After that, came a string of women in and out of our apartment. Some were nice enough, but others were like Daisy would call—mean. They had no interest in two little girls grieving for their mother, and it wasn't long before he gave up all pretence of taking care of us, and we were put into foster care.

The only blessing was that my sister and I managed to stay together. I was fierce about that and would not allow social services to split us up. We were a set, and we clung to each other as we came to terms with the loss of our parents and the only home we had ever known.

'Nathalie?' Seb says, and he leans towards me and elbows me gently.

I jump as he jolts me out of my memories.

'Penny for your thoughts,' he says, and the expression makes me turn and smile at him.

'Sorry, I was far away.'

'I could see that. Is there something I can help with?'

His tender words make me want to cry again, and I wish I could get a grip on my emotions. I haven't been sentimental and dwelling on the past like this for a long time.

I force a bright smile onto my face. 'No, it's fine. You're right. Of course, we can be friends. What else would we be?'

His relieved expression rips off another raw piece of my heart, and for the first time since the kitchen kissing, I feel a rush of rebelliousness. If he doesn't feel how deep this connection is between us, then he's the fool. I know I'm not imagining it, but if he wants to just be friends, then friends we will be.

And boss-employee, of course. It's difficult to forget that's what we really are when he pays me to live in his house.

Sebastian stands and whistles to catch Daisy's attention and calls her over. He asks who wants ice cream when she joins us. Daisy tugs on his hand so they can go and choose what she wants. I decline the offer, saying it's a bit early for ice cream for me, but I'd love a latte if they have one.

I watch them walk hand-in-hand towards the café and lose sight of his broad shoulders and dark hair as he disappears into the queue. My chest feels tight. Leaning back against the table, I look up at the sky and inhale deeply and release a couple of long, slow breaths.

That's it. I will do my job to the best of my ability and the year will fly by and then we'll go our separate ways.

I can't make him love me, so there's no point making more of a fool of myself trying.

CHAPTER 19

Nathalie

I hop off the tube—which I still call the metro in my head—at Knightsbridge and walk the few minutes to Juliette's flat. London is huge. I thought Paris was big until I tried to get my head around the size of London.

I've hardly been anywhere alone, out of the Richmond area. It's easy enough to get to Juliette's by train, and we sometimes go for something to eat or for a wander around the shops. When I have a day off, I try to get to see her unless I'm volunteering at the kids' centre. If I had to find my way around London alone, I'm sure I'd be lost in a heartbeat.

Juliette's expecting me and buzzes me up right away. Her flat is on an upper floor of a tall, elegant buttermilk-hued building near Hyde Park, and I run up the stairs two at a time and arrive to see her standing in the doorway waiting for me.

We kiss effusively in the French style, and she ushers me

inside. I walk to the window and admire the wide, tree-lined street from above. It's like a picture postcard and I'm reminded we are both living our London dream we talked about throughout university.

Calling out to Juliette, who is in the kitchen, I say, 'You're so lucky to live here. I told Sebastian where you live, and he said it's one of the most affluent neighbourhoods in London. Near to his hotel, actually.'

Juliette hands me a steaming cup of milky coffee. Her lips curve into a cheeky grin. 'Got to be some benefits for putting up with these annoying bureaucrats. They're enough to drive me crazy, sometimes.'

'Yes, I can imagine. Good for you, getting a place like this. *C'est trés chic*,' I say, as we chatter on in French. 'You're also lucky you get to speak French all the time. Apart from with you and the occasional call with Sabine, I barely utter a word these days.'

'I thought you were teaching the little girl to speak French,' she says.

'Teaching a five-year-old some basics is hardly conversation!'

'True,' she laughs. 'Well, you are welcome here anytime. You know that, I hope. I get lonely sometimes, and it's amazing having you nearby.'

We sink onto the sofa and drink our coffee and nibble at a selection of divine chocolate biscuits. My best friend then interrogates me in the Juliette style I know so well.

'Talking of your job, how is your sexy boss?' she asks, her eyes locking onto mine, willing me to serve the latest scoop.

She knows we had a bit of *thing* in the kitchen and since I told her, she never tires of asking for the latest news. Juliette is a hopeless, or should I say, *hopeful* romantic, and is always looking for the happy-ever-after in every story. Sometimes I wish I was as optimistic as her, but I lost my childlike innocence when my family fell apart.

'He's good,' I reply, humouring her after a sip of coffee. 'He took me and Daisy to Richmond Park this morning.'

'Yes, you mentioned you were going. And?'

'And, what?' I say, playing like I don't know what she's alluding to.

'You know. Did he say anything else about the "let's be friends" suggestion?' She purses her lips in a mock kiss. 'I mean, is he offering friends with sexy benefits, or just friends?'

'Oh that. Um. Not really,' I say, feeling like she's grilling me on a hot barbeque.

She is relentless, and my reticent reply doesn't put her off. 'Do you think he was really offering you friends with benefits, or perhaps nanny with benefits?'

I roll my eyes at her mischievous probing. A part of me wants to talk about him non-stop, but another part of me wants to keep my conversations with him between us. They feel sacred somehow, and like I betrayed him by telling her exactly what he said, so I'm not as forthcoming as I know she would like.

'You're pursing your lips,' she says. 'Honestly, I've never known you to be so hesitant talking about a guy you're into. What is it with this one? What makes him so special?' She pauses, and bites into another biscuit, then continues after I pull a face. 'I mean, he's super-rich, okay, and a big shot CEO, but he's still just a guy who has the hots for you.'

My cheeks are pink, and my face heats up more as she studies me.

'You've got it so bad. I can see it in your eyes. You're never usually like this when you're dating.'

I laugh, but there's not much humour in it, and the sound

is fake even to my own ears. 'Maybe because we're not dating!'

'Come on,' she says, 'for heaven's sake, dish the dirt. I can see there's more to this than you're telling me.'

I decide it will do me good to talk to her, and I know I can trust her, so I tell her the latest. 'Honestly, there's no dirt to dish! I only wish there was. Ever since our risqué episode in the kitchen, we've barely been near each other. I don't know how much more I can take of it, to be honest,' I sigh. 'I'm so hot for him and dream about him every night.'

She stares at me and then asks, 'And how is he behaving towards you?'

My heart clatters at the question.

'He's the perfect gentleman.' I sigh. 'But a total wanker, too, though, because he keeps apologising for what happened and it makes me feel like absolute crap.'

She laughs and nearly spits out her coffee.

'He obviously thinks it was a terrible mistake and regrets every second of it,' I vent.

'I doubt it,' Juliette says with authority, as if she knows something I don't, after studying me for a minute.

Granted, she has a lot more experience in matters of the heart than me, and her words cause tiny buds of hope to blossom within me, against my cautious judgement.

'What do you mean?' I can't resist jumping on her hook and taking the bait.

She narrows her eyes and says that she wouldn't be at all surprised if he's madly in love with me.

My heart beats faster as I listen to her words. The sound of them is like a soothing balm for my soul, and for a second, I relish the feeling washing over me. But then I remember how many romance novels she reads, and that my best friend is a total sucker for a happy-ever-after.

'Oh, Juliette, Juliette,' I say, shaking my head and hugging my knees to my chest. 'As much as I'd love for you to be right, this is real life, not one of your romance novels.'

She rolls her eyes and sighs as if I'm a lost cause.

I inhale sharply and tell her I think he went on a date last night.

'Hmm,' she says.

Looking at her expectantly, I wait to see what she makes of that crushing revelation. Surely that will puncture her romantic balloon.

'Do you know that for sure, or are you just catastrophising?'

I grimace. 'No, not for sure, but he went out for dinner, and it seemed like he was dressed for a date.'

'Don't jump to conclusions,' she warns me. 'If you don't know where he went, then there's no point imagining the worst scenario.'

True.

'Did he come home alone last night?'

I nod and tell her I heard him come in around eleven alone.

She takes a final swig of her coffee and places it on the wooden table.

'There you are then,' she says, nodding like a wise old sage. 'It wasn't much of a hot date if he came home early and alone.'

She fuels my fantasies, but I'm still wary, and I change the subject and suggest a stroll in Hyde Park.

When she walks me back to the station, she says, 'Have a bit of faith in love, ma chérie. If you're meant to be together, nothing and no one can stop it. And I have a feeling you two are meant to be.'

Whilst I appreciate Juliette's romantic philosophy, I'm not sure giving me hope in this hopeless situation will not do more harm than good. But I know her well enough to realise that my pessimistic attitude to love won't prevent her from predicting a great love for me and Sebastian, so I smile at her and think how blessed I am to have her as my best friend.

As we weave through the busy street, I say, 'I love your optimism, but to be honest, I don't think he can be my Romeo, no matter how much I'd like him to be.'

'Stranger things have happened,' she says. 'Time will tell. Time will tell…'

CHAPTER 20

Sebastian

We're approaching the opening of our new hotel in Cannes and the pressure is building. It doesn't help that my head isn't fully in the game. Usually, I would be all over it and excited at the thought of another hotel on the Rochester map. But instead of thinking about what needs to be done for a successful launch, I'm thinking about Nathalie. All the time. I can't get her out of my mind, and now there's a message from Grandfather and I call him back.

'Are we all set for the opening? This is high profile, and we can't afford for it to be anything less than perfect,' he says.

I tell him plans are all in place and we've received confirmations from several French dignitaries and celebrities who will attend the event.

'When are you arriving?' he asks.

'Arriving where?' I say, puzzled.

'Cannes?'

'I'm not arriving. Xavier, my deputy, is attending. Made perfect sense, seeing as he speaks fluent French and has worked on the project all the way through.'

'Hmm,' says Grandfather over the phone. I can tell he'd rather I was going in person. I do my best to keep him happy and live up to his expectations, but I'm confident they don't need me there. Xavier is more than up to the job.

'There should be a Rochester in attendance, for maximum publicity.'

'Okay, I can fly out on the morning of the opening if you think it's that important,' I offer, hoping he'll let it pass because I really don't want to go. I'm juggling so many projects and am rammed with work. And Daisy might go to her mother's soon, which in theory should mean I've got more flexibility, but I'm always wary she's going to change plans at the last minute. It puts me on edge and makes it more difficult than if she'd never said she'd have her in the first place.

Grandfather says, 'Hmm, yes, I think you should go.'

'Right, okay, I'll make the arrangements for a fly-in-fly-out visit,' I agree to pacify him. If he thinks it's important, then he's probably right. I don't underestimate his years of experience. He expanded Rochesters internationally and I don't kid myself we would be where we are in the business if it wasn't for him.

'Good call,' he says, as if it was my idea all along. It's subtle, but he's smart like that. 'How did it go with Lizzy Archer, by the way? I heard you had dinner.'

I can't help smiling at how he slips it into the conversation and I imagine him and her grandfather hatching their plan for world domination through the two of us.

'It was good,' I say. 'She's lovely.'

'That is wonderful news. I thought you two would hit it

off. She's a fabulous girl. Known her since she was a kid.' Then he adds with a wistful note, 'My goodness, when I look back, I don't know where the years have gone.'

He prods and probes for more details with the skill of a master interrogator and seems satisfied when I say we will be having a second date. Just as I think it's over and I can get back to work, he adds, 'I've got a suggestion.'

My stomach lurches. I'm familiar enough with his suggestions to know that I probably won't like what's coming. 'Go on,' I say, running my hand through my hair.

'How about surprising Lizzy with a trip to Cannes? Kill two birds with one stone.'

I wince at the idea of going away with her and crack a joke about his crass phrasing. 'Let no one say you're not a true romantic.' Dinner was enough of a challenge, but I don't want him suspecting I'm not being fully transparent about Lizzy.

'There's a time for romance, and there's a time for bold moves. I'll let you guess which time this is,' he chuckles.

'What do you have in mind? You know if I fly in for the opening, it's going to be hectic, with no time for anything other than business meetings and PR.'

'That's true, but remember that Lizzy knows the ropes. This is exactly why it's such a good idea to marry someone from the same background as you. She's been on business trips such as this with her grandfather for years. You realise she's the sole heir to Archer Banking? She's the only grandchild, you know,' he says. 'Ultimately, the business will pass to another branch of the family if she doesn't produce an heir.'

I hadn't realised, but I am quickly realising why he thinks this is such a perfect match. If I marry Lizzy, Archer Banking will be under the Rochester umbrella, within a generation.

Her father is a dynamic leader, so all being well, he should be at the helm for quite some time yet.

'Um,' I say, mulling over what he wants me to do. If I take Lizzy to Cannes for the grand opening, it's as good as making an official announcement that we are a couple. I suspect this is his real motive, despite all the business talk. 'Lizzy told me she is her father's right hand of London operations, so surely, she has just as demanding a schedule as me? I doubt she can take off for several days with such short notice. She must have commitments.'

Grandfather's sigh reaches me over the phone. 'Sometimes you forget there are perks to being the boss. It's not all hard work and sacrifice—occasionally you get to take advantage of being able to call the shots.' He pauses as if he's waiting for me to catch up.

I stay quiet and try to think of a graceful way to avoid inviting Lizzy to join me, without revealing we're not really dating.

'If there's one thing I'm certain of, it's that you can be extremely charming and if you want her there with you, I'd put money on the fact that she will be. One word to her father and I'm sure he'll see the wisdom in you two teaming up for such a high-profile event.'

I'm not sure what to tell him. The last thing I want is to travel to Cannes for a supposedly romantic business trip with Lizzy. I wish it was a trip with Nathalie.

Well, you shouldn't, you numpty. You and Nathalie are just friends, and you can't take her away. There is no future for you.

But the idea of whisking Nathalie away to the French Riviera excites the hell out of me. I imagine her blue eyes sparkling at the invitation, the way they did when I asked if she wants to visit Richmond Park again. She thinks I don't notice these little things, but I notice everything about her.

You get to know someone fast when you share a house with them.

What would she make of travelling on the private jet? Thoughts of sharing a bed with her at the new Cannes hotel, and strolling along the beach, hand-in-hand, spring into my mind and I struggle to focus on the conversation. She's given me glimpses of the difficult childhood she had, and there's nothing I'd like more than to give her a whole new experience of her home country. They say money can't buy happiness and I've found that largely to be true. But it can buy wonderful experiences and I'd love to treat Nathalie to a five star holiday.

'What's it to be, my boy?' Grandfather asks, puncturing my fantasy bubble and snapping me back to reality with a thud.

'I'm not sure. I'll see about shifting some meetings and making plans to go myself, but I don't think I'm ready for a weekend away with Lizzy just yet. We've only been on one date, Grandfather.' There's a tinge of resentment in my statement, and I take a deep breath and calm myself.

'Precisely,' he says. 'There's no reason to take it slow when we're dealing with a mutually beneficial marriage such as this. You want to make sure no one else steals her from under your nose. If you hadn't got involved with Madeleine when you did, and married her in such a whirlwind, I would have suggested this match with Lizzy then.'

He knows exactly how to get to me. He knows my weak spots—all of them. It's almost impossible for me to not rise to the challenge when he throws one out for me. I hate disappointing people who think highly of me, and I can't bear falling short of his expectations.

Maddy said it was my ego disguised as doing-the-right-thing, running the show, and I should stand up to my grandfather and not let him tell me what to do. Perhaps she had a good point, but it doesn't stop me from being programmed to please him. It does, however, explain why *she* wasn't his first choice. Besides, it's easy for her to say. In my opinion, she has too little regard for pleasing her family—if she didn't, we'd still be married, and I wouldn't be in this mess.

My siblings and I have been competing against each other all our lives. We love each other and have each other's backs, but we all know this is a competition. Some of us take it more seriously than others. Being the spare heir is a bit of a curse. Maybe that's why I'm so competitive. I'm always *almost* number one but not quite. I'm close enough for my grandfather to keep grooming me to step into his shoes should the need arise, but not close enough to feel it's ever going to happen. Not that I would want it to happen, anyway. It's Damian's spot, but I do want to keep my seat on the board and inherit more shares in the company, so I have a say in what happens with Rochesters & Co.

If I take Lizzy to Cannes, it will earn me major brownie points with Grandfather, and it could be a clever move, business-wise. The press will adore the idea of a Rochester-Archer collaboration, which will have a knock-on effect for the opening of the Rochester Cannes. My guess is we'll be all over the business news, and probably make the celebrity headlines too. Wealthy families like ours are in a kind of limbo between serious business news and celebrity gossip. People love reading what the rich and powerful are up to and although we're not as famous as movie stars, in our own world, we're famous.

Straddling the business and celebrity news is spot on for hotel publicity because that's our target market for luxury hotels.

But what about Nathalie?

Imagining her face when she learns I'm going to France with another woman crushes me, and I don't think I can go through with it. I know I don't owe her anything, but that doesn't change how I feel about her, no matter what I tell her —or myself.

Someone is going to be disappointed. The only question is who?

Lizzy and I agreed to go along with the dating charade and help each other out by buying us both some time to figure out how to get what we want. We said if we pretend to keep dating, it will get our grandfathers off our backs, and save us the hassle and humiliation of having to date a string of potential suitors while we search for a spouse, or in her case, convince her family to agree to her marrying the man she loves.

Fake dating, it is then. But in France?

In the restaurant, fake dating seemed like a good idea. Well, perhaps not a *good* idea. A good idea would be going home and knocking on Nathalie's bedroom door, and her opening it semi-naked and me proceeding to peel off her nightshirt. I know she wears a nightshirt because we've bumped into each other on the landing in the early hours when she was going to get something from downstairs.

Instead, when I came back from the date with Lizzy, I let myself in quietly so I wouldn't disturb Nathalie. I was dying to go up to her room and slip into bed with her. Ever since we nearly made love in the kitchen, I've been so sexually charged I could explode. I wake up every morning with a massive erection and relieve myself in the shower. Her face is everywhere, and I fantasise about what would happen if we resumed where we left off on the kitchen island. I would fuck her so hard, and she would moan loudly and lose all control, like she did when I made her come on my fingers.

I'm hard now, just thinking about her again, and I shift under my desk as I think about how to wrap up this call with Grandfather without pissing him off.

Finally, I tell him I'll have a think about it and see what will work.

He makes a satisfied sound, and it's clear he thinks his persuasive talents have ensured it's a done deal and he's going to read about his grandson at the official opening of the Rochester Cannes, with Lizzy Archer, heir to the Archer banking fortune, on his arm.

I get up and pace my hotel office and then gaze out the panoramic window at the sweeping views of Mayfair and the London skyline.

All this is at my fingertips, so why can't I marry the woman I love?

CHAPTER 21

Nathalie

It was an emotional shift at the centre today. We found out a kid's mother threw herself under a train. Her little boy had been waiting for her to visit and kept hassling to know when she was coming. Heartbreak is not enough of a word to explain how I felt watching him. Knowing he would soon learn that his mummy would never visit him again broke me.

My spirits are low as I sign out and grab my bag from my locker. The little car I normally whiz about in is in the garage for a service, so Sebastian said he'd send his driver for me. However much I'm struggling with our personal relationship, I'm touched by what a thoughtful boss he is. If only that was all I wanted from him; my job would be the best I ever had.

Richard, the centre director, follows me out. 'No car? Do

you need a lift home?' he asks. 'It's the least I can do after all your help today. You made a real difference with poor Jack.'

I thank him for his kind words and explain I'm waiting for my lift. He hovers chatting for a few minutes and then wishes me goodnight. He's joined me for coffee a few times in the canteen, but there's no space for any man in my heart except Sebastian, so I don't respond to his signals. A complicated relationship with one boss is quite enough.

It's dark, and I feel bad inconveniencing the driver at night, especially when I could easily have got a lift with Richard or called a taxi, but Sebastian insisted. Scanning the small car park at the back of the centre, I can't spot the Range Rover, so I shelter from the rain and stand in the light where I should be easy to see whilst I browse on my phone.

There's a beep and I look up. My eyes fall to a shiny black Porsche already parked near the entrance to the carpark, and I see Sebastian waving to me.

My heart hammers as I shove my phone in my bag, and hurry towards the car as all six-foot-gorgeousness of him springs out. By the time I cover the distance, he is standing, holding the door open for me like a gallant knight, ushering me in out of the drizzle.

The sight of him knocks the breath out of me and my heart races like it so often does when he's around.

'To what do I owe the honour?' I say in a teasing tone, trying to act cool and not sound like a breathy teenager. My heart is pounding like shotgun fire, and it's all I can do to get my words out.

He's sitting next to me now and flashes me another of his devastating smiles.

'Thanks for picking me up. Where's your driver tonight?'

'Couldn't leave you stranded,' he says. 'We were back much earlier than expected, and I let him clock off. Don't want you taking taxis at this time of night.'

'The centre director offered me a lift actually, so I could have spared you the bother.'

'It's no bother,' he says. 'Was that the guy who spoke to you when you came out?'

I nod and arrange my bag near my feet as I nestle into the low leather seat and turn to gaze at him. I'm never as happy as when he's nearby.

Fact.

It's surprising how much his presence affects me because I've not experienced this type of euphoria before. I like men well enough, and thought I'd had some satisfying relationships. After the dramatic events of my childhood, I steered clear of emotional drama and only went out with guys who had their shit together and treated me well. And that worked out okay, but I didn't fall madly in love with any of them. I started to think that's just the way I'm made, and suspected I'd been emotionally damaged to the point where I would always hold back a little piece, and not let myself truly open my heart in the way others do.

Juliette throws herself into love affairs with such glorious abandon, and I envy her ability to do that sometimes. But there's been many a time I've had to comfort her and help her put herself back together again after the latest heartbreak. Not that I disapproved, but I thought that would never happen to me. Part of me yearned for an epic romance, whilst part of me—the scared, hidden part—was relieved I wouldn't have to face that kind of pain.

Ever.

But now, as I sit next to him in the Porsche, every cell of my being radiates joy simply because of his proximity.

Is this love?

If it is, I have no control over it at all, so I relax against the seat, and we chat naturally like we do when I'm not trying to hide from or avoid him. I'm done fighting this feeling. It's clear it's a losing battle and the odds are against me escaping unscathed, so I decide to let myself feel every emotion and see what that's like. I'll do it for now, anyway. After the heavy day at the centre, I'm too weak to resist his magnetic pull.

'Are they good people you work with?' he asks.

I assure him they are very nice, but he continues.

'You can always take the car or call me when you need a lift. And if I'm not home, I'll send my driver for you. You don't need to ever go with anyone you don't trust 100%. Please be careful.'

I glance at him, trying to figure out what's behind his words.

Is he jealous? Of Richard?

'Thank you,' I say. 'That's so kind. I usually take the car, so it's not an issue, but I am careful, of course.'

'How was your shift?' he asks, as he handles the car smoothly and we glide around a corner.

'It was hard, to be honest,' I say.

He cocks one eyebrow at me, before moving his eyes back to the dark windscreen and the rain whooshes on the road as we whiz along. 'Oh, why?'

My eyes are watery as I picture the little boy's face.

'There's this little boy called Jack,' I say. 'We had some tragic news today, and the thought of him learning that his mother died—.'

Tears fill my eyes and spill down my cheeks as I talk. I'm helpless to stop them and for an inexplicable reason, I don't even try.

Sebastian reaches for my hand and strokes it, which makes me cry even harder.

'Hey, hey,' he says, handing me a tissue from the glove compartment. 'Tell me what happened.'

I blow my nose and wipe my eyes and offer him a tremulous smile. 'Sorry, I bet you didn't expect all this drama when you picked me up.'

The kindness in his eyes tells me all I need to know. He has a compassionate heart, and it's one of the many things that attracts me to him.

'The boy's mother threw herself under a train in London. He has no father or other family that we know of, so he's an orphan now. And he's been waiting for his mother to visit him for weeks, and it's just too sad,' I continue, sniffing and dabbing at my red face in a futile effort to stop my tears.

'That is tough,' he says. 'Poor kid. I don't know how you do it.'

His comment interrupts my meltdown and I pause. 'How I do what?'

'Handle these tragic situations with these neglected kids. I don't think I'd be able to face it. I'd want to bring them all home with me.'

The vision of him piling a load of disadvantaged kids into his Porsche makes me laugh.

'That's better,' he says. 'I don't know why the idea of me not being able to handle it is funny, but at least it brought a smile to your face.'

His hand isn't on mine anymore, but his warmth is all around me, comforting me like a warm blanket. I tell him I was thinking of him piling them into the Porsche and this time it's his turn to laugh.

'You're right though. I do want to bring them all home with me. It's hard not to want that, but as it's not possible, I do what I can, which is give them a bit of my time and attention.'

'You amaze me,' he says.

I'm not the best at receiving compliments, and I feel myself blushing, but his words hug me. I'm embarrassed to ask exactly why I amaze him, so I let the words drift on the air between us and turn to look out the window at the rainy summer's evening.

He's undeterred by my reluctance to ask what he means, and he continues. 'I mean you've got your hands full with Daisy, you're in a foreign country, and you still make time to volunteer at the centre every week. Like I said, you're amazing.'

My cheeks burn at his effusive praise, but I force myself to look at him. He's staring at me and if he wasn't driving, I think he might kiss me.

He looks away abruptly and changes the subject, asking some questions about the centre. When I tell him I'm impressed by the work they do, he says I should speak to his mum about applying for funding from Rochesters Foundation. 'Mum is always open to hearing about children's initiatives.'

The thought of asking his mum makes me nervous.

I shake my head to dismiss my silly thoughts and tell him I'm certain that Richard would be thrilled to have backing from their foundation. It's not fair to let my own insecurities get in the way of an opportunity to help the kids.

'That's the guy you were chatting to?'

I nod. 'Yes, I think he founded the centre.'

He studies my face again for a few beats and then says he'll talk to his mum about it.

We pull into the drive and the rain is strumming hard on the windscreen.

'It's so quiet at home when Daisy's away,' he says.

His words startle me. 'Why, where is she?' I ask.

He tells me her school friend invited her for a last-minute sleepover after the playdate earlier. 'I wanted to say no and keep her all to myself for the evening, but she was so excited, and they only live down the road. I couldn't think of a good reason to refuse,' he laughs.

'She'll have a great time with her friend. They've been playing together a lot lately,' I say, but it occurs to me the house is empty, and Sebastian and I are going to be alone for the first time in ages.

Silence fills the car, and then he says, 'Don't move. Wait there until I open the front door, or you'll get soaked. I didn't bring an umbrella.'

I sit there, my heart banging, trying to calm my breathing as I wait for him to open the door. He disappears inside for a minute and then reappears. He doesn't signal to me to get out, but he takes his jacket off and runs out in the rain and opens my car door. 'No idea where all the umbrellas have gone,' he says. 'There's never one around when you need it. This'll have to do.' He holds up his jacket and shields me from the pouring rain as we run inside, laughing, and our heads brush against each other's.

We remove our wet shoes and there's another heavy silence as we stare at each other. I don't want to leave him and go upstairs to shower and get ready for bed, even though I know I should. That would be the way to keep things simple.

'Fancy a cup of tea?' he says.

I nod and follow him into the kitchen, finding it difficult to swallow. It's like there's a hard knot blocking my throat.

My eyes fall to the kitchen island and memories of the last time we were alone flood into my mind. I wonder whether he ever thinks about that night.

He sets about making the tea and I ease onto a stool and flick through a magazine, but don't digest any of it. I meet his eyes as he places the cup in front of me and leans against the counter, close enough to touch.

His eyes are on me as I sip the hot tea. I smile at him and try to act as though my heart's not ricocheting in my chest like a trapped bird in a cage, and I can't construct one coherent sentence.

We lapse into silence again and focus on the tea.

The air between us crackles and fizzes and I try to think of something sensible to say, but I've got nothing.

He's looking at me now, and I return his gaze until I'm drowning in his gorgeous blue-grey eyes.

I am lost. Again.

CHAPTER 22

Sebastian

Her cornflower blue eyes undo me. I want her so badly I could scream. She's guileless and vulnerable—unlike any woman I've known. Now I look back, it seems like all the women I dated before getting married had an agenda. They all wanted something from me. Nathalie destroys me with her innocence. She only has to look at me and I'm lost.

I'm playing with fire, but I can't seem to stop myself. Even as I released my driver early from his shift, at the back of my mind, I knew it was because I wanted to surprise her at the centre. I don't kid myself that I'd be racing to collect the previous nanny, and I know I'm wading into treacherous waters with Nathalie. It was me who said we should just be friends, so why at every opportunity do I look for a way to get closer to her?

The Cannes trip is on my mind. Grandfather's right and

I've got no choice but to go if I want to do my best for the hotel, but I don't want to be there with Lizzy Archer. She seems great and if I just wanted to tick the boxes of a suitable Rochester wife, she would fit the bill perfectly. If only Lizzy and I wanted each other, this would all be straightforward. She messaged me earlier and I must get back to her.

Nathalie's nursing her cup of tea and I can see she's on edge. There's a heavy silence between us and my thoughts flick back to when I almost fucked her in this very spot. What would have happened if Daisy hadn't interrupted us then?

You know what would have happened, you numpty. You'd have been inside her in seconds—it was that close.

Would things be different between us now? She seems to have adjusted to the idea of us being friends and has stopped avoiding me, so I mustn't mess it up again. Even as I think these sensible thoughts, I'm yearning to cross the line again now we're alone. Knowing we've got the whole place to ourselves tonight is killing me.

A lock of damp golden hair has fallen into her eyes, and I look at her and feel a physical ache. I'm longing to hold her again. It's been weeks since I tasted her sweetness and held her in my arms.

The air is charged, and I see by the searing look in her eyes that she feels it too.

'What time is Daisy back tomorrow?' she asks, clearing her throat and steering us back into familiar territory.

We always talk about Daisy when we get into choppy waters. She's our safe ground—our ice breaker.

I tell her they will drop her off in the morning, and then the silence looms again, swirling around us and tormenting me. I look at her again and before I can stop myself reaching towards her, my fingers touch the lock of hair and move it gently away from her eyes.

Smiling at me shyly, she rests her cup on the counter and blushes slightly. I feel the effect she has on me, and it spirals through my lower body.

'Thanks for the tea,' she pauses, 'and for collecting me tonight. I appreciate it.'

'That's what friends are for,' I say, trying to sound casual and not let on that I'm desperate to crush her body against mine.

A shadow crosses her face, but she doesn't object. It's obvious she doesn't like it when I say we're friends. But surely that's better than me referring to myself as her boss.

'Well, I'd better get to bed. Got a busy day tomorrow, and it's getting late,' she murmurs, and slides off the stool, avoiding my eyes.

Looking at my watch, I say, 'Yeah, me too. Good plan.'

All I can think about is taking her to bed. What would it be like to have the entire night with her, undisturbed?

We are alone, which is so rare that it seems a dreadful waste.

My cock's straining against my crotch, imagining lying on the bed naked with her, licking her clit until she screams with pleasure. The memory of her moaning and begging for more when she was on the edge of exploding beneath my tongue and fingers taunts me.

I turn away and try to contain my heavy sigh as I place the empty cups in the sink. My heart's hammering to a ragged beat and I'm tempted to tell her how much I want her. But when I turn to face her, she's moved and is already by the kitchen door, about to slip upstairs to bed.

'Night, then,' she says, searching my face, a small, sad smile on her lips.

What is she thinking? Does she want me too or is she still upset about what happened at the centre?

'Night, sleep well,' I say, feeling like I want to howl with frustration.

How the fuck did I get myself into this ridiculous mess? The hottest woman I've ever met is not only living in my house, but she's sleeping in a bed a few doors away from my bedroom. And I'm the fool who created a rule where I can't touch her...

You're really smart, Rochester. Fantastic job.

After she's gone, I pour myself a small whisky and down it in a few large gulps as I gaze out at the starry, dark sky, lost in thoughts of Nathalie. After making sure the doors are all locked, I walk slowly upstairs, listening out for her movements. She must be in her room already. I imagine her sliding into bed between the sheets and laying her head on the pillow. Is she thinking about me too, or is it only me who's obsessed?

The light on the landing is dim as I head towards my bedroom door. It's strange not going to check on Daisy. Everything is different tonight—no wonder I feel restless.

I hover on the landing for a minute, reluctant to go into my bedroom and end any possibility of seeing her again tonight. My eyes close for a second as I try to get a grip on my emotions.

I'd be breaking my own rule if I went up to her room.

But then I open my eyes, and she's standing before me, her hair flowing over her shoulders. I was so lost in thought; I didn't hear her walking down the stairs from the top floor.

'You okay?' I ask, startled.

'Yes. I left something downstairs, that's all. Sorry, I didn't mean to creep up on you.'

'No, you're fine. I was in a world of my own,' I say.

I can only make out her shadow in the faint light and can just about see she's wearing some kind of skimpy summer nightshirt and her long legs are bare.

We both move at the same time, and my breath catches in my throat as we brush past each other and our bodies touch. It's like I've been burnt, and my senses explode with longing.

She smells of soap and flowers, and I inhale her scent like a dying man taking his last gasp.

Pausing, I say, 'Shall I get it for you?'

She teases me in a whisper as if we need to be careful that we don't wake Daisy up. 'You're the only boss I've ever had who asks what they can get for me. Isn't it supposed to be me —your employee—asking what I can do for you?'

I know exactly what I'd like her to do for me, and my blood's racing in my veins, making me dizzy and my head is pounding, but I say, 'That might be true if I were only your boss. But we said we are friends.'

'True,' she says. '*You* did say that.' She's standing so close to me, I could reach out and touch her, but I keep my hands firmly at my sides. My eyes have adjusted to the light, and I see her nightie is like a stripey man's shirt with buttons running down the front, and a slit up both thighs. The buttons reveal a tantalising glimpse of her tanned cleavage, but it's not an overtly sexy piece of lingerie. It's very tomboyish, but the effect it has on me is alarming. She's sexy whatever she wears. My already straining cock stands to full attention, and an overwhelming wave of lust shoots through me. My self-discipline is waning rapidly as my eyes drift to her pink lips, and I imagine running my tongue over them and kissing her all night.

Keep your hands off her, Rochester.

'Have you ever slept with a friend?' She murmurs and at first, I'm not sure I hear her right.

What?

I search her eyes and see a world of desire that matches mine.

'I don't think I have. But I'd very much like to,' I reply

softly, and before I can remind myself of my own stupid rule, our lips collide, and we melt into each other. She presses against me, and I feel her hard nipples through the thin fabric of her nightshirt. I'm on fire, and frantic with longing. Now it's happening I can't hold back. She's not holding back either and is completely opening herself up to me. We somehow manoeuvre against the wall as we kiss deeply, our tongues exploring each other's mouths. She's breathing heavily and I feel her warm breath on my face as I pause for a second and tilt her against the wall. She's tall but I'm taller and I bend my head to kiss her again and lift her slightly as one of her legs wraps around me.

We're both panting now, and my hard length presses into her flesh through my jeans, as she moans and pushes herself against me and drives me insane.

She rubs her hand over my crotch and fumbles with my zipper in the dim light. I'm so close to having her soft hands on me again, but I grit my teeth and force myself to pause and ask, 'What about our agreement to be just friends?'

I'm close to losing my mind, but I can't fuck things up between us again. It's not fair to Daisy, and I can't risk her quitting because of me, no matter how much I want her. The most we can have is a casual relationship and if she wants more, it's only fair to make it clear I can't give her that. *Ever.*

The words are bitter for me to say, but I push them out one by one through my dry throat, and don't relent. 'I can't offer you a serious relationship. It's complicated and to do with the terms of my inheritance.'

There's a wanton abandon in her eyes. 'I know,' she says. 'It's okay. I don't want anything serious, anyway.' In her alluring French accent, she adds, 'Friends with benefits, then?'

I need no further invitation, as she tugs on my zipper again and helps me pull my jeans and then my shorts down.

My aching need juts out and when she touches me with her warm hand and falls to her knees in front of me on the thick carpet, I think I may pass out from the bliss of her tongue rolling around my starved flesh.

'Nathalie,' I gasp. 'Oh, Nathalie!'

CHAPTER 23

Nathalie

I enter my room and lean against the door.

Merde!

I didn't want to leave him, but it seemed too obvious I'm mad about him if I stayed. He'll think I'm too needy if I keep loitering about waiting for him. This is the first time we've been alone in the house since we made out in the kitchen. Sitting, drinking tea with him and pretending I'm not burning up to feel his hands on me again was impossible.

Does he know how badly I've fallen for him? I can't stop thinking about him, and I'm at the point where I don't even care if we can't have something serious. I just want to be with him again.

There's a broken piece of my soul that believes I'm not worthy of being with a man of his status. I hate that I have that thought somewhere deep in my consciousness, but there's nothing I can do about it, no matter how much I beat myself up. You can't bully yourself into feeling worthy, and I know that I still feel not quite enough, no matter how much I work on improving myself.

Turning the situation over in my mind, during the long restless nights, I've asked myself again and again whether it is worth loving fully just once, if this is my only chance. This may be the only time we have together, and I've never felt like this about anyone. These thoughts make me feel wild and reckless.

A few days after I thought he'd been on a date, he mentioned casually that it was a meeting with a family friend. The pain in my heart lifted, and I hummed all day, feeling light and happy.

He's single, so why not be with him, whilst I can?

I don't want to die a lonely old maid, wishing I'd been bolder and courageous enough to go after what I want—*who* I want. It's not as if he doesn't want me sexually. There's a smouldering energy between us. Tonight, in the kitchen, it was off the charts, and I kept having flashbacks of how he swept me up onto the island the first time we kissed. Well, it was the *only* time we kissed. And okay, we didn't go all the way, but he transported me to places I've never been.

I've not managed to come when a man has gone down on me before, so I tell myself that it's no wonder the experience is scorched vividly into my memory. Just the thought of him running his tongue over my most sensitive place and making me orgasm so quickly, makes me shiver, and lust spirals through me. He's clearly a skilled lover, and I crave more of him. But it's bigger than that—I'm drawn to him like a moth to a flame and I've given up fighting the attraction.

Moving about my bedroom in a daze, I take a quick shower and change into my nightshirt. I have a busy day tomorrow, and should go to sleep, but my senses are racing and all I want is to go back downstairs and kiss him. Or even better, knock on his bedroom door and offer myself to him if he wants me.

What was it Juliette said? *Friends with benefits.*

It's time to take a risk.

Juliette said that as I like him so much, I should just go for it and take my chances, but then she's always been more adventurous than me. She's had her heart shattered, whereas my heart hasn't ever truly been tested in love. Things have always sort of fizzled out in my romances and we've called things off by mutual agreement, with no big drama. In all honesty, my love life has been dull. I've never been sexually attracted to anyone in the way I am to him. It's as though all logic disappears whenever he's around and I'm desperate to be close to him.

But I'm scared of being hurt and experiencing all those terrible feelings of loss, like when my parents died. Deep down, I know that's why I've always held back in relationships. It's safer to keep things neat and unemotional, and I've never felt the urge to open myself up to anyone in this way before.

Until Sebastian. Everything's different with him. An inner voice keeps whispering to me he's the one and I should trust my feelings for him.

I brush my teeth and examine my face in the huge mirror. It doesn't look like I'm going to sleep tonight. My eyes are shining, and I'm too restless to sleep. It's in that second, I decide that for tonight, I will not play it safe.

If you're not willing to get into the game, how will you ever win? I whisper to my reflection.

Taking one last look at myself in the mirror, and smoothing down my messy hair, my legs propel me to the door, even as my heart clatters. I'm pumped but also terrified and I wonder if I'm on my way to make the biggest mistake of my life.

Am I about to do something that will lead to me losing my job and having to return to Paris before the year is up?

Quietly, I glide down the stairs in a dreamlike state, to the landing where Sebastian's room is. My heart's pounding so loudly at the thought of how brazen I'm being. I feel disorientated. But I keep walking as though something beyond me has taken over. As my toes sink into the plush carpet and my bare feet approach Sebastian's bedroom door, he looms in front of me, and I jump.

I'm acting on impulse and am shocked to bump into him without a chance to prepare myself or reconsider my actions and flee to the safety of my suite.

He makes a slight noise as if he's just as shocked to see me, but I can't make out his expression in the pale night light.

Then he asks if he can get me something, which is so typical of him. He doesn't act like a mega-rich guy—well, not with me, anyway. The other rich families I've worked for have always been very clear that I'm there to serve them, not the other way around. And that's fair enough—they're paying me, after all. But Seb is different, and he's been different since the first day I arrived. He treats me like his equal, not like the paid help. Sometimes I wish he wasn't so well-behaved and would take the lead and come onto me again, but I know that's unfair. He made it clear that my position as Daisy's nanny is important to him, and I get why he doesn't want us to have a thing.

But lord, how I want us to have a thing, and I want it now, like I've never wanted anything. And when we brush past each other and accidentally touch, a tremor runs through me, and I know I'm going to make love to him tonight if he'll have me.

We move towards each other, and our lips merge as if it's

the most natural thing in the world, and before I can think what's happening, my back is against the wall on the dimly lit landing and he's touching me and I'm touching him and it's delicious and I never want it to end.

When he pauses to ask if I'm sure I want this even though we can't have anything more, I hear my words ringing out from a distant place, assuring him I don't want anything serious. My voice sounds confident and casual, like I'm speaking the truth and wouldn't dream of wanting a long-term relationship with him.

Liar.

Yes, I've become a liar, and I don't care. All I want is him, now, and I'll lie to him and to myself if that's what it takes to be with him. I'm conscious that all we have is tonight, and I'm going to make the most of it.

Tomorrow, everything will return to normal with Daisy at home, following me around like my little shadow and Mrs Johnson cooking in the kitchen, and the assistant housekeeper tidying the bedrooms, and the other part-time staff popping in and out to make sure the house and garden are pristine. Sebastian will go to work, and I'll miss my chance if I don't take it now.

He kisses me again and his hard mound pushes into the thin material of my nightshirt, and the feel of him drives me crazy. I tug on his jeans, desperate to touch his hardness. I want to taste him and give him the intense pleasure he gave me last time. I want us to pick up where we left off, and when I grip him firmly in my hands, he groans, which turns me on even more. The sound of him surrendering to my touch after fantasising about him for so long inflames me. My inhibitions evaporate, and I drop to my knees and take him in my mouth.

He groans again, louder this time, and when I hear my name on his lips, it sounds right, and like it is meant to be. I can tell he's losing it, and then he pulls me gently to my feet and leads me by the hand through the door into his bedroom. A light flickers on as we enter and I blink as I scan his bedroom for the first time. I've been tempted to open the door and have a quick look at his rooms when he's been in London, but I held myself back as it didn't seem fair. If he wanted me to see his room, he would show me around, but here I am in his inner sanctum, and a rush of joy darts through my chest.

He guides me over to the bed in the centre of the opulent room, and we sink onto the duvet with me sitting astride him, my nightshirt pushed up to my waist and my legs bare. He's naked apart from his T-shirt and I'm desperate to feel his skin against mine, so I clamber to help him pull it over his head and run my hands over his broad shoulders and down his chest.

The illicit thrill of being together like this in his bed has me so wet and ready for him, I can't wait for him to take me.

He opens the line of buttons of my nightshirt and my breasts spring out and my nipples harden in the cool air.

'My God, Nathalie. They're perfect. You're perfect.' He pulls himself up and lowers his head to take first one pink nipple, then the other in his mouth as though he's paying homage to them.

'They're like pink cherries,' he says. He licks them and it's like he's got a direct line to my clit, and I moan loudly. His beautiful cock stiffens and begs for my attention, but he holds me still with his large hands as he sucks on my nipples, and I writhe with desire as I straddle him.

'Fuck me, Sebastian. Please,' I say, and it's like a wanton dirty stranger has taken over my mouth.

Finally, he releases me, and he presses a button above the bed and the light dims, and all I can see is the outline of his hard torso bathed in the silver shards of moonlight seeping through the shutter slats.

I reach for his long, thick shaft, and stroke him with a firm grip and steady rhythm, and he lets out an animal like groan. I bend over him and swirl my tongue around the moist tip, and he gasps.

'That's beautiful, but I'm not gonna last like that. Let me taste you,' he says, and he pulls me higher so I'm directly over his face and I feel the ecstasy of his tongue flicking over me and think I might come there and then. His hands support me as I ride his hot mouth and jerk about in a state of erotic abandon that's entirely new to me. I place one hand on the wall to steady myself, and the other in his hair, too weak with the pure bliss shooting through my lower body, to hold myself up.

He sucks my clit until it's on fire, and the sweetest agony ripples through my groin and my legs stiffen. I cry out for more and then more. I keep exploding in his mouth, and he relentlessly sucks my sensitive bud until I lean my head against the wall and catch my breath as the waves consume me.

The floating gradually subsides, and I move down his body.

'Wow,' I say. 'That was incredible.'

'You're incredible. You taste amazing,' he says. 'I need to feel you on me now. Ride my cock, Nat, before I burst from wanting you.'

I tease him briefly with my mouth again, but he begs for mercy, and I laugh. 'I'm going to ride you now,' I promise, and I lower myself near his hard length, desperate for him to be inside me, but then I stop abruptly.

'What?' he says, his eyes gleaming in the moonlight.

'We need a condom,' I say. I feel awkward and don't want

to ruin the moment, but even with the intense heat between my legs, it's drummed into my brain to always be cautious.

'Ah, yes, of course.' He scrambles about with one hand and slides open a small drawer next to the bed, and I see him tear a packet open with his teeth. Watching him move his hand up and down his shaft in the moonlight, until it stands to stiff attention again, makes me so hot, I writhe in anticipation as he rolls the condom on.

'I can't wait to be inside you,' he says in the deep, gravelly voice which makes me wet in my dreams.

Lowering myself slowly onto him, I close my eyes as I feel his hardness fill me up and I groan and say his name as I move on him. I lose myself as he reaches for me and pulls me close to him with his muscular arms.

'You're so tight and wet,' he says, his voice turning me on as much as the feeling of him inside me, and the thud of his heart against my hot skin.

'It's been a long time,' I whisper.

'For me too,' he says, and the thought of him waiting for me and not being with anyone else undoes me.

'I'm coming again,' I cry.

'Beautiful. Come, baby, come,' he whispers, kissing me deeply.

I'm still on top of him, and we move together to our own perfect beat, until I forget my name, but I hear it on his lips as he explodes inside me, and I collapse in his arms, and we drift into a satisfied slumber.

CHAPTER 24

Sebastian

I'm in a sweet daze, hovering somewhere between sleeping and waking when consciousness seeps into my mind and I remember I'm in bed with Nathalie.

Oh fuck!

Her blonde mussed hair tickles my skin and the weight of her head rests on my shoulder. The duvet lies in a heap on the carpet where it slid off the bed during our night of passion. One of her long legs is tangled in the sheet and her breathing is steady. Moving my free arm tentatively, careful not to disturb her, I glance at my watch and see it's 7 a.m. Double fuck. The housekeeper will be here soon.

Monday morning and I'm not even out of bed yet. I'm usually showered and finished catching up on the business news by now. There's a text from my driver asking what time

I want to leave for the office. Reality forces itself back into my life, whether or not I'm ready for it.

The sun makes me wince, and I remember I forgot to close the shutters last night. Just as well we're not overlooked.

Despite my jumbled thoughts, I'm still buzzing, and I think how lucky that I had condoms on hand. That's the upside of not having sex for so long—an untouched packet of condoms and a sexual appetite that had me so insane for her we only slept for short bursts. She's even sexier than I imagined, and each time was hotter than the one before. We just fit together, and it was effortless. I woke up craving her again, and I reached for her in the hazy dawn light. Her eyes told me she was hungry for more too, and I slid my fingers into her wet pussy and fucked her until she quivered and came over and over until we both fell into a heavy, satiated sleep.

I can't remember the last time I had an all-nighter like that. In fact, who am I kidding? I've never had one like that—never had a woman like her.

My ex and I had some passionate nights in the early days, but when Daisy came along, our nights were sleepless for other reasons, and we had sex less and less frequently, until we barely slept in the same bed, never mind had sex.

It's been so long since I relaxed and let go completely.

But with Nathalie? For fuck's sake.

I can't seem to control myself around her. She seemed to be coming around to the idea of being just friends, so what am I doing?

At least I checked in with her first. She said she was fine about us having sex without a commitment. I hope she meant it, or things could get complicated, fast, after a night like that. She caught me by surprise when she suggested friends with benefits—it was the last thing I expected her to say—but I was too hot to refuse when she appeared like that.

But now, I'm not sure I want friends with benefits, as cool as it sounds. My feelings run too deep and if I let myself have her like this regularly, no matter how casual she says it can be, I don't think I'll be able to hack it.

Her head nuzzles on my shoulder, and she turns on her side towards me, her warm breath caressing my flesh as her hand flops onto me. I'm already semi-hard, and her touch ignites me into full morning glory. Even as I'm warning myself about being with her, I'm lusting after her again, and I pull the sheet up to cover the evidence.

Her eyes peel open, and she beams me a lazy, contented smile. 'Morning.'

'Morning, beautiful,' I say, dropping a kiss on her forehead. 'Sleep well?'

'Hmm, well, but not much! We only slept a little,' she says, throwing me an impish grin. She moves her head off my shoulder and sits up, stretching her arms in the air like a sleepy cat.

'You really do have the most divine tits,' I say, admiring her body. I feel myself twitch.

'You kept saying that last night,' she says, and her eyes wander to the hill in the sheet.

'Yes, well, your nipples have been on my mind since the day you arrived when you wore your wet swimming costume.'

She laughs, and her cheeks flush. 'Oh, please don't remind me. Sorry about that. I didn't know you would appear so soon.'

'Never apologise for letting me see your stiff nips,' I say, and although I know I should get ready for work, I lick one perfect nipple and then the other. The sight of them hardening is too much for me. I'm going to have to have her again, Monday morning or not.

'I should be on my way,' I murmur, but I keep licking her nipples and the way she moans arouses me further. Her eyes shine with desire, and I know she wants me as much as I want her.

She runs her hand over the sheet, and I'm so stiff, my cock throbs.

'This feels promising,' she says, teasing me, as she rubs her hand back and forth and palms me through the silky sheet.

I'm losing my mind and can't think straight now. All I can think is I want to be inside her again, so I throw off the sheet and flip her onto her back and lie on top of her, balancing my weight on my arms.

'Is this a good idea?' she asks coyly.

'I thought you said we can be friends with benefits,' I say, my voice low as a growl.

'True. But I mean, what if they drop Daisy off now?'

'They won't. It's the summer holidays,' I say.

'What time is it? Mrs Johnson will come any minute, won't she?'

I can see she wants me, but she's worried about us being discovered.

'Don't worry. We've got at least thirty minutes. Would you like to talk about who might arrive soon, or is there something else you'd rather do?' I move down the bed and trail my tongue lazily back and forth across her bean, gradually increasing the speed until she's feverish and has forgotten all about being discovered.

She surrenders to my mouth and when I cover her body with mine, she wraps her legs tightly around me, and I make love to her again, even though I know I shouldn't and I'm losing my heart to the nanny.

After a hurried shower, I find it almost impossible to

leave her sitting there so radiant on my balcony. I want to stay and spend the day with her, but work calls and we won't be alone soon even if I played my boss card and didn't go in. I don't want to put my foot in it, so I don't say much before leaving. If I tell her how I feel, it will ruin everything.

I can never give her more, and the guilt of taking her to bed overpowers me even though we had the most amazing night. It's been years since I was an immature fuckboy, and it seems taboo to sleep with an employee.

So, why does being with Nathalie feel so right?

If I want to keep my seat on the board, I'm going to have to play out the fake girlfriend charade with Lizzy in Cannes. I'm not sure I would have come up with the idea of fake dating if she hadn't suggested it. 'Lots of couples like us do it,' she said over dinner.

It reminded me of Caspian's set up. He told me he likes their fake relationship because he always has a suitable date on his arm when he needs one. He says proper dating is too tricky with the press watching our every move. Since the media hammered Damian again, Caspian told me he's being more careful. He and Isabella have a casual arrangement that works well for them because they genuinely like each other and both don't want to commit.

I don't know how he keeps his feelings under control if he's also having sex with her. But he says he never wants to marry, so he's clearly better at compartmentalising than me.

Nathalie doesn't know about Lizzy Archer, and I'm in no rush to tell her. No matter how much she might say she wants nothing serious, I understand women well enough to know that no good will come of her finding out. And so, I still haven't mentioned the impending Cannes trip. I haven't even mentioned it to Daisy because she tells Nathalie everything.

We're only doing it to pacify our grandfathers. I remind

myself it can't happen again with Nathalie, anyway, because she's going to get hurt, no matter what she says. I'm not free to be with her and it's not fair.

But all the way to the office, memories of her wrapped around me ricochet through my mind and I still feel the aftershocks of her touch on my skin, like she's branded my flesh. I miss her already.

Is it her heart I'm worried about breaking, or mine?

CHAPTER 25

Nathalie

We made love—again and again—and it was amazing. What a night. What a morning… I never want it to end, but it's getting late, and the housekeeper really will be here any minute now. My stomach lurches at the thought of her finding out I'm in Sebastian's room, but I can't bring myself to leave.

When I leave, it will all be over. He's looked at his watch a few times and I can tell he's getting restless.

'I must shower and get ready to leave for the office,' he says. His blue-grey eyes appraise me from under their lush dark lashes, and I dissolve with that one look.

He leans over and drops a quick kiss on my lips. It's over before it's begun, and I feel the distance reinserting itself between us. He jumps out of bed and pulls his pants on, and as he's doing them up, he says, 'Coffee?'

I nod, shyness overtaking me in the harsh morning light and making me feel vulnerable.

He strides across the room, and my eyes follow his bare back, wishing he would stay in bed with me, and this interlude could continue uninterrupted. I'm not ready to let him go yet.

His broad shoulders and sculpted torso make my throat dry, and memories of running my hands over his warm skin as he groaned with pleasure flood into my mind. I'm in a post-orgasmic haze and feel a bit tender, but it doesn't stop me from wanting to be in his arms again.

We can call it sex or fucking, but I know enough to know what we experienced last night was pure lovemaking, and I'm going to treasure the memories of that erotic night together forever.

It doesn't stop me craving the waves of ecstasy washing over me again. And that's just the physical ache in my groin. It's a strange thing about the closeness of sex with someone you're crazy about—the more you have, the more you want —and I'm definitely still craving him. There's a jagged stab in my heart, and I'm scared of the feelings I know are sure to follow now we are reverting to the status quo.

My cheeks burn at the thought of my words the previous night on the landing, when I would have said just about anything to have him. He asked me if I was okay with things as they are. I can't blame him—not that I want to—but it was me who suggested friends with benefits. Juliette's words made me bold, and I let my yearning for him call the shots.

I tell myself it was worth it. Spending the night with him was unreal, but now I must face reality.

He walks towards me with a steaming cup of coffee. 'I made it how you like it,' he says, an adorable pleased-with-himself expression on his face.

'Thank you,' I smile. He's been paying attention, so that's

something. My heart thuds as our eyes meet. 'I'm surprised you come downstairs at all,' I say, waving one hand around his room. 'My suite is comfortable, but this is something else.'

'I don't do it justice, really,' he says. 'There's a lounge and a kitchen through there, but I only make the occasional coffee here. I prefer eating downstairs with Daisy—and you.'

He pulls the shutters and opens the doors to reveal a long, secluded balcony lined with shrubs and flowering bushes overlooking the garden. 'You can see Richmond Park from here,' he says, pointing. 'Want to drink your coffee out here?'

He passes me one of his shirts and I slip into it gratefully and get out of bed carefully with my coffee. 'Have you time to join me?'

Shaking his head, he says, 'Regrettably not. I must get to the office. We've got a new hotel opening soon, and it's manic at work, but you take your time. I'll see to Daisy if they drop her before I leave, and I'll ask Mrs J to keep an eye on her until you come down.'

He's perfectly considerate and polite, but I can feel him restoring the boundaries between us as he speaks.

What did I expect? That we'd sleep together, and he'd declare his love for me and say we should get married and be together forever...

For one glorious night, I knew what it was to be loved by him and feel the bliss of being with the man I adore. It made me forget I am just the nanny, and we can never have a permanent relationship.

The finer details of how we made love ripple through my thoughts, and the thrill of his touch lingers.

Does he regret it? I know I don't. But I'm certain I will pay the price, and my heart aches for more.

He's keeping his distance and being business-like, which makes me think he probably does regret it. When he said we should be friends, he didn't suggest anything beyond that.

It was me who did that, and now I'm embarrassed.

He leaves the room to shower, and I sink into a sun lounger on the balcony, sipping my coffee, and gazing at the park in the distance. It's another idyllic summer's day, and here I am on Sebastian Rochester's private balcony, which I didn't even know existed until this morning.

Billionaires, aye?

What else don't I know about him?

Rays of gentle morning sun caress my skin, and I rest my empty coffee cup on the table and close my eyes as images of him waking me at dawn—his hard length pushing against me—dominate my thoughts.

As I lay there, I remember how I felt his stubble grazing my skin, and his musky smell teasing my senses, bringing me to the edge. There was a burning need in his eyes as he rolled me onto my side and his body moved flush against mine. We had barely slept, and when he entered me, we needed no warmup. Wet and ready for him, he slid into me, and I cried out as he made me his again before we collapsed into another lust-filled doze.

'Hey, sleepy head,' he says, popping his head out.

He startles me out of my daydream, and I open my eyes. He is ready to leave, and his dark, wet hair glistens in the sunlight. His driver will pick him up in five minutes and he's going to skip breakfast and get something later, he tells me.

The words wash over me, and I feel empty because I'm losing him. Losing him to his Rochester commitments and his inheritance. Is that even a thing? The thought crosses my mind that maybe he's only saying that to make me feel better about him not wanting anything serious with me.

'Daisy's not home yet. Her friend's mother just texted me to say the girls want to play some more and she'll drop her back later. I gave her your number so she can be in touch. Okay?'

I nod. I'm pleased Daisy's having a good time, and I'll have a chance to pull myself together before she gets home. But Sebastian's business-as-usual façade sends a chill through me, and I want to cry out that I love him. I want to ask him to stay longer.

But I don't. Of course. I smile at him brightly, as if everything is perfect in my world, and I couldn't wish for more.

It was me who proposed friends with benefits, after all, wasn't it?

My heart twists and my chest hurts as he rushes around, getting ready to leave.

He pauses at the door, turns to me, and says, 'Thank you for a lovely night.' There's a genuine smile on his shapely lips, but his eyes look dark and guarded, as if he's unsure what to say and what my reaction might be.

'I'm going to slip away now. See you later,' he says. His tone is casual.

No words come out of my mouth. My insides lurch and I feel like I'm being ripped apart.

Slip away.

I don't think I've ever hated two words more.

He opens the door, waves, and then he's gone.

'Bye,' I say, but it's too late for him to hear me.

I have no one to blame but myself for my heartache.

What a fool I've been.

CHAPTER 26

Sebastian

I've not been able to concentrate on work at all, which is bad because I've got a shitload to do. Reports with the latest sales figures are strewn all over my desk, and a meeting is scheduled with my executive team for later today. It's Monday and I usually hit the ground running and get a head start on the week.

But every time I try to focus, flashbacks of the night with Nathalie take over. I still feel her hands on my dick, and my mind plays dangerous tricks on me.

What if we sleep together but keep it casual?

Even as I think it, I know it's madness. It'll never work. I'm not the casual lover type, and besides, if Grandfather finds out I'm sleeping with the nanny, he'll go fucking mental. He's big on us upholding the standards we have for our employees, and we're not supposed to get any special treatment.

But the sexy, delirious thoughts keep coming, and I'm helpless to stop them.

Would Nat even agree to continue the arrangement, or am I losing it?

She was the one who came back downstairs and suggested it, so perhaps she would. Maybe she was being straight with me when she said she's not looking for anything more.

It could be true, but I find it unlikely.

I'm aware that could be my ego talking. As one of the most eligible single men in London, I'm used to being regarded as the ultimate catch, so it's a novel idea for me to consider that she doesn't want me long-term.

Ha...

I sit at my desk and flick through the reports, but I may as well be elsewhere. Her cornflower blue eyes told me how much she wanted me, so it's hard to know the truth. I trust her though. That much I do know. Trusting her with Daisy was the ultimate test, and she's passed with flying colours every step of the way.

The image of how she sucked me on the landing rushes into my mind and I harden in my suit trousers. This wanting her all the time is like an addiction, and you'd think a night with her would have given me some relief, but I only want her more. I push my chair away from the desk and stand up and pace back and forth in my office.

Like I said—not much is getting done today. The Cannes hotel opening needs attention, and that's what the exec meeting is about later, so I must get my head together.

She's monopolising my every thought and I ache for her again. The problem with my feelings for her is, it's not just sex. If it was just sex, I could fuck her out of my system and move on, but it's so much more than that.

For the rest of the day, I discipline myself to focus on work and not think about Nathalie. But I'm fighting a losing battle because she's *all* I can think about. No matter what I do, she's in every thought, somewhere. The more I try not to think about her, the more the images of her spin into my mind, like video reels playing over and over. And even when I'm not consciously thinking about her, my senses are overloaded by her touch.

This is ridiculous. I'm going to have to handle this, or it will become a real problem. Maybe if we sleep together for a while, we'll tire of each other, I reason. And on and on the thoughts go, whirring through my head and driving me insane.

I'm fucking obsessed.

I shake my head as if I can clear the fogginess from my brain.

After lunch, my assistant opens the door and says a letter has arrived for me. She places it on my desk, and I recognise my grandfather's writing. That's just what I need. I often tease him, he's the only man in England still writing his mail by hand. I quickly tear it open, apprehensive about what he deems so important he has to put it in writing. Greystone family dinner invitations rarely come in the mail and my heart rattles as I extract the sheet of my grandfather's embossed notepaper and scan his words:

Dearest Sebastian,

You're doing the right thing, my boy. I know things haven't been easy, and I want you to know I'm proud of you for honouring your family duty. John Archer told me Lizzy had a wonderful time at dinner, and she is looking forward to seeing you again.

An invitation to accompany you to Cannes will be the ideal next step in getting to know her better before we discuss details of the engagement.

Your loving grandfather,

And he signed off with an impressive flourish, as if he didn't just obliterate my world. My throat feels dry, and I can barely swallow as I reach for a glass of water.

Details of the engagement.

This is all going too fast. Lizzy and I came up with the beginnings of a plan where we said we will keep the pretence going so everyone thinks we're dating seriously. She's a smart cookie, and said that if we're seeing each other, it will put a stop to our grandfathers' matchmaking. Lizzy said she can't bear to date a string of candidates he's picked out for her, and this way we can nip it in the bud.

By the time we left the restaurant, I'd made a snap decision to go along with her plan and I told her I agreed and would be in touch.

But I haven't been able to make myself move forward with it and still haven't replied to Lizzy's latest text. She's lovely, and her plan makes perfect sense, but I hate it.

Fortunately, my antics don't capture the press's attention like Damian's do, and apart from a brief mention in one of the social columns about my dinner with Lizzy at the high-profile restaurant, I haven't spotted any more coverage.

Grandfather is pushing for her to come to Cannes. And her text was just two words: *What next?*

We're both caught in a trap, and I see the logic of us pretending to date each other—making the best of a bad situation—so why can't I bring myself to reply?

Nathalie's smile spins into my mind again, and I can't wait to go home and see how her day was. Is she thinking about me like this too? The only person I want to text is her.

The meeting with my execs is short and they're surprised it's over so soon. I don't usually let them off the hook so quickly.

'Is that it?' Xavier, my deputy, says. 'Aren't we ready to make detailed plans for the Cannes' opening?'

Shaking my head, I make some lame excuse about having to deal with something else this afternoon, and we'll reconvene soon. I haven't told him I'm coming yet, as I keep toying with the idea of not going ahead with the visit and having him represent me as originally planned. He'll be disappointed, I imagine, so I hold off telling him.

If there's one thing I hate, it's disappointing people I care about, so I keep the change of plan to myself just a little while longer whilst I decide whether this is really going to happen.

As CEO of Rochester Hotels, my head needs to be focused on this opening, and I know I need to decide soon so Xavier can make the grand opening plans. He's perplexed by my non-committal and says as much, but I brush him off and soon I'm alone again with my dangerous thoughts.

My phone rests on my desk and is calling to me. I'm tempted to call Nathalie, but I shouldn't. And if I text her personal messages, it's as good as saying I want us to continue where we left off. But if I don't text her, it feels cold, like I'm not bothering to check she's okay after our night together.

After finishing my coffee and deliberating, my resolve

weakens even further, and I pick up my phone and type out a message to her:

Hope you're having a good day and are not too tired.

I add some love hearts, but then hastily delete them. I'm like a lovesick boy, and I'm unsure how to behave around her. Reading the message again, I decide not to refer openly to what happened between us, and then I decide not to send it. Daisy reads quite well and who knows if she might see it and start asking her endless embarrassing questions, like when she went off on one about me not dating a mean girlfriend. Besides, I can't let myself fall into romancing Nat by text. I'm like a druggie where she's concerned, and she's my heroin, so I must keep her at a distance, somehow.

Pushing my phone aside, I distract myself by reading a report and signing off on something for my assistant. I don't recall being this unproductive, and it's not like me at all.

In the end, I conclude it's rude not to message her, and I settle for a middle of the road, non-committal friend/boss style message:

How's your day so far?
Is Daisy back yet?

The second I press send, I'm on edge waiting for her reply. I'm pretty certain she will respond soon, because effectively I pay her to update me on Daisy. That's why the message was a bit of a cop-out and I'm not thrilled with it. But I'm holding myself back from messaging what I really want to say, which is she's the most amazing woman I've ever known, and I can't wait to see her. Calling would be more enjoyable, but I'm scared she'll hear how much I want her, so that's a no-no. I'll have to have a stern talk with myself before I arrive home tonight, or this is going to become an impossible situation. Maybe going away to Cannes for a few days isn't such a bad idea...

There's the noise of a ping and I click to reveal the text. Adrenalin rushes through me, and my heart hammers and I feel lightheaded. Too much coffee and too little sleep.

Hi

All good, thanks. Daisy is on her way soon. I'll let you know when she's home.

Relief courses through me she's obviously okay, and not angry at me for taking advantage of the situation. That's something. Daisy took a backseat yesterday when I was overcome by wanting Nat, but I must keep reminding myself that our happy home scenario could go up in flames if I'm not careful. Daisy losing Nathalie as her nanny, just when she's flourishing and settled with her, is not an option and I won't allow it to happen.

I don't dare unravel the gloomy thoughts of what will happen if *I* lose Nathalie, but I tell myself as long as she's at home, at least I can see her. That's better than nothing, and if it comes down to it, I'll take that.

As the afternoon ticks by, the highs of the night morph into weariness and I almost nod off at my desk. I drink another coffee. We can't have slept for more than a couple of hours, and even that was off and on. I'll get to bed early tonight and make decisions about Cannes tomorrow.

I can't imagine how I'm ever going to sleep peacefully again, knowing Nathalie is in bed, just one floor above me. How am I going to resist her, especially if she says she wants me again? The only way I kept my distance from her since the kitchen incident was because she avoided me for most of it. If she's into this friends with benefits scenario, my gut tells me I'm doomed.

I've been self-contained and kept my sexual appetite firmly under control for years, but now I've tasted what I've been missing with Nathalie, I don't think I'm going to be able to keep myself so tightly buttoned up. My right hand has kept me from losing my mind, and I've had the occasional skin-on-skin encounter, but they make me feel worse when they're over.

If I get into this arrangement with Lizzy Archer, how will I stop Grandfather rushing me to the altar?

Memories of Nat riding me like a cowgirl in the moonlight send ripples of lust through my body. At this rate, I'm going to have to relieve myself in the shower at work just to get through the day. I don't remember being this hot for anyone.

Somehow, I push through the stuff on my desk but do a mediocre job, and I can't wait to leave. Before I wrap up for the day, I send another text, this time to Lizzy:

Fancy coming to Cannes for the opening of our new hotel?

A minute later, there's a ping, and I read her reply:

Yes. When is it?

. . .

I give her the dates, and she says she thinks it would work.

Lizzy: *Let's get together soon to discuss deets and give the media something to talk about!*

She adds a laughing face emoji. It's all a game to her. If it wasn't for Nat, I suppose I could have some fun with it, too. It's not like I'd be hurting anyone. But all I can think about is Nathalie's face, and how she's going to feel when she finds out.

Oh fuck.

CHAPTER 27

Nathalie

I've been panicking since he left for the office this morning. The boldness I felt last night has fled, and I feel vulnerable. What have I done? It seemed like the right thing in the madness of the moment, but now I'm not sure.

Daisy will be home soon, and I need to pretend everything's okay, but I'm in a state. What if Sebastian thinks we're going to continue like this? And even worse, what if he doesn't even want to?

There's a ping on my phone and I check my messages, expecting it to be an update from Daisy's friend's mother. But it's from Sebastian, and my hand shakes slightly as I click to read it.

My spirits plummet further when I see he's back to business as usual. No mention of our night together. He asks how I'm doing and then gets straight into what's happening with

Daisy. I don't know whether to be relieved or disappointed he's acting normal.

I reply in the same way I usually would when he's in touch about Daisy. We've never texted about anything else, so I shouldn't be surprised that today isn't any different.

But I'm sad. A tiny slither of me hoped things might change dramatically now, and he would see how good we are together and want more than the stupid arrangement I offered.

I text a cry for help to Juliette, and we message back and forth. She tells me to calm down, and everything will be okay. She thinks it sounds like he's crazy about me and it's just a matter of time until things grow more serious.

Tired of texting, we switch to a phone call, and I ask her if she's forgotten he's the son of a mega wealthy family that will never approve of a relationship with someone like me.

She asks what I mean by someone like me and says he'd be lucky to have me. I remind her I'm just the nanny, but she won't have it. Juliette is unfazed by my sob story about how I said I was up for a friends with benefits arrangement, and she is confident things will work out.

'Take it one day at a time, and see what he does,' she advises.

But she's such a romantic, so although I long to believe her, I can't be as positive as her.

She calms me down by the end of the call, and when Daisy arrives, I throw myself into keeping her entertained.

Sebastian doesn't text again, and I try to keep my mind off how awkward it will be when he gets home later. It's my fault for throwing myself at him and offering myself on a silver platter.

'Are you sad, Nathalie?' Daisy asks suddenly when we're in her room sorting through her many books.

'No. Why do you ask?'

'You usually smile a lot and today you look sad,' she says, studying me with a puzzled expression on her sweet face.

'Maybe I am a little sad, but it's nothing for you to worry about,' I say. 'But you know what would really help?'

She raises her eager brown eyes to mine. 'What?'

'A big hug from you,' I say, smiling.

We hug, and it really does help. She's such a lovely girl, and I don't want to think about my time with her ending. I decide to shake myself out of this melancholy mood. 'Want a swim?' I ask, knowing this is her favourite activity and we always have fun in the pool.

The weather is overcast now, but it's warm enough to swim in the heated pool and sit in the garden, so we change into our costumes and head outside.

Mrs Johnson is in the kitchen and promises us a round of freshly baked muffins by the time we finish swimming.

Daisy is giggling when we jump in and she swims doggy paddle next to me, and I pretend to race her. There's no deep end, so the pool is relatively safe, but we don't allow her to swim alone. She's thrilled at this unexpected swim. Hyper from her night at her friend's, she tells me they stayed up late to watch a movie and eat popcorn.

'I bet you're going to sleep well tonight,' I laugh, thinking that I hope I will, too. I'm exhausted after our night of passion, and a day of worrying about the consequences of my actions isn't helping.

'What did you and Daddy do?'

I gulp. 'Your daddy picked me up from the children's centre and it was already late by the time I finished work. We had a cup of tea and went to bed.'

Well, it's true!

She asks if her friend can sleep over soon.

I tell her she'll have to ask her daddy, but I imagine it'll be fine.

'The house was so quiet without you here—it was weird,' I say. 'We didn't like it.'

It might be for the best if we're not left alone again. It's too tempting, and I don't think I can handle it. That's only the second time we had the house to ourselves at night, and both times we've ended up kissing. If only I could be the fearless Nathalie, I was last night… But the truth is, my old insecurities have come back to haunt me and I'm dreading what's on the horizon. I can't see any good coming of it. Now I just want him even more. The sex was incredible and images of us in his bed keep monopolising my mind and it's hard to think clearly.

What was it he said about his inheritance? I can't remember the details, and on reflection, I'm not sure he gave me any. Why would he? He doesn't have to explain his situation to me, after all. I think he mentioned he's expected to marry someone suitable to satisfy the terms of his grandfather's will.

Arthur Rochester sounds like a formidable character, and I feel bad that he must have a marriage approved by some old guy, no matter who he is. No wonder Seb is still single.

My thoughts wander back to how he reacted when he saw Richard talking to me, and he mentioned asking his mum for funding. The idea of meeting her in person still fills me with apprehension. Would she like me, or would she pick up on what's going on between me and her son? Mothers are incredibly intuitive about their children. I've been a nanny long enough to know that.

Daisy's a proficient swimmer for her age, and can already swim without arm bands. We swim back and forth for a while and then play with a ball, jumping about and reaching for it in the air. The exercise and fresh air shift my mood and I feel a bit more myself by the time we dry off. I always bring a Rochester robe with me when I swim now, so I'm not caught semi-naked by Sebastian again, although after last night, that seems silly.

Mrs Johnson brings out a tray of sandwiches and muffins for a late lunch and we sit in the garden, chatting and eating.

Daisy asks if we can go on holiday together like her daddy promised. I laugh, and act as though it's not a big deal, but my heart skips a beat as I imagine how fabulous it would be to go on holiday with my two favourite people.

'He didn't promise,' I remind her. 'I think he was just floating ideas, but that doesn't mean we're going to do it.'

Daisy pulls a glum face. 'All my friends go on summer holidays with their families,' she says.

'Aww, *ma chérie*,' I say, squeezing her hand. 'Speak to your daddy and see what he says. I don't know if he has time for a summer holiday. You know how busy he is at work.'

We munch through a delicious freshly baked muffin each, and then I take her upstairs to shower and change, ready for Sebastian coming home.

Every sound makes me jump, and I keep looking at my watch, wondering when he'll arrive. I daren't think about what we'll say to each other and how we're going to get through the next weeks.

Will he invite me into his bed again, or will he go back to pretending nothing's going on between us?

With a sinking feeling in my stomach, I guess it will be the latter, and I know I'm going to struggle with the situation.

Maybe I should give in my notice and go home to Paris before this gets any more out of control?

But then Daisy places her hand in mine and says she had the most brilliant afternoon and thanks for swimming with her.

I don't know who I love more—Daisy or her gorgeous daddy...

CHAPTER 28

Sebastian

It's been strained at home since we spent the night together. She can't even meet my eyes over breakfast, and it seems like whenever I arrive home, she rushes out. I hate it, but I don't know what to do. It's not right to pursue a sexual relationship of any type with my daughter's nanny, never mind a casual one. The staff are bound to rumble us if we keep at it, and besides, I don't want her getting any more hurt than I suspect she already is. Her eyes hold a depth of sadness that wasn't there before, and I hate myself for doing that to her.

I can't handle a casual relationship, anyway, given the depth of my attraction to her. But now we're stuck in this limbo of being neither lovers nor friends, and it's confusing.

Lizzy Archer confirmed she will attend the grand opening of the Cannes hotel. We met for coffee to discuss our fake dating plan, and we agreed it makes sense. But I'm not sleeping well, and no matter how much I tell myself it's for the best, my heart rebels, and the future looks bleak.

The hotel opening is fast approaching, and I still haven't mentioned to Nathalie or Daisy that I'll be away for a whole week. It shouldn't be a big deal, but somehow it feels like it is, and I'm dragging my heels. Not that I get much chance to talk to Nathalie. One evening, I overcame my reluctance to pry, and I asked if she was off anywhere nice. She said she was doing an extra shift at the centre because they're short-staffed. This reminded me about the guy who was hovering when I collected her, and I know I have no right to be jealous, but I am.

The thought of her with someone else kills me, and I don't know how I'm going to get through it. Then, one morning at breakfast, Daisy brings up the summer holiday topic again and asks if we can go on holiday with Nathalie. Guilt grabs me by the throat as I think of what she's missing out on by not having her mother and father together. Her mother has cancelled the last few visits and is away on a trip with her new husband again.

Daisy asks if we can go for a holiday by the sea, like I said. I don't even remember, but she's got it firmly in her sights, and her eyes shine as she talks about us going on holiday to the seaside with Nathalie.

My heart drums and I'm apprehensive, but I know I need to break the news to them that there is no holiday on the horizon. If I wasn't avoiding mentioning it, I would tell them I'm away on business soon, and I must tell them before Daisy gets her hopes up any further.

Man up, Rochester.

We finish dinner and I pull Daisy onto my lap and glance at Nathalie to see if she's listening. Daisy's allowed to stay up for a later dinner in the summer holidays. Nathalie is actually here for dinner, for once, which is a pleasant change, and her eyes are on me as if she senses I'm about to say something important.

I wonder if she's dating that guy from the centre, and that's why she's out so much. Bile rises in my throat at the vision of them together. There's no one to blame but me, and I wish I didn't care so much about my position. I'd tell Grandfather he can do whatever he likes, and I refuse to marry someone of his choosing. But I'm too ambitious and have invested so much of myself into Rochester Hotels. It isn't workable and seems like an unfair choice.

Clearing my throat, I say, 'I'm going on a business trip soon, so I won't be able to take time out from work this summer holidays, but we'll definitely arrange a trip later in the year, okay, pumpkin?'

Daisy's eyes well up, and her disappointment eats at me. I feel torn, but I push on as I need to get this off my chest. Now I feel guilty about Nathalie, as well as neglecting Daisy, and it doesn't sit right with me. I have to make it up to them somehow, arranged marriage or not.

My eyes move to Nathalie's face, and I think I see disappointment in her eyes, too, until she looks away. I say, 'How do you feel about you and Daisy going for a seaside holiday without me?'

Surprise registers in her expression and I can tell she didn't expect that. 'Of course, we can do that if that works best for you,' she says carefully. She's been distanced and professional ever since our night together, and it's crucifying me.

'It's not that I wouldn't love to come, but I'll be out of the office for a week on this business trip, and although it's not a holiday, it will still be tricky for me to take more time away. We're in major expansion mode,' I say.

'Daddy, where are you going on your trip?' Daisy wriggles on my lap and stares up at me, waiting for my reply.

This is when I need to tell them. I still hesitate and wish the hotel opening was anywhere but France. It feels doubly treacherous, and like I should take Nathalie and Daisy, not Lizzy.

'The new hotel is in Cannes.'

Nathalie's eyes light up. 'I love Cannes! My parents took me and my sister there on holiday when we were little. Before my mother got sick.' Her gaze drops to Daisy, and she tells her, 'It's a beautiful place in France by the sea. In French it's called *Cote d'Azur*.'

Daisy repeats the words after Nathalie, and I marvel at how easily she's taken to speaking snippets of French.

Nathalie throws me a sweet look. 'If you like, I could travel to Cannes with Daisy, and we could meet you for a few days when your business is completed? It would be great for her to practice her French. She's been making good progress, but there's nothing like speaking in real-life situations.'

My heart hurts. This is even worse than I imagined. Clearly, she's ignoring our personal situation in favour of making it work for Daisy. I appreciate it, but this is just making things harder.

'Yes, Daddy. Pleeeeese, Daddy,' Daisy pleads, almost slipping off my lap in her excitement. 'Let's stay by the sea and speak French, *s'il vous plaît*.'

I hold my hand up, before she gets any more carried away, and say, 'Your French is coming along beautifully, but I'm afraid that isn't going to be possible as I'll be tied up with work.'

Nathalie says, 'Never mind. It was just an idea. Daddy needs to work, Daisy, so it will be just you and me. Don't worry, we will do some fun stuff, like we always do.'

Tears spill from Daisy's eyes now, and I feel wretched.

'But you're the boss,' says Daisy. 'Why do you always have to work?' She slides off my lap and gallops out of the room and I hear her little feet pounding the stairs as she rushes up to her bedroom.

'I'm sorry,' says Nathalie. 'I didn't mean to make it worse. That was my fault.'

'No, no, it's okay. She has to learn that things don't always go her way. If I could do it, I would, but the hotel opening will be full-on and then I'll need to get back to play catch up at the London office.'

'I understand,' she says, her blue eyes guarded, but her voice gentle.

'Thank you,' I say. I want to reach out and touch her hand, but I stop myself.

'For what?'

'For being so fantastic with Daisy and for trying to make her seaside holiday dream come true.'

'Of course,' she says. 'I can take Daisy somewhere without you, like you suggested if that's better, although I think she is set on us all going.'

She stands as if to leave the room.

'I'd love to take her for a holiday by the sea at some point.'

'I'm sure she would love it,' Nathalie says.

'And would you love it too?'

Her cheeks flush slightly beneath my stare.

'Yes,' she says. 'I hope you have a successful trip to Cannes. Don't worry about Daisy. I'll go and cheer her up now.'

'No, it's okay. I'll go,' I say, rising. 'She's upset with me, so it's only fair. Are you going out this evening?'

She shakes her head. 'No, they don't need me today.'

The thought of her staying at home pleases me.

If only I could tell her how much I love her.

CHAPTER 29

Nathalie

Sebastian left for Cannes a couple of days ago and although I miss him, in some ways, it's a relief.

I'm looking forward to spending long, lazy summer days with Daisy. There's a heatwave, and with her off school, we're having a lot of fun. We don't need to rush about, and there's plenty of time to swim, eat meals in the garden and play games. In the evenings, we curl up and watch a movie together on the big sofa. Now Sebastian is away, we've got the house to ourselves, and Mrs Johnson is the only staff member working every day and she makes sure we're well fed. I've taken the week off from the centre while Sebastian is in France, and it feels like a mini holiday for me, even though this is supposedly work.

Luxury home, gorgeous child, housekeeper, stunning location, and everything we could ever need at our fingertips. Sebastian gave me a credit card to use for whatever we want, so I'm living the dream. There's no money stress like when I was younger, and as I barely spend any of my salary, I'm saving most of it like I'd hoped I could.

Today we walked into town and then wandered down to the river and ate ice cream and played word games. The riverside comes alive in summer, with boats bobbing back and forth on the rippling water, and tourists and locals dining alfresco. There was a band playing today outside one restaurant and we watched them for a while. Daisy asked if she could put money in the hat. Luckily, I had some cash with me, and she was thrilled.

I've decided to take a break from dwelling on the awkward situation with Sebastian. We did what we did. It was great, but obviously he's not into me in the same way I'm into him. I'm just going to have to get over him and move on.

My heart hurts if I think about our night together too much. It made it harder for me to be around him, so in the past few weeks, I've been taking any shift I can get at the centre, just to be out of the house at night, once Daisy's in bed.

Her schedule is much more relaxed during the holidays, and she goes to bed late, so we are rarely alone. I couldn't risk a repeat of that night, as I don't trust myself not to let it happen again if he's up for it. I dread to think what he makes of how easy I was, and my ridiculous suggestion of friends with benefits.

Sometimes I think I catch him looking at me like he's pining for me too, but if he is, he's doing a fabulous job of pretending things are normal and we didn't sleep together.

For fuck's sake. I roll my eyes.

Sebastian is so sexy when he swears. You can't really swear when you're a nanny, and he doesn't when Daisy is around, but I roll the English swear words on my tongue, under my breath and think of him and smile.

Oops. Not supposed to be thinking of him, but here I go again. The more I try not to think of him, the more he pops into my head. Or maybe he just never pops out of my thoughts. It doesn't help that Daisy looks like him. She has a lot of his expressions and mannerisms too, and it's like a kick in the gut sometimes. Fortunately, she also has his good nature and is upbeat and easy to be around. Whichever lucky woman lands Sebastian and Daisy in her life will be blessed.

The thought of him remarrying and Daisy having a step-mother, cuts me like a sharp blade.

If only our situation were different and we were social equals, perhaps things would work out. But what can I do?

He acts like we didn't have the most mind-blowing sex of my life. Maybe it was all quite routine for him. If he had made some allusion to our night together, I wouldn't have closed myself off and fled to the centre at every opportunity, but the more he acted like nothing happened, the more wretched I felt, and the more I beat myself up for initiating sex with my boss.

What kind of nanny comes onto their boss?

I'm ashamed of my behaviour and am doing my best to be professional and fall out of love with him, but I'm not having any success. He still appears in my dreams every night, and I wake up aching for him. It's impossible for me to imagine life without him, and the thought of returning to Paris and never seeing him or Daisy again fills me with dread.

Daisy's playing a game on her tablet and I'm tidying up her toys when the post box clangs. Walking towards the front door, I bend to pick up the newspaper from the mat. Sebastian gets several newspapers and magazines delivered and there always seems to be something arriving. He's an avid reader of the business sections and sometimes I skim through the supplements in the weekend papers. It makes me feel like I'm a proper English citizen and reminds me of my mother.

What would she say if she could see me now, living in this amazing house in one of the most expensive areas in London?

If she were still alive, I think she would have adored to visit me here, and I know she would have loved Daisy. And Sebastian.

Stop it...

I drop the heavy newspaper on the table, and it lands with a satisfying thud, and the supplements slip out of the main newspaper and scatter across the surface. I'm just about to go back into the other room when my eye catches sight of a familiar face. My breath catches and I stare at the photo.

Stretching out my hand, I pull the supplement into the centre of the table and pore over the front cover. Sebastian's handsome face stares back at me, and my stomach churns as my eyes move to the glamorous woman at his side. She's got her arm in his and they look very much like a couple. By now, my heart is doing somersaults and I feel sick.

The woman is everything I'm not. She exudes wealth and confidence. I see by her expensive jewellery and outfit that she's no stranger to designer clothes and wears only the best. Reading the article, I discover her name is Elizabeth Archer, and she is the granddaughter of John Archer, the legendary banker. The article goes on to say that Lizzy attended the grand opening of the Rochester Cannes with Sebastian and then mentions a list of celebrities and business icons who were at the party.

I can barely swallow. My throat has closed over and it's like a deadly virus has struck me. My head hurts and I feel weak, so I sink into a chair with the article laid out in front of me.

Sebastian looks heart-stoppingly handsome in his tux, which reminds me of our night at the ball when we danced. I imagine him whirling Elizabeth Archer around the dance floor and my eyes fill with tears.

He didn't mention he was dating anyone, and he certainly didn't mention his trip to Cannes was also a romantic one.

Why would he, you idiot? He doesn't have to explain himself to you.

Thoughts are cascading through my mind, and my impulse is to run upstairs, pack my bags, and jump on a flight to Paris.

'Nathalie. Can we swim soon?' Daisy asks, wandering into the room. Her voice is squeaky, and I can tell she's excited. The sun is already high in the sky. It's a glorious day, and I promised we'd spend the afternoon in the pool.

'Yes, of course. Pop upstairs and put your costume on,' I say. 'I'll be up in a minute.' My voice doesn't sound like mine, and my throat is choked with emotion.

She wanders over and says, 'You sound funny.' As she approaches, I quickly wipe my eyes, so she won't notice I'm crying. But she's a sharp kid and doesn't miss a thing. 'Nathalie, why are you crying?' she asks. Her small arms shoot up to my shoulders and she stretches to hug me. 'Please don't cry, Nathalie.'

I raise my face to hers and look at her. She is the sweetest child and the concern in her eyes touches me and makes me feel even more emotional. 'I'm okay,' I say. 'I got some bad news from a friend, that's all. But it'll be fine.'

'What bad news?' she asks, ever curious.

'It's nothing. I don't want you to worry.'

Her father's photo catches her eye as she moves her head. 'It's Daddy! What do they say about my daddy?' Her face creases as she tries to make sense of the words and reads some of them slowly. 'What do they say, Nathalie? Please read it to me. Who is this pretty lady with him?'

'It's the business paper. They're talking about the hotel opening in Cannes, sweetie.'

She keeps asking what they say, and I struggle to reply as the tears block my throat.

'That the hotel opening was a success and your daddy's a brilliant CEO of Rochester Hotels,' I say.

'Are you crying because my daddy is with that lady, and we didn't get to go on holiday with him?'

I shake my head and fold the newspaper over so I can't see their smiling faces anymore. 'No, of course not.'

Clapping my hands, I stand up and touch her small shoulders. 'Everything is fine. Let's go swim, shall we?'

'Yay!' Her glum expression transforms into a sunny smile, and we go upstairs and change into our swimwear.

The afternoon passes in a haze, with images of Sebastian and his date swirling around my mind, as Daisy and I play catch in the water, and lounge about on the pool inflatables. I do my best to act normally for Daisy, but I'm counting the hours until I can be alone. All I want to do is cry, but I hold myself together and go through the motions of the day in a robotic fashion.

At dinner time, my phone rings and I see it's Sebastian. He rarely calls me, but as he's in France, I guess he wants to speak to Daisy.

'It's Daddy,' I call out to her. 'Come and answer the phone.' I don't want to speak to him and he's calling for Daisy, anyway.

I accept the call and hand my phone to her. 'Daddy,' she squeals and tells him all about our pool games and what a fun afternoon we've had.

I can hear his deep voice echoing through the phone. They chat for a few minutes, and she tells him we saw his photo in the newspaper with a pretty lady. After a while she loses interest and they say goodnight and she wiggles the phone at me. I jump like I've been bitten. The last thing I want to do is speak to him now.

He knows I've seen the photo in the paper. How embarrassing.

'Daddy wants to speak to you now,' she says, and hands me the offending phone and runs off to drink her orange juice, oblivious to the mayhem in my heart.

'Hello,' I say, trying to keep my voice calm, but I hear it waver.

'*Bonjour*,' he says. His voice melts me, and we exchange a few pleasantries. His French is decent, so it's not unusual for him to talk to me a bit in French, but today feels different. He asks after Daisy and says he's happy we're having a good time. He says he's missing us and can't wait to come home.

I don't say a word about the newspaper photo, but he brings it up. 'Daisy said I'm in the paper for the opening?'

'Yes,' I say.

There's a long, awkward pause as he waits for me to elaborate, but I don't. I can't. All my words have deserted me, and my heart feels like it's crashing in my throat.

'It's a business thing,' he says.

'What is?' I ask.

'The opening party,' he says, his voice smooth, like velvet.

All my senses are reeling as his words wash over me, but I still say nothing.

What is there to say?

'What does it say?' he asks finally.

I take a breath and try to calm my thudding heart. 'I didn't read the article,' I say. 'We just saw a photo of you with a woman on the front page.'

There I said it. I gulp. It's true. When Daisy arrived, I stopped reading because I couldn't hide my tears from her. I'll take it to my room and read it properly after she goes to bed. That way, I can cry in peace. Judging by my reaction to the photo and captions, I need to read it alone where no one can see how affected I am by my boss taking a date to the official opening of the Rochester Cannes Hotel.

'What did you tell Daisy?' His tone is subdued and not like Sebastian's usually carefree tone.

'Nothing. What would you like me to tell her?' I ask, forcing the words out.

'It's not important. Nothing at all.'

'Okay. I have to help Daisy get ready for bed now,' I fib.

'Nat?'

I can't breathe, and the concern in his voice crushes what little self-control I have left.

'Yes?' I whisper, and the sound barely registers over the line, but he hears it.

He makes a low noise, like he's sucking in his breath.

'I'm sorry,' he says.

'I'm sorry too,' I whisper, and press the button to end the call.

I dash into the bathroom as the tears stream down my face, thinking I can't live with him like this anymore. It's too much to bear.

But how can I leave Daisy?

CHAPTER 30

Sebastian

When she ends the call, my guts feel like they've been shredded. The hurt in her voice destroyed me and I didn't know what to say. I tried to avoid having a photo with Lizzy at the opening, but it was inevitable. If you don't give the media something to write about, they make up their own story, and that can be a lot uglier than the truth.

Grandfather is waiting to see the publicity pieces and won't be satisfied unless there are features in several of the most important publications in the business world. In his eyes, that was the main reason Lizzy attended the event with me, and he would regard anything less as missing the mark.

I racked my brains thinking of ways around it, like inviting them to photograph me alone and offering them an exclusive shoot. But Lizzy was on my arm at the official opening and the press clamoured for a photo of us together. She wanted to get her money's worth for her family too, so although I wouldn't call her mercenary, she knows that being photographed with a Rochester attracts the buzz both our grandfathers want.

I dread to think what they wrote in the article after all the questions they fired at us. Nothing excites reporters as much as a new couple they can be first to share the full scoop on. They didn't hold back and were throwing questions at me about our relationship and asking if I'm planning to remarry.

Subtle they are not...

Lizzy confided in me that her boyfriend won't like seeing us together, and I could see she was troubled and was just doing her duty. I know how she feels.

Fending them off as best I could, we got through it and to be fair, Lizzy is good company and knows how to conduct herself at this type of event, so it was a breeze in that respect.

But it was a complete nightmare for my relationship with Nathalie. I felt guilty the whole time, even though I didn't make any promises.

All the same, it doesn't feel right, and I can't stand the thought of her upset at home when she saw the photo in the paper. But what else could I do? I feel cornered and out of options.

When I called to see how they were doing at home, I was hoping Nathalie wouldn't have seen anything about the opening. She doesn't pay much attention to the papers, but it's sod's law she saw that one.

The worst thing is the publicity isn't over yet. Rochester Media lined up loads of interviews for me, and Damian said they wanted Lizzy involved as much as possible.

Thanks Damian.

He may suspect I like Nathalie because I saw him looking at us curiously at the ball, but I doubt he has any idea how far we went and how deep I've fallen. He is only conveying what

Grandfather asked him to. Lizzy is a great draw for the media, and the camera obviously loves her, so I won't hold it against him, but I'm upset all the same.

I was tempted to throw myself on his mercy and tell him the truth. I could have asked him to keep the coverage about me and Lizzy to the bare minimum, but I couldn't bring myself to say the words. It was too risky, and I would be betraying Nathalie's confidence. I'm crazy about her, but I'm also her boss and feel a certain duty of care. If what I said were to reach Grandfather, Nathalie could find herself in an untenable position, and I can't lose her. After thinking it through, I realised I had no choice but to go with the media circus and pray we all emerge unscathed.

My prayers weren't answered because I could tell from Nathalie's first syllable how much she was hurting. Even if I didn't hear her speak, I sensed something was wrong immediately. I always know when she's down, even when she puts a brave face on it. It's like we're connected by an invisible chord, and I feel her pain all the way from Richmond to the Riviera.

All I want to do is get on the private jet and fly home to Nathalie and Daisy. The Riviera is stunning, and anyone would think I'd be having a wonderful time. The hotel is one of our best and is a fabulous achievement, but I can't relax and enjoy it.

Lizzy suggested we go for dinner at a new restaurant with a sensational panoramic view of Cannes. I went along with it as she's helping me out by being here, and our fake dating ruse is just as difficult for her, but my heart's not in it. I'm trying not to be horrible company, and to get myself into a better head space so I'm not a complete bore, but I know I'm failing. All I can feel is Nathalie's disappointment, and what she must think of me right now.

'I'm sorry this is so hard for you,' Lizzy says, running her hand through her glossy styled hair.

Raising my head from the menu, I say, 'Is it that obvious?'

Empathy shines in her eyes as she nods and shrugs her shoulders.

'Please don't take it personally. Things are just awkward in my life, right now,' I say.

'Don't worry. I get it. Things are not great for me personally, either. I think I told you about my forbidden love?' She laughs, but the humour doesn't reach her eyes, and I see she's hurting too.

'I'm very grateful to you for taking the time to do this,' I say.

'It's a pleasure. I will be happy to fake date you anytime! My boyfriend hates it, but Grandfather is going to cut me off if I don't play nicely. It sounds like it's much the same for you.'

I nod and take a swig of cold beer. 'Yes, unless I want to risk losing my seat on the board, and perhaps even my position as CEO of Rochester Hotels, I must comply with my grandfather's wishes. He says I already made one fuck-up with my ex-wife, and he won't allow me to make another.'

'Was it that bad?' she asks.

'Yes, and then some. Although I got my daughter out of it, so it's not all doom and gloom.'

'It's rare to find such a devoted single dad. I'm impressed. Your daughter is a lucky girl.'

'I'm the lucky one,' I reply, and drain my glass of beer.

The server takes our order, but I've no appetite.

'You worried about your girlfriend?' she asks.

'Yeah, no,' I say, grasping for the right thing to say. 'She's not my girlfriend, to be honest.'

'I see,' she says, sipping her champagne cocktail. 'But you wish she were, I take it?'

'Something like that,' I say. 'It's complicated.'

'It always is,' she says.

'What about you?' I ask, steering her away from my impossible situation. As much as I long for Nathalie, I'm nostalgic for the days when I was numb to all feeling. I was only half-alive, but I was great at pretending I was fine. She stunned me back to life, and now I'm drowning in a sea of pain.

I keep telling myself I can handle this, and it will get easier. Family and business expectations weigh heavily on me, and sometimes I wish I wasn't shackled to all this success. But who would I be if I wasn't Sebastian Rochester, CEO of Rochester Hotels, and shareholder in the company?

Shaking my head, I sigh and pick at the fancy French cuisine. I'd much rather be sharing a pizza with Nathalie and Daisy, and a wave of homesickness rolls over me.

'You're miles away,' says Lizzy.

'Sorry,' I say. 'I'm not good company this evening. Please forgive me. You were saying?'

Over dinner, to the backdrop of the setting sun, she regales me with how she met the love of her life, and how she couldn't have fallen for someone more unsuitable if she tried. She rolls her eyes and is self-deprecating. I think how fortunate that she's a nice person and not a predatory type who would cash in on my predicament.

As we eat, a camera flashes, and I notice a guy snapping shots of us from a distance. I stand up, but the host hurries over and tells the photographer to leave.

'Paparazzi,' I say. 'No doubt, another glossy photo of us, this time sharing a romantic dinner.'

'Well, it's kind of working out exactly like we planned, isn't it?'

'Yes, it is. My grandfather and older brother are going to be pleased with the show we've put on,' I say.

'And what about the woman you can't stop thinking about?'

'This will be the nail in the coffin,' I say, and order another beer. Lord knows, I need something stronger, but I can't afford not to keep my head straight, so I resist the temptation to numb my torment.

The wheels of the jet hit the runway, and I'm relieved to be back in London. At least that media circus is over, and I can get home to Daisy—and Nathalie. I can kid myself all I like that she's not monopolising my every thought, but the truth is I haven't been able to get her out of my head throughout the whole trip. I kept imagining how amazing it would be if we took a holiday together, like the one Daisy begged for. If I'd agreed to Nathalie's suggestion, they could have met me after the final interview yesterday, and we'd now be enjoying the Riviera together. Perhaps we'd be swimming in the sparkling aqua waters of the Mediterranean. But I knew it couldn't work after a week of masquerading as Lizzy Archer's date. I won't risk trailing Daisy and Nathalie through the media with me, and someone would be bound to spot us after the high-profile week I've just had.

The short flight was enough for me to get up to speed on the articles in the press.

Fuck. It is even worse than I thought it would be.

I asked my assistant to organise a copy of the paper Nathalie saw so I would know what I was up against. It wasn't pretty. No wonder she was upset. The article looked and sounded like I'm in a serious relationship with Lizzy and am about to pop the question. I only met the girl for the first time a few weeks ago, but that doesn't stop them! Berating myself, I wonder what I expected. Like Lizzy said, it worked out exactly as we planned, and our fake dating was an immense success. It seemed like everybody bought it and thought we were the real deal.

There's only one person I really need to buy it, and that's Grandfather.

Damian calls on the drive home and congratulates me on a perfect match. He sounds genuinely happy for me, and it seems like I might have pulled off convincing the family that I'm dating Lizzy for real.

We talk about the new hotel, and I can tell he's impressed. I should be thrilled, and this is the time to bask in the glory of a job well done. It's rare Damian commends me—he's tough to please—all the more so since our father died, and his life unravelled piece by piece.

But this hard-won success doesn't ease the pain, and I don't feel the joy of victory.

'The interviews went well, and you and Lizzy are all over the media. It couldn't have gone better. And I'm enjoying not being the one in the spotlight. It makes a refreshing change,' Damian says, his tone teasing.

'Ah yes, and how is Jamie, by the way?' I ask, knowing this will deflect him from talking about me and Lizzy.

There's a chilled silence that only Damian could pull off.

He still doesn't speak so I say, 'I didn't get a chance to say goodbye to her. Had an idea I might see her around Greystone again.'

In a voice that could freeze icicles, he eventually replies. 'I don't know. I haven't seen her since the ball.'

'Sorry, Damian,' I say.

'Whatever for?' he asks and makes light of it as if he didn't fall for her. But I know there was something between them.

'Well, as long as you're alright. If you bump into her again, please give her my best. I liked her a lot.'

After we end the call, I feel bad for rubbing salt in his

wounds, but I had to change the subject and couldn't take any more talk of me and Lizzy.

It's been a long week, and I didn't sleep much last night, so I nod off in the back of the car, my head resting against the cool leather.

The car pulls into the drive and my weary eyes flicker open.

Home sweet home. So, why am I dreading going in?

CHAPTER 31

Nathalie

Sebastian is due home this afternoon and I swear my heart's been beating too fast since he texted me. He kept his promise after the first time we met. Since then, he always texts me to let me know he's on his way home.

For a while, I let myself imagine it's because he can't wait to see me, but really, I know he's doing it because he's my boss and he has impeccable manners.

Nathalie, pull yourself together. He's dating someone suitable now, and he's probably going to marry her, so you'd better get used to it.

Daisy hears the car first, and shouts, 'Daddy' and runs to the door and tries to open it, but it's locked. I move towards her, but Sebastian unlocks the door from outside before I reach it. And there he is—all gorgeous six feet of him—his blue-grey eyes lock on mine. I feel a tremor as if an electric shock runs right through me as I stare back at him, my heart thumping.

Daisy calls his name and waves her arms in the air frantically. 'Daddy, pick me up, Daddy!' The connection between us is broken, and he scoops her up and sweeps her around in the air like an aeroplane.

'There you are my little pumpkin. I've missed you so much,' he says.

Daisy garbles excitedly in his ear and then looks back and forth between us, and says, 'We've missed you too, Daddy. Nathalie said the house is too quiet without you.'

He drops his eyes to search mine, and I blush. I did say that, and I meant it. But that was before I saw his face in the paper with his future wife. But I can't look away when he stares at me like that. His eyes activate every cell, and adrenalin shoots through my veins and floods my body.

'Did she, now?' he asks, a playful note in his voice.

I've missed hearing his voice, and it caresses me all over, and I shiver as goosebumps coat my skin. I can barely breathe as his eyes fix on mine and he waits for me to respond. Images of our night together flash through my mind, and I shift from one foot to the other.

'She did,' I say, trying to make light of it and not show him how he affects me.

'And is she pleased I'm home now?'

His tone is teasing, and I almost let myself fall back into our usual banter automatically, but something in me won't allow it this time. 'Great to have you home. Daisy has been counting the days. Looks like you had a successful trip.'

I hope he doesn't see the hurt in my eyes. I'm doing my best to be pleasant and professional, but it's at a heavy price. My chest is tight and my stomach churns in his presence.

'Was it a good trip, Daddy? Who was the pretty lady in

the photo with you?' Daisy bombards him with questions, and he lowers her to the floor without answering.

He glances at me as if to gauge the effect of Daisy's words, but I look away and avoid meeting his eyes again. I know all I need to know about the pretty lady in the photo, and I turn to walk away.

'I've got something for you,' he says, before I can put any distance between us.

His words stop me in my tracks. I know without a doubt he's talking to me.

'Have you got something for me too, Daddy?' Daisy squeals.

'Of course. I've got a surprise for both of you. Let's move out of the hallway, shall we, and I can get your presents out?'

He brings his monogrammed leather case through to the living room and opens it on the coffee table. Daisy is bouncing up and down and can't contain her shrieks. Considering she's the only great-granddaughter of one of the wealthiest men in England, she is surprisingly unjaded and appreciative, which I love.

He extracts a colourful wrapped gift from his case and hands it to Daisy. 'What is it? What is it?' she says breathlessly, throwing herself on the rug and tearing the paper open.

He puts his hand back into his case, as if it's an Aladdin's cave, and a moment later I watch him extract another beautifully wrapped gift.

'This is for you, Nat,' he says. His voice is low and tender as he passes it to me.

He's not making this easy for me. I planned on withdrawing from him. Being distant is the best way forward, I decided. But this throws me off-kilter, and he's already melting my carefully constructed defences I put in place after the newspaper article hit me so hard.

I reach to take it and our fingers brush, and I draw away quickly. Holding the gift in my hands, I thank him. Daisy runs back and hugs him, saying she loves it.

'Look at my dolly, Nathalie,' she says, waving it about. 'Why don't you open your present too? I wonder what Daddy got for you.'

I'm clutching onto the small package, reluctant to open it and see what's inside. What does your boss who you slept with buy for you when he's away with his new girlfriend?

My fingers shake slightly, and I try to calm myself as two pairs of Rochester eyes stare at me, urging me to open the gift.

Fumbling with the wrapping, I slide it off to reveal a black velvet box.

I raise my eyes to Sebastian's, and he says, 'I noticed it in the window and knew it was perfect for you the second I saw it, so I went back to get it.'

Flicking the box open, I gasp at the exquisite blue stone twinkling in the box. 'My favourite stone. How did you know?'

'I didn't,' he says. 'But it complements your eyes.'

'It's called topaz,' I tell Daisy, trying to normalise the moment but feeling overwhelmed that he should buy me such an obviously expensive and personal gift.

I carefully unfurl the piece from where it nestles on the luxurious padding and, holding it up, I see it's a necklace.

'It's white gold,' Sebastian says. His eyes are boring into me as he waits for my response.

The reaction I want to give him is one that's off-limits. I'd love to throw my arms around his neck like Daisy did. I'd love to kiss him and relax in the safety of his arms. But I can't do that and I'm holding myself in check, because if I don't, I'm frightened he will see the emotions he's awakened in me, and I'll lose control and break down. I must keep it together and maintain my distance, or I'll be lost. Again.

Daisy is watching us. She may be only five years old, but she's observant.

'Put it on, Nathalie,' she pleads. 'Please, I want to see the pretty necklace.'

Sebastian steps closer to me and says, 'Here, let me.'

I pass him the delicate white gold chain and he spins me around and I feel his firm hands on my neck. His fingers ignite me like touchpaper, and I inhale sharply.

'There,' he says. 'Let's see.' He turns me around to face him and we're flush against each other. The fire erupts between us like it always does.

I step backwards and take a breath, trying to calm my pounding heart. His eyes draw mine back to his, and I say, 'Thank you so much. I love it. How thoughtful of you.'

His smile is genuine, and I see how pleased he is that it's a hit.

'What do you think?' I ask Daisy.

'It's so pretty, just like you. Isn't Nathalie, pretty Daddy?'

'She is. Absolutely stunning,' Sebastian says, and his words are like cool silk calming my feverish skin. Every sense is on alert, and I long for his hands to touch me again.

I move towards the mirror and take in my flushed cheeks and the gleam in my eyes. He's right. The topaz stone is a perfect match for my eye colour, and the white gold shimmers in my reflection. The emotion builds and tears well in my eyes, no matter how I fight to hold them back.

And suddenly he is standing behind me, watching me in the mirror. He sees the tears, and I glimpse a flash of pain in his eyes, which look more grey than blue, as he studies me.

'Sorry,' I say, wiping my face. 'I'm being silly.'

'Why the tears, Nat?' he whispers so close to my ear that his breath brushes over the sensitive skin on my neck, and I shiver. Desire courses through my veins and I'm desperate for him to hold me. I never want this moment to end.

'It's just that no one has ever bought me such a beautiful gift,' I say, trying to push back the emotion and stop the tears, but they're spilling out of my eyes faster and won't stop as he looks at me.

I'm embarrassed and look away.

Daisy flings herself at me and hugs my legs. 'Don't cry, Nathalie. Please don't cry again.'

I stroke her head and soothe her, saying they are happy tears, not sad ones. She seems satisfied with my explanation and runs off to play with her new doll.

'Don't cry, darling. It's beautiful. Just like you,' Sebastian says, and then he runs a hand down my bare arm. There's a pause where we just stare into each other's eyes. I don't know what to say, but I don't want him to stop looking at me like that. His eyes are full of love. 'I'm sorry about the article. That was a misunderstanding,' he adds.

I don't know how it can be a misunderstanding, but in that second, I don't care. I clutch at his words and hope leaps within me. I'm so overwhelmed by the necklace, and his touch on my bare flesh, I can't compose the right words to question him.

So, I just let myself drown in his kind eyes with the thick, dark lashes, and I breathe him in. His masculine scent envelops me, and the heat circles in my groin. I yearn to feel him against me again. He's so close I could tilt my face upwards and kiss him, but we just hang there in the hot air, unmoving but glued together like magnets that can't break apart even if they wanted to.

The room is silent but for our breath, and it's like we're standing in this vortex forever, but then Daisy rushes back in and calls, 'Mrs Johnson says tea and cake are about to be served in the garden.'

Sebastian searches my face, and I see regret in his eyes, but ours is to be an unfulfilled love. What does it matter if he desires me if we can't be together?

I've been reading about the Rochester family, and I found an interesting article saying it's well-known that Arthur Rochester laid out in the terms of his will that each of his grandchildren must meet his criteria to qualify for their full inheritance which includes shares in the company. The word is that their grandfather must give his approval for their marriage as part of the terms.

So, what did Seb mean by it being a misunderstanding? To me, it seems clear that Lizzy Archer must be the chosen one in his quest to meet his grandfather's approval.

Lucky Lizzy.

We walk into the garden and my thoughts are swirling as I try to make sense of what's happening. He must care for me at least a little to bring me such a beautiful gift. But then why would he buy me a personal gift when he was with his girlfriend and potential future wife?

He doesn't strike me as the cheating type. Everything I've observed in his character and what he's shared with me about Daisy's mother and their marriage makes me certain that he did his best to make it work, even if he made mistakes. They were career-oriented mistakes, not other-woman mistakes.

What is he doing, and why is he still leading me on like this if he's decided to marry her? It feels unfair, but I clutch at the fragments of hope he's relit in me by presenting me with the necklace.

None of it makes any sense, and I try to act normal and drink tea and butter a scone for Daisy and heap strawberry jam onto it which is her favourite. My actions and responses are robotic as I play the perfect nanny role and act like my heart isn't splintering into tiny pieces. But all the while, my head is foggy, and I can't figure out what any of it means. My heart hurt so much after reading the article and discovering he had started dating someone, but now I can't stop the fledgling seeds of joy shooting through me. I can't help it. No matter how bad it all looks, the necklace—and the way he touched me—say something different.

Don't they?

Daisy finishes munching her scone, and I wipe the bright red jam from her mouth with a napkin. Sebastian stands and goes into the house to take a call, and my eyes follow his retreating back. I can't take my eyes off him. His broad shoulders in the white shirt that tapers down into the waist of his trousers make my mouth dry.

Daisy leans over to me and whispers something. I can't make out what she's saying. 'What?' I whisper back, thinking she's playing one of her word games.

Her eyes are mischievous, and she has the cheeky grin on her face that I love so much. The grin that reminds me of her father and makes my soul sing.

'I think my daddy loves you,' she says, louder this time.

I look back at her, stunned.

'Shhh,' I say. 'Don't be silly, sweetie. Your daddy is my boss.'

But the blush slides over my cheeks and I look away, confused.

If Daisy knows there's something between us, who else does?

CHAPTER 32

Sebastian

Buying her the necklace seemed like a good idea at the time. I missed her so much when I was away. I always get something for Daisy, not that I've been away for more than a day or two during the past few years. After buying the latest doll with all the gadgets for Daisy, it just felt right to get something for Nathalie. I told myself she's doing such a fabulous job with Daisy, it's only fair.

But the effect the necklace had on her was devastating. And the effect it had on me was equally devastating. I didn't think it through. I should have realised that buying her such an intimate gift would confuse us both even more. What she makes of my behaviour, I don't know, but I saw the tears in her eyes. No necklace, no matter how lovingly chosen or expensive, could repair the harm I've done to her. She was a flawless jewel when she arrived, and I have damaged her. As much as I can't bear the idea of not being with her again, causing her even more pain would be worse.

And I told her the article about me and Lizzy was a misunderstanding. What was I thinking? All I know is I had to bring the life back into her eyes, and that seemed like the only way. How did we get so tangled up like this?

Since the divorce, when it hit me that I had been away from home too much on business, and not realised my marriage was imploding, I swore Daisy would be my number one priority. Always. Business is important, but it shouldn't supersede Daisy's wellbeing. I vowed not to let that happen again, and it was even more imperative after Maddy left. They barely see each other, so I'm all Daisy has. It's not strictly true, of course, because my mother adores Daisy and is always asking to spend more time with her. And Grandfather is close to her too, and when I take her to Greystone for family gatherings, she is spoilt rotten by my siblings. She's luckier than many, I remind myself. We are a big, close-knit family and we have each other's backs. Even so, every child needs a predictable routine.

Nice one, Rochester. You've fallen in so deep that now we're in danger of losing Nathalie.

I hate the idea that I've allowed my lust and selfishness to blur the lines on my commitment to myself about Daisy.

But then Nathalie's face floats into my mind, and all logic disappears when I think of her. Nathalie, the poor little girl who had only her younger sister for company. The girl who lost both her parents when she was so young and had no one to turn to when she was thrown into the foster system. No wonder she cares so deeply about the kids at the centre.

My eyes grow misty and the idea of her fending for herself and her sister breaks me.

Perhaps things aren't so bad after all. Daisy is incredibly well adjusted—Nathalie said so—and she's so used to not having her mother around that honestly, I don't think she misses her. From what I hear from Daisy, her mother treats her like a toy to show off to her friends on the rare occasion she takes her anywhere. And Maddy has been away so much lately, Daisy has barely seen her since Nathalie arrived. I'm not even sure, Maddy realises we have a new nanny with whom Daisy has bonded so closely. I know I told her, as I make a point of updating her on anything significant in Daisy's life, but I'm uncertain she registered it. Either way, she didn't comment in any meaningful way beyond her usual one-word replies.

If I let it get to me, her careless attitude toward Daisy's happiness makes me angry. So, I don't let it get to me. The divorce taught me to manage my emotions carefully, and until Nathalie shook my world, I was a tightly controlled machine where my heart was concerned.

More recently, I've discovered that trying to control and manage my emotions is an exhausting endeavour, and I'm failing miserably. I only need to see Nathalie's face or hear her voice and all the feelings roar to the surface, and I want to save her from experiencing pain. I realise this is a highly inconvenient way to feel about Daisy's nanny. And the irony is that I am the one who is causing her pain. She was fine until she came into my life, and I fell for her.

What the hell am I going to do?

I shouldn't have bought her such an expensive gift.

Why didn't I buy her chocolates or something useful she might want from her country of birth?

Because you dick, you wanted to wow her. You let your own emotions and your ego take over, instead of thinking about what was best for her.

Sighing, I confront the rotten truth that I've made the situation even worse. She saw the article about me and Lizzy, and goodness knows how many more she's seen since.

I almost grabbed her some French celebrity magazines as I thought she'd enjoy reading the gossip from home, but then I saw my name on the front cover of one of them. That would be vicious and make her think I had no regard for her feelings at all.

Damian messaged me again to say we're now all over the media and the press is great. There is lots of supposition about when we're to tie the knot and what a powerful alliance we'll make by joining the Rochesters and Archers.

Grandfather called to congratulate me and said that for once he's happy with the press, and Lizzy and I did a fantastic job. He asked me to bring Lizzy to visit as soon as it's convenient.

I'm dreading it. It's one thing letting the media think you're an item, but it's quite another to pull off a fake dating charade in front of your family. In fact, I doubt my ability to do it. My mind is so full of Nathalie, I didn't even pay enough attention to Lizzy when we were in Cannes to get to know her. I don't feel bad about that because she was equally distracted. It's not like she wants me any more than I want her. We're more like brother and sister, and the minute we could both disappear back to our own suites, we did. We make a good team, but I don't know how long we can do this. She said her boyfriend is handling it badly, no matter how much she assures him there's nothing between us.

And Nathalie? Well, I think it's clear she's not handling it well, and neither am I.

I woke up with a painful hard-on this morning and nothing I did would banish it. I'm insatiable with wanting her. The night together only made it worse and now we've not been alone since before the Cannes trip. I'm aching for her.

When I clasped the necklace on her slender neck and touched her arm, I had to physically pull myself back from swooping her into my arms and kissing her pink lips. Her scent tortures me and every bit of me yearns to be with her again. The sex was so hot, and as the memory of it grows more distant, it gets hotter and hotter. The more I know I can't have her—I shouldn't have her—the more I want her.

What makes it worse is I think I could have her. Unless I imagined the love reflected in her eyes when I put the necklace on her and looked at her in the mirror, she wants me just as much as I want her.

Part of me, the selfish, desperately horny part, wants to pick up where we left off with the friends with benefits arrangement. I want to fuck her till next Tuesday. My gut tells me she would go for it because she desires me too. But my conscience tells me that would be wrong, even if it feels so right when we're together.

If I take advantage of her feelings for me, and let our sexual relationship continue, even though I know I can't give her the legitimate and honest commitment she deserves, I will destroy her.

And I will destroy myself. The more I have her, the more I pine for her. This yearning for her at every hour of the day and night is too painful. If she wasn't so brilliant with Daisy, it might be for the best to find a different nanny and recommend her to one of my associates. But the thought of Nathalie gliding around someone else's house with someone else's children fills me with dread. The jealousy I feel isn't something I'm proud of, but I acknowledge it. I'm not sure I've ever felt this jealous, and it's not a trait I've encountered much before. I had the occasional jealous moment when I was younger, but even when Maddy left me for the footballer, I wasn't jealous. I felt disillusioned, and my primary emotion was disappointment that my family had crumbled, and I wouldn't be able to give Daisy the same epic kind of childhood I had. Even if I make it brilliant for her, she won't have a sibling from the same parents and that still makes me sad. And based on how I felt when the marriage ended, I doubted she'd have a sibling at all.

But Nathalie has changed me. She's pierced the hard shell that I encased myself in to protect me from feeling. Now I'm vulnerable and frightened of these feelings that I can't contain or control, no matter what I do.

The ordered life I fought so hard to create has shattered into chaotic shards and I'm spinning in a helpless cycle of yearning.

Somehow, I go through the motions and get through the day. By the time I get into bed, I'm exhausted and fall mercifully into a deep, dreamless sleep.

The birds are tweeting like a dawn chorus as I emerge from my heavy slumber. The second I open my eyes, clarity follows. I know what I must do, even though I hate the thought of it.

It's the only way to protect Nathalie from more heartache.

CHAPTER 33

Nathalie

The atmosphere is charged whenever we're near each other, and I'm wondering how or even if we can go on like this.

I've tried to accept he's seeing someone else, but it's hard. It's made even harder because he told me it was a misunderstanding, but hasn't said another word about it since. I tried to bring it up once after he came back from Cannes, but he changed the subject abruptly. He's rarely at home, but when he is, he's not his usual light-hearted self, and Daisy asked him if he's sad, which tore at me even more than my own sadness.

There's definitely something strange going on with him, and he's not being straight with me. My heart tells me so. I feel his pain and my own, and the result is a kind of prolonged agony I can't escape.

I'm not sleeping well, and I'm barely eating. Juliette says

I've fallen madly in love and she's happy I'm feeling this deep emotion at last. She says if you haven't experienced devastating love; you haven't really lived. I texted her back that if this is love, I'd rather have no part in it.

She says to have faith, and that it will work itself out for the best, but I'm struggling to get through each day, never mind be optimistic about the future. It sounds weak, I know, and once upon a time I wouldn't have imagined myself accepting this, but I don't want to visualise a future without him. When I do, I feel myself sinking into an abyss of black despair.

On the rare occasion I bump into him, he's withdrawn and acts as if he doesn't have a spare minute to spend with me. A voice deep inside me whispers that we're perfect for each other, and if it's true he's not with the woman in the photo, why won't he acknowledge it? It's not like I'm asking for a wedding ring. I understand he must marry someone eventually from the right background, but as soul destroying as it is, I already accepted that when I slept with him and said we could be friends.

It's not that I actually think we're only friends. If we are, then he's an unusual kind of friend. It's just that I was willing to let him kid himself there's nothing more serious between us if that's what it takes to be with him.

I told Juliette in our endless texts, which are the only thing that keeps me going right now through this madness, I realise it's pathetic to accept the minimum just so I can be with him.

She said she doesn't think it's pathetic at all. She thinks it's honest. But then again, aside from being a hopeless romantic, she's also French, and we're well known for having unorthodox affairs of the heart, so I suppose that's why it didn't seem so terrible for me to be with him without a commitment.

On the night we slept together, I think I would have said anything to feel his hands on me again. I blame the sex. It's so hot with him I can't think clearly when he touches me. Although, at that point, we hadn't even slept together, but the taste of him in the kitchen was enough to make me desperate for more. And how he made me come with his mouth has ruined me for anyone else, for evermore. He's my addiction, and I don't want to cut off my supply, even though I know I should.

I keep meaning to have it out with him and ask him what he meant by a misunderstanding. The only thing I can think of is he's seeing Lizzy Archer to get his family off his back, which makes sense. Whatever he's doing, clearly, it's not making him happy. In fact, I've never seen him so glum. He is usually all jokes and banter, but that's the old Sebastian and I miss him so much. It's not just the sex I miss, it's the connection, and how he used to look at me over the table, like he was ravenous for me, not breakfast.

'Friends who fuck,' I say aloud to myself, rolling the crude phrase over my tongue. Honestly, I'd go for that again if he offered it to me. It's better than not having him at all, and now we don't even talk. It's like being cast into hell and the only glimmer of light in my dreary, dark days is sweet Daisy. I love her so much and don't want to mess things up for her, but I truly don't think I can carry on like this much longer. Summer is coming to an end and I'm considering reaching out to the agency to ask if they can find me a new position. Every time I decide I'll do it, something pulls me back from the edge, and I wait a bit longer to see if anything changes.

What I really should do is return to Paris and forget all about Sebastian Rochester, but I can't bring myself to leave London. Not just yet. If I could get a new position, he and Daisy would still be nearby and the thought of it comforts me, even if I wouldn't be in their lives anymore.

It's a strange experience to love someone so deeply that all the things you thought were so important before, disappear into the ether and instead there's a certainty in your bones that none of it really matters. You are supposed to be together, and it's the only thing that makes sense. Why can't he see it too?

I never thought of myself as a romantic. Juliette totally has my back, which is a relief. I couldn't stand it if she judged me. She says to follow my heart and give love a chance to work its magic. Things have a way of working out, but you need to be patient.

I just hope love works its magic soon, or I'm going to have to put some actual distance between us and move out of this house. The more Seb avoids me, the more I suspect he wishes I would leave, but he's too kind to say. That makes me shudder with humiliation and I turn the thought over and over in my mind, torturing myself as I wonder whether it's true.

My shifts at the centre help keep me sane, even though I'm sad that Sebastian only arrives home a few minutes before he knows I have to leave, and he's upstairs in his room by the time I get home, even if it's not late.

And then one evening, just as my shift ends, Richard calls me into his office and asks if I have a few minutes. He wants to know how my nanny job is going and whether I see myself doing it long term, or if I'm open to something new.

The question piques my interest, so when he invites me to sit down and offers me a drink, I accept. What is there to rush home for, anyway? Sebastian will avoid me as usual, and Daisy will be in bed by now. We have a pleasant chat and I warm to him even more. He's been kind to me since I started volunteering and if I wasn't so in love with Sebastian, perhaps I'd respond to his obvious interest in me. He asked me out for a drink a while back and I politely declined, but I get the feeling he's the persistent type.

'You work for one of the Rochester brothers, I understand?' he says.

I'm startled he knows who I work for because I don't recall telling him.

He sees the confusion on my face and explains he saw Sebastian pick me up a while ago.

'Ah,' I say. 'I didn't realise you two knew each other. Come to think of it, I don't think I've mentioned your name to Sebastian.'

Richard smiles, and for no reason I can pinpoint, I get goosebumps. Something isn't quite right about his reaction.

He tells me they were both at Eton. 'I'm afraid we rather came to blows back in the day.'

I must look concerned because he says, 'Oh, don't be alarmed. That's all so long ago. I'm sure we'd be the best of friends if we were to get reacquainted. Boys will be boys and all that.'

My mind switches back to that fateful evening Sebastian collected me after work. It was raining and I remember every detail because it was the one night we spent together. He was odd about Richard talking to me and went all alpha on me, saying someone can always pick me up and I shouldn't trust anyone else. But I'm pretty sure he didn't know him, or if he did, he gave no indication of it. No, that was when Sebastian was open with me, and I can't imagine him hiding it if he recognised him from school.

Richard pulls me back to the moment when he asks whether I would consider working for him full-time at his head office in central London. He praises me profusely and says how impressed he is by my dedication to the kids, and how much I've contributed to the smooth running of the centre.

This was the last thing I expected, and I just stare at him as my mind ticks over and I process what he's saying.

I'm a nanny, not an administrator.

'Nathalie?' he says, when I don't reply after some time.

'What sort of job do you have in mind?' I ask after summoning my wits and piecing together a coherent question.

He asks if I've eaten dinner, and I shake my head. All I had was a hasty piece of toast before my shift. It crosses my mind that perhaps he has an ulterior motive, and this is his way of getting me to go out with him, but I banish the thought. Why should I think the worst of him? Maybe he has a job for me, and it dawns on me that it could be the solution to all my problems.

When I was lying in bed enduring another sleepless night, it occurred to me I'm not at all excited to take another nanny position, which surprised me because I've always adored my job. But I so enjoy caring for Daisy, that ditching her for another family doesn't feel right.

An office job might be just the change of pace I need and allow me to afford to move out of Sebastian's house and be independent.

Whilst the idea of moving out makes me nervous, I'm also aware I need to do something soon or I'm going to go mad. If Sebastian turns out to really be dating the woman he was with in Cannes, then it's only a matter of time before she rocks up to the house with him. That would be unbearable, and the thought of it spurs me into action.

Richard jumps up from his seat, beaming at me when I accept his dinner invitation. We grab our things and sign out before emerging into the dark car park. Luckily, I didn't drive my little car here today because it's in the garage. Sebastian's driver asked me if I want him to collect me, but I told him I'd get a taxi home. I don't want him hanging around waiting for me all evening when I can so easily get home from here, and I doubt Sebastian cares how I get home after what's happened.

The carpark lights flicker on, and my eyes adjust gradually. A tall figure, dressed in a white shirt with a jumper slung over his shoulders, is leaning against a car bonnet. My pulse quickens when I realise who it is. At the sound of our voices, he swivels around and faces me, and my legs turn to jelly.

Sebastian.

CHAPTER 34

Nathalie

'Sebastian, what are you doing here?' I ask. My voice is squeaky and doesn't sound like me. When I'm nervous, my confident command of English fails me, and my French accent is more pronounced.

My cheeks burn as I walk towards him.

He shoots me a charming smile. 'I waited for you. I heard you don't have the car, and you turned down the offer of a lift from my driver?'

'I—I didn't want to bother him when I can easily get a lift,' I stammer.

'I'm here to take you home. I told you. It's never any bother,' he says, his tone clipped.

His blue-grey eyes glitter as he surveys Richard coming up closely behind me. I watch as recognition registers and his eyes narrow to an ominous slit.

My heart's slamming as Richard reaches my side, clears his throat, and extends his hand to Sebastian. 'Well, hello, Sebastian. It's been quite some time, hasn't it?'

Sebastian stares at him coldly and makes no move to accept his hand.

I'm embarrassed by how awkward this situation is, and I scrabble for a way to smooth things over.

Richard stands there expectantly, his hand still outstretched like the spurned party, but I notice a slight smirk on his face.

What's the deal with these two?

Richard edges closer to Sebastian, and says in an obnoxious tone, 'Don't tell me you don't remember me, trust fund boy?'

My heart's pounding as I watch them, transfixed.

Sebastian's eyes widen. 'Ah, Tricky Dicky. Well, fuck me. I didn't recognise you now that you're slightly taller than four feet.'

I gasp as he insults Richard so blatantly, and his eyes blaze. This isn't the charming Sebastian I know, and I search his face as I try to figure out why he's so furious.

A matching flash of anger distorts Richard's features, and he moves his hand and casually lays it on my arm in a proprietorial manner.

'I think it's best we go now,' he says, looking at me briefly before glaring at Sebastian again.

I glance at Richard. I'm caught between my two bosses, like a mouse in a trap, not knowing how to diffuse the landmine that's about to explode.

'Where are you going?' Sebastian says. His voice is cold and there's a steel-edged undercurrent to his words.

Richard pulls himself up to his full height, but he's still a whole head shorter than Sebastian. He's heavy set and stocky next to Sebastian's lithe broad-shouldered beauty, which even in this tense moment makes me swoon as I watch him fight for me.

Richard says, 'We're going to dinner, so if you don't mind stepping aside, we'll be on our way. I'm sure Nathalie's had enough of this nonsense.'

Sebastian growls, 'Nathalie isn't going anywhere with you.'

I jump at the sound of my name, so gruff on his lips.

Merde! He's so hot when he goes alpha.

He swats Richard's hand off my arm like an annoying fly.

'Get in the car, Nathalie,' Sebastian commands.

His tone makes my hackles rise and for a second I consider disobeying his ridiculous command and showing him I'm a free agent and can go to dinner with whomever I want, without his permission.

I stare at him and don't move.

He locks his eyes on mine. 'Please get in the car,' he says, his tone more conciliatory now.

I'm about to object when the warning in his eyes stops me. There's obviously more to this than I realise and so I decide to trust him and go along with his command-like request. Casting a swift apologetic glance at Richard, I tell him I'm going home, and we can do dinner and discuss his proposal another time.

'Over my dead body,' Sebastian growls again, and he towers over Richard. 'You're not going out with this twat.'

'What?' I ask, stunned. I can't believe he's talking to Richard this way. It's so out of character for the usually charming Sebastian.

Richard looks outraged, and like he's about to protest again, but he remains quiet.

Sebastian's jaw is set into uncompromising hard lines and if I was Richard, I don't think I would take him on either. He looks like he's spoiling for a fight.

'Give us a moment. Wait for me in the car, please,' Seb says to me.

I don't know what to think, but he seems intent on getting me out of the way, so I do as he asks.

Once in the car, I look out the window and see him talking to Richard. A few minutes pass, and I can't see clearly what's going on, so I sink into the seat of the luxury vehicle and try to relax.

What was that all about?

Finally, the car door opens, and he gets in.

'Okay?' I ask.

He shrugs his shoulders, as Richard's car roars out of the carpark.

'He's a complete wanker. If I'd known you were working for him, I'd have found you a different role, immediately.'

I study his face to gauge if he's really serious.

'But I don't work for him. I volunteer at the centre because I want to,' I protest.

'I'll ask my mum to find you a volunteering role through our foundation, so you don't have to see him again. Mum knows everyone, so you can probably take your pick.'

Now, I'm even more confused.

'What?' he asks. 'What's that furrowed brow for?' He stretches his arm out and rubs his thumb across my forehead. 'I don't want you seeing him again. He's trouble, trust me.'

Whilst a part of me is thrilled he cares so much; the independent woman in me is outraged by his cavalier attitude, bossing me about like he owns me.

'I appreciate you think you're doing what's best for me, but honestly Sebastian, you're not my boss outside of my job.

I like volunteering here in my free time, and I plan to continue doing so.'

He sighs. 'Sorry. It was insensitive of me to demand it of you, but you'll see I'm right about him. I'm just trying to save you from learning the hard way.'

'But what did he do that's so terrible?'

We were at Eton together. 'He was a lying, thieving little snot of a bully. Damian and I had to kick his short arse more than a few times.'

'A bully?' I say, shocked. 'But he does all this amazing work for charity. That doesn't sound like the kind of thing a bully does. He must have changed. It's a long time ago,' I add.

'Leopards don't change their spots, Nat,' he says.

I smile at the quirky British expression, despite my confusion.

'Why were you going to dinner with him, anyway?' he asks as he manoeuvres the Porsche out of the carpark with one hand.

I say what's been on my mind since Cannes. 'Why? Am I not allowed to go to dinner with a guy you don't approve of, but you can just get engaged without even telling me?'

The words are out before I can stop them, and I hold my breath, my heart thudding. I've broken the unwritten rule of not mentioning anything about our relationship.

I look out the windscreen at the smatterings of oncoming cars and the headlights dazzle me as I wait for his response.

'I'm not getting engaged,' he says flatly.

I summon every fragment of courage and challenge him. This is something I've wanted to talk to him about ever since I saw the article in the paper, but I've been too afraid of the consequences to broach the subject. Not that I've had much of an opportunity with him avoiding me all the time.

'That's not what the media says.' My voice is small and soft, and I realise I don't want to keep pretending I don't care, as if he hasn't broken me with his dating antics all over the papers.

'They make it up as they go along and say whatever they want,' he snaps, lowering his foot so we pick up speed.

I'm frightened of the answer he might give, but desperate to know the truth, so I push the words out of my dry throat, 'Do you love her?' My cheeks burn again as I make myself look at him.

His face tells me all I need to know, and he shakes his head and there's resignation in his eyes. He runs his hand through his thick wavy hair, and I long to reach out and touch him.

'No,' he says.

He's not forthcoming and his monosyllabic reply tortures me. If I don't find out what's going on now, I may never know, so I push on despite my aching soul.

'Is it serious between you, though?'

He looks at me again, and sighs. 'No, it's not. If you must know, we're fake dating to please our grandfathers. That's all there is to it.'

'Fake dating?' I ask, relief rushing through me. 'What's that?'

'It's silly. Something my brother, Caspian, told me about. We Rochesters can't have any kind of personal life without the press hounding us and making up lies. Sometimes it's easier to put on a show for them so they've got something to talk about. You know, feed them a narrative, and throw them off the scent so they don't know what we're really up to.'

'What do you mean by your grandfathers?'

He flicks a button, and the car roof slides back and the evening summer wind rushes over us and soothes my hot skin.

'Lizzy Archer's grandfather and mine are old friends and

they want us to marry because they see us as the perfect strategic alliance for both our families.'

Inhaling sharply, I try to steady my breathing and act nonchalant, as if his answers don't mean the difference between life and death to me.

'And what does she think about it?' My voice is low, and my senses are spinning as I say the words.

'She's in love with someone else.'

The tension drains out of my tight chest and the knots in my stomach unfurl.

He doesn't love her.

That's all I take in and it's all that matters. The rest of it is just detail.

'Please don't go out with Tricky Dicky, Nathalie.' He shoots an appealing look at me, and I melt like butter. When he looks at me like that, he could ask me to do anything, and I doubt I'd be able to resist.

I'm curious and feel emboldened by the scene he made with Richard. 'Why shouldn't I? You don't want me, so why do you care if someone else does?'

'It's not that. Just not with him,' he says, and for a second I see a flash of a sullen little boy who is used to calling the shots.

His answer guts me. So, he doesn't care if I go out with someone else. The thing with Richard is just about his ego, and not about us at all. The two of them were doing a dick swinging competition and staking claim to me like I'm their property.

'Why didn't you tell me about you and Lizzy instead of avoiding me?'

'You are all questions tonight.'

'Please,' I urge, 'I need to know.'

He sighs again. Clearly, he doesn't like explaining his behaviour to me, but I don't back down. After that showdown at my workplace, I figure I hold a card or two and he owes me.

'I thought it might be better to leave things there. I will lose my seat on the board if I don't marry someone my grandfather approves of, and soon.'

'What will you do?' I ask softly.

'I won't marry Lizzy, but I don't know what the answer is. I'll have to find someone suitable to marry or I'll lose everything I've worked so hard for. It's a fucked-up situation, and I'd do anything not to be in it, but this is my life.'

'I'm sorry,' I say. 'It must be awful to feel like you don't have free will to make decisions about your own future.'

He looks winded by my words, as if he's not thought of it like that before.

'I do have free will,' he snaps.

'No, *mon chéri*, you don't. If you had free will, you wouldn't have to marry someone your grandfather chooses for you. You would marry or not marry whoever is right for you.'

He looks ahead and a heavy silence falls between us. All I can hear is the sound of the wind as the car whizzes along the road.

'Did you tell Tricky Dicky you work for me?' he asks suddenly.

'No, not that I recall. We haven't really talked about anything personal before, but he mentioned he'd seen you when he offered me a job this evening.'

'You don't need a job,' he quips, not missing a beat. 'You have a perfectly good one.'

'He offered me one and we were going to discuss the details over dinner.'

'I see,' he says, driving through a pair of tall iron gates. 'In that case, I'm even more relieved I showed up when I did.'

I recognise the gates to Richmond Park. 'Don't we have to get back for Daisy?'

He shakes his head. 'Not for a while. Mrs J is working late doing something or other in the kitchen, and she said she'd watch her.'

The car snakes along the deserted road through the park, and the dusky sky twinkles. 'I've never been here in the evening,' I say.

'I used to come here a lot to think. It's peaceful.' He pauses and then says abruptly, 'Why did that twat offer you a job?'

'He said he's impressed with my work and asked if I'm open to a change of career. I got the impression he was going to offer me an administrative role at his head office.'

'You can't work for my arch enemy!' he says, wincing.

'Arch enemy? What is that?'

He laughs. 'Your English is so good that sometimes I forget it's not your first language. An arch enemy just means someone you despise.'

'Okay. And why is he your arch enemy?'

'Damian and I got into terrible fights with him and his crowd for years.'

'I thought you said Damian looked out for you at school.'

'He did. I might not have explained exactly how he looked out for me. Sometimes we all came to blows,' he says with an impish grin.

'Naughty boys,' I say. 'Thank goodness Daisy is better behaved than you two.'

'Tricky wank-face must have known you worked for me and he's trying to get at me,' he mutters.

'I didn't tell him anything about you. I'm very discreet about my employment.'

'I don't doubt it,' he says.

A painful thought occurs to me. 'Don't you think he could

be offering me a job because he thinks I'm the best person for it?'

'Of course. He's worked with you. He knows how committed and wonderful you are, so that's not even a question. But he's also seen a chance for revenge. I'll give you all the funding you want for whatever charity, but I don't want you involved with him.'

He's talking to me again like he has a say in what I do. A heady feeling grips me as I imagine what it would be like to be with him all the time. His alpha weirdness is sexy and turns me on even more. All my senses are on red-alert and if he touches me, I'm going to make love to him. He's not with that woman, after all, and I'm past caring whether it's sensible to show him how much I want him.

But I provoke him a bit more and test how far I can go. 'I would like to know what he was going to offer me before I refuse the job.'

He shoots off down a narrow lane and the car comes to a smooth stop beneath a huge oak tree and he fixes me with a stare. 'You didn't answer me. Why do you need another job, Nat?'

My skin prickles as he keeps looking at me, and I know I've got to tell him the truth.

'I thought you were going to marry Lizzy.' I blink back the tears as they fill my eyes. 'I can't stay on with you, living in your house when you're going to marry someone else. It's for the best that I find another job.'

'Best for who?' he demands, and I hear the raw pain echo through his words.

I swallow the emotion rising in my chest and try to hold back the tears. 'Best for us all.'

'Daisy won't think it's best for her,' he says, his deep voice like gravel.

'I know. I don't want to leave Daisy, but given what's happening, I don't have much choice.'

'So, you want to leave me?'

'Seb, I don't *want* to leave you. But we're not together. The whole friends who fuck thing isn't going to work out, is it? I was stupid to suggest it.'

He tuts and a shadow falls over his face. 'Don't say that. We're so much more than that.'

'Are we?'

'You know we are.'

We fall quiet again for what seems like an endless time. My spirits are sinking even lower, and I don't know what else to say.

It's hard to force the words out because wanting him like this makes me feel naked, but an inner voice taunts me not to be a coward. I must tell him how I feel. I don't want to regret not telling him the truth whilst I had the chance. My insides tremble, and I whisper my deepest fear to him. There's no going back now. 'But you don't want me.'

The stillness in the car is terrifying. All I hear are the distant murmurs of nature in the vast park against the backdrop of my pounding heart.

Finally, he breaks the heavy silence. And when he speaks, his resonant deep voice is like soft velvet trailing across my skin. I shiver as all my senses heighten and I want him to touch me more than I remember wanting anything or anyone.

'What makes you think that?' he says. He swivels in his seat to look into my eyes, and the world spins around me as our lips touch.

CHAPTER 35

Sebastian

I'm not a violent man and like to think I'm reasonable. But when Tricky Dicky laid his hand on Nathalie, it was all I could do to restrain myself from knocking his lights out. My fists flexed and I held them forcibly at my sides while the little twat put on a smarmy show for Nathalie and acted as though we're old friends.

Who the fuck does he think he is, touching her like that? And when he said her name as if she's his property, my hands moved swiftly from my sides, and I swear I was just a second away from punching his smirking face.

He had the nerve to say he was taking her to dinner.

Oh no. I don't think so...

I see my aggressive behaviour confused Nathalie, but she doesn't know how we hated each other at boarding school. He was the only kid who got under my skin and our feud began on the very first day that I arrived, and it ran right through my years at Eton. Damian can't stand him either.

This is clearly a play for revenge and somehow, he found out Nat works for me and went after her. I kick myself for not paying more attention to what's been going on.

As it is, I've avoided Nat like the black death since the day I gave her the topaz necklace. She loved it so much, it ravaged my heart, and I knew it was a fatal mistake. I took it too far and let my feelings for her spill out all over the place.

After I heard her voice on the phone when she saw my photo in the paper, I was desperate to make it up to her, and delighting her with an extravagant gift seemed like the thing to do.

When you have abundant wealth at the push of a button, it's easy to think money can fix everything. *Ask your assistant to order a magnificent display of flowers or return home from a business trip with an extravagant box of expensive jewellery.* I soon learnt it didn't fix everything, or at least it didn't in my marriage. In fact, it fixed nothing.

But I forgot the hard-won lesson and slipped back into my old ways. I soon realised I only made it worse by giving Nathalie mixed signals, and she read more into it than I can give her. It was too much for me to sit across from her at breakfast every day, when all I could think about was the one night we spent together.

Avoiding her hasn't helped get her out of my mind though, and I dream about her every night and wake every morning pining for her. It's like a sickness that gets more intense with every passing day.

To make things worse, the day after I gave her the necklace, when I was reading Daisy a bedtime story, she asked if I'm going to marry Nathalie. Her innocent face tore at my heartstrings.

I just stared at her, gobsmacked, thinking what a fool I've

been. Letting my emotions sweep me into a grand romantic gesture was a wrong move. Even my five-year-old daughter can see I'm in love with her nanny. That's when I knew I had to put a stop to all this madness and establish boundaries before I destroyed Daisy's newfound stability and ripped Nathalie's heart to pieces.

Not talking to her during the past few weeks has been hell, and I've been waking Daisy early in the morning to spend time with her before I skip breakfast and leave for the office.

It's stupid. But I didn't know what else to do.

And now it's all come to a head. When Nat finally did as I asked and went to the car, I warned Tricky Dicky to stay away from her and threatened to tell her the details of his thieving, bullying past if he doesn't leave her alone. He looked sufficiently alarmed, so he obviously cares about his reputation amongst his staff. I'm hoping my threat will keep him away from her once and for all. I told him I don't want to hear about him asking her out to dinner or offering her a job ever again.

The longing to wipe the annoying smirk off his face was still intense. But I knew she was watching, and I didn't want to make things any worse. Tricky Dicky pressing charges against me for assaulting him wouldn't do any of us any good.

With all the menace I could muster without physical violence, I asked him if my demands were clear.

For a second, he looked like he might take me on, but suddenly he backed away, shrinking, like all bullies of his ilk when faced with someone who stands up to them.

Now, I'm in the carpark watching him scurry off. From the safety of his BMW, he shouts at me. 'You haven't heard the last of this, trust fund boy. You'd better watch your back.'

What a complete and utter wanker. How he came to be running a children's centre, I do not know.

I despair how he popped up like a floating turd, after all these years.

Back in the car, all I want to do is take her face in my hands and kiss her pink lips, but I'm keeping my instincts firmly under lock and key tonight, so I just look at her and start the engine, feeling empty.

Even after that childish scene, her eyes are loving. If I'd caused that kind of fuss about my ex-wife, she'd be spoiling for a fight and would waste no time in putting me straight and telling me how she doesn't belong to me.

Nathalie is no pushover, but rather than throwing a tantrum like Maddy would, during the drive, she asks me questions about why I behaved like a crazy person at her workplace. She doesn't say it in so many words, but I'm pretty certain that's what she's thinking and if the situation wasn't such a shitshow, I'd laugh at myself. It's been so long since I lost my temper like that, but the sight of Tricky Dicky and Nathalie together drove me to the edge.

Whilst I'm not a fan of being grilled and having to answer questions of a personal nature, I appreciate Nat's sensitive approach, and do my best to answer her many questions because I owe her an explanation after rocking up at her work like some crazed mafia dude.

On a whim, I drive towards Richmond Park. It's such a beautiful evening. The warm summer night is drawing in fast, and I want to get there before the gates shut.

Luckily, Mrs Johnson is staying on later tonight. She's baking fruit pies and stocking the freezer, which she does every season. I told her I might be out for a while, and she said not to worry. When I left, Daisy was tired and cuddled up, wearing pyjamas and half-asleep on the sofa watching her favourite show. She made no fuss about me going out and didn't ask to come with me like she normally would. It's no wonder, because I've been waking her up so early in the mornings even though it's the holidays. When my driver texted me to say he was clocking off and Nathalie refused his offer of a lift, I couldn't stop thinking about how she was going to get home. Perhaps it was my gut telling me to go, but suddenly, I yearned to be alone with her and I grabbed my car keys and left before I could talk myself into doing the sensible thing and staying away.

The truth is, I'm aching to touch and taste her again. I'm desperate to make love to her. Although I'm so horny from my painful abstinence, I might have to fuck her very hard a few times first to calm myself down before I can make love to her in the way I want.

Not that I'm going to act on my desires.

During the drive, when I'm answering another one of her questions, I tell her that Lizzy Archer is in love with someone else. I bite my tongue and just in time, I stop myself from adding 'too'. *She's in love with someone else, too,* would be the accurate version of events, and I almost let it slip, which would be an absolute disaster. I can't have her knowing I'm madly in love and have lost my mind over her, for fuck's sake.

What am I doing?

My heart beats much faster than it should all the way to the park, and I'm relieved when the gates are standing open. I can't bear taking her home just yet. I can't have her in the way I want her, but I need to be close to her just for a little while. I'm like a beggar, desperate for any morsels she might throw me, which is stupid because I see in her eyes that she wants me too.

I don't plan on having sex with her again. Another encounter, like the ones we had, will only rip me apart, which is why I've been working so hard to avoid her. Today, is just a little slip. I'm allowing myself to indulge in a brief glimpse of heaven by spending a few minutes alone with her away from the house, where no one can interrupt us. And I breathe easier, just knowing she's sitting next to me in the car. I don't let myself think about what could happen if I make a move on her, but my senses race as I turn off into a narrow lane and stop the car beneath a huge, ancient oak tree. This is my favourite place in the park, and I've sat here alone many times. We're hidden from prying eyes, not that anyone's around at this hour and the park buzzes with nature bedding down for the night.

My intentions are honourable, and I didn't bring her here for sex. But the pity in her eyes claws at me and tips me off the precarious balance I have. She says something about me not having free will if I can't marry who I want, and I can see she feels sorry for me.

How the fuck did that happen? I'm an heir to the mighty Rochester dynasty. She's a nanny with barely anything to her name. I don't think she even owns her own place.

And she pities me...

The realisation that she's right hits me. Despite all the money in the world, I don't have true freedom, and her words wound me even though I know she doesn't mean them in a hateful way. She genuinely feels sorry for me, which is even worse, and I can't stand it. The trapped feeling is suffocating and makes me want to break out of my familial chains and do something wild. My grandfather's face looms in my mind and it's all a haze as my thoughts toss and spin and I try to think how to free myself from this prison. I promised Lizzy we would keep the fake dating farce going until we both figure out what to do, but the thought of it exhausts me.

All I want is Nathalie. An image of the magical life we could have together with Daisy springs into my head.

Nat's right. Why can't I be with who I want?

What would it be like to surrender to this all-consuming desire I feel for her and disregard my Rochester duties? What's the worst that could happen?

I pull my thoughts back to the car when she abruptly ceases her questions and makes a statement that haunts my soul. She says I don't want her, and the pain in her voice breaks me.

I can't let her think that when every cell in my body burns to be close to her. So, when I see the longing in her eyes, before I can hold myself back, my lips merge with hers and we kiss feverishly for the first time in weeks. But it feels like a lifetime.

All my resolve melts away when I taste her, and my hands have a life of their own.

I surrender to the flame that is us.

CHAPTER 36

Nathalie

I tell myself I should be angry about how he behaved with Richard—acting like my jealous boyfriend, when we're not even together—but I'm not angry. Seeing him being all masterful and protecting me was thrilling and so unexpected. It was a primal call to my femininity, and I felt it deep in my bones.

He wants me just as much as I want him. He's not allowing himself to have me in the respectable marrying kind of way, but he wants me even if he doesn't want to want me. There was no mistaking the fury in his eyes when Richard touched me.

He's been avoiding me since Cannes, not because he doesn't want me, but because he *does*. And the revelation about him and Lizzy pretending to date was exactly what I needed to hear to forgive him for all the hurt I've felt since I saw that article. It all makes sense now and relief floods through me again.

He doesn't like it when I ply him with questions, but he answers them patiently, one by one, and my heart twists as I watch him grapple with his emotions. The second he takes a different route and doesn't drive straight home; I know tonight is going to be one of our nights. He takes me to his favourite place.

When his lips touch mine, I don't hold back. I've been having intense erotic dreams about being with him again and I'm wet and ready for him and just want him to take me. The passion crashes over me like violent waves as our tongues meet and he groans loudly. He tries to pull me onto his lap, but the car is too compact, so he opens the door and helps me out with his outstretched hand. I'm wearing stiletto sandals and the evening breeze catches the gauzy material of my dress and it billows behind me as I find my footing and look at him.

I glance around nervously, but we're sheltered by the sweeping branches of the giant tree, and the track is dusky and deserted.

'Don't worry,' he soothes in his deep hypnotic voice that calls to me in my dreams. 'No one's around—they'll be closing soon—besides, no one can see us in this secluded spot.'

My heart's dancing as he pulls me towards him and we kiss again, and this time I feel his hard desire pushing into me. 'Umm,' I say, and push back against him and he stiffens even more, and we move as one.

He reaches for my dress and lifts it up my thighs and in an instant his hand caresses my most sensitive place, and his fingers slot into my wetness and I moan.

'I've missed you,' I purr.

'You mean, you've missed this,' he says, in his gravelly voice. The one he uses when he's red hot and I know he's about to fuck me.

His fingers slide in and out of me, as I stand semi-naked in a royal park with the breeze rolling over my skin and Sebastian playing me with the skilled precision of a virtuoso.

I don't recall moving, but he's repositioned me so I'm leaning against the back of his car, and I arch over the boot as he rubs his thumb relentlessly over my clit and moves his fingers in and out of me simultaneously. Then he lowers his head and sucks my bud until my whole body is on fire. I'm completely at his mercy and I cry out as my orgasm races through my veins, and I come over and over whilst he continues to play me like a beloved instrument.

'I love it when you come for me like that,' he murmurs. His voice is low and so sexy that just listening to him would be enough to make me lose it. It's his voice I hear in my fantasies, alone at night in my enormous bed, trying to sleep while I ache for him.

And now my fantasies are coming true. Being in the dusky park like this has a dreamlike quality, and I know this is a night I'm going to remember for the rest of my life. The evening stars twinkle in the sky and it's still warm despite the breeze.

My fingers fumble with his buttons, and I'm mad with longing as I run my hand across his erection and his hardness pushes through the thin material of his shorts.

He groans again, more loudly this time. 'Nat, I warn you. I can't take much of this. It's been too long.'

The boldness I feel when I'm with him overtakes me, and I whisper, 'How long?'

'Since the last time we were together,' he pants. 'How can I be with anyone else when I've tasted you?'

My hand palms him through the material, teasing him, and the guttural noises coming from his throat are like dynamite to my already blazing desire. I drop to my knees on the dewy grass, and he helps me free him. His cock juts out and I remember how big he is as I run my tongue around the tip, and he cries out.

I sit back on my heels, still holding him lightly. 'Hush!' I whisper. 'What if the park warden hears us?'

'I don't care,' he hisses. 'Just please don't stop what you're doing or I might die.'

My hand slides up and down his hard, thick girth and his loud groans inflame me further as I place my lips over the head of his cock and suck, and my hand moves faster to an erotic beat.

'Turn around,' he commands.

I stare into his lust-filled eyes.

'What?'

'Turn around,' he repeats. 'I can't wait any longer. I need to be inside you right now.'

His hands are on me and he spins me around and positions me so I'm facing the back of the car. I'm still wearing my stilettos and he pushes my dress up and my knickers aside, and I feel the breeze on my bare skin. I'm throbbing with need for him and can't wait.

He brushes my thighs, and the tip of his hard cock nudges between my legs as he bends me over and enters my pussy from behind.

I'm so wet and ready, I immediately slam back onto him and we both groan as he fills me up and we rock to our unique rhythm. His big hands are all over me and he fucks me so hard, I grip onto the edge of the car to keep my balance.

We rut like wild animals in the park, and our need is so

urgent we soon explode together in a crescendo of exquisite pleasure and I collapse against the car.

He leans over me, careful not to crush me, and I feel his heartbeat slamming wildly against my hot skin as we catch our breath.

'You've ruined me for anyone else,' he says. Then he buries his face in my neck and whispers, 'I love you, Nat.'

CHAPTER 37

Sebastian

Being summoned for one of grandfather's family dinners couldn't have come at a worse time. I usually look forward to visiting Greystone and drive down at every opportunity, but this is going to be awkward.

Damian says Grandfather has been morbid lately, talking about not having any more great-grandchildren before he dies. Daisy will come with me, but I won't take Nathalie. Grandfather wants to see Lizzy and has been badgering me to bring her ever since Cannes, and this time the invitation explicitly invites her to accompany me. My instincts tell me he's ready for things to speed up and he's looking for an imminent engagement, so I'm not taking her either.

Nat looks wounded when I don't invite her. I've told her and Daisy so many stories about growing up at Greystone, and I mentioned she should come with us on our next visit.

Now I could kick myself. Me and my big mouth, getting carried away and not thinking of the consequences. Sometimes, my enthusiasm talks before I think.

I can't bring myself to tell her we're going until a couple of days before the dinner, and then I only tell her because I have no choice. I try to slip it into the conversation casually, hoping it won't seem like a big deal, but it's difficult because everything is a big deal with Daisy. She is almost levitating with excitement about seeing everyone, especially my mother—her grandma. When Nathalie is present, she asks if we can stay over for the weekend, and then I have no choice but to tell Nathalie what's going on. Guilt clutches at me as I try to act as if I'm not excluding her on purpose. It seems wrong because she's like part of the family, and if all this emotion wasn't bubbling between us, she'd come as Daisy's nanny.

I tell Nathalie we've got a family thing and give her the day off. I've tried thinking of a way around it, but there were too many sly comments after we danced at the ball. I can't risk anyone guessing there's something going on between us.

'Does that mean I have the weekend off?' she asks, after an awkward pause.

'Please come with us, Nathalie. Daddy, can Nathalie come with us?' Daisy asks.

I raise my head from the newspaper reluctantly. At least we're back to having breakfast together. I've been trying to act normal—whatever that is—and decided that rushing off to work without seeing her was only making things worse.

But now her blue eyes are locked on mine, and I'm forced to answer her.

'Yeah, of course.'

I don't like the idea of her going off on her own, but I can't expect her to stay here and not make the most of us being away.

Whatever I do, I hurt her. There's no way to avoid it in this impossible situation. I'm doing my best, but I'm failing miserably.

I keep telling myself, I'll figure it out so we can be together somehow, but even in my most elaborate fantasies, Grandfather will never approve of me marrying the nanny, no matter how amazing she is.

And if I tell him I'm going to be with whoever I want and not meet his terms, I'll lose everything. The hotel business is in my blood, and I can't imagine not leading that division after all these years of working so diligently to reach my dream role of CEO.

Daisy keeps pestering for Nathalie to come with us, and eventually I tell her that Nathalie needs a few days off. I daren't meet Nat's eyes after that.

Ever since the smouldering night in the park when all my defences crumbled, it's been even more difficult to stop myself from going to her room when Daisy's asleep and the house is silent. Every night when I walk to my bedroom is a fresh test, and I stare at the winding flight of stairs that leads to her door.

It would be so easy to slip into a routine with her. She didn't say she loved me in response to my declaration, but there was no mistaking the feeling between us. We were so close on the drive home it was painful to separate.

That was the most tempting night of all. But Daisy sometimes wanders into my room and gets into my bed when she has a bad dream, and I can't risk complicating things for her. If she couldn't find me in the night, she would panic and run up to Nathalie's room, so either way, she'd see us in bed together, no matter which room we chose.

The other reason I'm holding back is selfish. I'm in so deep, I'm losing myself and if making love and sleeping with her become a regular occurrence, giving her up forever, is going to be even more agonising. And give her up, I must, or lose everything.

Whilst we're not as traditional as some high-net-worth families who insist on arranged marriages and won't even contemplate a mere love match, I'm out of wild cards.

Grandfather has told me multiple times; he's not letting me repeat the same mistake. 'You're too romantic for your own good, my boy,' is one of his regular observations when discussing what he sees as my shambolic love life.

And maybe he's right. In a weak moment, I let it slip that I love her, and that was unfair to Nathalie. I realize I'm unsuited to marry for a strategic business alliance, which leaves me only one route if I'm to meet the terms of the inheritance clause in the will.

I must marry for love.

But when I think of it, all I see is Nathalie.

How am I going to fall in love with someone else when the love of my life sleeps one floor above me?

I can't. I won't.

The only answer—and it turns me cold—is to find her a new position, end her contract and hire a new nanny. A frumpy, Mrs Doubtfire type, like the one I expected. If my assistant hadn't hired Nathalie, none of this would have happened, and for a nano-second I blame her for the mess we're in. Sighing, I know it's pointless. She is the most efficient executive-assistant I've ever had, and she was only doing what I asked.

However it happened, I can't ignore that I'm digging a hole for both of us and we're both getting precipitously close to the edge. I saw the betrayal in Nathalie's eyes when I said we were going to Greystone without her. Treating her like a member of staff doesn't come naturally to me, and I had to force myself. It feels cruel, and my instinct was to sweep her up in my arms and give Daisy what she wants, which is for all of us to go together and have a wonderful weekend with my family. The irony is that's what I want, too.

It's a bright morning, and the sky is blue with only a whisper of cloud when Daisy and I set off. Hampshire isn't far, and we should be there in a few hours unless the traffic is heavy. Daisy was upset that Nathalie wasn't coming and asked at least five times before we left if she could come and stay over with us.

Nat avoided looking at me. Since the conversation about us going for the weekend, she's been withdrawn. For a day or so after we were together in the park, she was happy and glowing.

But I've fucked it all up again, and I can't see a way out. I tried to catch her eye several times at breakfast today, but she kept herself occupied and didn't look at me once.

There's a physical pain in my chest when she cuts me out like this. I don't know what she expects from me and feel bad enough as it is without her giving me the cold shoulder.

I don't blame her. I promised her nothing, and she's acting differently. She's losing patience and thinks I'm a dick, and to make matters worse, I think so too.

What if she leaves before I figure this out?

I'm on edge about her going to the centre when we're away, and I don't trust Tricky Dicky. He'll be itching for revenge and my instinct is he will keep hitting on her to get at me and I won't be around to protect her. I know I insulted her when I said he only offered her the job because he discovered she works for me.

Nathalie helped Daisy pack her bag and Daisy kissed and hugged her a thousand times before we left.

All I got was a stiff goodbye before she turned to go back into the house. As we drive away, I'm already missing her and a weekend seems like a lifetime without her, but I promised Daisy we'd stay over. Hopefully, I won't get too much of an inquisition from the family. I console myself that it will be great to catch up with everyone as I haven't seen much of them lately.

Marian told me Caspian is bringing his girlfriend so that should be interesting and take the heat off me. He never brings anyone home, so this is a sign that something important is going on. My siblings and I share an unwritten agreement where we don't take dates to Greystone unless it's serious. There's too much pressure and so we keep our dalliances to ourselves. It's easier that way, as there are no awkward questions and no pressure to make it formal.

I've never known Caspian to have a proper girlfriend, so I'm curious to meet this one. I wonder whether she's the girl he talked about when he was extolling the virtues of fake relationships for keeping the fam and the press off his back.

As the car thunders across the miles, I wonder casually what Damian is up to.

Personally, I would have loved to see him get together with Jamie. They were perfect for each other, but were the only two who couldn't see it. Even Grandfather was smitten. I got the sense that he might blur the lines for her, as they seemed to really hit it off.

A thought crosses my mind as I hit the accelerator and switch into a different lane. What if Grandfather would blur the lines for Nathalie?

I shake my head. Last I heard, Jamie was back in London, so I'm getting carried away. That's all over, and I imagine the pressure is mounting on Damian to make a suitable marriage. If I know my grandfather, he'll be pushing him into action after the latest fiasco in the press. I hope it'll divert his attention from his recent obsession with me making an arranged marriage.

The drive was smooth and lulled Daisy to sleep, and as we

slow down and wait for the security guy to open the barrier for us to enter the Greystone estate, she stirs.

'Are we here, Daddy?'

'Yes, pumpkin. You nodded off.' I smile at her through the reflection in the mirror and she rubs her sleepy eyes and flashes me a toothy grin. 'Hang on a minute, and I'll come and get you out to stretch your legs.'

Greystone Manor rises before us as we pull up in front of the grand old house. The sight of the familiar turrets takes me right back to childhood and returning home from boarding school. Briefly, an image of Tricky Dickhead, as I think of him, flashes into my mind, but I push it firmly away. I will not let thoughts of him ruin the first entire weekend we've spent with the family for ages.

It's bad enough I miss Nathalie already, and there's an ache in my chest which I can't seem to shake.

Is this true love? Always feeling incomplete when she's not nearby?

Before I can ponder any longer on the intricacies of love, Albert, the dear old butler who is as much a fixture of Greystone as the gothic turrets, opens the door and hurries across. He's slowed down during the past few years, but he still puts on a spurt, and his craggy face breaks into a welcoming smile. Honey follows at his heels, barking and heading straight for me. She jumps up and I bend down to stroke her silky, apricot-hued head.

'Hello there, lovely girl.' I say, and she kisses me enthusiastically. Daisy is by my side and Honey runs between us, barking and licking our bare skin and kissing us wherever she can.

'She's excited to see us,' I say to Daisy, who adores Honey and is on the ground tickling her.

Albert follows us in with our small bags, and Alice, the housekeeper, awaits us at the door as we enter.

'Good morning, sir,' she greets me. 'Miss Daisy.'

No matter how much I tell the household staff, Sebastian will do perfectly, and to drop the formality, they never do. It's a code they all adhere to.

We enter through the wide main doorway, Albert and Alice behind us and Honey spinning around our ankles, nearly tripping us up.

My mother appears in the hall, her eyes sparkling and a huge smile on her face. 'Daisy, my darling. I've been waiting for you. And my darling boy. There you are. I'm so thrilled you're staying for the weekend. We'll get a proper chance to catch up.'

After we exchange hugs and kisses, my mother leads Daisy by the hand in search of a glass of milk and cookies. The staff adore Daisy, so I know it'll be a while before I see her again.

Turning to Albert, I ask where my grandfather is. He tells me he is in his usual spot in the library, eagerly awaiting us. I'm the first to arrive, so I seize the moment and stride towards the library, right into the old fox's den.

Let's get the Lizzy interrogation over before the others get here.

CHAPTER 38

Sebastian

We gather for dinner and Daisy is hyper excited to wear the dress my mother bought her and to stay up late for dinner with the grown-ups. I've barely caught sight of her since we arrived, and she's been thoroughly spoilt.

'I really need to see more of Daisy,' my mother says to me at dinner. 'She's such a delight and I'm missing out. Perhaps she can stay on for the week.'

I tell her it's still summer holidays, so it should be fine. Daisy adores her grandma and loves running wild in the gardens at Greystone.

She nods. 'How quickly one forgets everything centres around school terms. I remember waiting anxiously for you kids to come home from boarding school so we could have you all to ourselves for the summer.'

We reminisce about the good old days, and I know that

both of us are thinking about my father, Julian, and how wonderful it was when he was with us. He's left a giant hole in our lives and even years after his sudden death, we're still hurting. I reach to cover my mother's hand with mine, and she gives me a grateful smile.

'Do you remember that awful kid at Eton we used to call Tricky Dicky?' I ask her after a pause.

My mum's still an attractive woman and suits her role of Rochester matriarch. She narrows her mossy green eyes as she casts her mind back. 'Oh yes. You mean that dreadful bully who used to steal from the other kids, and you and Damian kept getting into fights with him and his crowd?'

I tell her I bumped into him recently and give her an extremely potted version of events. It would only worry her if she knew how close I came to punching him and reverting to the violent encounters we used to have at boarding school.

She asks if he's improved as an adult, and I assure her he has not. 'Nathalie volunteers at a children's centre, and it turns out he's the founder. He was trying to lure her away from working for me and get her on full time in his office.'

'Nathalie seems like a lovely young woman. She was such a help with the annual ball. I was sorry not to meet her in person. I thought she might accompany you this weekend. But then Grandfather was hoping you would bring Lizzy, so I wasn't sure who to expect.'

I feel her eyes on me, appraising me in that omniscient way mothers have. She falls silent and waits for me to continue.

'Ah yes, Lizzy. She couldn't make it, but Grandfather has his heart set on her,' I say, my voice flat despite my efforts to sound upbeat. I redirect the conversation swiftly back to Nathalie before she can ask me any more about Lizzy. 'Daisy absolutely adores her,' I say carefully.

My mother nods and tells me Daisy talked her ears off

about Nathalie and that was one thing that made her realise she needs to spend more time with her granddaughter. 'Nannies come and go, but grandmas are in it for the long haul, and I realised I'm not seeing her enough. I'm happy Daisy's settled, but be careful about letting her get too attached. It's so difficult when nannies leave, and they always do at some point.'

If she knew how attached I am, she'd have an even more severe warning for me.

My heart rampages at the mere suggestion of Nathalie leaving, and I'm straining to keep my emotions caged. The last thing I need is my mother knowing I've fallen for the nanny. I'm concerned about Lizzy and Nathalie, and am more uptight than usual.

Grandfather grilled me earlier about Lizzy and was most disappointed I didn't bring her this weekend. I made up some story about her being too busy at work, and I don't know if he bought it, but it bought me some time to get my act together. When I left the library, I rested against the door for a breather before entering the sibling fray. If anyone is going to fire tough questions at me, and catch me off guard, it's that lot, so I'm wary.

Marian is seated on my other side and whispers, 'What do you make of Isabella?'

Caspian surprised us all when he said he'd be bringing his girlfriend for the weekend, and we've all been covertly observing them together.

'She's lovely,' I reply, my voice low. 'You?'

'Yes, I like her,' she says. 'She seems like a lot of fun. They've been friends for years, apparently, since they were at uni together. Caspian is a dark horse. Have you met her before?'

I tell her I don't think so, but he had so many girls at uni that it's no surprise I don't remember her. We gossip a bit about how unusual it is to see Caspian with a girlfriend, and then she deftly changes the subject to me before I see it coming. Marian is an expert at wringing information out of people, so I must be alert, or she'll wheedle information out of me before I've even had a chance to think about what I reveal.

She begins innocently enough, 'What about you? How's it all going?'

I take a breath and reply, 'Business is good. The Cannes hotel opening went very well.'

There's a lull in the conversation and my words resound around the long table in the elegant dining room where we eat when we all get together. Grandfather catches my eye. 'The Cannes hotel opening went extremely well. You handled it beautifully, Sebastian. And Damian, the media coverage was excellent. What a joy to open the newspapers and read positive press about at least one of my grandchildren.'

Damian scowls because he's the one who gets reams of bad press. I stifle a laugh. We're close, but there's a tinge of sibling rivalry that grandfather seems to encourage. He's old school, and I think he likes us fighting for the top spot in the Rochester hierarchy, which is ridiculous really because as the eldest, Damian is the primary heir and will succeed Grandfather's position as head of the family, whatever I do. But he likes to keep us on our toes, so we try to outdo each other as much to please him as to compete with one another. That's my theory anyway, so I may as well make the most of having done something right in his book.

My league table scores fell dramatically after the divorce. Grandfather is not a fan of divorce and would much rather we did whatever we had to do to stick with the marriage. Like I say, he's old school. Sometimes it irritates me because my grandparents had a wonderful, loving marriage right to my grandmother's death and he idolised her. It begs the question, what does he know about sticking with a failing marriage?

Most of the time, I focus on my work in the hotel division and never let Rochester politics tangle with my good humour. It's difficult to rattle me as I'm naturally optimistic. My priority is Daisy, and as long as she's thriving, I can handle anything life throws at me. But now I find myself in an unfamiliar spot and must play my cards with care. It's not helped because how things play out with Nathalie directly impacts Daisy's wellbeing and life.

Grandfather raises his glass and toasts me for the success of the Cannes hotel opening. 'Sebastian is doing a fine job as CEO of Rochester Hotels. Congratulations, my boy,' he says. Everyone joins in—even Damian. 'I'm hoping that soon we'll have another reason to toast him.'

I roll my eyes at his unwavering commitment to marry me off to Lizzy. Bessie's home baked apple crumble is served with ice cream and I'm thankful for the distraction from my personal life, as we all dig in. My mother oversees the menus, and the food is always top-notch at Greystone, so I relax, grateful that the worst of the interrogation is over and there will be no more talk of Lizzy or Nathalie tonight.

But how wrong can I be?

After a few spoonfuls of delicious melt-in-the-mouth crumble, Marian resumes the conversation where we left off and asks if it's true that I agreed to marry Lizzy Archer. Before I can reply, she adds, 'I knew her quite well when we were kids, you know. We're the same age and went to the same birthday parties.'

The crumble sticks in my gullet. Coughing, I reach for my glass of red wine and take a big gulp.

'You alright?' Marian asks, concern etched on her face, her eyes crinkling at the sides.

I nod. 'Where did you hear I'm marrying Lizzy Archer?' I ask, trying to sound casual, but knowing nothing gets past my sister.

'You're the talk of the town, dear brother. Don't you know your relationship with Lizzy Archer is headlines in all the celebrity magazines? You're one of the most eligible bachelors in London, if not the world.'

I snort. 'Is the term bachelor still a thing? Either way, I can't be a bachelor because I'm divorced. You, on the other hand, dear sister, will most definitely be classed as a spinster if you don't find some unsuspecting man to make an honest woman out of you.'

I'm not surprised when she punches me in the arm, but I shout and wince as if she's injured me. Old childhood habits die hard.

'Numpty,' she says, rolling her eyes. 'By the way, how is it that the word "bachelor" sounds so dashing and debonair and evokes images of Hugh Grant, whilst "spinster" makes me think of a dried-up old prune, knitting in her rocking chair until the movement lulls her to sleep for an afternoon nap?'

'You'd better get married soon, Mari, my love, or you'll be a spinster for the duration,' I continue, ribbing her and enjoying deflecting her attention away from my sorry situation.

'Seriously, though,' she says. 'Lizzy Archer is fabulous, but when I saw you together in the photo, the first thing I thought was she's not your type at all. There's the obvious thing—you usually go for blondes, and she's a brunette—but it's not just that. I can't put my finger on it. You don't look like a couple. It was as if they'd stuck you together in the photo, and you barely know each other.' She takes a huge swig of her wine and fixes me with a stare, her eyes challenging me to explain.

Nothing much gets past her, and we've always been close, so I'm not overly shocked that she's onto me. 'Perhaps, after the shambles of my marriage, I want a different type,' I say.

'Perhaps,' she says, narrowing her eyes. 'How is Nathalie, by the way?' Marian is shrewd and I don't doubt there is a motive for her question.

'Nathalie is great. Daisy is madly in love with her. To be honest, I don't know how well me getting married will go down with Daisy. She came home a while back asking me if I was going to marry a mean lady like her school friend's father did. What do you say to that?'

Marian laughs and then she comes right out and says it. 'My guess is she would approve of you marrying Nathalie, though, right?'

My heart's beating to a fast jagged rhythm as I toy with my napkin, and after a pause, I say, 'Don't be silly, sis. You know we Rochesters can't marry regular peeps.'

Marian rolls her eyes. 'Well, I'm going to marry for love,' she says. 'That's if I decide to marry at all. This whole expectation that Grandfather must approve our marriages is archaic.' She drops her voice and leans into me as she talks.

I laugh. 'Good luck with that. I agree with you, but Grandfather doesn't seem like he's about to change the terms of his will, so if you do marry without his approval, make sure they are worth it. You might just lose your shares and your seat on the board in the name of love.'

Dinner passes in a haze of laughter and chatting across the table, and then we retire to the drawing room. Daisy falls asleep draped across my mother's knee, so I pick her up and settle her into bed upstairs, leaving the night light on in case she wakes up and forgets where she is.

Honey escorts us upstairs, wagging her tail, and then follows me back downstairs and into the drawing room where the others are lolling on the sofas looking lethargic after the heavy meal.

Caspian wanders over to stand beside me and we talk about the usual football and business highlights. Isabella is talking animatedly to Marian, and they look as though they've hit it off.

'Isabella looks right at home.' Lowering my voice, I say, 'What's going on with you two? I thought you were just having a relationship of convenience. Must be heating up for you to bring her here?'

Caspian shakes his head. 'Not really, but Grandfather's been dialling up the heat on me and insists I start thinking about marriage. Issy has her own family dynamics to deal with, so it seemed like a good idea for us to act like we're serious.'

'And?' I ask.

'And what?'

'And have you fooled him? Did Grandfather fall for it and think you're in a genuine relationship?'

He shrugs his wide shoulders and runs one hand through his thick shock of dark hair. Caspian is famous for his striking looks. Whilst some say we're a good-looking bunch, Caspian has a way about him that drives women out of their minds. His rebellious nature makes him seem unattainable and for as long as I can remember, he's had droves of girls chasing him. He's never given any of them much attention, so this is significant, no matter what he says.

'Are you considering marriage?' I probe, hands thrust deep in my pockets as I mull over the Rochester marriage conundrum.

'I'm not sure what to do, to be honest. Issy would make the perfect wife, and she's drop-dead gorgeous and from a comparable family, but I don't know if I'd be able to live with a marriage of convenience even if she were to agree to it,' he says, his voice laced with brooding.

'How about you and Lizzy Archer?' he says, diverting me away from his situation. 'Was the Cannes dating for real or was that just a cover?'

I sigh. 'Was it that obvious?'

Caspian chuckles. 'Only to me, perhaps. I've had enough experience of fake dating to recognise it when I see it. Even if it is in print.'

Silence falls between us and we stand there, both lost in thought about how we're going to fulfil Grandfather's criteria.

'Poor Grandfather,' I say in a whisper, even though he already retired for the evening. 'None of it is real. You and Isabella. Me and Lizzy.'

Caspian says, 'We're all living a lie.'

'We're no closer to marrying or, in my case, remarrying. And Marian swears she'll only marry for love *if* she marries at all.'

'It's a difficult business,' Caspian says.

'That's for sure. I don't know how to tell Grandfather that Lizzy and I will not take it any further. He was so set on it when I talked to him earlier.'

'Well, I'm not sure I'm the best person to ask,' he says, his eyes drifting to Isabella as she chats with the others and seems to fit right into the family.

Later, I'm in my old room, and it's hours until I fall asleep and I have to stop myself from texting Nathalie.

My head and heart are full of her and give me no peace.

CHAPTER 39

Nathalie

It took me by surprise when Sebastian said he and Daisy were spending the weekend at Greystone. Without me. Stupid, I know, but I'd begun to hope he might want to be with me.

When he slipped it into the conversation, as if it was no big deal at all, even though Daisy begged him repeatedly for me to go with them, my hopes of us ever having a proper relationship spluttered and died a horrible death. It was like the ground was slipping away beneath my feet, and I was falling into the abyss.

What was I thinking? Daring to imagine there'd be more for me with him, even though I'm just his employee. And now, because of our relationship, I'm not even getting the usual benefits of being a nanny. If there was nothing going on between us, I'm sure he would have expected me to go to

Greystone Manor with them to help look after Daisy. No one would have thought it strange for me to accompany them, so it's clearly Seb who doesn't want me there. He must be worried they'll pick up on something between us.

And it hurts. The word doesn't describe just how much it hurts. It's like he peeled the lining of my insides away and ripped it off until I'm raw and bleeding. After they drove off this morning, I felt discarded, like a used rag. I'm not good enough to be his girlfriend or, God forbid, a Rochester wife, but he also daren't risk taking me to his ancestral home as the nanny. I'm gutted about him choosing not to include me. I've wanted to visit Greystone since I first took the job. Sebastian has talked about the estate where he and his siblings grew up, so much. It's got an almost legendary reputation now, and I wanted to see it for myself.

Naively, I expected something to change after our passionate lovemaking in the park. He told me he loved me of his own volition. It's not as though I pressured him or told him how I feel, so I believed him. But he's been so distant since that night that I'm wondering if I only imagined the magical words I wanted to hear. But no, he said he loved me, so why is he being so cold?

As the hours tick by, I feel less and less like going out and making the most of my weekend off. Juliette invited me to stay at her flat, but I haven't been able to rally myself into leaving the house, and I'm angry about my lethargy. I sit by the pool, letting the gentle late summer sunshine wash over me, trying to read a book and failing. I can't concentrate. All I see is his face, and my heart feels bruised from the disappointment of recent events.

The house is still and silent without Sebastian and Daisy's voices ringing out through the rooms. Mrs Johnson isn't needed for the weekend, so she's not here either. It's just me roaming around this big place, and I've never felt so alone.

I'm in the house of my dreams, but it means nothing if he doesn't want me. He's not texted, and why would he? Daisy is with him for the weekend, so there's no reason for him to be in touch in the casual way he usually is.

I am expendable, and it cuts like a knife.

As the evening sets in, the air chills, and my spirits sink lower until an ominous thought floats into my mind. It makes me shiver and I clasp my robe around my swimsuit and pull the towel over my tanned legs. I can't face going inside to make something to eat, even though my stomach's growling and demanding its next meal. It all seems so pointless without him.

The thought hovers in my mind, plaguing me until I can't ignore it any longer.

I have to leave Richmond.

I have to leave Sebastian and my sweet Daisy.

I must leave now.

It occurs to me, if I'd never known love like the love I feel for him, and the overwhelming joy I feel in his presence, I'd be perfectly happy living in a luxury London home and caring for the most wonderful little girl.

But I did meet him, and I've tasted what it's like to love someone so completely that everything around you ceases to exist. At this moment, I know I can't do this to myself anymore. I've been torturing myself for months with thoughts that I'll never be able to be with him properly for all the obvious reasons, but a glimmer of hope burst into a flame when he said he loved me.

I thought that once he acknowledged he loved me, he'd find a way for us to be together, despite his family duty and inheritance clause. We're perfect together in every other way that counts, and I thought he understood we can't carry on like this.

But now it's clear, it makes no difference that he loves me.

He's a Rochester first and foremost and his actions this weekend speak more clearly than any whispered words of love in a weak moment of post-sexual passion.

He still sees me as just the nanny. The irony is that if he came to me on bended knee and declared his love for me was greater than his inheritance and he would give it all up for me, I'm not sure I would let him do it, anyway.

I will never know now.

The last thing I want is for him to give up his company and position in the business, and then a few years down the line, resent me for being the reason he lost everything.

No. That can't happen, even if he was willing to risk everything to be with me. But as it happens, he's shown me he's willing to risk nothing. He won't even risk taking me to his family home.

So, what's the answer?

It's a predicament of the worst kind, and I see no way out for us. I love him too much to wait around for the occasional crumb he throws me. I've struggled with my self-esteem, and usually I would beat myself up and think this is all my fault.

I'm not loveable enough.

But when we're together, I feel his love, and for the first time in my life, I know I am enough.

If I wasn't enough for him, he wouldn't keep seeking me out and tormenting us both. He wouldn't have bought me the topaz necklace that I keep under my pillow and think about every night as I try to fall asleep without him beside me.

The sun is setting as the light in the garden fades, and wearily I collect my things and move into the house.

My heart feels like it's hardly beating, and my legs are so heavy I can barely make it up to my room. I throw myself onto my bed and sob like the wretched being I am. I'm rarely alone in the house and I've contained my emotions so much recently, I'm like a tightly strung guitar, finally allowing its strings to be plucked. The tears roll down my cheeks and I wail like a distraught child. There's no one to interrupt me, and no one to worry about in this large empty house, so I let it all out. I cry like I haven't cried since my mother died, and it feels like a similar pain. It's the agony of loss and abandonment, and the coming to terms with a grief so fierce that there is no way around it, only through it.

I don't know how long I sob, curled up on my bed with the covers up to my chin. Eventually, I drift off into a deep sleep and when I awaken; the room is in darkness and my heart pounds as I scramble for my phone next to the bed to see what time it is.

It's only 10 p.m. and it strikes me how slowly time passes when you're miserable. I get off the bed and begin organising my things with robotic movements. My emotions are raw, and I'm all cried out now.

Sebastian's beloved face floats into my mind, and a sharp pain runs through me as I think of leaving him forever.

The cold realisation of what I must do is clear in my mind. The second I opened my eyes after sleeping, I just knew. When he left for Greystone, I knew it was over, but I wasn't quite ready to admit it to myself. He made his choice, although he may not realise it yet.

I can't continue like this. We can't continue like this. The pain is too great and we're going to destroy each other. And Daisy deserves a better life than this. He thinks we can just carry on as we are, but I can't do it, and our feelings for each other will get in the way of him finding someone his family will approve of whom he can marry when he's ready.

I don't know how I know what he's thinking, but I do. We're connected by an invisible bond, and I feel his feelings. I must go somewhere he won't find me even if he looks for me because I suspect he will.

He can marry Lizzy Archer without me getting in the

way. He said she doesn't want the marriage either, but if he makes a proper proposal, perhaps she'll be willing. Her family is pressuring her too, so it's only me standing in the way. Daisy will have a proper step mum and enjoy the stable home life she deserves. After the initial sadness of me leaving, she'll be fine. I hope she'll get her dream holiday by the sea.

I must get on with my life and forget him. And I know I can't do that while I'm living in his house.

I will leave before he returns, or I won't have the strength.

CHAPTER 40

Nathalie

I make a cup of coffee to clear my head despite the late hour. It's not as though I'm going to get much sleep tonight, anyway. Juliette answers when I call, and we have a long chat. She assures me she's got my back whatever I decide to do, and she's there for me, which is a great relief. Sometimes you just need a friend to listen while you vent, and that's what she does for me, and I'm reminded how fortunate I am to have her. By the end of the call, my face is wet with tears, but my heart feels a glimmer of light. It's good to know I'm not completely alone, which is how I've been feeling all day. I didn't want to worry my sister, so have been pretending everything is going great and haven't told her a thing.

Juliette tells me to sleep on my decision and see what I want to do in the morning. It's too late to leave now, but I doubt I'll have a change of heart overnight. I don't want to leave at all, but I know I must, and I don't see that changing by tomorrow morning.

I play some music and wearily pull my case down from the top of the wardrobe. All the emotion has worn me out and I'm mentally exhausted. It's just as well I didn't bring much and haven't bought many things since I've been in London. I always travel light just in case a nanny post doesn't work out and I need to leave at short notice. It's never happened until now, but families often change their plans, and there have been a few times where I've had to move from one house to another in the middle of a posting.

This is the first time I'll be ending a contract before the agreed date, and I hope my track record with the agency will speak for itself and not ruin my prospects of working with them in the future. That worried me a lot when I first considered ending the contract early, but I've realised that I'm reaching the end of the road of my days as a nanny. My sister and I text regularly, and she is thriving in her new career, just as I'd hoped. I've got savings, and for the first time in my working life, I can choose to do what I want, rather than the sensible thing.

It's a shame that all I want to do is stay with Sebastian and Daisy when it is not an option.

My thoughts flit to Richard at the centre. I'll have to let him know I won't be around for any more shifts. There's no long-term commitment to volunteering, so although I'll miss the kids, I'm not letting anyone down. Perhaps Richard really has a job for me in his organisation. Seb's name for him makes me giggle, even in my melancholy mood.

No, I can't work for Tricky Dicky.

I'll never see him in the same light again. Besides, Sebastian would hate it if I did. I'm not sure why that's so important, but even if we don't see each other again, which we probably won't, I want him to have good memories of our time together, and not think of me as ditching him and Daisy, to work for his arch enemy.

I fold my clothes quickly into neat piles and pack methodically, so everything fits into my small case.

Daisy. Dearest, sweetest Daisy. I'm going to miss her so much, and I feel bad about leaving her like this because I know she's grown as attached to me as I have to her.

But if I wait to see her or Seb again, I won't leave. It's too hard to leave even when they're not here. This is the right thing to do for us all. She'll soon bounce back, and it is for the best in the long run.

I'll probably see a headline about Sebastian marrying Lizzy Archer when I pass a newsstand one day, and I steel myself for the inevitable.

That night, I toss and turn and barely sleep for more than thirty minutes at a time, and I'm grateful when the long, dark night is interrupted by the dawn stirrings of nature and the birds tweet their joyous songs. It reminds me that there is always light after dark, and one way or another I'll get through this, even though I feel like I'm heading for hell.

My phone pings, and I check my messages, thinking it'll be Juliette checking in on me after our emotional call last night. But it's from Sebastian. My heart bashes in my chest as I click on the message.

Morning Nat. Hope you enjoyed a relaxing day without us! Just to give you a heads up, in case you're at home today, I'll be heading back early evening. Daisy wants to stay at Greystone for a week with grandma, so you will have a free week. Sorry for the short notice. See you later. S x

For a second, my heart does a happy jig and I'm tempted to wait for him. But it's a terrible idea and I know it. The inevitable will happen when we're alone, and if he gets a sniff of me leaving, he'll be all over it and will charm me to stay. I find it impossible to resist him, so if I'm serious about going, today is the best time. It's even better now because Daisy will be with her grandma for the week, and the agency will have plenty of time to line up a temporary nanny by the time she gets home.

The Rochesters have tons of family and staff members, so it's not like no one will fill my spot, especially in the summer holidays, when her schedule is flexible. If the agency really can't find a suitable replacement at short notice, I imagine Daisy can always stay on at Greystone until they do, whilst Seb works.

I read his message again. It's friendly but business-like, apart from the one surprising kiss. The spare heir, as he laughingly calls himself, has one kiss to spare for me. We've always been careful, given our professional status, but based on that text, no one would guess we were making passionate love to each other recently.

Well, it's not enough, Sebastian. You've had time to figure out what you want to do, and it looks like you have—nothing.

My resolve deepens and a feeling of calm descends upon me. I'm done being his bit on the side for when he feels horny. When he gets home, I won't be here.

Enough is enough.

It's Sunday and I've still got the house to myself, which is good because it gives me plenty of time to get organised before I need to leave. I want to make sure I don't forget anything, because when I go—that's it—I have no intention of coming back. A clean break is what I need.

I make myself a bowl of muesli even though my stomach's swirling and the last thing I want to do is eat. It's going to be a long day and I need my strength. After washing up the few dishes, I sit at the kitchen island where we first kissed, and for a moment, I wonder whether I'm doing the right thing.

There's something in me that keeps whispering that he loves me.

But no, if I carry on like this, I'm going to be a wreck. I'm already a wreck, for God's sake, so I pick up a pen and write him a letter on the Rochester Hotel notepad. I owe him that much, and as I write, the tears flow and I wipe them from my eyes, so they don't fall on the paper. Just as I'm finishing, a tear slides through my fingers and lands on the bottom of the letter. I blot it with a piece of kitchen paper and hope it doesn't stain. This is a hateful letter, and I can't bear to rewrite it. I come close to ripping it up and throwing it away. Perhaps a text message will be better, after all. I can't call him because the sound of his voice will break me.

I read the letter once more, sign my name and fold it carefully and write his name on the front. Placing it on the desk in his office, I lay the box with the beautiful topaz necklace inside, next to the letter. It was never supposed to be mine and I can't keep it, no matter how much I love it.

And then I get ready to leave Richmond for the last time.

CHAPTER 41

Sebastian

I whistle as I exit Greystone Village and take the road to London. Nathalie didn't respond to my text yet, which is unlike her, but she's not working this weekend, so she's probably out.

Tricky Dickhead's irritating face enters my mind and I push him firmly away. She works for him too and after my outburst; I realise I have no right to tell her not to see whoever she wants. I've offered her nothing, and it's unfair of me to expect her to fit in with my likes and dislikes beyond her job.

But all that is going to change starting today. I don't know how I'm going to work this out, but something about my conversations with Marian and Caspian disturbed me profoundly.

I don't want to live a lie any more than they do. Marian

said she's only going to marry for love, and Caspian is playing along with Isabella to fool Grandfather. It just seems so wrong, and as much as I think the inheritance clause in the will is unfair to us, I know Grandfather is only doing it to protect us and the company he's worked so tirelessly to build. After all, we won't inherit fully until he passes away, so the repercussions of our choices won't impact him personally, but if we make disastrous marriages, we all stand to suffer, and it will damage the legacy for future generations. And I want Daisy to have something remarkable to inherit. A marriage to Lizzy Archer would be the best strategic move I could make, and I reconsidered it this weekend. Lizzy is involved with someone else, but if I genuinely wanted to make it happen, I think I'd be in with a chance of persuading her to agree to an arranged marriage for the good of both our families.

I even let myself imagine briefly what it would be like to be married to her, but all I could see was Nathalie, and the thought of giving her up forever made me die inside.

I can never marry Lizzy or anyone else who isn't Nathalie. No matter how much my grandfather wants me to do it for the company, I don't believe he truly wants a loveless marriage for me. He must be counting on us growing to love each other over time.

In the middle of the night, I woke up and an eerie calm fell over me and I just knew. I must find a way for Nathalie and me to be together. I know I must do something now or I'm going to lose the most incredible woman I've ever known.

It's going to take some time for me to figure out how to break it to Grandfather, and maybe we don't need to tell him for a while. My mother has a way of getting through to him, so I consider appealing to her romantic nature. I know she's not altogether comfortable with the will arrangement, but

Grandfather calls the shots. Perhaps if my father had lived to take over the company, he would have softened the rules around marriage and had more of a modern view, but we'll never know.

My thoughts tick over as the car eats up the distance back to London, and I form a plan. Nathalie and I can see each other with no one knowing and keep things under the radar for a while longer. I don't doubt I want her forever, but given the situation, it's wise to take it slow. Damian can have his people work discreetly on making the story about Lizzy disappear, or that will look awful when the news about me and Nathalie breaks, which it inevitably will when we go public. I shudder at what will be a busy day for the media: *Spare Heir to the Rochester dynasty in torrid affair with daughter's nanny.*

Daisy is Nathalie's top fan—well, after me—so I'm certain she'll be thrilled if we make it official, but I can't risk getting her hopes up in case it all turns to shit somehow. I need to be smart about this and so I decide to enlist Damian's help once he's back in Chelsea.

The traffic is heavy as I enter London and I wait for what seems like forever for a set of temporary traffic lights to turn green.

Come on, come on.

There's a ping on my phone, and I see a message from Nathalie flash up on the screen, but then the lights change. It said something about her going, but I couldn't catch the details.

Where is she going? I tell myself to calm down—I just gave her the week off so she might have gone away for a break. I hope she's still in when I get home because I'm desperate to see her. I'm not sure whether I'll tell her everything that's on my mind just yet, until I decide how to handle the volatile situation, but I will tell her how I feel about her. Again.

What if I've misread the depth of her feelings?

I couldn't get a minute's peace this afternoon, which is the downside of being surrounded by a big family and a young daughter. I ummed and ahhed about writing something more personal on the text message, and I even started to tell her how I feel and that I want us to be together, but then it sounded silly, so I deleted it. Don't want to scare the poor girl off when I'm not there to gauge her response. For all I know, she's not ready for a commitment like that, anyway. She looked startled when I told her I love her after the red-hot car fuck, which is partly why I backed off.

I restrain myself from speeding in my eagerness to turn into the first service station and check her message. Maybe she wants me to meet her somewhere.

It seems ages until I can pull over and read the message. An icy dagger slithers through my heart and I just stare at the words, wishing I could unsee them:

Dear Sebastian, I'll be gone when you get home. I left a letter on your desk to explain. Thanks for everything, and sorry to leave on such short notice. Nathalie.

My hearts crashing against my chest like a wild thing, and I claw at my hair and a strangled scream escapes my lips.

What the fuck have I done?

My head's spinning and I don't trust myself to drive, so I just sit in my car for I don't know how long, as people come and go, laughing and joking as if my world hasn't crashed and burned around me.

I've been so stupid. All this time she's been at home

waiting for me, wherever I went, and I didn't stop to think that one day she might not be there. Now she's gone and I see the signs I missed. The long silences since the evening in the park, and not meeting my eyes when I look at her. I thought she was embarrassed and didn't know what to say, but I didn't think she was planning her getaway.

I went to Greystone, determined to take some time to think, which was another reason I didn't invite her to come with us. But what about *her* feelings? I berate myself for being so selfish and not seeing things from her perspective. All I thought about was what was good for Daisy and me, and the stupid bloody inheritance clause. I've taken her for granted, and it serves me fucking well right.

What a complete and utter twat you are, Rochester.

I grind the words out aloud, but they give me no respite from the searing agony running through me. I've lost her and there's no one to blame but myself. My head sinks against the steering wheel and I physically stop myself from howling like a wounded animal in the middle of the service station carpark.

I've made the biggest mistake of my life.

I bash the steering wheel several times and stare into space again, unseeing. How long I sit there like that I don't know, like everything is pointless now she's gone and there's nothing to go home for. Daisy's not there either, and I hate the house when it's empty.

Eventually, I realise I can't stay here, so I pull myself together somehow and drive to Richmond on autopilot, but it barely registers when I arrive at the house. Knowing Nathalie will not be inside ever again is more than I can take. When I punch in the security code and enter the house, there's a tiny piece of me praying that she changed her mind and didn't go.

Maybe she waited for me, after all?

But once I'm in, I rush from room to room, calling her name, but the house is deserted and silent. I run up to her suite and knock, but there's no reply, so I enter, my heart thumping.

She didn't bring many personal possessions, and there's nothing I can see that wasn't here when she moved in. I wander into the bedroom and notice the sheets have been stripped from the bed and there's no trace of Nathalie. *Anywhere.*

I sink onto the edge of the bed and uncontrollable anger courses through me. Why did she leave without talking to me first? My chest feels strangely hollow, and I stumble downstairs to my office, remembering she said she left me a letter.

There it is on my desk, with my name written across the front in neat script. Never have I hated the sight of a letter more than when I stare at that piece of paper that I'm certain will rip my heart out and leave me even more hopeless than I am now.

And she's left the box with the topaz necklace next to it.

I sit on the corner of the desk and unfold the piece of paper and make myself read it…

CHAPTER 42

Sebastian

Dear Sebastian,

I am sorry to have to leave like this. I hope you understand why I can't stay on any longer. I just can't do it anymore. Wanting you is tearing me apart, and we're going to destroy each other if we continue like this. It's not fair on any of us, especially Daisy, because we're confusing her with our situation.

I've tried to talk to you about how I feel, but I understand you're in an impossible situation with your family, so I must leave, and I can't face seeing you first because I won't have the strength to go if I do.

I asked the agency to organise a temporary nanny to give you time to find a suitable replacement. Please give my love to sweet Daisy and make whatever excuse for my leaving that you think is best. The most important thing is that she knows it's not because of her. It has been a joy to know you both and to take care of her. I hope things work out for you as you wish. Please don't try and find me. It's easier this way.

All my love,

Nathalie x

I sit there staring into space until I swipe at the tears on my face with the back of my hand. I haven't shed tears since my father died. There were none left when my ex went—I was numb and hurting for Daisy, and still mourning my dad.

Now it's all going to shit for Daisy again. And even if it wasn't entirely my fault when my marriage fell apart, this catastrophe certainly is. My darling daughter will suffer because of my actions.

At this moment, I couldn't feel more contempt for myself, and I'm dizzy as the painful emotions consume me and grip my throat like a tight band. I let her slip through my fingers—seat on the board—or not. I've been in a stupor—focused on appeasing my family and fearing their disapproval, and now it's too late. She's gone.

The coffee cup is cold, so she must have been gone a while, and I curse that I didn't leave Greystone earlier. Daisy was having a brilliant time with the family, and I could easily have left earlier, but I wanted to make sure she was settled before leaving her there for the week. It's the first time she's wanted to stay over at Greystone without me, and apart from the very occasional week with her mother, she's not been away from home as long as that before.

Where the hell has Nat gone?

The question runs through my mind repeatedly like a relentless ticker tape. It's Sunday, so I can't call the agency until tomorrow, and they are the only ones I can think of who might have a forwarding address. Racking my brains, I try to remember names of friends she's mentioned. There have been a few of Daisy's friends' nannies, she's hung out with at local kids' activities, but no one special jumps to mind. Tricky Dicky's face looms in my mind again, and I force myself to consider she may have taken the job he wanted to talk to her about.

I'm ashamed of the way I behaved. Nathalie didn't deserve to be bossed around like that. I told her to not even consider it, claimed her as my own in the most primal way in the park, and then retreated into my shell in a panic about how to handle my feelings.

A chill runs through me, and I shake myself into motion and walk to my room. I can't rally my limbs to move fast like they normally do, and when I open my bedroom door, memories of the night she lay in my arms attack me and I sink onto my bed and my head falls into my hands.

It was warm when I left Hampshire, but there's a bite to the air now, so I pull on a sweatshirt like I'm sleepwalking.

I've been like a lame horse all this time, even though I fell for her immediately. I've held myself back from letting myself feel what I want to feel for her, and I've been so scared of disappointing Grandfather I've ignored my own needs. And hers.

As I stare out the window, wondering what to do, I experience another startling flash of clarity.

I must risk it all if I'm going to have any chance of winning her back.

Why didn't I see it before? The feeling keeps rolling over me and I know I must face the disapproval of my family if I'm ever to stop living my life according to my grandfather's rules. I see how ridiculous it is now.

I call Nathalie and hold my breath whilst I wait to see if she'll pick up. There are only a few places I can think of that she would go. There's the centre, as well as her friend Juliette, who is a translator, but I don't have her address. Her name stuck in my head, and I recall she lives in Knightsbridge, but that's about it. I can ask my assistant if she has a number for Nat's sister in Paris.

But surely, she wouldn't leave London without seeing me first?

Nathalie's phone rings and rings. It strikes me that if she doesn't answer when I call, then she's unlikely to respond to me reaching out via her sister, so that's pointless. That's the second time I've called since she messaged earlier, and she hasn't picked up or messaged me back. The phone clicks into voicemail and I blurt out: 'Nathalie. I'm sorry. Please don't leave. I've behaved like a fool, but I love you. Please call me or come home so we can talk.'

The centre should still be open, and there's a chance she went there, so I jump in the car and race out the drive, tapping my hand on my thigh as I wait for the traffic lights to turn green. I can do without another run in with Tricky Dickhead, but the centre is my only tangible lead, so I must see if she's there.

Easing my legs out of the car, I hurry to the main entrance and push the buzzer. I introduce myself over the intercom and ask if I can see Nathalie. There are some jumbled voices, and I can't make out what they're saying.

'Hello?' I repeat. 'I'm a friend of Nathalie's and I need to speak to her urgently, please.'

There's a silence and then a familiar voice booms over the speaker. 'She's not here, Rochester, and even if she were, it's none of your business.'

I restrain myself from making a rude gesture at the camera where I guess he is gloating—it is a children's centre, after all, and I have gained some restraint since we were at school.

'Come on, Dicky, I say. I need to get in touch with her. If

you care about her at all, let's put our differences aside. Please tell me if you know where she is.'

'I'm afraid I can't do that, even for a mighty Rochester. For once, you can't bend the rules. We have data protection for our people, and if you don't know where she is, then it's not my place to tell you. Your position holds no sway with me. I suggest you leave her alone.'

'Thanks for nothing. Charming as ever,' I mutter, and cover the distance to my car in a few strides. He has always had the ability to infuriate me, and today is no different. That wanker has not lost his touch.

I consider hiring a private investigator. But what will I tell them? The nanny resigned her post and I want them to find her? It sounds ridiculous even to me in my current state. She's gone because she wanted to go, and there's a letter explaining why.

She's gone because you're an utter twat, and you treated her so poorly.

No one except me is going to think the situation warrants an emergency search, even if I throw money at them. I shelve the private investigator idea for now and keep it as a backup in case I can't find her through other means.

The thought of her disappearing forever out of my life makes me shake.

My gut tells me she's not in the centre and she's not with Tricky Dicky. He's the type who wouldn't be able to resist rubbing my nose in it if she was there. And if she's taken a job with him, I doubt he'd be able to stop himself from bragging, especially after our almost punch up.

Possibilities of places she may have gone roll through my mind like a torturous conveyor belt. Her friend in Knightsbridge seems a likely place for her to have headed to this evening. Of course, she could have checked into a hotel, but why would she when her best friend lives in London? I'm angry at myself for not paying attention and asking more questions. I didn't want to be intrusive, and it didn't seem important at the time. She's stayed over at her friend's flat once, as I recall, but that's all I know. A hazy memory floats into my mind that Juliette is connected to the French embassy, somehow, so that's a lead.

I can call them to get her address, but they'll be closed on a Sunday. And knowing how embassies operate, I'll be lucky if they answer on Monday.

I try to calm down by telling myself she'll be in London at her friend's, and I'll get an address for her tomorrow. Maybe she'll be in touch when she sees my missed calls.

Anything is better than thinking about the worst option that landed in my head and lurks there like a parasite.

What if she's on her way back to Paris?

That night, I barely sleep, only nodding off in fitful bursts.

Daylight is a welcome relief and I check my phone again, but there's nothing from Nat, just the usual torrent of work updates from my assistant. My head is throbbing, and I need to pull myself together, so I'll deal with those later. A hot shower with the water pumping at full blast revives me, and I dress hurriedly and head out to the garden to drink my coffee. It's still chilly, but there's a promise of late summer warmth to come, and the familiar chatter of birdsong fills the air. Normally, I love my garden, but today the beauty of it passes me by and all I can think about is that Nathalie won't be in this garden or swimming in this pool anymore.

It's still too early to call the agency or the embassy and I have a morning meeting at my London office. Thank goodness Daisy stayed in Hampshire, or yesterday would have been an even bigger nightmare. I don't want to think about breaking the news to Daisy that Nathalie has gone, and the thought propels my weary body into action.

My driver's waiting outside, and I'm just about to leave for the office when the doorbell rings and shatters the uncharacteristic silence of the house. My heart thuds as I stride across the hall and fling open the door, ready to do whatever it takes to get her to stay and never leave again. Relief courses through me and I'm ecstatic she's come home.

I'm ready to admit how much I want her now.

But standing on the doorstep, is a small neat looking middle-aged woman. Disappointment slithers through me as I look at her and I can't summon a smile, but I do my best to be polite. 'Yes? May I help you?'

She rests her case on the ground and looks up at me. 'Mr Rochester? I'm the temporary nanny, Ms Thorpe. Pleased to meet you.'

My mouth drops open and all I can do is stare. This is *so* wrong. She looks like the type of woman I expected to find when I came home to Nathalie in nothing but her swimming costume.

'I'm sorry, there must be some mistake. We don't need another nanny,' I blurt out, unthinking.

Now she looks confused. 'The agency called me yesterday and asked me to do emergency cover because your nanny had to leave unexpectedly? Just until they find you a long-term replacement,' she says, flashing me an uncertain smile.

'You'd better come in.'

Letting her in seems like an admission that Nathalie has gone forever, and I hate it. I want to shout at her we don't need a new nanny. But I won't be rude to this woman who has come all the way here at such short notice, so I stand aside.

Whilst she takes a seat, I call my assistant, who answers on the first ring.

'I messaged you she was coming,' she says. 'The agency

emailed me late last night to say Nathalie asked them to provide emergency cover because she had to leave.'

'But I don't need her now.' I try not to snap, but I'm irritated as fuck. All I want to do is get to London and be done with my meeting so I can search for Nathalie.

I thank the nanny for coming but explain that Daisy won't be here until the end of the week. Extracting a wad of crisp bank notes, I press them into her hand and tell her that should cover the inconvenience and travel expenses incurred. 'I'll tell the agency to pay you for the whole week,' I say, so you're not out of pocket.

The bewildered woman leaves in a taxi, and I lean against the door, fervently hoping I won't see her again. The reality of employing a new nanny hits me hard, and my stomach is in tangles.

Nathalie, Nathalie. Where are you?

CHAPTER 43

Sebastian

My long-suffering assistant has instructions to find Juliette's address whilst I take care of urgent business on the way to the office. She calls me back soon after to tell me the agency only has Nathalie's phone number and doesn't know her whereabouts. 'And the embassy wouldn't give me any details about their staff. Understandably,' she adds. 'They will not divulge private information about embassy employees, just like that.'

'Yes, I suppose you're right, but it was worth a shot.' I sigh.

But she hasn't been my executive assistant for years without knowing how to conjure rabbits out of hats. 'I found her surname, though. She's called Juliette Laurent, so I shall begin a search for listings that may have her Knightsbridge address, and I can track her down that way.'

My chest stirs with wisps of hope, and I release a long,

measured breath. 'You're a star. Let me know as soon as you have anything.'

Fortunately, she knows better than to pry and ask why it's urgent to find our runaway nanny in Knightsbridge!

She must think I've lost my mind, but the most important thing is to find Nathalie, so I brush those thoughts aside.

The morning meeting trickles by until I can't stand anymore and bring it to an abrupt end. Glancing out the window at the London skyline, I see dark clouds have submerged the earlier promise of sunshine and it looks like rain is coming. By the time I step out of the hotel, it's spitting, but the air is clammy. We crawl through the busy streets, and I ask my driver to drop me near Hyde Park. He does his best to stay close in case I want to jump back in the car, but it's impossible in the morning madness, and soon he's out of sight.

My mind is elsewhere, and I don't notice the rain tickling my face as I stride towards the French embassy. I get through security and speak to a receptionist who confirms they don't give out personal information in any circumstances.

My assistant texted she uncovered the names and addresses of the embassy staff residences and I decide to go there myself and search for Juliette's flat. I start ringing buzzers on the outside of the first elegant apartment building and only get one response. It dawns on me that as these are embassy staff homes, most of the residents are probably at work on Monday morning. One finally answers and asks me what I want in a French accent that isn't Nathalie's. She says she's never heard of Juliette Laurent and, as far as she knows; she doesn't live here.

The rain is lashing down and as I race from building to building, cutting through the perfectly manicured communal gardens, the water drips off my hair and bounces onto my face and shirt. I'm wearing a suit and no overcoat, and I'm drenched as I press buzzers and ask if Juliette lives there. I'm on a wild goose chase and curse my stupid idea.

Did I really think I'd ring a few buzzers in Knightsbridge and Nathalie would just miraculously be there waiting for me?

No one has heard of Juliette, and I'm losing faith in my plan and wondering if she is a figment of my imagination. It's not as if I've ever met her. I might have got the wrong end of the stick altogether and she doesn't even live in an embassy flat. Perhaps this isn't all the residences and I'm in the wrong spot. The last tall buttermilk-hued Georgian building in the row looms before me, and I buzz the first doorbell. My suit is soaked, and I shiver as the ominous sound of thunder rolls through the sky.

I'm desperate now and for some reason, I decide to ask for Juliette in French. I've nothing to lose and they clearly all speak French, so maybe it'll help.

No luck. Again. I've pressed all the buzzers now and have nowhere else to try. If Nathalie did come here to Juliette's, they must both be out now. I linger, not wanting to give up, but not knowing where else to go.

I hover near the entrance as lightning cracks through the grey sky like rich veins of gold.

Grabbing my phone, I type another message to Nathalie:

I'm outside the embassy garden apartments in Knightsbridge. It's raining. Hard! And thundering and lightning. Are you here?

Nothing. I try again. I'm persistent:

I've been a total fool. Forgive me. And if by some wild chance you are here, please let me in. My shoes are full of water, and I'm drowning!

My phone pings.

Nathalie: *I'm here. But I can't see you.*

Me: *Why not?*

Nathalie: *I explained in my letter. It's too hard to leave if we see each other.*

Me: *Then don't leave. Nat, please come out and talk to me. Or let me in!*

I wait for what seems hours and there's no response. It's no good. She won't see me and there's not a damn thing I can do about it. I lean against the entrance wall to catch my breath and wait for the rain to ease. The thunder and lightning are still twirling through the sky and it's a beautiful sight, but my heart is breaking. I'm a broken man.

After a few minutes, I try again:

I'm still here. Soaked. I might even die from pneumonia on the doorstep if you don't let me in. You don't want to step over my dead body when you go out, do you?

I add a sad face emoji to strengthen my case. A few more minutes pass and I'm too wretched to leave, so I just stand there waiting and hoping. The door clicks and startles me out of my pity-fest. And then she is in front of me and her beauty steals my breath away. My heart clatters so hard I can't form any words and we just stare at each other.

Finally, I say, 'Thanks for not leaving me to die.'

'Well, you're a hard man to ignore.'

'I missed you.'

'It's only been a few days,' she whispers, a light blush staining her cheeks.

'A few days too long,' I say. 'Nat. Please. I should never have let things go on like this without talking to you. I figured we'd work things out somehow.'

Her cornflower blue eyes are shining, and she straightens her shoulders as though preparing for battle. 'I told you. I can't do this anymore. I'm Daisy's nanny, not your girlfriend, and it's obvious I can never be your girlfriend. It's too painful.' Tears spill from her eyes, and she looks away, embarrassed. 'This is why I can't see you and leave you at the same time,' she mutters, pointing to her face.

'So don't leave me! I've been a fucking idiot, but I want us to be together.' I drop onto one wet knee.

'Nathalie Dubois, will you do me the honour of being my girlfriend?'

The tears stream down her face as she looks at me.

'But I'm the nanny.'

'Okay, so I'm firing you. You're not the nanny anymore!'

She struggles to speak but takes a deep breath and says quietly as tears mingle with the raindrops splattering on her face. 'I can't let you lose everything you've worked so hard for, just to be with me.'

'But don't you see, baby? You *are* everything! Nothing is worth anything without you. I know that now.'

'And Daisy,' she whispers.

'And Daisy, of course.'

I get up and move towards her, and she stumbles into my arms. The rain is coming down even harder and splashing onto our heads, but I don't care. I kiss her lips and we devour each other's mouths and hold on to each other so tightly, like we're each other's oxygen and can't breathe if we're not touching.

Her stiff nipples poke through her wet t-shirt, and I have a raging hard-on at the sight of them. It reminds me of the day she burst into my life, and it was never the same again.

'You're so wet,' she whispers a while later when we finally unglue our lips, and she runs her hands through my hair.

'You're soaking too.' I laugh. 'You're not the easiest woman to find, by the way. I've been like Sherlock fucking Holmes since you left.'

She pulls me inside the building, laughing too now.

'Let's go up to the flat and we can dry off.'

'Does drying off involve us getting naked?' My tone is teasing, but I'm desperate to feel her skin against mine and I'm praying that Juliette really isn't at home.

'It might do,' she says. A coy smile spreads across her wide mouth, and as we walk up the stairs, her hand nestles in mine. Something tells me we're going to be fine. More than fine. My heart's blazing with love for her and nothing has ever felt so right.

My seat on the board, my shares in the company and my position as CEO aren't worth anything without her.

I'll give it all up for her in a heartbeat, if that's what it takes. And *whatever* happens with my family, I'll spend every day, starting today, making sure she knows she's the love of my life.

'You didn't give me an answer,' I say.

She looks at me. 'To being your girlfriend—are you serious?'

'Of course, I'm serious. I've never been more serious.'

'In that case, yes.' She nods and the look of pure joy on her face tells me all I need to know.

'I love you, Nat,' I say, unable to hold back any longer.

'And I love you too,' she says. Her eyes shine as she opens the door of the flat, and the second we're inside we strip each other's sodden clothes off and make frantic, passionate love on the sofa.

Much later, when Nat's out the room, I reach for my suit jacket and extract a box from the pocket and flip it open. The topaz necklace gleams on the velvet lining, and when she returns, she sees it and gasps. She sits on my knee, and I gather her thick golden hair in one hand and sweep it over one shoulder, and then I place the necklace around her neck and close the clasp.

'This belongs to you,' I say, admiring how perfectly it matches her eyes.

She touches the necklace and I can see how much it means to her as she leans over to kiss me.

As soon as she's got used to the idea of being my girlfriend, I'll make another proposal. The kind that requires a ring.

I can't wait for her to be my wife—Mrs Nathalie Rochester.

EPILOGUE

Nathalie

I release a contented sigh and rest my magazine on the table beside the sunbed. It feels great to be back in France and I'm loving this holiday. The glint of my topaz engagement ring next to my wedding band catches my eye, and my heart flutters at the memory of Sebastian searching for me in Knightsbridge and turning up soaked with the topaz necklace in his pocket.

Being Mrs Nathalie Rochester still feels surreal. Who would have believed I'd marry Sebastian when I took the position of Daisy's nanny?

Certainly not me. A Parisian orphan who grew up in foster care.

Juliette, the eternal romantic, said the fates always knew we were destined for each other, and she never doubted it from the first. I think back to our wedding day and how thrilled she was to be my maid of honour. I hope to return the favour for her one day soon when she finds someone who meets her fictional book boyfriend expectations.

Daisy's shrieks whistle through the air, and I hear splashing from the pool.

Sebastian asked whether it would be okay with me if we invited his mother to come on holiday with us. He wanted to make Daisy's family holiday dream come true. Vivian is a wonderful mother-in-law and we've grown close after working together on Rochester Foundation projects, so I didn't hesitate. She's popped out for a wander around the old town, and we've got the place to ourselves for a while. I love being part of a big close-knit family, and she's a great help with her granddaughter. We have a private chef at the villa, but we skipped organised childcare because this holiday is all about Daisy.

Sebastian blew me away when he asked me to move back into the house as his girlfriend, and I accepted once I saw he was sincere. He was willing to risk it all for me, and I had to know that because I couldn't be the reason he lost his family's goodwill and position in the company if he wasn't prepared for the potential consequences.

We kept our relationship secret for a couple of months while he figured out how to handle the situation. He took me to visit Greystone, as Daisy's nanny, to ease us all in gently. Soon after, he returned to break the news of our engagement to his grandfather.

Arthur Rochester took it better than expected. He admitted that he was disappointed Seb wouldn't be creating the all-powerful business alliance by marrying Lizzy Archer, but then he said that, ultimately, he only ever wanted to stop him from marrying the wrong woman again.

I was shaking when Seb took me to see his grandfather after our romantic engagement in Paris—I was so worried he would think I wasn't good enough for his grandson. But he was kind and courteous and laid my fears to rest. He said that the most important thing was his grandson and great-granddaughter were happy and he could see that I am definitely the *right* woman for that. He gave us his approval to marry and promised Seb he would honour the inheritance terms accordingly.

We didn't wait... Sebastian may have been the most impatient fiancé in England, and I was equally keen, so we married soon after in a small but elaborate private ceremony at Greystone Manor. Only our closest friends and family attended, and it was the most wonderful day of my life. Daisy was thrilled when we told her we were getting married, and she was the cutest, most hyper flower girl you could imagine. And Damian gave me away.

And now here I am, one year on, in a glorious villa, on a terrace overlooking the dazzling Mediterranean Sea with winding steps that lead down to the secluded beach where we've been swimming every morning with Daisy. It's just like the house by the sea in Daisy's dream holiday scenario.

An orphaned girl from the suburbs of Paris married to one of the wealthiest men in Europe. When it gets overwhelming, which it sometimes does, I remind myself that the important thing is how much we love each other and how well matched we are. I couldn't love Seb more, or Daisy for that matter, and I can truly say I have never been happier. Sometimes I worry it's all too good to be true. I don't deserve this good fortune and I'll lose my hard-won happiness in some freak disaster. I've never truly forgotten the trauma of losing both my parents, and sometimes it still haunts me. Once when I awoke in a panic in the depths of the night, I confided in Seb about my anxiety, and he said whenever I can't sleep, I must wake him, and he'll hold me until I fall back to sleep.

He makes everything right and I feel safe with him.

Rising from the sunbed, I wrap my silk sarong around my waist and slip my tanned feet into my flip-flops and pad towards the end of the huge terrace near the pool where Daisy is laughing hysterically. Seb is throwing the ball to her, and she is leaping about in the water trying to catch it, but more often missing and collapsing into the pool with an enormous splash. Her sweet face is a picture of delight and my heart fills with a fierce tenderness for this little girl who came into my life so unexpectedly, and who is now officially my stepdaughter.

'Nathalie, Nathalie,' she shouts. 'Please come in and play with us. We're playing an amazing game of catch.'

Seb looks up at me and beckons me in after he wipes his dripping hair out of his face. 'Yes, I second that. Come and join us. The water's fantastic.'

I walk to the steps, remove my flip-flops and sarong, and slide my sun-warmed body into the pool, gradually, grimacing as the cool water washes over my stomach.

'It's not that cold,' giggles Daisy, her butterfly float wiggling about. 'It's heated,' she promises and jumps up and down whilst I wade a few steps and then plunge under the water and swim towards them.

When I emerge, Seb reaches for me and says, 'Ah. Just how I like it. My two girls together.' Daisy paddles towards us and lunges to wrap her wiry cold arms around my neck and I swing her about.

Vivian appears and walks towards us. 'Having a good time?'

We chat a bit and then she says, 'The old town is beautiful. Why not go in for dinner this evening—just you two?'

'Don't you want to come?' I ask.

She shakes her head. 'I've had a long day and can think of nothing better than curling up in the villa with my granddaughter. Want to watch a movie and eat pizza with Grandma?'

Daisy cheers, and Seb and I exchange a look.

Date night on the Riviera.

'Perfect,' he says. 'How about one more swim before we order your pizza and Nathalie and I get ready to head out?'

Daisy paddles frantically, her freckled face wreathed in smiles as we both swim slowly alongside her.

'Where's my favourite swimming costume?' asks Seb, when Daisy's out of earshot and her grandma is helping her out of the pool.

I smirk. 'You mean the one that shows my nipples, I suppose.'

'Of course.' His eyes stray to my cleavage. 'You're a sight for sore eyes in that bikini, but it's hard to beat that costume. It's got a lot to answer for.'

'I'll wear it for you tomorrow,' I say, laughing. He always goes on about that costume, which is the only reason I brought it. I've got far more expensive and prettier costumes, courtesy of Marian's designer label, than that old one.

'Is that a promise?'

'Absolutely,' I say.

'Come here, Wife. Just the thought of you in that costume drives me crazy.' He pulls me into his arms and his hard body presses against me and I feel him stir. I wrap my legs around him as he lifts me up in the water and our lips meet. 'Can we get ready for our date, now?' he says, and I know exactly what kind of getting ready he has in mind.

Daisy and Vivian are settled in the snug, ready for pizza, and we wish them goodnight. Just as we're about to leave, Daisy calls, 'This is the best summer holiday *ever*. Thank you, Daddy. Thank you, Nathalie.' She runs over to hug us both.

Our driver arrives and we slip into the backseat of the car and Seb reaches for my hand and turns it over and plants a kiss on my palm.

'Thank you for being so incredible with Daisy and my mother. I've not seen either of them so relaxed in years, and it's all down to you.'

My eyes well up at the raw emotion in his voice, and I think for the thousandth time, I must be the luckiest woman in the world.

I lean over to kiss him and run my hand through his shiny, damp hair. 'Thank you for being *the* most incredible husband and for making me the happiest woman alive.'

We hold hands all the way into the old town until the car pulls up outside the restaurant and we get out. The scent of his aftershave teases my nose and I'm as buzzing to be out with him for the evening as I was on our first date.

He's all mine and I couldn't be more grateful.

The thing about falling in love with someone who's forbidden to you is that if the universe realigns and by some miracle, you're able to be together, you never take it for granted. It's always special.

My hand grazes my stomach, and excitement fizzes through me.

I received a confirmation email when Seb was in the pool with Daisy, and our date night on the beautiful Riviera is the perfect time to tell him the news.

I put my hand over my wine glass and shake my head at the server, smiling.

Seb tilts his head to one side. 'No wine on date night? That's unusual,' he teases. He knows how much I appreciate fine wine.

My heart's thumping, and the adrenalin rushes through me as I raise my eyes to his. 'There's a reason I shouldn't drink wine.'

He looks at me quizzically.

I study his handsome face and drop him another clue. 'It will continue for quite a few months of date nights.'

A look of pure joy flashes into his blue-grey eyes and he leaps up and dashes around the table, and pulls me gently to my feet. He wraps his arms around me and whispers in my ear, 'Are you saying what I think you're saying?'

Tilting backwards slightly, I nod. 'Yes. We're expecting.'

Seb lets out an earth-shattering whoop and picks me up and swings me around and then kisses me as people at the nearby tables stop eating and stare.

His enthusiasm is contagious and everyone's looking at us curiously now, and I feel the need to explain. I look around, smile, and tell them we just found out we're having a baby.

It's a small bistro and the diners from the surrounding tables stand up and raise their glasses to us in a noisy toast, like a scene from a romantic comedy. '*Bravo!*'

We thank everyone and sit down. Seb can't stop smiling, and he clasps my hands and says, 'I love you madly.'

'And I love you more,' I reply.

The three of us are such a happy family and I can't wait to tell Daisy she's going to have a little sister or brother.

Enjoyed this book?

I hope you did. I'll be forever grateful if you take a moment to leave a quick review or rating on Amazon or Goodreads. It makes such a difference to Indie Authors like me, and will help me to write more Rochester books for you.

Thank you so much,

Rachel x

WANT MORE SEBASTIAN & NATHALIE? (BONUS CHAPTER)

Download the bonus chapter *The Proposal* to your inbox:

https://rachelhenke.com/sh-bonus/

This bonus chapter is told from Sebastian's perspective. He surprises Nathalie with a luxurious, romantic trip to Paris and proposes with a grand gesture.

READ CASPIAN & ISABELLA'S STORY

Pre-order on Amazon: *Rebellious Heir*

ALSO BY RACHEL HENKE

The Rochesters

Arrogant Heir - (Damian & Jamie)

Rebellious Heir - (Caspian & Isabella)

Twin Flames - (Cara and George)

Twin Flames

The Uprising

The Runner

The Covenant

ACKNOWLEDGMENTS

Thanks to Russell Cooper, my partner, editor and constant cheerleader. I couldn't do this without you, my darling.

And special thanks to Anita Davis, Amy Henke, Ella Henke, Clare Horrocks, Kim Kaase, Emily Mace, Shelley Moench-Kelly and Donna Peerce for the support, enthusiasm and advance reading. I appreciate you so much.

Thank you to my wonderful readers who recommend and review my books.

With love,

Rachel

ABOUT THE AUTHOR

Rachel's novels are angsty, steamy, romantic tales about soulmates, destined to be together against all odds. She has a soft spot for tortured heroes and the sassy females who redeem them.

She writes contemporary and historical romance and dreamt of being a novelist since she was seven years old. Her debut historical time travel romance series, *Twin Flames,* hit the Amazon bestseller lists in 2020 and stayed there for several years.

Rachel lives with her partner in the beautiful Surrey town of Weybridge, where the Rivers Wey and Thames meet. She spends her days drinking excellent coffee, telling tales, and meeting the incessant demands of their bossy toy poodle.

Printed in Great Britain
by Amazon

23812392R00179

A RAMAZ DONADZE THRILLER

NO MURDER FORGOTTEN

AJ LIDDLE

ISBN-13: 978-1-8381911-7-7

PRAISE FOR NO MURDER FORGOTTEN

A welcome and thrilling return to the streets of Tbilisi. With Donadze at the helm, AJ Liddle once again proves himself a master of taut, intelligent crime fiction. Brutal, haunting, and utterly compelling—No Murder Forgotten marks another standout in this outstanding Georgian-set series.

-GR Halliday

Set against the vibrant backdrop of Tbilisi, Georgia, AJ Liddle's No Murder Forgotten is a masterfully crafted thriller that immerses readers in the gripping world of local police Lieutenant, Ramaz Donadze. No Murder Forgotten weaves a complex tale of murder, conspiracy, and rough justice, blending rich cultural details with razor-sharp suspense. Liddle's deep understanding of Georgian history and society adds authenticity to the narrative, while his compelling characters and intricate plot will keep readers hooked until the very last page.

-Adam Oyebanji

No Murder Forgotten is a hugely enjoyable detective thriller with a likeable yet tough protagonist. This is crime writing for the aficionado.

-Mac Logan

The hunt is on for a killer in a crime thriller that is as enigmatic, intriguing and engaging as the Georgia setting.

-Gordon Brown AKA Morgan Cry

AJ Liddle writes with style and undoubted authority.

-Craig Robertson

A gripping read with a thoroughly likeable detective.

-Lydia Travers

Writing as sharp as a blade.

-Andrew James Greig

ALSO BY AJ LIDDLE

THE RAMAZ DONADZE THRILLERS

No Harm Done
No Way Back
No Rules Apply
No Murder Forgotten

For Georgia, a country which has given me so much.

There lay between them, separating them, that same terrible line of the unknown and of fear, like the line separating the living from the dead.

-Leo Tolstoy, War and Peace

He is a man of courage who does not run away, but remains at his post and fights against the enemy.

- Socrates

ONE

'Where are you going?' Nini demanded, leaving the party to follow Rusiko into the bedroom.

'I told you—home,' Rusiko said, attempting to locate and extract her jacket from the mound heaped upon the bed by fellow party guests. 'I've got a class tomorrow, remember?' she added, laughing as her friend's face collapsed, her shoulders sagging in theatrical disappointment. 'Sorry.'

'Skip the class, it won't make any difference,' Nini urged.

Maybe not to you, it wouldn't, Rusiko thought. She was two years into her law degree, the first girl in her family to go to university, the weight of her parents' expectations heavy on her shoulders. Not that these expectations were ever spoken; they didn't have to be. Her father's ill-health had stopped him working and her mother cleaned offices and stacked supermarket shelves to earn what little money she could. Her days started early and finished late, putting in more hours at minimum wage than employment laws allowed. Rusiko's heart broke when she looked at her mother: exhausted, stooped, prematurely old.

Rusiko was twenty, she could be contributing to her family's finances instead of putting additional strain on them. Something she was acutely aware of. *It's what they want*, she told herself, knowing that to be true. But it didn't ease her sense of guilt, anticipating the day when—her studies complete—she would secure a well-paid job and support the family so that her mother could do more than just exist.

She couldn't say any of that to her friend, whose father was a medical doctor and comfortably well off, happy to indulge his daughter's half-hearted studies until she limped over the finishing line with a mediocre degree.

Rusiko found her jacket and slipped it on. 'You should stay,' she said, walking into the hall.

'No, it's okay. I'll come with you,' Nini said, her reluctance poorly disguised.

Rusiko kissed her friend and whispered in her ear, 'Stay. Vazha would be *so* disappointed if you don't.'

'You think so?' Nini said, glancing over her shoulder and flashing a warm smile at the young man who was watching them, a beer bottle to his mouth.

'Definitely.'

'You're not *actually* going to *walk* though, are you?'

'No, of course not. I'll call a taxi.'

'If you're sure...'

'I am, see you tomorrow,' she said, winking at her friend. 'You can tell me how you got on with Vazha.'

Nini gave her friend a quick hug, already calculating how to further attract the young man's interest.

Rusiko let herself out of the apartment, closing the door behind her and negotiating the worn steps. The lighting was dim with many of the lamps blown or removed by landlords to reduce electricity costs, the stairway tricky to negotiate safely if not sober. But Rusiko was completely sober, having faked the quantity of alcohol she'd consumed. She intended attending her class *and* being in a fit state to learn.

She reached the bottom of the stairs and pressed a button to unlock the front door, stepping out into the fresh but warm and humid air. Contrary to what she'd told Nini, she had no intention of taking a taxi. It wasn't that she couldn't afford the fare, more that taxis somehow symbolised a waste of her parents' money. It was only a four kilometre walk, she'd be home in less than an hour.

Rusiko Darsalia never made it home. Head down and listening to music on her earbuds, she didn't see the man standing in the shadows or hear him move swiftly behind her, clamping his hand over her mouth and jerking back her head to cut deeply into her throat. He held her tightly, his own body trembling as she thrashed and bled. She soon lost consciousness and he dragged her into the fetid alley, dropping her onto discarded food containers, used vapes and other city detritus, pausing only long enough to watch her die.

TWO

Lieutenant Ramaz Donadze's phone buzzed. He forced his eyes open and reached for the device, swinging his legs out of bed, his pulse quickening. It was five in the morning. Calls this early usually meant a new murder investigation, most killings being committed during the dark hours, the dead discovered only as the city awoke.

He carried the phone from the bedroom, trying not to disturb Tamuna. 'Irina,' he said, his voice low. 'What have we got?'

'Hey, Ramaz,' his partner Irina Jaqeli greeted him brightly. 'Rusiko Darsalia, a twenty year old student.' She paused a moment. 'It sounds pretty brutal.'

'Okay, I'll pick you up in twenty minutes,' Donadze said, ending the call.

Tamuna had woken anyway. She shuffled into the living room, cinching her dressing gown around her waist. 'Irina?' she guessed. She filled the kettle with water, holding it wearily for Donadze to see.

He nodded his thanks. 'I'll take it with me, if that's okay.'

'It's okay by me, Ramaz,' she said.

He crossed to the bedroom, washed and pulled on his clothes then returned to the living room to retrieve his pistol and ID.

Tamuna pointed to the travel mug she'd left on the breakfast bar. 'Give it a few minutes to cool,' she said, yawning.

'You should go back to bed.'

'There's not much point, Eka's going to be up soon.'

'I know, sorry I woke you,' Donadze said, acknowledging that their daughter rarely slept beyond six.

Tamuna took a sip of her own coffee. 'That's okay,' she said. 'Enjoy your new case.'

'Enjoy it? Someone's been murdered, Tamuna.'

'You know what I mean.'

'I suppose so.' He picked up his cup, kissed Tamuna goodbye then crept into Eka's room, watching his daughter for a moment as she slept, her chest slowly rising and falling as she snored softly in her cot. She was twenty months old now and growing much too quickly for Donadze's liking. He leaned into the cot and kissed her then turned and left the apartment, taking the elevator to the block's underground parking. His car *blipped* a welcome as he unlocked its doors and pulled himself into the driver's seat. The small SUV was a wedding present from Tamuna and still his pride and joy.

He eased the car out of its parking slot and manoeuvred up the ramp to street level, thinking of Tamuna's comment about enjoying his new case. It was true that he'd been bored lately. His last murder investigation—a drunk beaten to death by his abused wife—was over two weeks ago. That case had been opened and closed on the same day, the speed of closure useful when homicide clear-up statistics were assessed. It was hardly a challenge though; the woman herself had reported the crime and had met the responding officers in blood splattered clothing, the cast iron skillet she'd used to smash her husband's head still lying on the kitchen floor beside him. Donadze certainly hadn't enjoyed *that* case, especially as his sympathies lay with the perpetrator. He hoped his new investigation would be more challenging, if not actually enjoyable.

Jaqeli was waiting for him with her fiancé, Misha Arziani outside the apartment they shared. Arziani had been recently promoted and appointed commander of Mtatsminda Station, which made him Donadze's boss. Still in his early thirties, such rapid career progression was unusual. Donadze liked Arziani and couldn't deny he deserved his appointment. However, his own career had been stalled at a senior level—specifically, by Colonel Gabrieli Meskhi. It felt unfair, even though there was much about a command role—the bureaucracy and distance from real police work—that he knew he would hate.

He shook these dark thoughts from his head and wound down his window. 'Misha, Irina,' he said.

'Hey, Ramaz,' Arziani returned his greeting. 'Sounds like a bad one.'

'Aren't they all?'

Arziani shrugged. 'Some are worse than others.'

'Yes, I suppose so,' Donadze agreed, thinking again of his last case—the abused woman. 'I'll let you know how we get on.' He turned to Jaqeli. 'Ready Irina?'

'Always,' Jaqeli gave her customary response. She kissed her fiancé and got into the car.

Donadze watched Arziani in his rear view mirror. 'How are the wedding plans going?' he asked.

Jaqeli shook her head. 'They're going.'

'Family politics?'

'No, it's not that. Don't ask,' she added as Donadze was framing his next question.

'Okay, I won't.' He glanced at the car's clock. The traffic was picking up but still reasonable. 'Fifteen minutes,' he said.

❖

Donadze saw two patrol cars in the distance and slowed to park behind them. He and Jaqeli got out of his car, noting that the uniformed officers had already strung crime scene tape to close off the area from curious bystanders. An officer standing by the tape recognised him, lifting it to let them pass.

Donadze inwardly groaned when he realised that Natia Gagua was duty crime scene investigator. She was the most skilled and conscientious of all her colleagues he thought, but a chronic tease, with Donadze her favourite victim. She was kneeling over the body, measuring the dimensions of a neck wound and passing her observations to her technician who jotted them down on his clipboard. She straightened after a moment, her hands on her lower back and nodded to the technician, their work done. She noticed Donadze and placed her hands over her heart, fluttering her false eyelashes at him. 'Ramaz, you're here at last,' she gushed.

Donadze ignored her teasing. 'Hey, Natia,' he said. 'What happened here?'

'Well, you're no fun,' she said in a lispy Marilyn Monroe-type voice. Tormenting over, she became fully professional again, taking a moment to further appraise the scene. 'Okay, this looks pretty clear to me.' She held up an ID card and pointed to the body with it. 'This woman was Rusiko Darsalia, a twenty year old student at the Faculty of Law, TSU. As you can see, she was killed by a single, deep cut across her neck, severing her carotid artery. Judging by the depth of the wound and its clean edges, it looks to me like a very sharp blade was used, slicing rather than sawing across her neck.'

Donadze winced at Gagua's graphic description. 'Okay, so the blade was sharp but not serrated?'

'Correct. Not that that will help you much. There'll be thousands like it. There's something else though, Ramaz. A single cut as I said, but slicing upwards; that's difficult to achieve unless the head's pulled back and held out of the way. Is that something you would have learned during national service?'

Donadze had spent a year conscripted into the Army. 'Not me. I was just a trench monkey. It's a technique the GSOF are taught though,' he said, referring to the Army's elite Georgian Special Operations Forces. 'But anyone could learn it, I suppose. You just need a good knife and to be cold enough to take a life that way.'

'There's so much blood,' Jaqeli said, grimacing.

Gagua smiled. 'No more than five litres,' she said. 'But you're right, Irina, it always looks more, even to me. You can see that most of it was spilled out on the street and here in the alley. I think it's obvious what happened. The victim was attacked in the street and that's where her throat was cut.

She was still alive but—judging by the volume of blood lost—unconscious or nearly unconscious as she was dragged here, into this alley.' Gagua pointed to two haphazard trails connecting the blood pools. 'The victim's heels made these tracks as she was dragged in here and dumped.'

Donadze realised that Gagua was referring to Rusiko Darsalia as *the victim*, depersonalising the young woman as a self defence mechanism, he thought. Like him, she saw too much brutality and death. 'Can I take a look?' he asked.

'Of course.'

Donadze put on the one piece protective suit given to him by Gagua's technician, pulling the hood over his head and the boots over his shoes. He approached the body, avoiding the blood pool, knelt and looked up the debris-strewn alley. A familiar coppery smell of violent death mingled with the ammonia tang of urine, the alley clearly used by drunks relieving themselves on their way home. He stared into the dead girl's white, waxen face, her eyes open but sightless, the ugly gash on her neck drying to the colour of aged beef. 'What a terrible place for you to die, Rusiko,' Donadze said. He placed a gloved hand on her cold head and promised to find her killer.

❖

Donadze forced his way into the traffic, moving slowly passed the police barriers. 'What did you make of that, Irina?' he asked.

Jaqeli leaned back on her seat, her eyes closed, thinking. 'For me, what stands out most is the brutality of the killing, the sheer volume of blood. But it was more than that, it was cold, efficient, impersonal, almost like…'

'Almost like slaughtering a farm animal?'

'Yes, something like that. A single deep cut, massive bleeding, a quick death. We'd say it was humane if a farm animal had been killed that way.'

'Cold and efficient, yes. But it also seems casual to me. Like something a slaughterman would do day-in and day-out and never lose any sleep over.'

Jaqeli nodded. 'And that somehow makes it worse, don't you think? What about the military angle? Do you think a soldier or ex-soldier could be responsible?'

'It's possible, but let's keep an open mind. There are plenty of special forces *wannabees* out there, maybe one of them learned the technique and wanted to try it out.'

Jaqeli shuddered. 'The people we deal with…'

Donadze took his eyes off the road to glance at his partner. She was pale, her features drawn. 'The trick is not to let them get to you,' he said softly.

She sighed. 'That's easier said than done though, isn't it?'

'Yes,' he agreed. 'It's something I've never managed.'

'Okay,' Jaqeli said, refocusing. 'If this was *impersonal* and *casual* then that suggests Rusiko didn't know her killer.'

'I think so. She was probably just in the wrong place at the wrong time.'

'That's not going to help her parents…'

'No, it won't.'

Donadze stopped his car beside a sign prohibiting parking in that area. 'What do you think?' he asked.

Jaqeli shrugged. 'Leave a note on your dash,' she said. 'We won't be long.'

The Darsalia family's apartment block had been built

during the Soviet era and the elevator never replaced. Donadze followed Jaqeli into the small metal box and pressed a worn button for the third level. The door closed and the elevator eventually lurched upwards, its single, dim light doing little to lift the gloomy interior or Donadze's sense of claustrophobia. He was relieved when the box shuddered to a stop and the door opened, releasing them onto a bright corridor smelling faintly of the bleach used to scrub it clean.

They walked a short distance to the Darsalia family's door. Donadze pushed the bell and it was quickly opened by a woman he took to be Rusiko's mother. Her relieved smile collapsed when she saw Donadze and Jaqeli on her doorstep. He knew she recognised them for what they were—police—and understood why they were here.

'Rusiko…' she said, her throat constricted, her tired face draining colour.

Jaqeli showed her ID. 'May we come in, Mrs Darsalia?' she asked.

'No, I'm sorry,' the woman said, forcing a smile and indicating the supermarket uniform she was wearing. 'I'm already late for work.'

Jaqeli smiled and touched her arm. 'Please, Mrs Darsalia,' she said.

Donadze could read the conflict in the woman's face. He knew that denial is a common response to bad news: if you don't hear it, then it hasn't happened. 'Let's go inside, Mrs Darsalia,' he said, more firmly.

Her thin shoulders sagged, realisation and despair settling on her like a suffocating smog. 'I'm sorry,' she said. 'Please come in.'

She led the way into a small, homely room, a window

open to freshen the air. A man was sitting on a padded easy chair, gaunt, his skin an unhealthy yellow, a television blaring a mindless daytime show.

'My husband,' Mrs Darsalia said, crossing the room to turn the television off.

The man stayed seated, nodding at Donadze and Jaqeli as a tear welled in his eye and rolled down his white-stubbled cheek. 'You've found her then,' he stated.

'I'm so sorry,' Jaqeli said.

'How?' he asked, hesitantly.

Jaqeli looked between the man and his wife. 'Rusiko was murdered, sir.'

He shut his eyes, trying to absorb the devastating news. 'How?' he asked again after a moment, his duty as a father to learn how his daughter had died overcoming his dread of being told.

Jaqeli looked to Donadze and he nodded. 'With a knife, sir. We're so sorry,' she repeated.

'Stop saying you're sorry,' Mrs Darsalia snapped, her voice now firm. She turned her gaze onto Donadze. 'Are you going to find the monster who did this to my girl?'

'Yes, Mrs Darsalia, we'll find him,' he said.

'And then what?' Mr Darsalia asked.

'He'll go to prison.'

Rusiko's father reached to lift a cup from the floor and took a sip, his tear-filled eyes fixed on the blank television screen. 'It's not enough.'

Donadze nodded. 'I know,' he said. 'It never is.'

THREE

'Let's take the stairs,' Donadze said to Jaqeli as Mrs Darsalia closed her door on them.

'Suits me, I wasn't too keen on that contraption either.'

Donadze's car had escaped being ticketed. He unlocked it and they both got in.

'Who should we speak to first?' Jaqeli asked.

Donadze thought for a moment. Statements had been taken from Rusiko's parents, trying to determine if they'd noticed anything out of the ordinary with their daughter or if she'd been worried about anything recently. Both had been clear that there was nothing of note and that Rusiko wouldn't have kept anything from them if there had been. Donadze was sceptical though, knowing that there are topics that young women—and young men for that matter—wouldn't share with their parents. 'What's her friend called? Nini…'

'Nini Tabagari,' Jaqeli reminded him. She retrieved the

mobile number provided by Rusiko's parents, hesitating before calling. 'What will I tell her?'

'Just that we need to speak to her about Rusiko.'

'She'll guess something's wrong.'

'I know, but it can't be helped…'

It took several moments before Jaqeli's call was answered. Donadze could hear the student's voice through the phone's speaker, initially groggy with sleep but becoming almost hysterical as she realised something awful had happened to her friend.

Jaqeli hung up. 'That probably wasn't the best approach.'

'Maybe not, but it's done now.'

'She was still in bed by the sound of it. The life of a student…'

Donadze started his engine. 'I wouldn't know,' he said.

Nini's apartment was close to the university on Chavchavadze Avenue.

'A bit more upmarket than the area where I lived as a student,' Jaqeli said.

'Expensive,' Donadze agreed. He pressed the security panel's call button and the door immediately buzzed unlocked. 'Come up,' a tinny voice said.

Nini was waiting for them as the elevator door opened, wide eyed, bare footed, her hair dishevelled, blue jeans and a faded red sweatshirt pulled carelessly over her slim frame. 'It's Rusiko, isn't it?' she said.

A door was open along the corridor and Donadze turned towards it. 'Let's talk inside.'

She led them into her lounge. It was expensively furnished with a soft leather suite and matching polished wooden tables and cabinets. Warm, humid air breezed past the open balcony door's voile curtains but the skunky, spicy tang of recently smoked weed still lingered.

Donadze noticed a man's shoe, a wine bottle and two used glasses lying by the sofa. 'Is there somebody else here with you, Nini?' he asked.

She glanced at the open lounge door, her face reddening. 'No, of course not.' She shook her head. 'But why would that matter anyway? This is about Rusiko, isn't it?' she repeated, her voice rising. 'She's been killed, hasn't she? But how? How could that have happened? She promised me she'd take a taxi...'

'What have you heard?' Jaqeli asked, her voice soft and low.

'I checked my social media after you called. It's all over Instagram. A girl's body was found, murdered. There wasn't a name but I knew right away, it had to be Rusiko. I tried calling her but she didn't answer...' she added, her voice trailing off.

'I'm sorry, Nini,' Jaqeli said. 'But I'm afraid it's true. Rusiko was murdered last night.'

It took a moment for the young woman to absorb the horror that her friend had been killed. Her hands went to her head, her long hair falling over her face like a curtain coming down on innocence. 'But I told her to take a taxi,' she whispered at last.

Donadze and Jaqeli returned to his car. 'Are *you* on Instagram, Irina?' he asked.

'Yes, a private account.'

'What does that mean?'

'It means I control who can see my content and—'

'That's okay, you can explain it to me later,' he interrupted. 'Can you bring up the post Nini mentioned?'

'Ramaz…'

'What?'

'Don't ask a question if you don't want to hear the answer.'

A moment passed whilst Donadze absorbed his reprimand. 'Okay, sorry,' he said. 'But can you bring it up?'

Jaqeli sighed. 'Probably.'

Donadze leaned back on his car seat, thinking while Jaqeli searched for the relevant post.

'This looks like it,' she said, taking a moment to read before passing her phone to him. 'It's from an account called *Fenrirgeo.* A single post.'

'Strange name.'

'It probably means something: *geo* could be short for Georgia and *Fenrir* could be a name or a nickname—Georgian Fenrir, something like that maybe.'

'Yes, maybe something like that,' Donadze agreed. He examined the phone. The post consisted of a single image of the entrance to the alley where Rusiko Darsalia had died. Donadze could make out crime scene tape and he recognised the responding officer standing by it. The caption accompanying the image read, *So, this is one girl who didn't make it home!*

'It's definitely the correct location and it looks like the picture was taken after the body was found and also after the patrolmen had arrived,' Jaqeli said.

'Yes, but before Natia or you and I got there. That's quite a narrow window which means there couldn't have been many people with the opportunity to take it.'

'One of the patrolmen?'

'No, they wouldn't be that stupid.'

'Let me take a look at it again,' Jaqeli said, holding out her hand to take the phone. She tapped the screen. 'The account was created this month…'

'Before Rusiko was killed?'

'Probably, it doesn't specify a date. It's like Fenrirgeo set it up for this post.' Jaqeli paused a moment. 'The thing is, Ramaz, posting this type of thing isn't illegal. It wouldn't even contravene Instagram's contents policy. But there's no information about Fenrirgeo or his account other than it being based in Georgia…'

'Anonymous then?'

'Effectively. Let me try something else.' She tapped her screen several more times then read from it. 'Wow,' she said, handing him the phone. 'So, this is Fenrir…'

Donadze read from the online encyclopaedia entry. *Fenrir: a wolf from Norse mythology who, during Ragnarök, is prophesied to participate in setting the world on fire and killing the god, Odin.* He returned the phone to Jaqeli. 'So, our Fenrirgeo is a wolf…' he said.

'There's something else, Ramaz,' Jaqeli said. 'Take a look at the comment at the bottom. It's by Fenrirgeo, responding to other people's comments.'

Donadze took the phone and read, *There* WILL *be more. Where there are sheep, the wolves are never very far away.*

FOUR

'Does Colonel Meskhi make you nervous?' Jaqeli asked.

'No,' Donadze said, not entirely truthfully. 'Why should he?'

'I don't know why exactly, but he *does* make me nervous. I can't keep up with him sometimes.'

'Well, he's got a big brain—but so do you. And if *you* can't keep up with him, what chance do I have?'

'You do okay, Ramaz,' she said, drumming her fingers—nervously—on the dash. 'This *is* about Fenrir, isn't it?'

'*Fenrir*? Are we calling him that as well now?' He reversed into a vacant slot in the Ministry of Internal Affairs' car park and stopped his engine. 'But, yes, that's almost certainly what Meskhi wants to discuss.' He unclipped his seat belt. 'Let's find out.'

They crossed the car park and picked up security passes at Reception, taking the elevator to Meskhi's office.

Donadze looked at Jaqeli. She nodded her readiness and he knocked on the door and opened it.

Meskhi looked up from his desk. 'Lieutenant, Detective,' he greeted them. He was meticulously dressed as always in his trademark black suit, white shirt and tie, his shaved head, aquiline nose and unblinking stare reminding Donadze—not for the first time—of an eagle, perched and ready to swoop. He read from his screen a moment longer then pushed his keyboard away. 'Join me,' he instructed, unfolding his long, lean frame out of his chair and crossing to a small conference table.

He waited until Donadze and Jaqeli had taken their seats. 'Tell me about this *wolf murderer*,' he said, steepling his fingers and closing his eyes, a mannerism Donadze had become familiar with.

'We're going with *Fenrir* as a working name, sir.'

Meskhi opened his eyes, frowning. 'Fenrir, yes, that's appropriate, I suppose. Especially as the wolf, Fenrir was ultimately defeated and killed by Vídarr—as I'm sure you already knew, Lieutenant.'

'Of course, sir. Killed by Vídarr, Odin's son.'

'Yes, Donadze, you're correct, Vídarr was indeed Odin's son,' Meskhi said, his tone dry. 'Tell me about the *Fenrir* case then.'

'Yes, sir. The victim, Rusiko Darsalia was a twenty year old student. We don't think she was targeted for any specific reason; just unlucky to come across Fenrir when she did. She was either followed to the alley or intercepted there. Probably the latter, we think.'

'What do you make of Fenrir's appearance on social media?'

Jaqeli looked at Donadze and he nodded for her to answer. 'He's a braggart, sir. Arrogant. He's going to set the world on fire and kill a god and he wants an audience when he does it. For him, setting the world on fire means more people will die. He's Fenrir the wolf and, *Where there are sheep, the wolves are never very far away.*'

'Ah yes, the Plautus quotation. Do you think he sees himself as cultured? A superior intellect, perhaps?'

'Possibly, sir. Norse mythology and Roman playwrights are obscure topics for most people. I hadn't even heard of Fenrir or Plautus before this.'

'Unlike the Lieutenant,' Meskhi said, his mouth turning down. He looked at Donadze. 'So, this Fenrir intends killing more people. How will he be stopped?'

Donadze took a moment to answer. 'His arrogance, sir. The Instagram post, he's giving too much of himself away. It's how we'll catch him in the end.'

Meskhi nodded. 'I think you're right. Fenrir wants an audience as he sets the world on fire and kills a god. He's got his audience, thanks to social media. Which god do you think he has in mind?'

'The god who will do battle with him during *Ragnarök*. In the myth, it was Odin.'

'And here, today in Georgia?'

'I don't know, Colonel. Ragnarök stands for Doomsday, that's not something Georgia—let alone the world—is facing right now.'

'But Fenrir may be judging this his personal Doomsday. Who's standing against him?'

'We are—the police. Are you suggesting Fenrir might try to kill Irina or me?'

'More likely you, Donadze,' Meskhi said, his tone suggesting indifference. 'It's something you should consider.' He paused a moment. 'But this Fenrir: he's not a wolf, he's a vain and deeply flawed man—find him and bring him to justice.'

'Sir,' Donadze and Jaqeli said, a beat apart.

Meskhi took a moment to appraise his detectives. 'Good luck,' he said, their meeting over.

❖

Jaqeli waited until they were in the elevator. 'Why do you do that?'

'Do what?'

'Wind up Colonel Meskhi in that way. *Vídarr: of course I know he was Odin's son—doesn't everyone?*'

Donadze shrugged. 'That's not quite what I said. But anyway, it was just harmless fun, no big deal.'

'It might be fun, Ramaz, but it's not harmless, not for you anyway.'

'Meskhi and I don't enjoy the best relationship, Irina. We're never going to be friends.'

'You don't have to be friends. But you should at least show him some respect.'

The elevator door opened. 'I do, just not as much as he'd like.'

They dropped off their passes and walked back to his car in the pleasant, morning warmth.

'So, Fenrir is arrogant and a braggart,' Donadze said, starting his engine. 'You're the psychologist—do you think he's also a psychopath?'

'Do you want the academic or the popular definition?'

'Whichever one you think I'll understand.'

'I think you're easily capable of understanding both, Ramaz,' Jaqeli said. She took a moment to gather her thoughts. 'You already know the popular view from movies, television and books. Psychopaths: cold hearted killers, scheming, bold, egotistical. Sometimes even sexy.'

'Other than sexy, that sounds like Fenrir, doesn't it?'

'Yes, it does. *Psychopathy* is a psychological disorder and Fenrir—from what we know of him so far—exhibits its typical characteristics: definitely a lack of empathy towards others and feelings of self-importance. Not many people get to kill gods after all. But, just to be clear, as far as practitioners are concerned, there is no definitive diagnosis of the condition.'

'And you remembered all that from university?'

'It wasn't that long ago, Ramaz.'

'Well, like I said—big brain.'

'If I really had a big brain, I wouldn't stay partnered with you,' she said, glancing at him and trying but failing to stifle her laughter.

'Yes, you would, you'd miss these stimulating conversations.'

They drove the remaining distance to Mtatsminda Station in companionable silence, Donadze considering Jaqeli's advice about not antagonising Meskhi and knowing she was right.

Misha Arziani was working in his office when they returned to the detectives' bureau. He stood and opened his door. 'Ramaz,' he said, signalling for Donadze to join him.

'Go ahead,' Jaqeli said. 'I'll make a start writing up the case file.'

'How did you get on with the Colonel?' Arziani asked as Donadze sat down.

'Fine, he just wanted an update on Fenrir,' Donadze said then smiled. 'Oh, and to tell me that I might be the god Odin.'

Arziani frowned. 'What does that mean?'

Donadze shook his head. 'It's nothing, just something Meskhi came up with. He thinks that if the killer is hung up on Norse mythology, then he might see me as Odin.'

'And try to kill you?'

'Well, that's what Meskhi said. But I think it's unlikely. And it wouldn't be for a while yet. He's still got to set the world on fire and murdering one young girl is some way from doing that.'

'I don't know, Ramaz. Are you taking any precautions?'

'You obviously think I should be.'

'It wouldn't do any harm, at least for a while. Break up your routine a little, check your car before you get in, take different routes. Standard stuff, easy to do.'

'Okay, but it's only an idea Meskhi had, there's probably nothing in it.'

'Probably not, but you don't have to take unnecessary risks.' Arziani paused. 'That's not what I wanted to talk to you about. Your investigation, it's going to be too big, you can't run it from your desk.'

Donadze had already had the same thought. 'The Major Incident Room then?'

'Yes, you'll need the space and resources.'

'We could certainly do with someone to answer the phones and help with admin. But I want to keep things as tight as possible.'

'Okay, get yourself set up and let me know what you need.'

Donadze left Arziani and walked to Reception, asking the Desk Sergeant for the MIR's key. 'I'll be keeping this for now, Dato,' he told him.

It'd been a while since Donadze had been in the MIR. He pushed the door open, turned on the lights and went in, sniffing the stale air. The room was set up, ready to go: dedicated phones; writing pads and pens laid out on desks; flip charts armed with new and partially used pads of A1 paper; whiteboards cleaned but still showing faint marks from previous investigations. Donadze felt his pulse race, here were the tools he needed to catch a killer.

'We'll be working out of here for the time being,' Donadze told Jaqeli. 'Let's make sure it's locked when no one's here.' He handed her the MIR key. 'Give this to Dato to look after overnight.'

'You're worried about leaks?'

'It wouldn't be the first time, would it?' Donadze said. He gestured towards the walls. 'Could you start marking up these boards? We'll also need a street map of the city with pins identifying where the party was held and the spot where Rusiko was killed. Her parents' address as well. Anything else you think would be useful.' He lifted his jacket from the back of his chair. 'And think about what help we need. Nothing too much for now, maybe just someone to take calls and double up on admin. We can ask Misha for more than that if we need it.'

'Will do. Are you going somewhere?' Jaqeli asked.

'Just to my apartment, I'll be back in about an hour.'

Donadze left the station and walked to his car. He was in the driver's seat and about to press the start button when he remembered Arziani's advice about inspecting it before getting in. He'd been trained to conduct vehicle security checks during Army service and it took some time to do properly—time he wasn't prepared to invest. Donadze held his breath and started the engine.

There was no explosion of course but he'd learned during a previous investigation that car bombers sometimes used mercury tilt switches to detonate explosives as their target vehicles moved away. He gritted his teeth as he took his foot off the brake and the car—uneventfully—eased forward.

This is crazy, he thought, resolving not to worry about Fenrir trying to kill him unless he had evidence that that was actually the case. But Meskhi had put that corrosive thought in his head and he changed his usual route home, checking his mirrors for anyone following him, deliberately taking the wrong lane at junctions to make any pursuer more conspicuous—not that lane discipline counted for much in Tbilisi.

The drive was uneventful and Donadze parked his car and took the elevator to his apartment. He could hear Eka crying as he opened the door. Eliso, her nanny was feeding her lunch.

Donadze's mother had previously provided most of the child care they'd needed but they were forced to hire a nanny after she'd died. Their first nanny had married and left Tbilisi and Tamuna had replaced her with Eliso about a month ago. She was in her mid-forties, unmarried and with sound qualifications and an impressive work history—which Donadze had discreetly checked. Tamuna liked her and she and Eka seemed to get on well. She was particularly good at distracting the little girl when her parents left to go to work.

Good child care was in demand and Donadze knew they were lucky to have her. But his mother had always been there for him and Ana, his sister when they'd been children in their home region of Abkhazia. She'd also been there for him after Ana had been murdered and the rest of the family had fled to Tbilisi. There was no practical alternative but Donadze didn't like a non-family member looking after his daughter.

Eka spotted her father and stopped crying, holding out her arms to be lifted. Donadze picked her up and nuzzled her face, observing Eliso's mouth turn down in disapproval.

'I'm just getting something from the bedroom,' he told her. 'Is she okay?'

'Eka's fine. It's her age, she's discovering her own mind. And now she's too distracted to eat her lunch,' she added.

'Sorry,' Donadze said, the nanny's reprimand landing. He gave Eka another kiss then put her back in the high chair. The little girl started crying again. 'I'll be home for bedtime, *chemo gogona*. Be a good girl for Eliso.'

He went to the bedroom and noisily opened and closed drawers as though searching for something, then crossed to the apartment door, not wanting Eka to see him leave. He pulled the door open but hovered by the landing for a moment, listening to the sounds coming from the living room. All he could hear was Eliso singing a nursery rhyme and he shut the door, locked it and took the stairs to his car. He thought the nanny had guessed the real reason he'd returned to the apartment—to check up on her. But his daughter was in good hands, he told himself, thinking of how much he still missed his mother.

FIVE

A young man snapped to attention as Donadze entered the MIR.

'You've met Officer Patarava?' Jaqeli asked.

'Yes, of course,' Donadze said, although he couldn't remember having done so.

'Koka is joining our investigation. He'll be taking calls and helping us with the admin,' Jaqeli said. 'As you requested,' she added as Donadze looked at her blankly.

'I'd guessed that,' he lied. 'Relax, Koka. Take a seat.'

'Thank you, sir,' Patarava said, lowering himself smartly onto a chair to face Donadze, his back straight, legs pressed together.

'Relax, Koka,' Donadze said again, appraising the young officer. He looked about sixteen but was probably in his early twenties, his uniform neatly pressed, his black boots highly polished. 'Your first posting?'

'Yes, sir. I graduated from the Academy in April.'

'Well, congratulations. Has Irina briefed you on this case?'

'Yes, sir. We were discussing it when you came in: Fenrir, the wolf.'

'You know about Norse mythology?'

'A little. I play *God of War* on my PlayStation, that's where I first learned about Fenrir. Then I—'

Patarava paused as one of the desk phones started ringing.

'Take it,' Donadze said. He waited while Patarava spoke to the caller, jotting notes onto a pad.

He thanked the caller and put the handset down. 'Someone who thought he'd seen the victim walking home.'

'Good, we'll talk to him,' Donadze said. 'Did you get his name and address?'

'Yes, sir.' Patarava patted the note pad. 'But the times don't work, unfortunately. He thought he'd seen her on his way into work—but that was after the body had been found.'

Donadze sighed. 'Okay, that's a pity.' A thought occurred to him. 'How did you know when the body was found? You've only been with us for—what—about an hour?'

Patarava pointed to the white board where key dates and times had been recorded. 'From there, sir.'

Donadze nodded. 'That's very observant, Koka,' he said, watching the young man colour. 'You were telling us about your PlayStation.'

'Yes, sir. I'm a gamer, spend too much time on my console, at least that's what my parents say. PlayStation's definitely the best platform. Some people think Xbox is okay but if you want—'

'That's okay, Koka. I agree, PlayStation is best,'

Donadze interrupted, having never played video games on any brand of console. 'What's PlayStation got to do with our investigation?'

'It's where I first heard about Fenrir, sir. He's a character in the *God of War* PlayStation game. Series of games actually. He's an ordinary wolf who dies but is resurrected into a giant hellhound. He's featured in other games like *Assassin's Creed* as well.'

'Instagram's already picked up on the gaming aspect,' Jaqeli said.

'A giant hellhound.' Donadze shook his head. 'That's all we need.' He thought for a moment. 'I've got to go out again. Irina, can you sit with Koka and take a look at this game? Let's see if this Fenrir has any relevance to our investigation.'

'Okay. Where are you going?'

'The morgue. Metreveli's doing Rusiko's autopsy.' He checked his watch. 'In about half an hour and he doesn't like hanging around.' He turned to Patarava. 'Good to have you on the team, Koka. We'll talk later and—'

The desk phone rang again. 'You'd better take it,' Donadze said, standing to leave the room.

❖

'Glad you could make it, Donadze,' Metreveli said. He waved his hand over the autopsy table and the body bag which lay upon it. 'We can start now that the Lieutenant is finally here, Tariel,' he told his technician. 'You may open the bag now.'

'Sorry, Doctor, traffic,' Donadze said, trying and failing to block out the pervasive stench of disinfectant and death.

'Quite,' Metreveli sniffed.

The technician snipped a seal and unzipped the body bag to reveal Rusiko Darsalia's corpse; her clothes and hair matted with dried blood, her face pale, her lips blue, the gaping wound across her neck deep and incongruous.

'How did this young lady arrive here, Lieutenant?' Metreveli asked, then held up his hand to silence Donadze before he could answer. 'Try to get a good view of her neck,' he instructed the technician.

'Yes, Doctor,' Tariel said, crouching in front of the table, his camera angled close to the wound.

'The young lady, Donadze?' Metreveli repeated, impatient now.

'Rusiko Darsalia, Doctor. A twenty year old law student at TSU. Killed whilst walking home.'

'Ah, yes, the *Fenrir* murder.' Metreveli shook his head. 'How tragic.' He waited until the technician had finished taking photographs of the still clothed and unwashed body. 'Let's take a look at her hands now, Tariel.'

The technician removed protective bags from the body's hands.

'Do you think DNA recovery is likely, Lieutenant?' Metreveli asked, as he bent over the table to swab under Rusiko's painted nails.

'I don't know. Let's hope so.'

Metreveli grunted noncommittally and straightened, looking down on the corpse. 'Well, if it's there, we'll find it. Do you wish to examine my patient before we undress her?'

Donadze knew that, beneath Metreveli's gruff exterior, his compassion for his *patients* was sincere, an aspect of the medical examiner's character that he liked. He doubted that he would learn anything new about Rusiko's murder today, although that possibility, however slight was why he had to be here. But there was something else. It wasn't just an obligation, he *wanted* to be here. It was something he didn't fully understand but knew it involved protecting his victims when they could no longer protect themselves, their broken bodies respected and cared for even in death.

He stepped closer to the table and looked along it, crouching and changing his angle of view. 'Can we turn her over?' he asked.

Metreveli nodded his approval. 'Very thorough, Lieutenant. Tariel?'

The technician bent his knees and slid his hands under the body, straightening to turn it on its side.

'That's fine, Tariel,' Donadze said. 'There's nothing there that I can see.'

Metreveli looked at the wall clock. 'We're running late,' he grunted. 'Let's remove her clothing now, Tariel.'

Donadze looked away as the technician cut off the dead girl's clothes, glancing at Metreveli to see him once again nod his approval. 'Yes, someone's daughter,' he murmured.

The body was inspected again. 'No, nothing,' Donadze said.

The technician bagged the soiled clothes as Metreveli took more pictures. 'Let's get this blood washed off,' he said, stepping back from the table.

Tariel picked up a hand held water jet. 'Stand clear, Lieutenant,' he advised, spraying the body, blood washing off it in red and brown streams, a rusty mist floating over the table until Rusiko Darsalia's sad, pale body was fully revealed; cold, soft flesh lying exposed and vulnerable on cold, hard steel.

Donadze once again examined the body and shook his head.

Metreveli sighed. 'Okay, Tariel. Let's prepare our patient for internal investigation.'

The technician raised Rusiko's body while Metreveli slid a rubber block under her back, positioning it so that her arms fell clear of her raised chest.

Donadze grimaced as the medical examiner lifted his scalpel, preparing to make the familiar Y-incision from both shoulders to the sternum and down to the groin for ready access to the body's major organs.

Metreveli paused, looking at Donadze. 'Tariel and I can take it from here, Ramaz,' he said. 'I'll let you know if we find anything.'

Donadze drew his eyes away from the slight form lying on the table, defenceless and about to be sliced open by Metreveli's knife. Too young, too innocent. A familiar anger built inside him. He welcomed it as his friend and his enemy, it would drive him to find the killer, regardless of the personal toll taken. 'No, that's okay, Doctor,' he said. 'I'll stay until you're finished.'

❖

The early summer sun was low in the sky, its rays now subdued but welcome after the morgue's refrigerated chill. Donadze strolled to his car feeling strangely elated, the autopsy reminding him that, whilst death was pervasive, *he* was alive and life was good. He knew the everyday intrusions of city living: dense, slow-moving traffic; jarring, senseless noise and the press of too many people packed into too tight a space would soon return. But—for now—he felt good: still young, fit and able, determined and convinced that he would catch his killer. *Fenrir:* Viking wolf or gamers' hellhound—it didn't matter—his days on the streets were numbered.

Donadze got into his car, the wheel and trim hot to his touch. It was just after five thirty but it had been a long, difficult day and he was tired. He was determined to spend time with his family that evening, to take them for an evening stroll and buy them ice cream. It was a happy thought and he started his engine, rolling down the windows and cranking up the fan to blow out the hot, sticky air.

It was a bad time to travel. Patience, he told himself, trying to preserve his positive mood, already thirty minutes into a journey that should have taken ten. Traffic congestion in Tbilisi had been awful for as long as he could remember. The new roads, underpasses and bridges couldn't accommodate the continuous influx of people into the capital seeking work and a better education for their children, their beat up Soviet vehicles replaced over time by more desirable—and more expensive—Japanese, Korean and European models. The flood of Russians escaping the draft and Putin's war against Ukraine hadn't helped. Everyone wanted a car it seemed, but no one knew where to put them all.

Pekini Avenue was painted red on his route guidance app. Traffic was either slow moving or—more likely—gridlocked and Donadze turned left onto Tashkenti Street, hoping to save a few minutes on the drive. The deviation achieved little and he crept along, bumper-to-bumper, trying not to think of the poisons spluttering from oily exhausts, polluting the still air and choking his lungs.

The graffiti artists were getting bold, he thought, it

wasn't even dark yet. A young man of about eighteen was taping a stencil to a medical centre's brick wall, an aerosol spray poised ready for use on the pavement beside him. Donadze wanted to ignore him, graffiti was everywhere, a tide that couldn't be turned back. But that wasn't his way. He sighed and switched on his hazard lights, stopped his engine and got out of the car, ignoring the horn blasts and gestures of disbelief from the drivers whose lane he'd just blocked.

The young man straightened from his task as Donadze walked towards him, his ID extended.

'*Gamarjoba*,' Donadze said. 'Welcome to Georgia.'

'What?'

'Welcome to Georgia. You *are* Banksy, aren't you? The famous English street artist?'

The young man shuffled his feet. 'No, I'm Irakli. A student.'

'Ah, my mistake. What are you spraying today, Irakli?'

'Who said I'm spraying anything?'

'That aerosol and the stencil does. I've seen your work around the city, haven't I?'

'No, it wasn't me.'

Donadze unrolled the stencil. '*Fuck Russia,*' he read. 'Not exactly subtle, is it?'

'It's not meant to be. It says what it's meant to say.'

'*It says what it's meant to say*? Definitely not Banksy then. But listen, Irakli, if you really want to fuck Russia, why not get yourself a gun and fight the Russians in Ukraine? Why pick on a defenceless wall?'

Irakli shook his head. 'You're funny. Are you going to arrest me or not?'

Donadze smiled at the young man. 'No, I'm not arresting you today. Take that stencil down and get out of here. Don't let me catch you defacing private property again.'

He returned to his car, waving cheerily to a passing driver whose hand gestures suggested that Donadze was insane.

You're not wrong though, Irakli, he thought, starting his engine and resuming his slow drive home. The war in Ukraine was dragging on, tens of thousands killed on both sides. *Fuck Russia.*

SIX

Donadze woke early, his thoughts immediately turning to his investigation. Getting back to sleep would have been impossible and he slipped out of bed.

'Is that you up now?' Tamuna asked, her eyes still closed.

'Yes, I thought I'd get an early start.'

'Fine, but not this early,' she said, turning over. 'Eka will be up soon, she'd love to have breakfast with her father.'

Donadze leant over the bed and kissed the top of her head. 'No problem.'

He straightened and looked down on his wife. He was lucky to have her: a beautiful, intelligent and kind woman, his partner and best friend. Lucky that she was—usually—prepared to endure his long, erratic work patterns, his moods and frustrations whilst working cases. Lucky that she was such a good mother to their daughter, the other love of his life.

'Are you still here?' she mumbled.

'No, you must be dreaming,' he said, leaving the room.

Preparation was everything and he set about getting ready for Eka wakening: making her breakfast and laying out a fresh nappy and clothes, conscious that her nanny would probably change them for something she'd consider more practical.

He'd finished his preparations and was rewarding himself with his first coffee of the day when Eka began crying.

Seeing his daughter in her cot, awake, her tears turning to smiles, arms outstretched to be lifted was always a joy. He picked up the little girl, her chubby arms tight around his neck and carried her to the living room. He sat with her on his lap, father and daughter enjoying the quiet, intimate time together. It couldn't last, of course and she soon remembered her toys, squirming off Donadze's knee and walking—steadily now—to her toy box. She dropped onto her bottom and selected the animals she wanted to play with, their unlucky colleagues tossed nonchalantly over her shoulder. It was an opportunity for Donadze to finish his coffee and he let her play for about ten minutes before picking her up and blowing a raspberry on her tummy. 'Okay, *chemo patara*, let's get that nappy changed now.'

Breakfast was over by the time Tamuna joined them, showered and dressed ready for work. She stifled a yawn. 'Thanks, Ramaz, I needed that.'

'It wasn't very long.'

'Long enough.' She crossed the room to kiss Eka in her high chair then kissed Donadze. 'I've got her now if you need to get away.'

'Okay, thanks.' He returned to their bedroom, ran his electric shaver over his face, showered and dressed then kissed Tamuna and Eka goodbye.

He drove to Mtatsminda Station and parked, entering the building and nodding to the Desk Sergeant. 'Do you have the MIR key, Dato?'

'Your new guy, Patarava has it, Lieutenant. I think he's in there with Irina now.'

'Keen,' Donadze said, noting the time, it was still only seven forty.

Patarava jumped to his feet as Donadze entered the MIR.

'Please stop doing that, Koka,' Donadze said.

'Sir?'

'I appreciate the respect but let's dial it back a little, okay?'

'Yes, sir,' Patarava said, shuffling his feet and looking at Donadze uncertainly.

'You can sit down again. You don't need permission for that.'

Jaqeli was trying not to grin. 'Would you like to see what Fenrir looks like, Ramaz?'

'In the computer games, I assume?'

'Unfortunately, yes. Koka, show Ramaz your video.'

'Ma'am,' Patarava said, picking up a remote control and powering up the MIR's wall-mounted screen.

'It's Irina, remember?' Jaqeli said.

'Yes, sorry, Irina.' Patarava reached for his keyboard and mouse to cast a YouTube video onto the screen. 'I *was* going to bring my PlayStation in...'

'But I told him that wasn't necessary,' Jaqeli said. 'This video covers it.'

Patarava shrugged. 'I searched for this on the Internet.

It's a compilation of all the scenes from *God of War* which have Fenrir in them.'

'Okay, let's see it.'

Patarava clicked the mouse and the video played: stunning graphics of a young boy being told by his father that his pet wolf was going to die. The boy comforted the wolf, whispering something to him as he cradled the dying animal in his arms.

'Atreus is casting a spell,' Patarava explained. 'That's how Fenrir's soul transferred after he died.'

'So this is a true story then?'

Patarava missed the sarcasm. 'No, sir. It's just part of the game.'

The next scene showed the boy and his father approaching a cave where a giant wolf was cowering. The boy recognised the wolf as Fenrir and tells his father, *It's giant magic.*

'That's probably enough, Koka,' Jaqeli said.

'Oh, okay,' Patarava said, pausing the video.

Donadze stood and examined the screen, the boy frozen as he stroked the giant wolf's muzzle. 'So, is *our* Fenrir a gamer?'

'Yes, sir, I think so,' Patarava said.

'Why do you say that?'

'Because your Fenrir—'

'*Our* Fenrir, Koka.'

'Yes, our Fenrir. I think, like me, he came across the character in God of War, or maybe Assassin's Creed and that's what took him to the Norse myth. Thousands, maybe millions of people play these games but not that many are familiar with Norse mythology.' Patarava paused, suddenly embarrassed. 'Well, that's what *I* think, anyway.'

'What do *you* think, Irina?' Donadze asked.

'Koka's right, it was probably the games that first sparked his interest.'

Donadze nodded. 'That seems about right to me as well. Thanks, Koka, that was useful, great work.'

'So,' Jaqeli asked, 'How do we find this game-playing god killer?'

❖

'Koka, could you ask Captain Arziani and Detective Chichua to join us if they're free.'

'Sir,' Patarava said, jumping to his feet.

'What do you have in mind, Ramaz?' Jaqeli asked.

'Fresh eyes. Misha and Soso might help us to see if we're missing anything.'

'That's a new concept for you, isn't it, Ramaz, team working?'

'Is it?' Donadze asked, surprised and a little hurt by her observation.

'Different styles, that's all. You still get results doing things your way.'

Patarava returned with Soso Chichua a moment later, the detective fighting his eternal battle to prevent his oversized trousers slipping down his oversized waist. 'Ramaz, Irina,' he said in greeting, extracting an off-white handkerchief from his pocket to wipe his face and neck. 'You wanted to see me?'

'Yes, take a seat, Soso,' Donadze said. He looked at Patarava expectantly.

'The Captain said he'll join us in five minutes. Do you want me to stay, Lieutenant?'

'You're part of the team, aren't you? Of course I want you to stay.'

'I was just going to get myself a glass of water, Soso. Would you like one?' Jaqeli asked.

Chichua smiled at her. 'Thanks. I hate this time of year. Months of summer to *look forward* to.'

Donadze set the air conditioning lower. 'I want your help with the Fenrir case, Soso,' he said.

'I'd guessed as much. You're under some pressure with this one, aren't you, Ramaz?' It had been two days since Rusiko Darsalia's murder and media interest—traditional and social—hadn't abated. Questions were already being asked about the effectiveness of the police investigation and the likelihood that Fenrir—as he was now widely known—would be caught before he killed again.

Donadze shrugged. 'A little, I suppose.'

Chichua nodded. 'Don't worry, you'll get him.'

'Yes, no doubt about it.'

Jaqeli returned to the MIR with Arziani, giving him a warm smile as he held the door open for her.

Clearly a couple, Donadze thought, knowing they found their situation awkward. 'Thanks, Misha,' he said. 'I hope this won't take up too much of your time.'

'That's okay. It feels good to be doing some real police work for a change.'

Chichua nodded his thanks as Jaqeli handed him his water. 'How do you want to do this, Lieutenant?'

'Informally. Irina will summarise what we know so far. Chip in with any questions or thoughts as we go along. Koka, jot down anything that comes up on that flip chart.'

'Yes, sir.'

'Irina,' Donadze invited Jaqeli to begin.

She paused a moment. 'Okay, Rusiko Darsalia was a

twenty year old student at TSU, killed whilst walking home from a party. Fellow guests were obvious suspects and we identified everyone there. They were all interviewed and dismissed from our enquiries.'

'Are you sure about that?' Arziani asked. 'From what I remember of student parties, things were sometimes a bit fluid: people coming and going, couples disappearing into bedrooms and reappearing later. Plenty of alcohol, drugs. Memories got distorted. Are you sure you got honest accounts from everyone? Is it possible that someone left the party and followed Rusiko without being noticed?'

'We're as sure as we can be, Misha. All the statements were cross-referenced, no one stood out.'

Arziani nodded. 'Okay, that sounds reasonable.'

'So no follow up required there,' Donadze instructed.

'How about boyfriends?' Chichua asked. 'Current or ex?'

'No one current, according to Rusiko's best friend, Nini Tabagari. Some boys in the past but none of them serious…'

'Maybe one of them was more serious than Rusiko realised.'

'What do you think, Irina?' Donadze asked.

'No, that doesn't feel right to me. Rusiko and Fenrir came across each other by chance, he wasn't someone she knew.'

'Yes, I agree, but let's rule that possibility out if we can. Go back to Rusiko's parents and ask them about her boyfriends. There might be something more they can tell us. And get back to Nini Tabagari. Rusiko would be more likely to confide in her than to her parents, especially if she'd been dating a boy they wouldn't have approved of. Ask her if

Rusiko had been seeing anyone she thought was a bit strange. Someone who was overly possessive, perhaps. An acrimonious breakup, maybe. Anything that rang alarm bells for her.'

'Okay, but it still feels like a long shot to me.'

'It probably is,' Donadze agreed. 'This is good though. Let's keep going.'

'Rusiko left the party early to walk home,' Jaqeli continued. 'She told Nini she'd take a taxi but decided to walk.'

'Do we know why?' Chichua asked. 'Could she have agreed to meet someone outside?'

'Well, Nini thought it was to save money…'

'What, five *lari*?'

'Maybe she just wanted fresh air and exercise,' Donadze said. 'In any case, the time between leaving the party and her murder was too short to have met up with anyone first.'

'Yes, it was too tight,' Jaqeli agreed. 'But let me check the timeline again, just to be sure.'

'Okay. Keep going.'

'Rusiko had about four kilometres to walk and was about fifteen minutes from home when she was killed. We think the killer got behind her and cut her throat before dragging her into the alleyway where she bled out and died.' Jaqeli paused as if expecting a challenge. When none came, she continued, 'What struck Ramaz and me most about this killing was how cold it was, almost casual.'

'And—in a sick way—skilful,' Donadze added. 'It's not easy to use a knife that way.'

'A military technique, wasn't it, Ramaz?' Arziani asked.

'Yes, sometimes called a stealth killing. It's how a soldier might take out a sentry, for example. But that doesn't necessarily mean Fenrir is military or ex-military, it could be something he's learned.'

'Have you checked any websites, Lieutenant?' Patarava asked.

'What kind of websites?'

'I don't know the specific sites, sir. But there are people who are fascinated by the military, particularly by special forces like the British SAS or American SEALs. There are sure to be websites set up for people like that, maybe some of them discuss training—including how to kill people quietly. Fenrir could be active on some of these platforms.'

'That's your job then, Koka. Identify these sites and see if anything stands out. If we're lucky and Fenrir was on them posting anonymously it might have been as *Fenrirgeo*. But look for any names with a wolf connection.'

'Like *Lobo* or *G'mork*?'

'Are these wolf names?'

'Yes, sir, real and fictional. I found them on a Google search. *Lobo* is Spanish for *wolf*. He was a real wolf, living in New Mexico in the 1890s. The settlers there tried to kill him but he was smart, avoiding their poisons and their traps. *G'mork* is fictional but he sounds a bit like Fenrir.'

'There's a theme here, isn't there? Wolves too smart to be caught.'

'Yes, Lieutenant, although if it's any consolation, the settlers did catch Lobo eventually and G'mork died in chains.'

'Good, because we *are* going to catch Fenrir and it's going to be soon, not eventually.'

'What if Fenrir *does* have a military background?' Arziani asked.

'We need to follow up on that. Irina, could you check Army records? I'd be interested in anyone discharged from Special Forces in the last ten years, especially if it was a dishonourable discharge.'

'Okay. What about Fenrir's use of social media?' Jaqeli asked. 'Bragging that he's a wolf and the rest of us are sheep. And not just any wolf, a wolf powerful enough to kill a god.'

'Tell Captain Arziani and Soso about Fenrir in *God of War*, Koka,' Donadze said.

'The PlayStation game?' Arziani asked.

'You've played it, sir?'

Arziani smiled, 'No, I used to play Xbox, but I've kind of outgrown it now.'

'Well, there's a giant wolf in God of War called Fenrir.'

'We think our Fenrir might be a gamer, identifying with the wolves in God of War *and* the Norse myth,' Donadze said.

'You said you've outgrown Xbox, Captain?' Chichua asked.

'Yes, different priorities now, I suppose.'

'Would you say gamers tend to be younger, Koka? Say thirty five or less?'

'Most of the gamers I know are about my age but there are still a lot of older people who play.'

'Okay, surprising, I would have guessed it was a young person's thing.'

'So being a gamer doesn't give us any indication of age,' Donadze said.

'No, but he's probably relatively young if he left the Army recently.'

'It depends how long he served. We'll keep it in mind

but not rule anyone out based on age.' Donadze was becoming impatient. 'Is there anything else?'

'No, sir,' Patarava said as Jaqeli shook her head.

'Good. I think that covers it then,' he said. 'Thanks Captain, Soso, plenty there to think about.'

Arziani remained seated. 'Could I have a word with Lieutenant Donadze in private?' he asked.

He waited until the others had left the MIR. 'Don't take this personally, Ramaz. You're the best choice to lead this investigation and I have full confidence in you. But, unless you get lucky, you're not even close to catching Fenrir, are you?'

'It has only been two days, Misha.'

'Yes, but Fenrir's going to kill again. Possibly soon. And you need to be ready for that. I don't have to remind you how Rusiko's murder is already playing out. That can only get worse if someone else dies. You'd have my support and Colonel Meskhi would give you as much cover as he could. But the arm chair experts would come after you. You know that don't you?'

Donadze attempted a smile. 'Well, if I didn't, I do now.'

Arziani didn't return the smile. 'I know how you like to work, Ramaz. But you're not on your own. Come to me if you need help.' He stood and offered Donadze his hand. 'Good luck, Lieutenant,' he said, winking and turning to leave.

'Thanks, Captain,' Donadze said to the MIR's closed door.

SEVEN

Donadze calculated that it had been a year or more since he'd last visited Beka Gabelia, much longer than he'd intended.

'Donadze?' Gabelia said, answering his phone.

'How are you, Sergeant?'

'Just the same as when you last saw me. What can I do for you?'

'I need your help.'

'I'd guessed that, you're not exactly one for social calls, are you? What do you want?'

'You still have your bar?'

'For the moment…'

'You're there now?'

Gabelia sighed. 'Where else would I be?'

'Good, I'll be there in thirty minutes.'

'Can't wait,' Gabelia said, hanging up.

Donadze drove to Kurdiani Street and parked outside *The Squad,* the bar named by Gabelia in honour of the Army units he'd led. Its exterior was tired, the paintwork faded and peeling, spidery cracks feathering across the windows, green mould seeping into the redbrick walls. Much as Donadze remembered from previous visits.

Gabelia had been an inspirational leader and mentor to the young, nervous infantrymen assigned to his squad. He was no businessman though, his bar being run more like a military welfare facility than a profit making enterprise. But it was a safe and reassuring place for serving and former Army personnel to gather, to be with their own kind, to remember old comrades and tell and retell each other their faded tales.

Gabelia had enlisted as a professional soldier and was already an experienced NCO when Russia and Georgia went to war. He'd kept his squad safe throughout the fighting, all his conscripted men eventually returning home. Gabelia had found his own home in the Army and would still have been there if his *Cobra* armoured car hadn't overturned on rough terrain, hitting a tree and taking his leg. After a period of recuperation and drift, he'd used his compensation money to open his bar. It wasn't long before other soldiers found and colonised it.

Donadze almost never socialised in bars but he was grateful to Gabelia and visited him on occasion to check his wellbeing, his visible association with The Squad deterring gangster selling protection, entitled police officers mooching free drinks and government officials fishing for bribes. Donadze didn't expect gratitude and it was never offered.

He pushed open the heavy wooden door and entered the building. It was dark and damp, its painted walls faded and nicotine stained. Prints of famous land battles—ancient and modern—competed for space with framed displays of medals, recruitment posters, cap badges and other military memorabilia. Green plastic-covered benches lined the walls with small tables and hard wooden chairs placed opposite them. Six or seven customers were seated at the tables drinking vodka shots with beer chasers. Most turned to stare at Donadze, the police not welcome here.

Gabelia was polishing glasses with a grubby dish towel. 'Lieutenant Donadze,' he said, nodding in greeting.

Gabelia had been a young man when Donadze had served with him and he was now in his early forties. He had never married or had children and had never mentioned other family members. He was short and as lean as he'd been in his Army days, his face gaunt and hungry looking with sunken cheek bones and short, dark, greasy hair. He was wearing shapeless blue jeans and a loose fitting olive green T-shirt, his wiry arms decorated with fading tattoos. Gabelia had been both respected and feared by the soldiers in his squad and Donadze knew that, despite losing a leg, he was still a hard, dangerous man.

'Sergeant Gabelia…' he returned the greeting.

'It's been a while, Ramaz.'

'Yes, it has. Sorry.'

'No need to be.'

'How's business?'

Gabelia gestured towards his few customers. 'How do you think?'

Donadze nodded. 'Can we talk?'

'Sasha,' Gabelia said, barely raising his voice.

A middle aged man looked up from his beer glass.

'Look after the place, I'll be in the backroom.' He gave

the glass he'd been holding a final polish, held it to the dim light then returned it to its shelf, dropping the dish towel onto the bar. 'This way,' he said, walking stiffly on his prosthetic leg.

Gabelia lived in the backroom. It too was dark and damp with the feral tang of the undomesticated man who occupied it, its only natural light and ventilation coming from a single window above a narrow door which provided access to the outside lane. The kitchen area consisted of a cracked and stained ceramic sink and a small electric hot plate. His bed, a military style cot, made up with a sleeping bag and a grimy pillow was pushed against a wall.

'Sit down,' Gabelia said, pointing to a small table with two wooden chairs. 'Do you want a drink? Coffee?'

Donadze was reluctant to drink anything prepared in that room but accepted a coffee.

Gabelia made the drinks and placed two chipped mugs on the table, lowering himself carefully onto the free chair. 'So, what can I do for you, Ramaz?'

'I'm going to show you some photos. They're not easy to look at,' he warned, taking a folder from his backpack. He showed Gabelia the photo Rusiko Darsalia's parents had given to him, a young girl dressed for a night out with friends: beautiful and full of life. 'This is Rusiko. She was nineteen when this was taken, a year after starting university.'

Gabelia reached to take the photo, examined it then nodded and handed it back.

'And this is Rusiko a year later,' Donadze said, showing him a picture of the girl taken at the crime scene, her body lying in a pool of blood in the squalid alley where she'd died.

Donadze gave Gabelia time to absorb the image, watching his mouth tighten. He took it back and handed him a photo of Rusiko's body in the morgue as it was about to go under Metreveli's knife.

'Her neck…' Gabelia said, his fingers on the image.

'Yes.'

'The man you're calling *Fenrir*?'

'Yes.'

'A soldier?'

'Maybe.'

'You think it's someone *I* know?'

'It could be. Or it could be someone one of your customers knows.'

Gabelia took a last look at the photo, shook his head then handed it back to Donadze. 'I'll ask around,' he said.

❖

Jaqeli and Patarava were in the MIR, waiting for Donadze as he'd instructed.

'Okay,' he said, dropping onto a chair. 'What have you got for me?'

'I checked the timeline to see if Rusiko could have met with someone after leaving the party,' Jaqeli said. 'And it's confirmed, she couldn't have, there just wasn't enough time.'

'What about ex-boyfriends then, anything there?'

'Unfortunately not. I spoke to Rusiko's mother again. She was only aware of one serious boyfriend, someone Rusiko had been to school with. They'd been together for nearly two years but split on good terms when he left Tbilisi to work in Switzerland. He was close to the family and phoned Mrs Darsalia when he heard the news, promised he'd be home for the funeral. So nothing there, at least not from Mrs Darsalia.'

'But from Nini Tabagari?'

'As you thought, Ramaz. Rusiko didn't share everything with her parents but she did share with her best friend. Nini told me Rusiko had had a few casual relationships after splitting with her boyfriend. But there was nothing creepy about any of them, no one she was worried about.'

'So you're confident we can rule out ex-boyfriends?'

'Yes, and given the way she was killed, that was always a long shot anyway. No, this confirms what we always thought, Rusiko and Fenrir came across each other by chance. They weren't known to each other.'

'Okay, well it was worth checking out. What about the military angle?'

'Not so clear, unfortunately. I've been promised a file with the names of all Army personnel discharged over the last ten years—but that's more than sixteen thousand individuals, most of them men.'

'That's a lot but we're mostly interested in soldiers discharged from Special Ops, especially anyone dishonourably discharged.'

'Yes, and that's where the Ministry of Defence gets a little coy. They won't even say how many men serve in Special Ops, let alone give us the names of any who have been discharged, honourably or otherwise.'

'We could force the issue, couldn't we?'

'Maybe, but it would take time.'

'I'll speak to Meskhi if that becomes necessary, see if there's anything he can do.' He turned to Patarava. 'You were looking at websites, Koka…'

'Yes, sir, there are plenty of military sites, lots with an interest in Special Ops, including their fighting—and killing—techniques.'

'Techniques like killing with a knife?'

'Definitely, even videos by retired soldiers demonstrating how to *take out* sentries. Some of it's pretty gruesome.'

'It'd be too much to expect Fenrir to be posting on these sites?'

'There was nothing from anyone called *Fenrir* or *Fenrirgeo* that I could see. And no obvious wolf names either. But I'll keep looking.'

'Okay, do that.'

'How did you get on, Ramaz?' Jaqeli asked.

'With Beka Gabelia? He's got his ear to the ground and he'll help if he can. He's a strange man but he does have a strong sense of right and wrong. He recognised Rusiko's neck wound for what it was and I could tell he was angry that a fellow soldier might have done that. He would see it as dishonourable, I think. Bringing shame on the Army.'

'Getting his help would certainly be quicker than extracting information from the Ministry of Defence.'

'Yes, it would.'

'It doesn't feel like we've achieved much,' Jaqeli said.

Donadze shook his head. 'It's early days, Irina. Fenrir's still out there but we'll find him, I'm sure of it.'

Levan's here. When will you be home? Tamuna's message read.

Donadze glanced at the bureau's wall clock, it was almost seven and the worst of the traffic should have been over by now. *Thirty minutes*, he replied.

An accident had closed Kostava Street in one direction and his journey took twenty minutes longer than expected.

He left his car in the underground car park and took the elevator to the fourth level, yawning deeply. He was pleased that his friend and mentor, retired police officer, Major Levan Gloveli had come to visit but Gloveli rarely made purely social calls and Donadze knew something was on his mind.

The welcoming aroma of Tamuna's cooking met him at the apartment door. The meal was ready and she was placing dishes on the breakfast bar. Gloveli was sitting on the settee with Eka, his goddaughter, already in her pyjamas and clutching her favourite bedtime toy, on his knee. Both were engrossed in a cartoon featuring singing ducklings.

'*Gamarjoba*, Major,' Donadze said. 'So, Veronika's finally thrown you out?' Veronika Boyko was a twenty one year old Ukrainian who'd been a material witness in one of Donadze's investigations. Agreeing to give testimony had put her life at risk and he'd placed her under Gloveli's protection, staying with him in his home in the village of Shindisi. She'd met Lasha there and they'd married in Georgia due to the ongoing war between Russia and her home country. Gloveli had become extremely fond of the young woman and, having no children of his own, had signed over ownership of his house to the couple. The arrangement worked well, Donadze thought as Veronika and Lasha had a home of their own and Gloveli continued to live with them, enjoying their company and receiving the support he needed as he got older.

Gloveli shook his head. 'Is he always this irritating?'

'Yes, always,' Tamuna said.

Eka had seen and heard enough of the ducklings and squirmed off Gloveli's knee, running to her father, her arms outstretched, demanding to be picked up. Donadze lifted her and blew a raspberry on her neck, the little girl tucking her head in to stop him but still squealing with delight.

'It's past this girl's bedtime, Ramaz,' Tamuna admonished. 'Don't get her too excited.'

'Oops,' Donadze said, winking at his friend.

'The food's ready, you can start.'

Donadze gave his daughter a kiss, whispered something in her ear and passed her to her mother.

'We'll wait for you, Tamuna,' Gloveli said.

'It's okay, go ahead. I know you have things to discuss.'

Gloveli rose stiffly to his feet and leaned forward to receive a good night kiss from his goddaughter.

'Are you okay on these stools, Major?' Donadze asked, watching the old policeman limp to the breakfast bar.

'Fine, I'm just a bit stiff from sitting too long. Let's have some wine.'

The wine had been made by Gloveli from grapes grown in his garden. Donadze opened the re-purposed plastic water bottle and filled two glasses. Gloveli lifted his glass and held it to the light. Satisfied, he swirled it and held it under his nose, inhaling deeply before nodding his approval. '*Gaumarjos*,' he saluted, gulping down a generous mouthful.

'*Gaumarjos*,' Donadze responded, sipping from his own glass. He placed plates containing cheese, salad and freshly baked *khachapuri* in front of Gloveli.

'So, you have a new case,' he said, lifting a slice of the cheesy bread.

'Yes, quite nasty, as I'm sure you've heard,' Donadze said, always amazed by how well informed Gloveli still was.

'Well, people tell me things.' He smiled. 'It's because I'm so approachable.'

'I'm sure that's the reason, Major,' Donadze said, deadpan.

'This psychopath, what is it the media call him? Fenrir?'

Donadze shrugged. 'Yes, Fenrir. It's caught on, we call him that as well now.'

'You know how this could turn out, don't you, Ramaz? Catch Fenrir and you're a hero, don't and they'll hang you out to dry.'

'Is that why you're here, Major? To warn me?'

Gloveli finished selecting his cheese and salad and pushed the plates back to Donadze. 'No, of course not, you already know that without me telling you. But I'm always available if you want to talk about it.'

'Yes, I know you are. And I appreciate it.' Donadze paused. 'So why *are* you here?'

Gloveli filled their glasses. 'To make you an offer. A friend of mine, someone I've known from the old days wants to retire. His company told him to find a replacement before they'll let him go.'

Donadze knew that the *old days* was a reference to Gloveli's service in the KGB when Georgia was still a Soviet republic, something he was now coy about admitting to.

'And your friend thinks I could be his replacement?'

'No, *I* do. He asked if there's anyone I would recommend for the job. I said there is but I didn't tell him it's you. And I won't put your name forward unless you want me to.'

Donadze took a sip of his wine. 'What's the job, Major?'

'Security manager at the Tbilisi Grand Hotel.'

'I don't know anything about hotels.'

'No one's asking you to clean rooms or serve meals. But you do know about fraud, theft, vetting staff, gambling, dealing with rowdy customers. You could do all of that easily enough.'

'Okay, you're right, I could. But so could just about any police officer. Why me?'

'I wouldn't recommend *any* police officer, it's my reputation I'm thinking about as well. Anyway, you should consider it. It'd be office hours and nearly double your police salary.'

Donadze nodded. 'It would certainly get me out from under Meskhi.'

'What's Meskhi got to do with it?'

'It just feels like I'm going nowhere with him looking over my shoulder.'

'Promotion, you mean. You haven't exactly made it easy for him, have you?'

'Maybe not.'

Gloveli refilled their glasses again. 'Think about it, talk it over with Tamuna, let me know what you decide.'

'Okay, I will. Thanks for thinking of me.'

Gloveli took a sip from his glass, appraising the younger man. 'You've no intention of taking this job, have you?'

'None whatsoever.'

'That's what I thought,' Gloveli sighed, stabbing a chunk of cheese with his fork.

EIGHT

'Do we have to?' Connor asked, looking at the line of hopefuls desperate to get passed the doorman and into The Bridge, the best nightclub in Tbilisi, according to Dea.

She gave him her best smile, the one she knew he couldn't resist. 'Come on, it's early. You'll love it.'

'It's *not* early. One o'clock in the morning *isn't* early.' Connor took out his phone. 'Actually, it's nearly one thirty,' he sighed, taking her hand and offering only token resistance as she dragged him across the road.

'Don't worry, this place is really popular, we probably won't even get in,' she assured him.

'So why are we even trying?'

He patted his pocket for the hundredth time that evening. The ring was still there, of course. He'd intended proposing over dinner but hadn't found the courage, worried that she would say no and even more worried that his proposal would scare her off, that he'd lose her completely. He knew that asking her to marry him this early in their relationship was crazy. They'd only met four months ago, a ridiculously short period of time to choose the girl you wanted to spend the rest of your life with. Even if that girl was as gorgeous as Dea Lapachi.

'What?' she asked, her smile curious.

The air blanketing Tbilisi was still warm and dank and he pushed his mousy-blond hair off his damp forehead. 'It doesn't matter,' he said, deciding to keep the ring in his pocket for another night.

She took his arm and led him to the back of the queue, smiling artfully at the doorman as they passed the club's entrance.

The doorman returned her smile.

We'll definitely get in, Connor realised.

It took twenty minutes to reach the front of the queue. The doorman looked Connor up and down, clearly not happy with what he saw but Dea said something to him and he laughed, stepping aside to let them enter.

The heat and the noise inside the concrete structure hit them like a wave.

'Come on,' Dea shouted into Connor's ear. 'Let's dance.'

She took his hand and they merged into the mass of clubbers on the dance floor. Moving in time with the music, she slipped her arms around his neck and pulled him close. 'Didn't I say it'd be great?'

Connor kissed her. '*You're* great,' he said.

Dea shook her head, unable to hear him over the pounding beat.

'Nothing,' he mouthed.

Mesmerised by the music, he lost track of time but Dea eventually cupped her hands and shouted into his ear, 'Come on, we'd better go.'

'Are you sure? We could stay a bit longer if you want,' he shouted back.

She shook her head and mumbled into his shoulder, 'Do you know how much I love you, Connor MacLeod?' She kissed him again then took his hand and led him off the dance floor and out of the club, smiling at the doorman as they passed.

The Syrian was a patient man, he had to be. He'd stalked the couple all evening, following them from restaurant to bar to club. He didn't know who the girl was, but that didn't matter, she would have to die with MacLeod. He tugged his cap lower on his head, at one with the still, sparse trees in whose shadows he waited, his time would come soon.

He watched the couple cross the wide road to the river embankment, MacLeod holding the girl tight. *They're in love*, he realised. The Syrian didn't know how that felt; he'd never loved anyone, although he could easily imitate the emotion. Something he'd found useful in the past. He crossed the road and fell in behind them as they continued walking along the embankment, their happy laughter and the gurgling of the river mingling in the still air.

The couple stopped a few minutes later and the Syrian also stopped, removing his phone. He murmured nonsense into the device while he watched and waited. MacLeod was trying to persuade the girl to come home with him. He didn't succeed and she gave him a last kiss before running across the road, turning to wave before continuing up a side street.

So, it's just you then, Connor, the Syrian thought, grateful that his task had become simpler.

MacLeod resumed walking. There was no one else on the embankment and the Syrian picked up his pace, closing the distance to his target. It had been a long night and there was more to do. He picked his spot, close to a park in a shadowed area halfway between the ornate lamps which lined the walkway. He felt a familiar, almost sexual thrill as he removed the switchblade from his pocket, caressing its polished-horn handle. It was Italian, a beautiful weapon. He pressed the release button, the blade springing out and locking with an exquisitely engineered *snick.*

He moved closer to MacLeod as he entered the shadows.

MacLeod heard footsteps and half turned, surprised but not yet alarmed. He nodded to the Syrian and had started to speak before his mouth was covered and his head jerked back, his pupils dilating with terror, his neck exposed. The razor-sharp blade slashed, deep and savage across his neck, blood immediately spurting from his severed carotid artery. The Syrian eased MacLeod onto the low concrete wall by the river's edge. He bent and lifted his legs, sending him—not yet dead—over the wall and into the mud and shallow waters below.

The Syrian looked at the knife wistfully for a moment then threw it into the fast flowing river. He leaned over the wall but could barely see the body below. He briefly wondered how the girl would feel when she learned the man she'd loved was dead. But then he shrugged and walked briskly away. He really didn't care.

NINE

Donadze's phone buzzed him awake. He forced his eyes open and lifted the device, carrying it out of the bedroom. 'Soso,' he croaked.

'*Gamarjoba*, Lieutenant,' Chichua said. He paused a moment. 'Sorry, I've just come up a fire ladder, not something I'm built for.'

Donadze didn't ask for an explanation, knowing Chichua would explain his fire ladder remark in his own time.

'That's okay, Soso. Catch your breath.'

Donadze grimaced and held his phone away from his ear as Chichua coughed and spluttered.

'That's better,' he continued. 'I'm on the East bank of the river, Ramaz. We've got another body to deal with, a foreigner this time, British.'

Donadze guessed what Chichua was going to tell him next. 'You think it was Fenrir.'

'Yes, I think so...'

'Do you have a name?'

'Connor MacLeod, male, twenty eight years old.'

Donadze thought Chichua had mispronounced the victim's surname. 'Do you mean Connor *MacLeod?* As in the Highlander movie?'

'I've not seen that movie, Lieutenant.'

'Never mind. You said you're on the East bank?'

'Yes, near Gotua Park. It looks like the victim was attacked on the walkway and pushed over the wall into the mud. Luckily the water level's low so the body's not been washed downriver. But it's still not that easy to get to.'

'And that's why you asked the Fire Department to rig a ladder for you?' Donadze guessed.

'That's right.'

'Have we identified the next of kin?'

'Not yet. I was hoping Irina would contact the British Embassy and get them to help.'

'Have you called her?'

'No, you were first on my list.'

'That's okay, I'll do it.' He hesitated. 'You didn't tell me why you think it's Fenrir.'

Chichua tried to pronounce the dead man's surname then gave up. '*Connor* had his throat cut, Ramaz.'

Donadze sighed. 'That certainly sounds like Fenrir. Okay, stay where you are.' He glanced at the wall clock. 'I'll be with you in thirty minutes.'

He returned to the bedroom where Tamuna was awake and sitting up on their bed. 'Another one?' she asked.

'Yes.'

'Is it the same killer?'

'It could be, probably is.'

'Ramaz…'

He paused while pulling fresh clothes from his drawer. 'What?'

'I know this investigation is important to you. But try to remember, it's not everything.'

'What do you mean?'

'Your family—Eka and me. Work's important but it's still only work.' She reached across the bed to take his hand. 'Don't let it take over everything else in your life.'

'You know I'd never do that.'

'I hope not.' She squeezed his hand then held it to her mouth for a moment. 'Be careful,' she said.

Donadze nodded then returned to the living room, pulling on his clothes as he called Jaqeli.

'Yes, Ramaz?'

'I'll pick you up in fifteen minutes. We've got another murder, a young man this time, British. And his throat's been cut.'

Jaqeli paused a moment. 'That sounds like—'

'Yes, it does,' Donadze said. 'See you in fifteen minutes.'

❖

Jaqeli and Arziani were waiting for Donadze outside their apartment block.

'Hey, Misha, Irina,' he said, as he pulled up alongside them.

'Ramaz,' Arziani greeted him. 'So, two now?'

'Looks that way, but a foreigner this time.'

'Yes, I heard. British.' Arziani looked thoughtful. 'That's going to complicate things.'

'It shouldn't.'

'I know it shouldn't—but it will.'

'Yes, you're right,' Donadze acknowledged. He looked at Jaqeli. 'Ready, Irina?'

'Always,' she said, getting into the car.

It was a short drive to President Heydar Aliyev Embankment, named in honour of a former president of Azerbaijan, a neighbouring country and the source of significant government income from the oil and gas pipelines which traversed both countries, the new *Silk Road*.

Donadze and Jaqeli parked behind a patrol car. Traffic was already backing up along the two lanes the police had left open and irritated drivers edged forward, pointlessly sounding their horns and turning to glare and gesture at the uniformed officers who stood stoically behind the barriers, ignoring the abuse.

Too many cars in this city, Donadze thought as he got out of his own, admitting to himself how reluctant he'd be to give it up.

He paused and assessed the immediate geography as Jaqeli walked towards Chichua. The area was familiar to him. It was daylight now but he pictured how it would have looked during the early hours of the morning: the street lighting dim, little traffic on the road, the walkway hidden in deep shadows. Gotua Park was about thirty metres on the other side of the road. He thought about the drunks who occupied its benches overnight, swigging cheap wine and vodka, their memories unreliable even if they could be tracked down and persuaded to talk. All in all, a good place to commit murder, he concluded.

Donadze ducked under the police barrier. Jaqeli and Soso Chichua were standing by the embankment's low wall looking down on the river's edge three metres below. A body was lying in the grey mud, its head unnaturally twisted, a deep, brutal gash across its neck. There was little blood, most of it having been washed away by the trickling rivulets, with only small pools of reddish, brown water remaining.

Natia Gagua was bent over the body. 'Hey, Natia,' he said, raising his voice over the churning, grumbling river. 'Don't you ever take a day off?'

She looked up and smiled. 'I could say the same to you, Ramaz,' she said, for once deciding not to torment him. 'We'll be finished here soon.'

A fireman whom Donadze recognised from an earlier investigation stood by the ladder he'd rigged to provide access to the river bank. Two wooden pallets had been placed in the mud at the foot of the ladder to afford a stable landing area and relatively dry access to the body. He searched his memory for the fireman's name. 'Good of you to help us, Giorgi,' he said.

The fireman seemed pleased to have been remembered. 'No problem at all, Lieutenant.'

Donadze turned to Chichua. 'Any ID, Soso?' he asked.

Chichua took an evidence bag from his backpack. 'Yes, this. A British driving licence.'

Donadze examined the plastic card through the bag, noting MacLeod's fuzzy image, his date of birth and his home address in Perth, Scotland. 'And that's definitely MacLeod's body down there?'

'No doubt at all, Lieutenant.'

Donadze returned the bag to Chichua. 'Who found him?'

'A runner. He noticed blood on the wall and stopped to

take a look.' Chichua paused. 'There's something else you should see, Ramaz.' He removed another evidence bag and showed Donadze a small jewellers box. He prised the box open inside the bag to reveal a diamond ring on a mud-stained, satin mount. 'Natia found it in Connor's pocket.'

Donadze remembered carrying Tamuna's engagement ring for weeks before she'd finally agreed to marry him. 'At least he had someone special in his life,' he said. He placed his hand on Chichua's shoulder. 'Okay, Soso, good work. Irina and I can take it from here. Get some rest.'

Chichua yawned. 'Sounds good,' he said, hitching his trousers and walking to his car.

Donadze turned to Jaqeli. 'After we've inspected the body, contact the British Embassy. Tell them one of their citizens, Connor MacLeod has been murdered but don't go into too many details at this point.'

'Do you want me to phone them?'

'Better go in person. Try to find someone who knew him. See if they can tell you how long he's been in Georgia and what he's been doing here.'

'Okay.'

'The girl he was going to propose to might get in touch when she doesn't hear from him. It's possible she was with him last night and can tell us what their movements were.'

'You realise it's possible he did propose but the girl turned him down and that's why the ring was still in his pocket?'

Donadze hadn't considered that scenario and he hoped MacLeod had been spared the pain and disappointment that such a refusal would have caused. 'Well, let's find the girl and ask her,' he said.

The fireman had been listening to their conversation. 'Connor MacLeod,' he said. 'Wasn't he that guy in the movie? *Highlander*? An *Immortal*, someone who couldn't be killed?' He shook his head. 'That's kind of ironic, isn't it?'

'I don't know what you're talking about,' Donadze lied.

Gagua left the body and climbed the ladder, smiling at the fireman as he took her hand to steady her. '*Madloba,* Giorgi.'

'How are things looking down there, Natia?' Donadze asked.

Gagua shrugged. 'Very much like Rusiko Darsalia. A deep cut by a very sharp knife, severing the carotid artery and crushing the larynx.'

'Was his head held back?'

'Almost certainly. And like Rusiko, one deep cut, angled upwards. What was it you called it, a stealth killing?'

'Yes, a special forces technique. Can we look at the body now?'

'Go ahead.' She smiled at the fireman again. 'Giorgi and his friends will help bring the victim up when you're done.'

Donadze looked down on the body. 'Are you okay on that ladder, Irina?'

'Why wouldn't I be?'

'After you then.'

He waited until Jaqeli had stepped onto the pallets before following her down.

The body was slim, average height and with fair hair, dressed in tight blue jeans and a T-shirt which had once been white.

'Not really much more to see, Ramaz,' Jaqeli said after a while.

'No, you can go to the Embassy now. I'll see you back at the station.'

Donadze stepped to the side, allowing Jaqeli access to the ladder. He watched the river flowing a few metres beyond the shallows where the body had been dumped, the water rapid, tumbling over exposed rocks, occasional items of flotsam and jetsam washing downstream. He knelt on one knee, ignoring the wet mud which clung to the pallet's wooden slats and stared into MacLeod's face, his hair matted, eyes open but sightless, the gash on his neck deep and ugly. He placed a gloved hand on the dead man's cold, damp head and promised him he would find his killer.

❖

Donadze had anticipated Meskhi's call. '*Gamarjoba*, Colonel,' he said.

'You're still at the crime scene?' Meskhi asked, skipping any pleasantries.

'Yes, sir.'

'And *Connor MacLeod*,' Meskhi said, his pronunciation perfect, 'was killed in the same way as your other victim?'

'Yes, the same military technique.'

'*Technique*? Be careful with your choice of language, Lieutenant. You're describing how a murderer kills his victims, not how an artist applies paint to canvas.'

Donadze took a moment to answer. 'Yes, sir,' he said, eventually, thinking Meskhi's reprimand had been petty.

'You're not convinced, are you, Lieutenant? Well, that's no concern of mine. How soon can you get to my office?'

Donadze looked over the wall to the river bank where Giorgi and his firefighter colleagues were doing their best to dislodge MacLeod's body from the sticky mud. There was little more for him to do here but he wanted time to think before meeting Meskhi. 'We're not quite finished, Colonel,' he said. 'I need about an hour.'

'Very well. Ten o'clock then,' Meskhi said, ending the call.

Donadze took his phone from his ear and looked at it for a moment before slipping it back into his pocket.

Natia Gagua caught his expression. 'Trouble with the boss, Ramaz?' she asked, smiling.

'Kind of. Can you send me your interim report when you have it?'

'Will do, but there won't be much in it that you don't already know.'

'I'm sure that's right but we've got to go through the motions, haven't we?'

Donadze rubbed his chin, he hadn't shaved and his stubble, unlike Misha Arziani's, never looked trendy. He attempted to remove river mud from his trousers but it was still wet and rubbing it only made the staining worse. His shoes were filthy. He considered using the time available to return to his apartment to shave and change his clothes but decided against it. *This is what policing looks like,* he thought. *Too bad if Meskhi doesn't like it.* He returned to his car and started the engine—he intended buying himself a coffee before meeting the Colonel.

Three quarters of an hour later and with caffeine and sugar kicking in, Donadze drove to the Ministry of Internal Affairs' HQ and parked. He crossed to the building and made his way to Meshki's office. The door was closed. He checked the time, he was ten minutes late. He knocked on the door and listened for the faint instruction to enter.

Meskhi and Misha Arziani were sitting on either side of Meskhi's desk. 'You should have been here by ten, Lieutenant,' he said, his face reflecting his disapproval of Donadze's dishevelled appearance.

Donadze chose not to apologise. 'Yes, sir. The crime scene was difficult, I got here as soon as I could.' He crossed the room—noting Arziani's conspiratorial wink—and took a seat.

Meskhi appraised him for a moment before speaking. 'Well, you're here now,' he said. 'I asked Captain Arziani to join us as this matter concerns both of you. But let's discuss this latest killing first. What do we know about Connor MacLeod?'

'Not much at the moment, sir. He was a British citizen from a city called Perth in Scotland. Detective Jaqeli is at the British Embassy now. We should have more information when she returns. There is one thing though, we found an engagement ring in his pocket. Someone will be looking for him.'

Meskhi shook his head. 'Well, that's quite sad.' He paused a moment. 'But at least this lady might be able to shed some light on why the killer chose MacLeod.'

'If there was a reason. He may have been chosen at random.'

'Yes, that's possible, of course. Nothing on Instagram from Fenrir?'

'Not yet, Colonel.'

'But MacLeod's murder is on Instagram and there's plenty of chat about it already,' Arziani said.

Meskhi shook his head again. 'Not surprising, is it? The slaughter of a young woman and a young man in our capital city, the same brutal method employed. Everyone's at risk and the police are no further forward in catching this god killer. You would have to question their competence, wouldn't you?'

'That's pretty much what's being said, Colonel.'

'Then we have to change that unfortunate perception.'

'Yes, sir. But we're going to need additional resources to do that.'

'You're right, Captain. But we also need a different approach.' Meskhi turned to Donadze. 'You'll remember we discussed my intention to fight criminality using, what I termed, *unconventional means*?'

Donadze had guessed this was the reason for being summoned to Meskhi's office. 'Yes, sir,' he said.

'It's something I've wanted to do for some time now. It's been too difficult up to this point but circumstances have changed and I believe the time is now right.'

Donadze nodded. 'Yes, sir. I agree.'

'I'm glad you concur, Lieutenant,' Meskhi said dryly. He turned to Arziani. 'I'm setting up a special unit with immediate effect. Donadze will lead it. He and his team will continue to work out of Mtatsminda Station. You will have oversight of their activities and will provide support as required—but Donadze will report directly to me. Questions?'

Arziani cleared his throat. 'Fighting criminality using *unconventional means*, sir,' he said. 'What exactly does that entail?'

'This unit will work within the law, of course. But there will always be grey areas which Donadze has a gift for finding and exploiting. You and he have worked together for some time now, I'm sure you can think of examples.'

Arziani nodded thoughtfully. 'Yes, sir. But why do we need a *special unit?*'

'To provide focus. And because I don't want any of this coming back on you. That's why Donadze will report to me. It's my job to handle the politics, the politicians and the public's unrealistic expectations and let you both get on with your work.'

'You mentioned my team, Colonel,' Donadze said. 'Do I get to choose who's in it?'

'No. You already have Officer Patarava providing admin support. I'm assigning you one additional detective. I'll speak to him later today and let you know if he accepts my offer. Your other team member is Detective Jaqeli.'

'No, sir, that won't work.' Donadze glanced at Arziani. 'Irina is one of the best but she wouldn't be happy in that role. She'd rather be assigned somewhere else.'

'And you know that how, Lieutenant?'

'The cases we've already worked together, sir. The grey areas you mentioned, she's not happy in them.'

'And that's one of the reasons I want her on your team. As I said, we'll be working within the law and you, Donadze need a moderating influence. Jaqeli will provide that.'

'But—'

'Let me make this easy for you, Lieutenant. Speak to Jaqeli, explain what I want you to do and let her decide if she wants to be part of it or not. Anything else?'

'Colonel,' Arziani said, his tone tentative. 'There's something I should tell you. Detective Jaqeli and I—'

'Are engaged. Yes, I'm aware, Captain. This has nothing to do with your awkward predicament—which I expect you to resolve soon. No, I want Jaqeli in the team because she's most suited for that role.' Meskhi looked at his wall clock. 'Anything else?'

'No, sir.'

'Nothing, Colonel.'

'Good.' Meskhi reached for his keyboard and hit a button to waken his screen. 'You may return to your work, gentlemen,' he said.

TEN

'*Unconventional means,* Ramaz?' Arziani said as they took the elevator to ground level. 'That sounds like *The Untouchables* to me.'

'And that would make me Eliot Ness? Well, it's a great movie and people do say I look a bit like a young Kevin Costner.'

Arziani glanced at Donadze and shook his head. 'No, I'm not seeing it,' he said.

The elevator door opened and they dropped off their passes and left the building, walking in silence across the parking area.

Donadze thought Arziani had something on his mind. 'You're worried about Irina?' he asked.

Arziani didn't immediately reply. 'I know I shouldn't be but yes, I am. She'll want to be on your team, Ramaz. Colonel Meskhi knew that—I do as well.'

They stopped beside Arziani's car. 'I can try to talk her out of it, if that's what you want.'

'No, don't do that. Just give her an honest assessment of what she's committing to and let her make up her own mind.'

'Do you want to discuss it with her first?'

'No, I can't. I'm her commanding officer, I can't interfere. In any event, it wouldn't make any difference. Just, you know…'

'It's going to be okay, Misha. I've got my own family to think about—we won't be taking any unnecessary risks.'

Arziani grinned. 'Good, that's what I wanted to hear. And this conversation…'

'Never happened.'

'We should probably drop that *Untouchables* joke.'

'What joke is that?'

'Right.' Arziani drummed his fingers on the roof of his car. 'Tell me, Ramaz,' he said. 'Did you deliberately set out to antagonise Meskhi just now?'

'Not really.'

'*Not really*? So it *was* intentional. And he was abrupt with *you*. What's going on?'

'It's nothing, just a personality thing.'

'Another personality thing? Listen, be careful, Ramaz. If you get into a fight with Meskhi, you're the one who's going to lose.'

'I know, Irina told me the same thing.'

'You should listen to her.'

'I do, Misha. Most of the time. When you get back to the station, tell her I'll be there in about an hour. Ask her to check social media for anything on MacLeod. Maybe Fenrir's posted something by now.'

'Where are you going?'

Donadze held out his hands, suggesting the answer was obvious. Most of the river mud had dried and fallen off his shoes, either in Meskhi's office or in the MIA's corridors but his trousers were filthy and his stubble was itching. 'To get cleaned up,' he said.

He drove back to his apartment, the dank stench of the river still in his nostrils.

Eka and her nanny were waiting on the other side of the elevator door when he reached the fourth level. Eka was in her buggy, a blanket tucked tightly around her even though it was nearly thirty degrees outside.

'Oh, Lieutenant,' Eliso said, surprised. Her eyes were red and puffy. 'I was just taking the little one to the park. She needs to get out of the apartment and run around in the fresh air for a while.'

Donadze placed his hand on his daughter's tummy to signal that she couldn't get out of the buggy. 'Is everything okay, Eliso?' he asked.

She put a hand to her face. 'Of course, it's just this time of year. Everything's so dusty and it affects my eyes. I'll take something for it later.'

'Are you sure there's nothing wrong?'

'Yes, I'm completely fine.' She pressed the elevator call button and the door opened. 'I'd better get this little girl to the park. Say goodbye to Daddy, Eka.'

Donadze leaned over and kissed his protesting daughter. He held the elevator door open while Eliso manoeuvred the buggy inside. He watched the door as it closed, not believing the nanny's explanation. *What's going on, Eliso?* he thought.

❖

'How were the Brits?' Donadze asked as he entered the MIR, noting Patarava resisting an urge to jump to his feet.

'Concerned,' Jaqeli said. 'Have you heard of someone called Rory MacLeod?'

'No, but I'm guessing he's related to Connor.'

'His father. He's also a senior minister in the UK government—the Home Secretary.'

Donadze pulled a chair alongside Jaqeli and sat down. 'That doesn't sound very senior to me.'

'It is, though. One of the top four political jobs in the United Kingdom.' She pointed to her screen which displayed an image of a man standing behind a podium, a digital representation of the British flag behind him. 'That's him.'

Donadze examined the image. MacLeod appeared to be in his early sixties. He was dressed in a dark blue business suit with a white shirt and blue tie. His full head of hair was greying at the sides and an unlikely shade of brown on the top. His eyes were raised to the sky in a contrived noble pose but his chin was soft and his face red and puffy.

'MacLeod heads up the Home *Office*,' Jaqeli added. 'Think of him as the equivalent of our Minister of Internal Affairs.'

'With responsibility for UK policing?'

'Amongst other things.'

Donadze sighed. 'Misha did say this would be complicated. Who did you speak to at the Embassy?'

'A liaison officer initially but the Deputy Head of Mission came to see me when I mentioned Connor's name. A woman called Janice Patterson.'

'She's going to contact the father?'

'Yes, she said she'd organise it. She thought MacLeod

would take—what she called—an *active interest* in our investigation.'

'That's understandable, most fathers would. What do we know about Connor?'

'An online journalist, some would describe him as a *blogger*. He finds stories, writes them up and posts them online. Or at least he used to…' Jaqeli moved her mouse and clicked a button to change her screen's display. 'This is his website, *JournoTruths,* he called it. But he hasn't posted anything on it since this…' She clicked the button again and a new window opened, the headline proclaiming, *Met Paedophile Ring Exposed!*'

'Can I read it?' Donadze asked.

Jaqeli turned her screen and gave Donadze the mouse. The story was an exposé of how a group of paedophiles working within London's Metropolitan Police had been able to operate with impunity, protected by senior officers whose priority was to preserve the reputation of their service over the safeguarding of children. It had been posted just over a year ago.

'I seem to remember something about this,' Donadze said. 'But I don't remember anything coming of it.'

'I only remembered it vaguely as well but Koka's done some digging…'

Patarava sat up straight on his chair. 'Connor's story got some attention in mainstream news outlets for a while, Lieutenant,' he said. 'There was an internal investigation but nothing was found to support his allegations. Connor himself was heavily criticised when his sources were discredited and it was found that he hadn't properly verified the information he'd been given.'

'Is that why he's not posted anything recently?'

'Possibly, we really don't know.'

'But he didn't retract the story or take it off his website?'

'No.'

'Maybe he continued to believe it was true,' Jaqeli said. 'In any event, the whole thing caused embarrassment to the Met and—'

'The Home Office, which Connor's father heads.'

'Yes, it damaged MacLeod politically. He has oversight of the Met and his opponents must have loved it when his own son led the charge against them. He's not considered party leadership material now, which means he'll never be prime minister.'

'That would hurt an ambitious politician.'

'You would think so. Connor came to Georgia a couple of months after all this blew up.'

'So what's he been doing here if not blogging?'

'Well, he had an apartment on Gotua Street, nothing too fancy. The Embassy lady thought he was okay for cash, the family's wealthy. But maybe he picked up some casual work here and there.'

'He must have had enough money to buy a ring.'

'Yes, although the Embassy didn't mention a girl, which means she's probably someone he met over here.'

'Yes, probably.' Donadze leaned back on his chair. 'Okay, this is all good information.' He turned to Patarava. 'Could you give us a minute, Koka?'

'Should I be worried?' Jaqeli asked after Patarava had closed the MIR door.

'No, but you have a decision to make. Colonel Meskhi is making changes and he wants you to be part of them. You don't have to agree and I think you should seriously consider the implications if you do.'

'It's okay, Ramaz. I've already thought about it.'

'I haven't told you what it is yet.'

'You don't have to, you've talked about this before. The Colonel wants to set up some kind of team within a team and you're to lead it. Why does he want me?'

'He said you were best suited for the role.'

'And you tried to persuade him otherwise?'

'No, well yes. But not in that way.'

'What does Misha think?'

'He's worried, but he's keeping out of it.'

'Good. What else did Colonel Meskhi say?'

'That you'd be a moderating influence on me.'

'And would I be?'

'You usually are.'

Jaqeli smiled. 'Okay, Ramaz. You've talked me into it. I'm in.'

ELEVEN

Jaqeli laid her phone on her desk, leaning back on her chair.

'Everything okay, Irina?' Donadze asked.

She looked at him, eyes glistening.

'What's wrong?'

'Connor's girlfriend...'

'You've found her?'

'She found me.' Jaqeli ran her fingers under her eyes. 'Dea Lapachi—she's my cousin, Ramaz.'

'I'm sorry, Irina.' Donadze hesitated. 'Are you and Dea close?'

'We were as children but haven't seen much of each other lately. No real reason for that, just leading different lives.'

'It's a small world sometimes. Did Dea say when she last saw Connor?'

'Just before he was killed, she thinks. They'd been walking along the river embankment together. She'd expected him to call this morning…'

'I wonder if she saw the killer when they were walking, maybe without even realising it?'

'It's possible. What a thought, that a monster like that was stalking you.'

'What else did Dea tell you?'

'Nothing really, she's very upset, could barely put a sentence together. It'll be easier in person. I said I'd go over and take her statement. She lives with her mother—my aunt. She's there now, waiting for me.'

'Do you want to take a few minutes, maybe talk things over with Misha first?'

'No, I'll speak to him later.'

'Give me five minutes and we'll head over.'

'Would you mind if I go on my own, Ramaz?'

'Why, do you think she won't talk if I'm there?'

'No, it's not that. I just want to spend some time with her, as her cousin, not as an investigating detective. I'll take her statement and we can get back to her if we have to.'

Donadze shrugged. 'Okay, if that's something you feel you should do. But be careful what you say to her, she may be your cousin but you'll still be conducting a formal interview.'

'Yes, I understand. I'll record the conversation so there's no doubt what was said.'

'Okay, I'll take a look in Connor's apartment while you're out. Call me if you hear anything important.'

'Will do, thanks, Ramaz.'

Donadze walked to Misha Arziani's office. 'Hey, Misha,' he said. 'I spoke to Irina as Meskhi instructed.'

'And she's in?'

'Yes, sorry.'

'Don't be, I knew she'd go for it. I don't get it myself, but she seems to like working with you…'

'I don't get it either. Anyway, there's something else you should know. We've found Connor MacLeod's girlfriend. Irina's left to take her statement.' Donadze paused. 'She's Irina's cousin. Her name's Dea—'

'Her cousin? Is she okay?'

'Who? Dea?'

'Well, yes, of course Dea. But I meant Irina, is *she* okay?'

'Not really, she's very upset.'

Arziani shook his head. 'You shouldn't have let her go out on her own, Ramaz. Not if she's as upset as that.'

'It's what she wanted, Misha.'

'I'll call her,' Arziani said, reaching for his phone.

'No, don't do that. She said she'd talk to you later, you're better leaving it at that.'

Arziani paused, undecided, then put his phone down.

'How are the wedding plans going?'

'Okay, no date yet. We've still got a few things to figure out. Why do you ask?'

'It can't be easy for you working together.'

Arziani sighed. 'It's not. Irina thinks I'm overprotective.'

'And are you?'

'You know I am.'

'Well, that's something you need to work on then.'

'Thanks, Mother. I wish it were that easy.'

'I don't suppose it is.' Donadze paused a moment. 'So, this Dea Lapachi, have you met her?'

'The name sounds familiar.' Arziani shut his eyes, thinking. 'But no, I don't think so. Irina must have mentioned her at some point.'

'Well, let's see what she comes back with.' Donadze stood and pointed to Arziani's phone. 'But don't call her, Misha. Let her do her job. She'll talk to you when she's ready.'

❖

Donadze found a parking space and walked to Connor MacLeod's apartment block. It was set in a good location on a slight rise above Heydar Aliyev Embankment, looking down on the Kura River. One of the many new residential blocks constructed to house the growing number of people living in the capital. He estimated that MacLeod had been murdered about one hundred metres from home.

Donadze jabbed a button on the entry system's keypad at random and identified himself as a police officer to the woman who answered. She took his word for it and he pushed the door open when he heard it unlock.

MacLeod's apartment was on the sixth level. Donadze walked to a door strung with crime scene tape. A key had been recovered from MacLeod's body and he removed it from its evidence bag, unlocking the door and pulling the tape aside to enter.

He walked slowly from room to room, trying to sense how Connor MacLeod had lived. The apartment was spacious with good quality fittings and furniture but there was little to reflect the personality of the man who'd occupied it.

MacLeod had designated an area within the lounge as his office. It contained a small desk with a screen, keyboard and mouse. There was no computer but a disconnected Hewlett Packard power cable was lying on the laminate floor.

A drawer pedestal had been placed alongside the desk.

The top drawer was empty apart from a few items of stationery, a set of ear buds and MacLeod's British passport. The lower drawer contained several suspension files, all of which were empty.

Donadze left the lounge and walked to the master bedroom. A king-sized bed dominated the room. It faced floor-to-ceiling windows with stunning views of the river and the city beyond. There was plenty of storage space but most of it was unused, clearly not required for the limited amount of clothing MacLeod appeared to own. A few items of women's clothing hung from a cupboard rail with female underwear and other items neatly arranged in two of the drawers.

Donadze continued into the spare bedroom. It was empty apart from an exercise bike which faced a wall-mounted television. There was no sign of the computer he believed belonged to the disconnected Hewlett Packard power cable and he messaged Jaqeli to ask Dea where it might be.

He returned to the lounge and slid the balcony door open to look down on the river below. He identified the location where MacLeod had been killed, remembering how the body had lain in the mud, discarded like a worn mattress.

His phone rang. Colonel Meskhi.

'Good news, Lieutenant. I've appointed your new team member. Sergeant Roman Ketsbaia will join you tomorrow.'

'Ketsbaia? Do I know him?'

'He knows you. You worked together some time ago. You may remember, a raid on premises in Samgori Street.'

'Was he part of the tactical unit you sent in, led by—'

'Led by Lieutenant George Losava. You and he didn't get on, did you?'

Donadze had come close to blows with Losava, the commander of the police tactical unit which had stormed a vehicle chop-shop containing hijacked cocaine. 'That was just a misunderstanding, sir,' he said.

'Hardly. Anyway, don't let your history with Losava influence your relationship with Ketsbaia. Understood?'

'Yes, sir.'

'Very well. You know what's at stake here, Lieutenant. No distractions, I want your best work,' he said, hanging up.

Donadze looked at his phone. 'Tell me when you haven't had it,' he said to the empty room.

❖

It was after five before Jaqeli returned to Mtatsminda Station, pale and tired looking, her eyes red and puffy. Arziani was working in his office, contriving not to notice that his fiancée was back and clearly upset. Giving her space, Donadze realised.

'Let's talk in the MIR,' he told her.

'Okay, but let me speak to Misha first…'

'No problem, I'll make the coffee.'

Donadze watched as Jaqeli crossed to Arziani's office, shaking her head and raising her hands to stop him hugging her. The few people still in the bureau were also interested, looking up from their desks or peering over their computer screens, curious observers or looking for evidence that the boss was playing favourites. Not easy for Jaqeli and Arziani to continue working together, he thought, wondering again how they would resolve that issue.

Donadze made their coffee and returned to the MIR. The police had an established procedure for managing major incidents, including specifying team members and detailing their roles and responsibilities. Donadze had no intention of following that procedure. He'd told Jaqeli that he wanted to keep the team small to limit the possibility of information leaks. Although that was a concern, the real reason was that he wanted to conduct his investigation hands-on, not to be spending time delegating and managing people.

Koka Patarava had left for the evening but had updated the MIR's boards and timelines, pinning on the city map the location where Connor MacLeod had died. Donadze examined the map, seeing no similarity between the two places.

He pointed to Jaqeli's coffee mug as she entered the room. 'How was Dea?' he asked.

She nodded her thanks. 'Devastated. I've never seen her like that, not even when her father died.'

'Are *you* okay?'

Jaqeli sniffed, dabbed her eyes with a handkerchief then determinedly stuffed it back into her pocket, her back straightening. 'I'm fine, Ramaz. Thanks for letting me spend that time with her. We both needed it.'

Donadze shrugged. 'She was probably more open with me not being there. Anyway, what did she tell you?'

Jaqeli took out her phone. 'This is Connor MacLeod,' she stated, handing it to him.

Donadze examined the image: a smiling, unremarkable looking man, his glass raised in salute to the photographer—Dea, presumably. He zoomed in on MacLeod's face; he looked older than his driving license photo but younger than twenty eight, his age when killed and his personal clock stopped.

'What did Dea say about him?' he asked, handing back the phone.

Jaqeli smiled. 'She'd only known him for about four months but it was a real love story. He told her he was a blogger but had run into trouble with the Metropolitan Police post that we saw. He was angry with himself for not verifying the information he'd been given but said he stood by his allegations. His father—Rory MacLeod—asked him to take the story down and apologise, but Connor refused. So MacLeod told him he should go somewhere he wasn't known and wouldn't be pursued by the media. And that's what brought him to Georgia.'

'Okay, but why Georgia?'

'No visa required and it's not difficult to get residency status here. He'd also been told about Georgia by a friend who'd worked for an American oil company in Tbilisi and he wanted to see the country for himself.'

'And his father?'

'They didn't get on well, even before the Met post. Connor told Dea how the family would be posed for photo shoots: Rory MacLeod, the great family man. But the reality was that Rory's career always came first...'

'Did the two of them stay in touch?'

'Up to a point. They exchanged occasional WhatsApp messages, a call every month or so…'

Donadze nodded. 'Better than nothing, I suppose. What's he been doing in Tbilisi?'

'Living quietly in Gotua Street, picking up work in the Old Town tourist bars.' Jaqeli paused. 'And working on his website.'

'So he hadn't given up his blogs. What was he working on? Something new on the Met story?'

'Dea didn't know, but she said he was excited about it. He said he needed it,' Jaqeli checked her notes, '*to get back in the game*.'

'To get back in the game… Another exposé?'

'She didn't know that either. Connor played it close to his chest, didn't like talking about his blogs. It was a sensitive subject after what happened with the Met story.'

'What about when Connor was killed? Did she notice anything unusual? Maybe he'd had a row with somebody while they were out? The embankment would have been quiet at that time in the morning, did she notice anyone following them?'

'No rows and she didn't notice anyone following them. They'd been dancing at The Bridge nightclub and were walking home. Connor asked her to come home with him but it was late and she wanted to get back to her own apartment.'

'It's probably a good thing she left him when she did…'

'She knows that. It doesn't make her feel any better.'

'No, it wouldn't. Was there anything she told you that would link Connor's murder to Rusiko's?'

'No. She didn't recognise her name or face and didn't think Connor had ever mentioned her.'

'What about his computer?'

'He had one, a laptop. It was always in his apartment from what Dea could remember. I assume it wasn't there when you visited?'

'No. And I think his documents and papers could be missing as well.'

'But there wasn't any sign of a break in, was there?'

'There wasn't and that would mean whoever got in must have had a key or knew how to pick the lock.' Donadze shrugged. 'But maybe there's another reason why the laptop's not there.' A thought occurred to him. 'Did you mention the ring to Dea?'

'I did. I wasn't sure if I should, but I did anyway.'

'Did she know Connor was going to propose?'

'She'd had no idea…'

'Did she say what her answer would have been?'

Jaqeli nodded slowly. 'She did. It would have been yes.'

❖

'How would you like to go to Shindisi this evening?'

'This evening? Are you missing Levan already?' Tamuna asked.

'No, it's not that,' Donadze said. 'There are a couple of things I'd like to run past him and I thought it'd be good for us to get out of the city for a few hours.'

'It's okay, Ramaz, I know what Levan means to you. You don't have to justify seeing him to me. And you're right, Shindisi would be lovely, when are you picking us up?'

'Half an hour, depending on traffic.'

'Okay, we'll be ready.'

Donadze ended the call, waving to Jaqeli as he left the detectives' bureau. He crossed the car park, walking through thick, moist summer air. A good evening to escape into the hills, he thought. He got into his car and set off to his apartment, the traffic immediately and inevitably dense.

It took Gloveli some time to answer his phone. 'Sorry, Ramaz,' he said. 'It's not easy getting out of my chair these days.'

'That's okay, Major. Your goddaughter wants to see you. Can I bring her to the village this evening?'

Gloveli brightened. 'Of course you can. Tamuna as well, I hope. I'll let Veronika know.'

'Thanks. About an hour or so?'

'Perfect, see you then.'

He brought his car to yet another stop, his half hour estimate for the journey home optimistic.

Tamuna understands how he feels about Gloveli, Donadze thought, pondering his relationship with the old policeman. It was certainly unusual: Gloveli was more than thirty years his senior, his former boss and now his best friend and mentor. But he was more than that, a father figure perhaps?

He remembered his own father as a tired and broken old man, lost to the family after Ana, his daughter—Donadze's sister—had been raped and murdered in their family home during the Abkhazian War. Killed by neighbours his father had considered friends. He had failed to save Ana, failed in his role as the family's protector, his purpose and self-worth taken with his daughter's life. Or so he had thought. Did he, Donadze, crave a replacement for the father he'd lost years before he'd died?

He put these dark thoughts out of his head and called Tamuna, giving her ten minutes notice. She was waiting on Kandelaki Street with Eka as he pulled up. He got out of the car and gave the little girl a kiss before strapping her into her car seat. 'Shindisi then,' he said, buckling his own seat belt.

'Shindisi,' Tamuna agreed.

Donadze followed the familiar, twisting road, chatting to Tamuna and singing songs to Eka, smiling and making faces at her in the car's rear view mirror.

He waited until she was distracted by her dinosaurs. 'How was Eliso today?' he asked.

'Eliso? Just as she always is. Why are you asking?'

'I had to go home earlier today and I ran into her. She was upset about something and I could tell she'd been crying. She said it was dust in her eyes but I knew there was more to it than that.'

'Because that's what you do?'

'Yes, that's what I do. I know something was worrying her and, whatever it is, we need to make sure it won't affect Eka.'

'Of course it won't affect Eka, Ramaz. We all get upset from time to time. If something is bothering her then it's probably personal and she wouldn't want us interfering.'

'I know, but I think we should keep an eye on her all the same.'

Tamuna sighed. 'You mean *I* should keep an eye on her, don't you? Yes, I'll do that, Ramaz. And I will speak to her—*if* I think it's necessary.'

They arrived in Shindisi and Donadze pulled up on the rutted, unpaved road outside Gloveli's home.

Veronika met them at the garden gate, delighted to see Eka, lifting her out of her seat and carrying her into the garden. Gloveli stood, holding himself steady against a plastic chair, with Lasha, Veronika's husband standing close by in discreet support.

'*Gamarjoba*, Major, Lasha,' Donadze said, shaking hands with both men.

'Welcome, Lieutenant,' Lasha said, assuming the role of head of the house, Donadze realised.

Gloveli winked, letting Donadze know he wasn't concerned. 'Thanks for bringing my girl to see me, Ramaz,' he said, sitting down heavily and holding out his hands to take Eka onto his knee.

'I couldn't have kept her away, Major.'

'Sit down, please,' Veronika said, her Georgian now fluent with only a trace of a Ukrainian accent.

'Pour the wine, Lasha,' Gloveli said, although his own glass was already full and the bottle half-empty.

'How are your mother and sister, Veronika?' Tamuna asked. 'Are they still in Mykolaiv?'

'Yes, they're still there. I'd like to bring them to Georgia of course, but my mother is so stubborn, refusing to leave home.'

'She shouldn't have to,' Gloveli said. He waited until the wine had been poured then lifted his glass to salute Ukraine and her heroes. '*Gaumarjos slava Ukraini – Geroyam Slava*,' he spoke in Ukrainian, giving the toast which had become popular after Russia had invaded its neighbour.

'*Gaumarjos*,' Donadze and Lasha toasted, taking smaller sips from their own glasses.

The table had already been laid with salads, cheeses and breads and Veronika bustled inside to continue preparing their hot dishes.

'I'll see if she needs help,' Tamuna said. She kissed Eka on the top of her head. 'Keep your eye on her, Ramaz.'

Gloveli filled their glasses and picked up his own, looking at it wistfully for a moment before returning it to the table, undrunk. 'I need to cut back on my drinking,' he said, pausing a moment for effect. 'Either that or make more wine.'

'Make more wine, Levan,' Lasha said, offering a rare, shy smile.

Gloveli picked up his glass and drank half its contents, sighing contentedly. 'That's the best advice I've had for months.'

Donadze had heard the routine before but smiled politely.

Lasha held out his hand to Eka. 'Would you like to feed the hens?' he asked.

Feeding hungry birds was a better option than sitting on her godfather's knee and she squirmed off, running towards the hens which were scratching in the dry soil at the foot of Gloveli's garden. Or Lasha and Veronika's garden, Donadze reminded himself, keeping a watchful eye on his daughter.

Gloveli leaned towards Donadze. 'What do you know about cryptocurrency, Ramaz?' he said, his voice lowered.

'Like *Bitcoin*? I think they tend to call it *crypto* now.'

'Do they? There are quite a lot of them out there now, apparently. Not just Bitcoin. Do you think they're worth buying?'

'It depends. I do know they're risky, you could lose all your money.'

'Or make a lot more?'

'Yes, I suppose so. I would imagine buying crypto is like any other form of gambling; don't do it unless you can afford the hit if you lose. Are you buying some?'

'I'm thinking about it.' He glanced across the garden. 'Lasha is trying to convince me it's a good idea.'

'Has he bought any himself?'

'No, he doesn't have the cash.'

'Doesn't that tell you something?'

'He's just trying to establish himself, Ramaz. It's not easy living in another man's house.'

'It's his house now though, isn't it? You signed it over to him and Veronika.'

'Yes, but I'm still here and that may be the issue. Anyway, if I do buy the crypto he's talking about, it won't be much. I'm old school, money's best kept in the bank or under the mattress.' Gloveli picked up his glass and finished his wine. 'Let's have another,' he said, reaching for the bottle. 'So, Meshki's finally given you your own unit?'

'He's talked about it long enough.'

Gloveli shrugged. 'The time wasn't right. Meskhi has a good feel for politics. People want this man caught and they aren't too worried how that happens. But it *does* have to happen and you're in the firing line if it doesn't.'

'Lots of people are telling me that. What's your take on Fenrir?'

'The same as yours probably. He's a narcissist, arrogant. You'll catch him. Just hope that happens before you run out of time.'

'How long have I got?'

'Impossible to say. You already have two killings on your hands…'

'And if he kills again?'

'Oh, he will kill again, it's just a question of when. He'll keep killing until you stop him. But you *will* stop him, Ramaz.' He gulped down his wine and returned the empty glass to the table. 'Just make sure you don't take too long.'

TWELVE

Donadze's new team member, Sergeant Roman Ketsbaia was in the MIR with Jaqeli and Patarava.

Ketsbaia appeared to be in his mid to late thirties, slim and of average height, his dark hair greying and buzzed almost as short as the stubble on his face. He didn't look comfortable in his suit, shirt and tie which—Donadze guessed—had been purchased on his appointment to detective. He crossed the room with a loose, athletic gait to offer his hand.

'We've met before, haven't we, Roman?' Donadze asked.

'Yes, sir. About two years ago. My unit supported one of your investigations; a raid on premises on Samgori Street. Successfully, as I recall, that was a very large cache of coke we recovered.'

'Yes, it was certainly successful, although one of the gang members was killed trying to escape.'

'Killed before he could kill *you* as I remember it, sir.' He glanced at Jaqeli; she had shot the gang leader's son before he could shoot Donadze. 'Irina had no choice, Lieutenant, we all thought that at the time.'

'Your boss didn't.'

Ketsbaia smiled. 'Yes, I remember that as well.' He paused, choosing his words carefully. 'Lieutenant Losava isn't always the easiest—'

'Okay, I understand,' Donadze said, sparing Ketsbaia disloyalty to his previous commander. 'So tell me, Roman. Why do you want to join Irina, Koka and me?'

Ketsbaia patted his new suit. 'I've been in uniform all my life, Lieutenant, Army then Police. But I'm thirty nine now, time for a change.'

'How long were you in the Army?'

'Six years.'

'So, you weren't conscripted?'

'No, professional. You, sir?'

'A trench monkey. Served my twelve months and got out.'

'The Army's not for everyone.'

'No, but it wasn't all bad either.' Donadze paused. 'Has anyone told you what we've been asked to do?'

'Yes, sir, Colonel Meskhi did. It sounds like he's looking for results.'

'You're right, he is.' Donadze gestured to the case file which Ketsbaia had been studying. 'What do you think?'

'Nasty, a young girl returning home. A student, she didn't have much but her money and jewellery and her phone were all still on the body. No sexual violence.' He hesitated. 'One thing that does stand out though, the way she was killed. It was almost like—'

'Almost like an Army stealth killing?'

Ketsbaia nodded. 'That's the first thing I thought when I saw the photos.'

'What about Connor MacLeod's murder?'

'That looks very similar, Lieutenant.'

'It is.' Donadze paused. 'Have you ever come across an NCO called Beka Gabelia?'

'Gabelia? Didn't he open a bar in Kurdiani Street? Some kind of military theme, mostly for old soldiers.'

'That's right. Have you ever been there?'

'No, the Army was the past, I've moved on from that.'

Donadze nodded. 'That's often for the best. Gabelia was my squad leader in 2008.'

'Good soldier?'

'He was born to it. He'd still be there now if he hadn't lost a leg. I've spoken to him, if our killer is ex-military, he might know him.'

'Yes, that's certainly possible. It's nearly all ex-servicemen who use that bar.'

'Where did you serve, Roman?'

'Infantry then, my last two years, special forces, sir.'

'Well, welcome to the team, Sergeant.' Donadze looked at his watch. 'I'd like you to work with Irina and Koka this morning. Get yourself up to speed then visit Rusiko's parents. Go with Irina and introduce yourself to them. Remember, they're victims as well. I'll speak to you later this afternoon.'

'Where are you going, Ramaz?' Jaqeli asked.

'The airport, there's someone I've been told to meet.'

❖

Donadze left his car at the airport's parking area and walked the short distance to the terminal building. He was late and the security manager who met him was clearly annoyed. 'Ramaz Donadze?' he said without greeting. 'Your ID please.'

Donadze showed him his badge. 'Sorry, I got held up in traffic,' he said.

The manager grunted noncommittally. 'I take it you're armed?'

Donadze patted his shoulder holster through his jacket. 'Of course.'

'Well, you can't take your weapon airside. Follow me,' he said, leading the way to a small office. The floor space was limited and he had to squeeze passed Donadze to get to his desk, reaching under it to retrieve a small steel box—a gun case. He placed the case on his desk and opened its lid, looking at Donadze expectantly.

Donadze was also becoming annoyed. 'What?' he asked, deliberately obtuse.

'Put your weapon in there,' the manager instructed. 'Please,' he added, reluctantly.

'Of course.' Donadze took his pistol from its holster, checked the safety was on then laid it flat on the case's foam interior.

The manager shut the lid and snapped on a combination lock, spinning its dials.

'I hope you've got a good memory,' Donadze attempted to joke.

'It's good enough.' The manager patted the case. 'I'll make sure the pistol's returned when you're back landside.'

'Landside?'

'Haven't you been briefed?' The security manager sighed, glancing at his watch. 'Mr MacLeod's flight will land in about ten minutes. The Minister of Internal Affairs and your Colonel Meskhi will meet him on stand and welcome him to Georgia, offering all the usual courtesies. The Minister and the Colonel will then leave and you will join Mr MacLeod and escort him to the morgue where he will view his son's body.' He glanced at his watch again. 'If you're ready,' he said, standing and holding his office door open.

He led the way passed the check-in desks and into a small departure area where he walked to the front of a short line of people waiting to go through body scanners. 'This is the general aviation area,' he explained. 'Private aircraft, helicopters, government and police.'

Donadze nodded apologetically to the man who'd been about to go through the scanner ahead of him. 'I'm in the right place then.'

The manager ignored the quip and punched a code to unlock a door leading to the apron where an airport-branded van was waiting, its rooftop light flashing yellow. 'Get in, Lieutenant,' he instructed, taking the driver's seat and starting the engine. Donadze had barely closed his door before the van accelerated away, the sign-posted speed limit ignored.

Two black SUVs and a TV station van and crew were on stand. Donadze recognised Meskhi's car. 'You'll make sure I get my pistol back?' he asked as he got out of the van.

'I said I would, didn't I?'

'*Didi Madloba*,' Donadze muttered as the van accelerated away.

Meskhi's rear window wound down. 'Join me, Lieutenant,' the Colonel said.

Donadze walked around the car and got in the back, pulling its heavy door closed.

Meskhi pointed to an aircraft on final approach, the British flag painted on its tail, a red, white and blue roundel on its fuselage. 'The Royal Air Force,' he said.

'For a government minister travelling on private business?'

'No one in England will object. His son's murder has attracted a lot of media attention over there and the British people are very sympathetic. Why wouldn't they be? A parent grieving and in pain, something we can all identify with.'

'Are they blaming us for Connor's death?'

'Not explicitly, not yet anyway. But Scotland Yard has, of course, offered its support.'

'Are we accepting it?'

'I hope not, but that may be out of my hands. That's why it's important that MacLeod's visit goes well. Take him to see his son, tell him everything he wants to know. Be positive but realistic. The UK is an important ally, Lieutenant. Make sure the Home Secretary understands how seriously we view his son's murder.'

'And Rusiko Darsalia's murder, Colonel?'

Meskhi appraised Donadze for a moment. He gestured towards the other car whose driver was holding its back door open. 'You know, Lieutenant, the Minister wanted *me* to escort MacLeod to the morgue. I advised him it should be you as you are closest to the case and therefore best able to answer the Home Secretary's questions. Am I going to regret giving him that advice?'

'No, sir.'

Meskhi opened his door. 'Use my car to escort MacLeod. Stay here, I'll bring him to you.'

Donadze sat back on the leather seat. 'Yes, Colonel,' he said.

⁂

The aircraft door opened and its steps unfolded to the ground. Two uniformed crew members left the aircraft first, taking up position at the foot of the steps like an honour guard. MacLeod must have spotted the television crew, Donadze thought, as he paused to strike a pose at the aircraft's door before taking the steps down, stopping to thank the crew and shake their hands.

Donadze got out of the SUV and waited by its open door. The meeting between the British and Georgian politicians was brief but warm, the Georgian minister's face dripping sympathy for his bereaved counterpart, their double-handed handshakes extended for the benefit of the television camera.

Meskhi stepped forward and said something to MacLeod then led him to his car. 'Home Secretary, this is Lieutenant Ramaz Donadze. Lieutenant Donadze is leading the investigation into your son's murder. His investigation also covers the earlier murder of a young female, possibly by the same person.'

Donadze offered his hand. 'I'm very sorry for your loss, sir.'

'Thank you, Lieutenant. Do you have any idea who killed my son?'

'We have a number of leads, sir. I can't tell you how long it will take us, but we will find the person responsible.'

'You sound very confident.'

Donadze glanced at Meskhi, ignoring his frown of warning. 'Yes, sir, I am.'

'Well, Lieutenant, let's hope you mean that.'

MacLeod nodded to Meskhi then got into the car, turning his face one last time to the camera: devastated, strong, determined. He slumped in his seat as soon as the car pulled away, sighed deeply and smiled at Donadze. 'Your English is very good, Lieutenant.'

'Thank you, sir. We learn English at school as a second language. Some of us, like my wife learn German or other European languages as well.'

'In preference to Russian now, I understand.'

'It's where most people see the future of our country, Mr MacLeod; the EU and NATO.'

'Indeed,' MacLeod said, noncommittally. 'You're taking me to see Connor now?'

Donadze spoke to the driver and confirmed that they were going directly to the morgue. 'How long will it take?' he asked.

'About thirty minutes,' the driver said. 'Twenty if I use the lights.'

'Leave them off,' Donadze instructed. 'Yes, we're going to see Connor now,' he told MacLeod.

The car stopped at a security barrier where Donadze was relieved to have his pistol returned. He slid it into its holster as the car accelerated onto the public road.

'When did you last see your son?' Donadze asked.

MacLeod didn't have to think. 'In person, last August. His mother's birthday.'

'But you've spoken since then?'

'Occasionally, our calls were brief.'

'What brought him to Georgia?'

'I suspect you already know the answer to that question,

Lieutenant. An unfortunate Internet post concerning the Metropolitan Police.'

'A post about paedophiles in the Metropolitan Police and senior officers who covered for them?'

'Officers who are *allegedly* paedophiles and senior officers who *allegedly* covered for them…'

'So, none of it was true?'

MacLeod shrugged. 'Connor couldn't substantiate his story.'

'What do *you* think, Mr MacLeod? Do *you* believe it was true?'

'I'm not sure that matters anymore.'

'It doesn't matter that children were abused and the perpetrators protected?'

'*Allegedly,* Lieutenant.' MacLeod straightened in his chair. 'What does any of this have to do with my son's murder?'

'Policing is no different here than in England, sir. We need to identify motive, if any.'

'You're surely not suggesting Connor's murder had anything to do with that post, are you?'

'Were you aware that Connor hadn't given up blogging? What if he'd found a way to substantiate his story?'

'He would have told me.'

'Would he have though, sir?'

MacLeod's shoulders slumped. 'No, probably not.'

'No one was prosecuted as result of Connor's allegations, were they? Are they all still in post?'

'Of course they are, there was no evidence to justify prosecution or even to take disciplinary action.'

'So, these people have a lot to lose if the story was ever substantiated—we would consider that a credible motive.'

'But you think Connor was killed by the same man who killed that young female. Why on earth would the Met have wanted *her* dead?'

'I don't know, but we can't rule out any possibility at this stage.'

MacLeod was getting angry. 'That's ridiculous. Don't you also consider *means,* Lieutenant. Do you really believe an English bobby travelled all the way to Georgia to kill my son?'

'Connor's murder in Georgia might have been difficult to arrange, but it wouldn't have been impossible.'

MacLeod shook his head. 'My God, what a mess.'

'I'm sorry, Mr MacLeod, I know how upsetting this is for you.'

'I want my son's killer found, Lieutenant. That's all I care about.'

'Understood, sir,' Donadze said, although he suspected MacLeod would also want to protect his political career.

The car pulled up outside the National Forensics building. Metreveli, the chief medical examiner stood by the door, waiting to greet his important British visitor. Donadze introduced the two men in English then added in Georgian, 'I hope Connor isn't still on your autopsy table, Doctor.'

Metreveli shook his head but didn't respond, offering MacLeod his condolences in hesitant English. 'Come with me, please, sir,' he said, turning to lead the way down a corridor, the sweet, rotten stench of death and strong chemicals permeating the air.

The body had been taken to a chapel of rest where it lay on a table, covered by a white sheet. Metreveli held the door open, giving Donadze a wounded look as they entered. The room was dimly lit and cool, a grapevine cross of Saint Nino hanging on the wall.

The three men gathered around the table, Metreveli at the head. 'Are you ready, sir?' he asked.

The politician took a deep breath then nodded. Metreveli drew the cover back, revealing Connor's head and shoulders. Donadze thought he looked peaceful in death, his neck wound hidden by a white cotton bandage.

MacLeod stepped to the head of the table, stared at his dead son for a long moment then bent and kissed his forehead. He attempted to say something but his legs gave way and he clutched the table for support. Metreveli took his arm, instructing Donadze to bring a chair.

MacLeod lowered himself onto it. 'Thank you, gentlemen,' he said, wiping his eyes.

'We'll leave you alone. Take as long as you need,' Metreveli said, ushering Donadze out of the room.

'Thank you, Doctor,' Donadze said after he'd closed the door. 'I think Mr MacLeod will take comfort from this visit.'

Metreveli snorted. 'Really, Lieutenant. *Still on my autopsy table,* indeed. Why would you say such a thing? You should give me some credit for professionalism.'

'I do, Doctor, but I felt I should ask. It's not as if your patients can speak for themselves.'

Metreveli shook his head. 'You clearly know more about my profession than I do, Donadze. Please give my respects to Mr MacLeod and tell him I have another patient to see.'

'Thank you, Doctor,' Donadze repeated to Metreveli's retreating back.

MacLeod spent about twenty minutes longer with his son before leaving the chapel. 'When can I take Connor home, Lieutenant?' he asked in a small, defeated voice.

'The coroner usually needs about a week, sir. How long will you be in Georgia?'

'Until tomorrow. I have to visit the Embassy and arrange Connor's repatriation.'

'Good, so you have some time. There's someone I think you should meet.'

THIRTEEN

Donadze had called and suggested to Dea Lapachi that they meet in a coffee shop on Rustaveli Avenue. She'd been reluctant at first, believing that Connor and his father had been virtually estranged and that Rory MacLeod would have no interest in seeing her. He'd persuaded her that that wasn't the case, that she and MacLeod were grieving the loss of the same man and both would benefit from meeting and talking to each other. He'd assured her that he would stay with them and take MacLeod away if she felt uncomfortable at any time.

Meskhi's driver pulled up outside the coffee shop and Donadze led the Home Secretary inside.

A young woman stood and gave them a tentative wave. They crossed to her table. 'Dea? I'm Ramaz.'

She took his hand, looking expectantly at MacLeod.

'And this is Mr Rory MacLeod,' Donadze added in English. 'Connor's father.'

She took MacLeod's hand. 'I'm pleased to meet you, sir,' she said.

'Please call me Rory,' MacLeod replied, placing his free hand on top of hers. 'Thank you for agreeing to see me, Dea.'

'I'm so sorry. It must be terrible for you, a father, to lose your son in that way.'

'Yes, it is. And I'm sorry for your loss as well.' He paused a moment. 'May we sit?'

Dea gestured to the empty seats. 'Please.'

They sat in silence as the waitress interrupted to take their order before bustling away again.

'I'm sorry,' Dea said. 'My English is not very good.'

'And my Georgian is non-existent,' MacLeod said, his smile extending to include Donadze. 'What is it about the British, eh, Lieutenant?'

Donadze realised that MacLeod was attempting to charm the young woman, something he was good at. A useful skill for a politician, he thought.

'Don't be too hard on yourself, sir,' he said. 'Half the world speaks English, why would an Englishman learn anything else?'

'Or indeed a Scotsman for that matter,' MacLeod smiled again.

'Connor was the same, he always insisted on being called Scottish,' Dea said.

MacLeod's mouth twitched, his smile lost for a moment. 'When did you meet Connor?' he asked, his tone gentle.

'Only four months ago, we didn't have a lot of time together.'

'No, that wasn't very long at all.' He smiled again, tentatively this time. 'Dea, don't answer this if you don't want to, but did Connor ever talk to you about his family, about his mother and me?'

'A little. But he really didn't have much to say about his life in Scotland.'

MacLeod shook his head sadly. 'I made him hate me.'

'No, that's not true. Connor loved you. He was proud of you, proud of everything you've achieved.'

MacLeod swallowed hard, brushing his eyes. 'Is that really true?'

'Yes, of course it is, I wouldn't lie about something like that.'

The waitress returned, taking longer than necessary to unload her tray, clearly curious about her customers.

'*Madloba,*' Donadze said, dismissing her.

Dea pushed the cafetière's plunger and distributed their cups.

'You must forgive me,' MacLeod said eventually. 'I've been selfish, talking only about my own relationship with Connor. What about you? How close were you?'

'I loved Connor, Mr MacLeod… Rory,' she corrected herself. 'We didn't have much time together, but I loved him.'

'I can see that.' MacLeod hesitated. 'Connor was very unhappy when he left the UK. How was his life in Georgia? Did you make each other happy?'

'Are you asking if he loved *me*? Yes, I think so.' She turned to Donadze. 'Can I tell him?' she asked in Georgian.

'I think you should,' he said.

'Connor was carrying a ring, Rory. He was going to ask me to marry him.'

MacLeod leaned forward and took Dea's hands in his. 'And he would have been lucky to have had you.' He held her gaze for a moment longer. 'I wish we'd met in different circumstances.'

Dea brushed her eyes. 'Yes, I do too.'

Donadze sat back in his chair allowing MacLeod and Dea to chat, exchanging happy memories of the man they'd both loved.

They finished their coffee and Dea caught Donadze's eye, signalling that she wanted to leave now.

'Shall I take you to your embassy, Mr MacLeod?' Donadze asked.

MacLeod nodded his agreement but kept his attention on the young woman, taking her hands again. 'Dea, this might be asking too much, but would you come to Scotland to meet Connor's mother?'

'Scotland?'

'Yes. Lesley would love to meet you, to know how happy you'd made our son. It would mean a lot to her. I could arrange everything through the Embassy.'

'I'm not sure…'

MacLeod released her hands. 'I understand, it's too soon. Forget I asked.'

'No, that's okay, I'd be very happy to meet Mrs MacLeod, if you think that would help…'

❖

Donadze paid the bill and left the coffee shop, blinking in the bright sunlight, his skin prickling in the sticky heat. MacLeod and Dea followed a few minutes later, the Home Secretary looking uncharacteristically awkward, uncertain how to say goodbye. Dea appeared to notice his discomfort and put her arms around him before breaking off to kiss his cheek.

'Thank you, dear, for everything,' MacLeod said.

She shook her head. 'I didn't do anything.'

'Yes, you did. I'll tell Lesley you're coming to see us in Scotland. You'll like her, Connor was much more like his mother than me.'

'No, Rory. I don't think so. I can see a lot of Connor in you.'

MacLeod swallowed hard, blinking away tears as Meskhi's car swooped in, drawing up alongside them, the driver jumping out to hold the rear door open.

'The Embassy, sir,' Donadze prompted.

'Of course.' MacLeod patted Dea's arm and pulled himself into the SUV.

The driver slammed the door shut and got back into the car, letting Donadze know he wasn't important enough to have his door held for him.

Donadze joined MacLeod in the rear and the car pulled away, the driver forcing his way into the slow moving traffic.

'What a lovely young woman,' MacLeod said.

'I'm glad you were able to meet, sir.'

'That only happened because of you, Lieutenant. Thank you.'

The car suddenly braked, the driver blasting his horn. 'Draft dodging bastard,' he snarled, as the driver of the car in front thrust his arm out his window, his middle finger raised.

'Road rage,' MacLeod said, smiling. 'Just like at home. Not surprising in this heat.'

'It's more than the heat, sir. That's a Russian car, the driver's probably in Tbilisi to avoid being conscripted.'

Meskhi's driver blipped the car's siren and sped past. 'Fucking aggressor,' he muttered.

'That's enough,' Donadze told him.

The driver looked in his rear view mirror, meeting Donadze's gaze. 'Sorry, Lieutenant,' he said.

'Let's just get to the Embassy in one piece.'

'Yes, Putin's war with Ukraine,' MacLeod mused. 'Something my government feels very strongly about. Things may change if there's a new American president but the Prime Minister is convinced that the free world cannot allow Russia to win.'

'Third time lucky, perhaps,' Donadze said, referring to Georgia's war with Russia in 2008 and Russia's annexation of the Crimean Peninsula in 2014, both events going largely unpunished by the West.

'I beg your pardon?'

Donadze shook his head. 'I was talking about Russia's recent history, sir…'

'Yes, I understand. I read about Russians coming to Georgia to escape the draft. Several thousand in your country now, I believe.'

'More than a hundred thousand, mostly in Tbilisi. Not everyone has welcomed them.'

'They haven't assimilated?'

Donadze shrugged. 'Some have, some have even opened businesses here. But there are others who think they're something special, that Georgia is still their vassal state. Most have money and they've forced prices up: property, food, restaurants, bars. Most Georgians can't compete.'

'It sounds like you're not too fond of your Russian guests either, Lieutenant?'

'I was in the Army in 2008. Russia invaded my country. I shot at Russians, they shot at me. How would you expect me to feel about them now?'

'I understand, emotions run deep. I'll speak to the Ambassador and ask him to brief me on the situation.'

'He won't be able to add much,' Donadze said, thinking that the British politician had no real interest in Georgia or its problems.

'No, probably not.' MacLeod took a business card from his wallet and wrote on the back. 'This is my personal number, call me if there's anything new on Connor. Or if there's any way I can help.'

Donadze nodded, giving MacLeod his own card. 'I'll be in touch, sir.'

❖

Donadze returned to the airport to pick up his car then drove to Mtatsminda Station. Misha Arziani wanted to see him and he went straight to his office.

Arziani was working on his laptop as usual, a situation he purported to be unhappy about. But if he was unhappy, it never showed, his breezy disposition almost never changing.

He saw Donadze walking towards his office and stood, rolling his shoulders.

'That thing's going to kill you,' Donadze said, pointing to the laptop.

'Not if I kill it first.' He glanced at the wall clock, it was after six and the bureau had emptied. 'I thought you'd defected.'

'Defected to the UK?'

'You know what I mean. How was the Home Secretary?'

'Quite slick, as you'd expect. But overall, I thought he was okay, fairly decent, at least for a politician.'

Arziani grinned. 'And I bet he loved you, too.' He twisted the kinks out of his neck and sat down, gesturing for Donadze to do the same. 'I want to talk to you about Roman Ketsbaia.'

Donadze shrugged. 'Okay…'

'I know you report directly to Colonel Meskhi now but you remember what he said, that I've to retain oversight of your work?'

'That's okay, Misha. I know you're still my boss.'

Arziani made a dismissive gesture. 'So, Sergeant Ketsbaia. I asked him to come to my office for a chat, a chance to get to know each other.'

'You hadn't met before?'

'No.' Arziani hesitated. 'Generally, I liked him. He seems smart, conscientious, enthusiastic…'

'And that's all good?'

'It should be...'

Donadze waited as Arziani searched for the right words.

'I know Ketsbaia's background: police tactical, Army special forces—high adrenaline stuff,' he said. 'The thing is, Ramaz, he didn't get into these roles by accident—he sought them out. I'm worried that he's joined your unit to get the same adrenaline fix. And if that doesn't come naturally, he might find ways to force it.'

'How would that happen? Do you think he'd take chances, put himself at risk?'

'Maybe. And it wouldn't just be him at risk.'

'You mean Irina?'

'I mean everyone on your team.'

'What did Ketsbaia actually say, Misha?'

Arziani leaned back in his chair. 'Nothing specific, it was just an impression he gave.'

'Well, your instincts are usually good. Do you want me to speak to him?'

'When the time's right, yes. Set his expectations about what you and your unit are about. You're not *The Untouchables*, remember?'

'I remember. I'll keep an eye on him. If he needs an adrenaline fix then he might have to go back to Losava's unit to get it.'

❖

Donadze's phone buzzed with a message from Tamuna reminding him that Lela Tabagari, her best friend and colleague at the Medifirst Clinic would be joining them for dinner that evening. He'd forgotten she was coming and inwardly groaned. He liked Lela and they got on well together. He'd previously helped her escape an abusive relationship and she in turn had advised him how to deal with a senior police officer who'd been sexually preying on women. But he was tired and had been looking forward to a quiet evening alone with his family.

Tamuna had asked him to be home by seven and he was only a few minutes late arriving at their apartment. Lela was already there and she and Tamuna were in the living room, sitting together on the settee drinking wine. Eka lay on her play mat, her collection of plastic animals—farm, wild and extinct—demonstrating an unlikely model of peaceful coexistence. She saw her father and squealed with delight, jumping to her feet and scampering to greet him, her little arms outstretched.

Donadze lifted his daughter and threw her a short but thrilling distance into the air, catching her and landing a wet kiss on her neck.

'That's what I call a welcome,' Lela said, standing and leaning past the little girl to kiss Donadze's cheek.

'Me too,' he agreed. He crossed to the settee—his daughter clinging to his neck—and managed to bend far enough to kiss his wife.

'Everything alright?' she asked.

'Never better. How was the clinic?'

'Busy,' Tamuna said as Lela nodded her agreement.

Eka squirmed to be put down and Donadze returned her to the mat, picking up a T-Rex and whispering to it, 'Watch out for the tiger!' He excused himself and went to the bedroom to shower and change out of his work clothes.

'There's wine in the fridge,' Tamuna said as he returned to the living room.

The mat and plastic animals had been abandoned and Eka was cuddled on Lela's knee, her eyes heavy.

Donadze retrieved the open bottle of *Tsinandali* and tipped what little was left into a glass. He opened another bottle and topped up all their glasses. '*Gaumarjos*,' he said, taking a sip of the pale, golden liquid. 'You two seem to be in a good mood.'

'We're celebrating. Lela's had some great news,' Tamuna said.

'Oh?'

'I've not decided yet, it's only an option at the moment…'

'What's only an option?'

'A job offer, in Germany.'

'As an obstetrician?'

'That's what I do, Ramaz,' she said, smiling.

'Germany's hiring Georgian obstetricians?'

'Not *just* obstetricians…' Lela said, glancing at her friend.

Tamuna nodded. 'All specialties, including orthopaedic surgeons apparently. If they can speak German.'

'And you can. Are you thinking of applying, Tamuna?'

'No, of course not, there's no way that would work—not for me, anyway. But it's a great opportunity for Lela. A brand new hospital in Stuttgart. And promotion, Lela would be deputy head of department.'

Donadze took another sip of his wine, glancing at his wife. Despite her apparent enthusiasm, he could tell she was unhappy at the prospect of her best friend leaving the country. And something else, he thought, possibly a little jealous that she couldn't also go.

'It's a great opportunity,' she repeated, unconvincingly.

'Yes, it is, but I haven't made up my mind yet,' Lela insisted. 'There's a lot to think about.'

Donadze guessed her thinking included her boyfriend, Paata, a serious relationship according to Tamuna. He held up his glass. 'Well, here's to opportunities,' he toasted.

'Did you get your parcel?' Tamuna asked.

'What parcel?'

'It was lying by the door when Lela arrived. I brought it in and left it there. Didn't you see it when you came in?'

Donadze returned to the door to retrieve a padded envelope, a printed label with his name and rank but no address attached. He carried it to the living room and pulled it open, spilling its contents—a folded sheet of paper and a woman's white linen handkerchief—onto the breakfast bar. He unfolded the handkerchief to reveal a name embroidered in blue thread: *Rusiko.* He laid it on the breakfast bar, staring at it, his gut clenching.

'Something wrong, Ramaz?' Tamuna asked.

He turned to Lela. 'When did you get here?' he asked her, keeping his tone even.

Lela shrugged. 'Just before six, I think.'

Donadze unfolded the paper, placing it alongside the handkerchief. The message was printed in large, upper case font and was brief, bold, and angry: MACLEOD WAS NOT ONE OF MINE!!!

❖

'What's wrong, Ramaz?' Tamuna demanded, alarmed.

Donadze blinked, his grim thoughts interrupted. He gazed at the breakfast bar, the package and its contents that he'd placed there. He realised his hands had balled, his jaw had tightened. He took a deep breath, forcing himself to relax.

'Tell me what's wrong, Ramaz,' Tamuna demanded once more, her voice rising.

He glanced at his daughter, asleep on Lela's knee. 'It's nothing to worry about,' he said.

'It's certainly not *nothing.*' Tamuna stood and crossed to the breakfast bar. 'What does this mean?' she said, reading the note. 'MacLeod, he's your murder victim, isn't he?'

Donadze nodded. 'He's one of them.'

'And these,' she said, gesturing to the handkerchief and the note, 'were left by the man you're looking for? *Fenrir,* isn't it? He's telling you he didn't kill Connor MacLeod?'

'Possibly.'

'So this Fenrir, this killer knows where we live—*possibly*?'

Donadze raised his hands in a conciliatory gesture. 'It

doesn't help to jump to conclusions, Tamuna. We don't know for certain who left the package. Even if it was Fenrir, he's not made any threats, he just wants me to know it wasn't him who killed MacLeod.'

'But he's angry you thought that in the first place.' She pointed to the handkerchief. 'Rusiko, isn't she the girl he killed?' Her eyes widened in horror. 'Oh, my God! He must have taken it from her body.'

'That's her name but it'd be easy enough to buy a handkerchief like that.'

'So this is just a hoax then?'

Donadze shrugged. 'Maybe.'

'But you don't believe that?'

He hesitated. 'No, I don't.'

'So, what do we do now?'

'I really don't think we have to do anything. Any grievance Fenrir might have is with me, not with you or Eka.'

'And that makes it alright?'

'No, of course not. But at this point all he's done is send me a message. It's not something we need to be too worried about.'

'Well, I think we do need to be worried. This job of yours, the monsters you go after…'

'It's what I do, Tamuna,' Donadze said, echoing what Lela had told him earlier.

'Yes, but it's not something you *have* to do.'

'What else is there?'

Tamuna shook her head. 'We've both got options, Ramaz.'

'You want us to move to Germany?'

'I don't know, maybe it's something we should think about.'

'Maybe it is. But not just because I was given a note…'

'Tamuna,' Lela said hesitantly, 'you know that you and Eka are welcome to stay with me. At least until Ramaz finds this man.'

Tamuna shook her head. 'Thanks, Lela, but no. That's not the answer.'

'Okay.' Lela looked down on the sleeping child and smiled. 'It's getting late, I should go.'

'I've spoiled your evening…' Donadze said.

'No, it's not your fault, and anyway, the evening wasn't spoiled.'

'Listen, I have to call my boss. Why don't you stay a bit longer?'

Donadze excused himself, taking his wine glass onto the balcony and drawing the sliding door closed.

Meskhi picked up almost immediately. Donadze described receiving the package, stating that he believed it was genuine, that the handkerchief had been taken from Rusiko's body and that someone other than Fenrir had killed Connor MacLeod.

'Even though the same method was employed?' Meskhi asked.

'Yes, it was a copy—a good one. It fooled us.'

'Both killers would need the same knife skills.'

'Yes, they would.'

'So why did MacLeod's killer want us to think Fenrir was responsible?'

'MacLeod was targeted for a reason, not killed at random as Rusiko was. Copying the method disguised the motive.'

'Do you have a view what that motive was?'

Donadze wasn't ready to share his suspicions about London's Metropolitan Police with Meskhi yet. 'It's something we need to work on, sir.'

'So how do you intend doing that?'

'We extend the investigation, start looking for a second killer.'

'And make our information about the second killer public?'

'Yes, of course.'

'No. That's exactly what Fenrir wants. You said he's angry—that's good. Let's make him furious. Sending you that note was a mistake. Let's ignore it and see what other mistakes he makes. And as for MacLeod's killer, let him think he has us fooled. At least for now.'

Donadze looked at the two women and his daughter through the balcony's glass door. 'Fenrir's angry with me, sir. But it might not be me he chooses to go after, at least not directly.'

'Your family?'

'Yes.'

Meskhi hesitated a moment. 'Two people are dead, Lieutenant. More may die. We have to give ourselves the best chance of finding these killers. Your family will be protected if necessary.'

Donadze didn't respond.

'We ignore the note. We do not go public about a second killer. Is that clear?' Meskhi pressed.

'Yes, sir,' Donadze said, eventually, thinking about a future life in Germany.

FOURTEEN

The MIR's door was open and the lights on when Donadze arrived. 'Been here long, gentlemen?' he asked.

'Not really,' Patarava said. 'About half an hour.'

'An hour or so,' Ketsbaia added. 'I wasn't sure what you meant by *early morning.*'

Donadze grimaced. 'I'll try to be more specific in future.'

'It's okay, I don't sleep much these days anyway.'

Donadze waited, thinking Ketsbaia would elaborate. He didn't, changing tack instead. 'Something new, sir?'

'Let's wait for the others,' Donadze said. 'And you don't have to call me *sir* or *lieutenant* all the time. Ramaz will do when we're on our own.'

Ketsbaia smiled. 'I always find it safer to err on the cautious side. We were never invited to call Lieutenant Losava, *George.*'

'Is Losava also ex-military?' Donadze asked, curious to know more about Ketsbaia's previous commander.

'He likes people to think that but no, not really, he just did his national service.'

'The same as me then.'

'I'd say that's about all you and Lieutenant Losava have in common, sir—I mean, Ramaz,' Ketsbaia said, correcting himself.

'I'll take that as a compliment.'

Ketsbaia smiled but didn't respond.

'Did we keep you waiting?' Arziani asked, walking into the MIR ahead of Jaqeli.

'Hey, Ramaz,' Jaqeli said, nodding to Ketsbaia and Patarava. 'You've got us intrigued.'

'Sit down, I've got something to show you.' Donadze opened a folder and extracted a photo of the package he'd received, passing it to Arziani. 'This was left outside my apartment yesterday.'

Arziani examined the image. 'Hand delivered,' he noted, passing it on.

'Just my name, no address. There were two items inside.' He handed Arziani a second photograph. 'Can you read the name?'

'Rusiko…'

Donadze nodded. 'And this was also in the package,' he said, passing the last photo to Arziani.

'MacLeod is *not* one of mine,' he read.

There was a moment of silence as the significance of the note was absorbed.

'Do you think it's real?' Jaqeli asked eventually. 'Fenrir didn't kill Connor?'

'I do. In some respects I wish it *weren't* real.'

'I don't blame you, Ramaz,' Arziani said. 'Your

investigation just got that bit more complicated. But I don't see what Fenrir was hoping to achieve by giving you that note.'

'I do. We know he's arrogant and a narcissist. But there's genuine anger here as well. It's like he sees himself as an artist whose best work has been copied.'

'So, two killers to find now,' Jaqeli said. 'An artist and a counterfeiter.'

'And the artist knows where you live, Lieutenant,' Ketsbaia said, his tone flat.

Donadze nodded. 'That fact hadn't escaped me. I briefed Colonel Meskhi; he instructed me not to go public with the note and not to reveal that there's a second killer. He thinks that will make Fenrir more angry and more likely to make mistakes.'

Jaqeli shook her head. 'That's easy for him to say. Fenrir's not been to *his* home.'

'No, the Colonel's right, Irina,' Ketsbaia said. 'We've obviously got under his skin, we might not even have realised there was a second killer if he hadn't paid the Lieutenant a visit.'

'Okay, but Ramaz has a family to think about.'

'Yes—but I don't.'

'What does that mean, Roman?' Arziani asked.

'I think we need to deflect Fenrir's attention away from Lieutenant Donadze, sir.' He paused. 'If Fenrir's going to be angry, let's make him angry with *me*. We know how sensitive he is and that works in our favour. I'll take the next media briefing, find a way to goad him so his focus is on me.'

'You want to make yourself a target?' Arziani asked, exchanging a look with Donadze. 'What difference would that make anyway? It'd just be you at risk instead of Ramaz.'

'With respect, sir, I think we're talking about the Lieutenant's family, not the Lieutenant himself. I don't have anyone at home to worry about. And—also with respect—I'm better trained for this type of thing.'

'What do you think, Ramaz?' Arziani asked, frowning.

'No. I'm in charge of this investigation and Fenrir knows that. He also needs to know he can't intimidate me.' Donadze hesitated. 'But, thanks, Roman, I appreciate your offer.'

Ketsbaia shrugged his acceptance of Donadze's decision.

'Ramaz,' Jaqeli said, 'you know you're going to have to protect your family now, don't you?'

'I do know that. Meshki's posting a patrol car outside our apartment. Tamuna's going to hate it.'

There was silence for a moment. 'Before jumping to conclusions, we'd better confirm that the handkerchief actually belonged to Rusiko,' Arziani said.

'Yes, I'm going to ask her parents if they recognise it. But I'm already convinced it's hers.'

'And then we need to figure out why Connor was killed and why the killer wants us to think Fenrir was responsible.'

'Connor's laptop and his missing documents must factor into this,' Ketsbaia said.

'Absolutely,' Donadze agreed. 'This is all about information suppression. Connor had information on his laptop, information in these documents, information in his head. Someone didn't want that information coming out and that's what cost him his life.'

'And,' Jaqeli added, 'that's why Connor's killers want us to think Fenrir was responsible: to throw us off the scent.

This was a one-off killing for a specific reason—to stop Connor revealing something. By blaming Fenrir, his killers want us focused on the murder, not the real motive behind it.'

'That's the way I see it,' Donadze said.

'You said *killers*, Irina. Are you saying more than one person was involved?' Ketsbaia asked.

'Yes. I think the man who killed Connor was a professional: skilled and cool enough to imitate what happened to Rusiko and then finish the job by breaking into his apartment to steal the laptop. But I also think he was acting under instructions—from the people who wanted to keep the information secret.'

'So,' Donadze said. 'Put simply, someone hired a hitman to bury something Connor was ready to make public.'

'The Met story?'

'Maybe…'

Jaqeli nodded. 'Connor may have backed up his laptop to the cloud. I'll speak to Tech, see if it's there and if there's any way to retrieve it.'

'Okay,' Donadze said, standing. 'Koka, you stay here and man the phones. Roman, you come with me. We're going to visit Rusiko's parents.'

❖

Ketsbaia's car was like an excitable dog whose master had returned home; its doors unlocking, lights coming on, the driver's seat rolling back to ease entry. All it needed was a tail to wag, Donadze thought.

He settled into his cream leather seat, the car's interior immaculate and perfumed by polish and a dangling air freshener. A nice car, he thought, and a significant investment for his new colleague. It occurred to him that Ketsbaia might be supplementing his police sergeant's salary illicitly but he quickly dismissed that notion; the car wasn't new and Ketsbaia had no family to drain his finances. Donadze loved his own car which was modest in comparison but he knew that certain people—certain men in particular—prioritised prestige cars over other spending, the value and power of their vehicles reflecting their self-esteem, sometimes even their masculinity.

Donadze was a nervous passenger, preferring to be in control when navigating Tbilisi's congested, ill-tempered streets. But he had to acknowledge that Ketsbaia was a good driver, assertive but safe as he made steady progress towards the apartment Rusiko Darsalia had shared with her parents.

'May I ask a question, sir?' Ketsbaia asked, lapsing into formal address.

Donadze let it go. 'You don't need permission to ask me a question, Roman. What is it?'

'Two of us, driving across the city to verify evidence seems like a waste of time to me...'

Donadze resisted pointing out that Ketsbaia had made an observation, not asked a question. 'You wanted to go on your own?'

'I didn't *want* to go on my own, Lieutenant. But you've probably got better things to do than escort me.'

'I've certainly got *other* things to do—but they're not more important than this. Rusiko isn't the only victim here, her parents are as well and they're entitled to our time. Besides,' he added, 'I want us to have a chat and the station's not the best place to have it.'

Donadze watched the other man stiffen. ‘Don’t worry, Roman,’ he said. ‘It’s nothing ominous, just a chat. We’ll grab a coffee after this.’

‘Sir.’

Donadze smiled to himself; Ketsbaia was clearly more comfortable addressing his superiors formally—a consequence of his military background and service under a pompous former commander, he thought.

They arrived at the Darsalia family’s apartment block and Donadze headed straight for the stairs, avoiding the Soviet era elevator. He was slightly out of breath by the time they reached the third level but Ketsbaia didn’t appear to have even exerted himself.

Rusiko’s mother was waiting for them by her open door. She ushered them into her living room where a small table with food and drink had been placed in front of her two-seat couch. ‘Please sit,’ she said, taking her own place on an upright chair.

Donadze manoeuvred himself onto the worn, sagging couch, leaving room for Ketsbaia to join him. ‘Is Mr Darsalia not at home?’ he asked.

‘No, he went for a walk. The doctors told him he has to keep exercising. He doesn’t go very far…’

Donadze thought the father had taken Rusiko’s murder even harder than his wife and was probably avoiding the pain of speaking with the police again. ‘Don’t worry,’ he said. ‘We won’t take up too much of your time. How have you been?’ he asked, lifting a slice of cold *khachapuri* and taking a polite but unwanted bite of the greasy, cheesy bread.

She shook her head. ‘It doesn’t get any easier, Lieutenant. I don’t think it ever will. I keep thinking Rusiko will come home soon, that we'll talk, that she'll tell me about her studies, the boys she likes, her plans for the weekend. I know that sounds foolish but…'

'No, it's not foolish at all, she'll always be with you in that way.'

'Yes, I hope so.' She paused a moment. 'I saw on the news that that monster—*Fenrir,'* she spat the name, 'has killed again, a foreigner this time. Is that why you're here?'

'No, it's not that,' Donadze said, feeling guilty that he couldn't tell her there was a second killer. 'We wanted to see how you were doing but also to ask you to look at something.'

Ketsbaia took his cue and reached into his jacket pocket to retrieve an evidence bag containing the linen handkerchief, the embroidered name visible through the clear plastic. He stood and showed it to the woman. 'Did this belong to Rusiko?'

Mrs Darsalia gasped, holding out her hand to take the bag and rubbing the handkerchief through the plastic. A tear welled in her eye and rolled down her cheek. She brushed it away with the back of her hand. 'We gave them to her on her birthday, a set of four. I think the other three are in her drawer, do you want to see them?'

'In a minute.' Ketsbaia held out his hand and the woman reluctantly returned the bag.

'How did you come by my daughter's handkerchief?' she asked, her eyes narrowing.

Donadze had anticipated the question but hadn't decided how to respond. He realised that she deserved the truth. 'The man who did that terrible thing to Rusiko took it from her. He delivered it back to me yesterday, along with a message.'

The woman started to speak but Donadze cut her off. 'I'm sorry, Mrs Darsalia, I can't tell you what the message said—but I can tell you it wasn't about Rusiko.'

She sat back on her chair, appraising the two detectives. 'I understand,' she said, eventually, her voice now strong. She fixed her gaze on Donadze. 'When you first came to this apartment you promised me you would find the man who killed my daughter. Do you intend keeping your promise, Lieutenant?'

'Yes,' Donadze said. 'Nothing's changed.' He turned to Ketsbaia. 'Sergeant?'

Ketsbaia hesitated a moment then nodded. 'Yes, Mrs Darsalia, we'll find him.'

⁂

'The stairs will be quicker,' Donadze said to Ketsbaia after they'd left the Darsalia family's apartment.

'You don't like that elevator, do you, Lieutenant?' Ketsbaia guessed.

'You've clearly got a great future as a detective, Sergeant,' Donadze said, smiling to soften his sarcasm.

The car went through its welcoming routine as Ketsbaia approached. 'Where to?' he asked, sliding into the low seat.

'We're going for that coffee and chat.' Donadze said. 'There's a place on Mtatsminda Street—we can drop off your car at the station and walk there.'

Ketsbaia raised his eyebrows but didn't comment, starting his engine and moving smoothly away.

Donadze waited until he'd manoeuvred into the traffic. 'So, definitely two killers then,' he said, conversationally.

'At least we're sure now.' Ketsbaia hesitated. 'Your promise to find Rusiko's killer, Lieutenant...'

'*Our* promise, wasn't it?'

'Yes, our promise. But what if we *don't* find him?'

'Let me ask you something, Roman: when you made that promise to Mrs Darsalia, did you mean it?'

'Yes, of course I did.'

'But you think I forced you into it,' Donadze said, turning to look at the other man. 'And now you're on the hook, committed to something you might not be able to deliver, worried that you'll let that poor woman down? It's not fair, is it?'

Ketsbaia shook his head. 'It's not a question of *fairness*, Lieutenant…'

'Well, fair or not, that's where we are. That's where *you* are, Roman. It's where I *want* you to be—committed.'

Ketsbaia glanced at Donadze, smiling. 'And I thought Lieutenant Losava was hard.'

'No, George is a pussycat compared with me.'

'Maybe I should transfer back to his unit?'

'Do you want to?'

'No, definitely not.'

'Good, then let's get that coffee.'

Ketsbaia parked the car and the two men walked to Mtatsminda Street. The only other table in use on the coffee shop's terrace was occupied by four young men. They had clearly been drinking and one stared, glassy eyed at Donadze and Ketsbaia as they passed.

'Russians,' Ketsbaia said, sitting down.

'Ignore them,' Donadze instructed.

The waitress came to take their order, noticeably avoiding passing too close to the Russians' table. Donadze read her name tag. 'Everything okay, Nino?' he asked.

She glanced at the other table. 'Yes, no problem, they're harmless. Just too much time on their hands and too much to drink.'

She left, ignoring a comment one of the Russians made as she returned indoors.

'Okay,' Donadze said. 'Let's not get distracted.' He turned to face Ketsbaia. 'Captain Arziani asked me to speak with you. He thinks you're fitting in well but he wants to make sure you understand how we work, what Colonel Meskhi had in mind when he set up our team.'

Ketsbaia frowned. 'Okay…' he said.

'Special forces and police tactical: that must have been pretty exciting for you?'

'Some of the time it was, a lot of the time we were sitting around, gathering intel, waiting. I don't understand what this is about, Lieutenant.'

Donadze was beginning to regret initiating the conversation. 'Okay, let me just say it outright. Captain Arziani is concerned that you won't get the same buzz from this job as you've had in the past.'

'And then what? Does he think I'll do something to generate that buzz and put you all at risk? That I'll put *Irina* at risk?'

Donadze nodded, impressed by Ketsbaia's insight. 'Yes, that's his concern.'

'And is that also *your* concern, Lieutenant?'

'It's something I've thought about,' Donadze admitted.

The waitress came out of the coffee shop carrying a tray. As she passed the Russians' table, one reached out and grabbed her wrist, throwing her off balance and causing the tray's contents—cafetière, water jug, glasses, cups and plates—to fall to the ground and shatter.

Ketsbaia looked at Donadze. He nodded and both men stood and crossed the patio.

Ketsbaia showed his badge. 'I assume you'll want to apologise to your waitress and pay for this damage,' he told them in Russian.

The man who'd grabbed Nino's wrist glanced at his three friends, making sure they would support him against the two Georgians. He pulled himself to his feet, a sly smile playing on his lips.

Donadze took a step to the side, watching the other men and calculating which one to hit first. They stayed seated, grinning, content for the moment to see how things played out between Ketsbaia and their friend.

'I wouldn't do that if I were you,' Ketsbaia said, taking a step backwards.

The Russian had clenched his fist behind his back, a subconscious signal that he was about to strike. He'd also mistaken Ketsbaia's backward step for fear. His eyes flicked to the side—another subconscious signal.

Ketsbaia stepped forward and low-kicked the man's outer thigh, his body twisting for maximum force as his shinbone impacted the Russian's sciatic nerve, freezing his leg.

The Russian howled in pain and surprise, reaching for the table top to stop himself falling.

'No!' Donadze shouted, his open hand close to the face of the man nearest to him, his other hand positioned to strike.

Ketsbaia's demonstration of violence and Donadze's posturing were enough to spike the Russians' adrenaline—fight turning to flight—and they fell back onto their seats, mumbling vague and improbable threats involving people they knew.

Donadze briefly considered arresting the main trouble maker but thought his bruised thigh and humiliation would be punishment enough. 'Get your wallet out,' he told him. 'Two hundred *lari* to pay for this damage and a hundred to Nino to say you're sorry.'

'Are you alright, Roman?' he asked as they returned to their own table.

Ketsbaia turned and faced Donadze. 'Did I behave recklessly just now?'

'No, you were always in control. You used minimum force. No one was seriously injured.'

'Did I put you at risk?'

'No, you showed these men that they couldn't win a fight, faced them down and stopped the situation escalating.'

Ketsbaia raised his hands and held them outstretched in front of Donadze—they were completely steady. 'I'm not looking for any kind of *buzz*, Lieutenant—I just want to do my job.'

Donadze nodded and put his hands on Ketsbaia's, pushing them down. 'Okay, Sergeant,' he said. 'Point taken. Let's have that coffee.'

FIFTEEN

'How were Rusiko's parents?' Jaqeli asked.

'We only saw her mother. She's strong. It'll take time, but she'll be okay,' Donadze said.

'And the handkerchief was definitely Rusiko's?'

'Yes, definitely. We're looking for two killers now—although Mrs Darsalia doesn't know that yet.'

'Was it difficult keeping the truth from her?'

'I try to think of it as not passing on all of our information.'

'That's one way of looking at it.'

'It's the only way—at least as far as Meskhi's concerned.'

Jaqeli shrugged, unconvinced. 'I've heard from Tech. Bad news, it looks like Connor didn't do cloud backups.'

'He didn't do backups or our tech people couldn't find them?'

'Well, I think their logic is: if they can't find something, it's because it's not there.'

'That doesn't sound right. It means Connor was prepared to lose everything if his laptop went down.'

'Not necessarily, Lieutenant,' Patarava said. 'He might have used an external hard drive or a memory stick. That's what people did before we had the cloud. You can store a terabyte of data on a stick now.'

'I know but Connor wasn't carrying a stick or any other memory device when we found him. And there was also nothing in his apartment.'

'That doesn't mean he didn't use one. It's good practice to keep your backups separate from your computer in case—'

'In case there's a fire or some other issue at your home or place of work,' Donadze interrupted. 'And someone breaking in and stealing your laptop could be one of these issues.' He turned to Jaqeli. 'Irina, did you ask your cousin if Connor had left anything with her.'

'I did ask that and he hadn't.'

'We know cloud accounts can be hacked by third parties,' Ketsbaia said. 'What if Connor *did* have data on the cloud but someone got in and deleted it.'

'That someone being?' Jaqeli asked.

Ketsbaia shrugged. 'Whoever was responsible for taking his laptop, his documents—and his life.'

'The Metropolitan Police?'

'Don't you think that's possible?'

'Theoretically, yes…'

'But improbable?'

Jaqeli sighed. 'It just seems a little farfetched to me.'

'Maybe not, Irina. Not if there really was a paedophile ring operating and Connor had found new evidence to prove it.'

Donadze had been listening to the discussion between Ketsbaia and Jaqeli. 'Okay,' he said. 'If our tech people can't find anything then the chances are that there never was a cloud backup. But even if there *was* and someone—let's say the Met—deleted it, then they've covered their tracks too well.'

There was a moment's silence before Ketsbaia spoke, 'This may be a stupid idea...'

'There's no such thing, Roman,' Donadze said. 'Go ahead.'

'Well, we agree that it's possible Connor did have a cloud account that was deleted. Our own people didn't find anything but that could be because they don't have the expertise, networks or equipment to properly check. Other organisations do have that capability—including England's MI5.'

'You think MI5 would investigate the London Met on our say so?'

'Not on *our* say so, Lieutenant. On Connor's father's—the British *Home Secretary's*—orders. And we wouldn't ask for the Met to be investigated, just for MI5 to look for evidence of tampering.'

Donadze shook his head. 'No, MacLeod wouldn't go for it. There's no proof, only conjecture on our part. The Met story has already hurt him. And he's a politician, he couldn't be seen to be using his position for personal reasons.'

'It's only personal because Connor happened to be his son, Ramaz,' Jaqeli said.

'He wouldn't be interested, Irina. You would know that if you'd talked to him.' Donadze hesitated a moment. 'But it's an idea. Let me think about it, maybe there's a way we can get his attention,' he said.

❖

Donadze's phone buzzed. 'Ramaz, it's Lela.'

'Is something wrong?'

'No nothing's wrong. But there's something I need to discuss with you. Could I buy you a coffee?'

'What's this about, Lela?'

'It's about Tamuna, but let's talk over a coffee. Are you at the station?'

'Yes.' Donadze checked his watch. Colonel Meskhi had instructed him to report to his office and he should already have left. 'Where do you want to meet?'

'I could be with you in about fifteen minutes. Is there somewhere private we can talk?'

Donadze considered bringing Lela into the station but he knew that an attractive young woman coming to see him on personal business would set tongues wagging. He directed her to the coffee shop that he and Ketsbaia had visited earlier in the day.

He wrote a text to Meskhi, *Delayed 1 hour.* He hesitated then changed it to read, *Apologies, sir. Delayed 1 hour. I'll get to your office as soon as possible.* He read the text once more then sent it; his family came first and Meskhi would have to wait—but there was no point in being deliberately rude.

Donadze had already guessed what Lela wanted to discuss. He returned to the MIR and told Ketsbaia he would be going home after meeting Meskhi, then left the station, thinking unhappy thoughts.

He took the table he'd sat at with Ketsbaia.

Nino was still on duty and she smiled and patted his arm shyly as she took his order.

Lela arrived a few minutes later. She kissed him and took a chair. 'How are you, Ramaz?' she asked, a tentative smile on her lips.

'Intrigued,' he said.

Lela waited while their coffee was served—accompanied by biscuits and pastries which Donadze hadn't ordered.

'This is on me,' Nino said, blushing. 'I didn't get a chance to thank you and your friend earlier.'

Donadze smiled. 'It was nothing.'

'Now *I'm* intrigued,' Lela said, as the waitress walked away.

Donadze reached for the coffee pot. 'Just some drunks making a nuisance of themselves.' He filled their cups. 'So, you want to talk about Tamuna…'

Lela sighed. 'I hate doing this, Ramaz. And you're probably going to tell me to mind my own business, but—'

'You've made up your mind; you're going to Germany.'

She sat back on her seat, surprised. 'How did you know that?'

'I'm a detective, Lela. You're going to Germany and you want Tamuna to go with you.'

'Wow, that's really impressive...'

'Not really. Did Tamuna *say* she wants to go with you?'

'No, but I know she does. And it's not *with me* as such...'

'How do you know she wants to go? You heard her say she wouldn't split up her family and she knows *I* can't go.'

Lela raised her hands to soften her words. 'Don't you think it's more accurate to say you're not *prepared* to go, Ramaz?'

Donadze nodded. 'Maybe that's true,' he acknowledged.

'That's okay. Tamuna understands that, she knows you'd find it difficult to leave. The thing is, I don't think Tamuna would want to leave either. Not permanently anyway.'

'Okay, this is getting too subtle for me, Lela. Why don't you just tell me what's on your mind?'

'Yes, that's probably best.' She took a deep breath. 'Please believe me when I tell you this is very difficult for me. But I want what's best for Tamuna and—in the long term—for you and Eka as well.' She looked at Donadze, waiting for him to signal his understanding.

'Okay…' he shrugged.

'You must know that Tamuna is ambitious,' she continued. 'But she's put her career on hold for Eka. And—being honest—also for your mother whilst she was still alive. I think she feels that, at some level, it's her turn now. If she doesn't go to Germany, she'll regret it, maybe even resent it. She might come to resent you, Ramaz. You like the movies, don't you? What's that line, *maybe not tomorrow, but soon and—*'

'*And for the rest of your life*. It's from *Casablanca*.'

'Yes. I think this is something Tamuna needs to get out of her system. And I think you should encourage her to go.'

'And Eka?'

'You know she wouldn't go anywhere without Eka.'

Donadze hesitated. 'For how long?'

'The Germans are offering us one-year contracts…'

Donadze shook his head, 'That's a long time.'

'It is, and I'm not saying it would be easy—for any of you. But it's not like you wouldn't see each other. You'd both have holidays, long weekends. You could make it work.'

'I don't know, Lela. I'll have to think about it.'

'There's one more thing to consider, Ramaz. This case you're working on, the parcel left at your apartment, the police car parked outside. None of that's easy for Tamuna. Going to Stuttgart would take her out of that situation.'

Donadze laughed. 'Well done, Lela, saved your ace for last, didn't you?'

She turned her gaze on him, eyes flashing. 'That's cruel, Ramaz. You should know me better than that.'

Donadze sighed. 'Yes, I do.' He drained the last of his coffee and placed the cup back on its saucer. He closed his eyes, a dull ache in his gut, his world falling apart. 'Thanks,' he said, eventually. 'It sounds like we have a lot to talk about.'

'I'm sorry, Ramaz.'

'Don't be. You're a good friend.'

She lifted her bag to leave, stood and kissed him on the cheek. 'It'll work out, you'll see.'

Donadze watched her walk from their table, turning to wave and offering him an uncertain smile. He didn't return it. He knew Lela had spoken reluctantly and that her intentions had been good. But her advice had been unwelcome. Donadze's fear—which he was reluctant to even acknowledge—was that he and his wife and daughter would drift apart, that temporary separation would become permanent, that he'd lose his family forever.

❖

Donadze left sixty lari on the table, more than enough to pay for the coffee and food which the waitress had said were complimentary. He knew that certain police officers were happy to accept free meals and drinks from obliging restaurants and bars but he viewed that practice as low-level corruption and always paid his way.

He checked the time. He'd told Colonel Meskhi he'd be about an hour late for their meeting but the traffic was building and he thought it would be closer to two hours.

He hurried back to his car. It was cooler now, a breeze whispering through the cobbled streets. He drove to the MIA building, parked and went through the familiar routine of picking up a security pass and making his way to Meskhi's office.

A uniformed senior officer was leaving as Donadze arrived, a clipboard in his hand. One of Meskhi's bureaucrats, he thought.

The officer held the door open for him, looking at him curiously; the Fenrir investigation and associated publicity had raised his profile, if nothing else.

Donadze nodded his thanks, standing in the doorway as Meskhi looked up from his desk.

'Sorry I'm late, sir.'

'Come in, Donadze. Something important, no doubt?'

'Yes, sir.'

Meskhi waited for him to elaborate and when he didn't, said, 'Are you always going to play this game, Lieutenant?'

Donadze wasn't in the mood for games either. Not today. 'It was a personal matter, sir.'

Meskhi nodded. 'Thank you. That's all you had to say. Is there anything I can do to help?'

'No, sir,' Donadze said. 'But thank you anyway,' he added.

'Very well. Take a seat.'

Meskhi took a moment to appraise him. 'How is Sergeant Ketsbaia settling in?' he asked eventually.

Donadze knew he hadn't been summoned to discuss

Ketsbaia. 'It's early days, Colonel, but yes, he's settling in well.'

'Good.' Meskhi paused. 'Do you know a lady called Janice Patterson?'

'I seem to know the name, sir...'

'She's Deputy Head of Mission at the British Embassy.'

'Yes, I remember now. Detective Jaqeli spoke to her in connection with Connor MacLeod's murder. She helped us with his movements in Georgia.'

'Tell me about MacLeod.'

Donadze was surprised by Meskhi's sudden change of direction. 'We've confirmed he wasn't killed at random, Colonel. We believe he was targeted because he'd uncovered sensitive information and was preparing to post it on his website.'

'What sensitive information?'

Donadze paused, reluctant to share his suspicions about the Metropolitan Police. He'd had an idea how to enlist Rory MacLeod's support in discovering if his son had a cloud account but knew any dealings with the Home Secretary would be politically sensitive.

'What information, Lieutenant?' Meskhi repeated.

Donadze paused, considering how much to disclose.

'MacLeod had previously written an exposé on paedophiles serving in the London Met and a conspiracy at a senior level to protect them,' he said. 'The exposé went nowhere because it couldn't be substantiated. We think it's possible MacLeod found new evidence to support his allegations.'

Meskhi sat back in his chair. 'And you're only telling me this now?'

'It's only one line of enquiry, Colonel. There's no proof, nothing in writing that we could find.'

'Your gut?'

'We know MacLeod hadn't withdrawn his allegations. But whether he'd found anything new or not...'

'In that case we should not jump to unwarranted conclusions about the Metropolitan Police. Or any other country's police force for that matter. Understood?'

'Yes, sir.'

'And MacLeod's killer?'

'We think he must have been hired for the job, Colonel. He knew what he was doing and he might have got away with it if it hadn't been for Fenrir.'

'So, a conspiracy to murder then.'

'Yes. That's the only way to see it. Why did you ask if I know Janice Patterson?'

'Take a look at this.' Meskhi tapped his keyboard and swung his screen around for Donadze to read.

The BBC News website was open on an article titled, *Georgian Police Search for Wolf Killer.* There was an image below the title showing Donadze leaving Mtatsminda Station. He scanned the article which described how Connor MacLeod, the son of the Home Secretary was thought to be the latest victim of the killer known as *Fenrir.* The murders had, according to the BBC, created a climate of fear in the city, as Georgians believed Fenrir would kill again if not caught. Links provided readers with a detailed description of the Fenrir from Norse mythology and the character in the video game. The article went on to name Donadze as the detective leading the investigation and included a quote from the Home Secretary, *Whilst I have full confidence in the*

Georgian Police, Connor's loss has been devastating for his mother and me and I have requested our embassy in Tbilisi to offer Lieutenant Donadze and his colleagues their full support. And I, of course, will continue to monitor any developments as the police investigation continues.

'Patterson has already offered her support?' Donadze guessed.

'Yes, it was very generous of her,' Meskhi said, dryly.

'And the Home Secretary is monitoring our investigation?'

'A little more than that. He's been in touch with our own minister. We discussed your case earlier today.'

'I'm sure he was equally supportive.'

'Of course he was.'

'What do you want me to do, sir?'

'Janice Patterson will be in touch. Give her as much information as you're able.'

'Should I tell her that Connor wasn't killed by Fenrir?'

'No. Our tactics haven't changed, no one's to know. Fenrir's angry, let's see if he makes another mistake.'

'And the Met?'

'Leave the Met out of it for now.'

'Yes, sir.'

Meskhi swung his screen back into position. 'I'm sorry you've become caught up in this nonsense, Lieutenant. But don't let it distract you from your work. Understood?'

'Sir.'

'Anything else?'

'No, sir.'

'Good luck, Lieutenant,' Meskhi said. 'You may go.'

'Thank you, Colonel,' Donadze said, standing and walking to the door, his thoughts immediately returning to his conversation with Lela and the discussion he would have with his wife.

❖

Donadze left Meskhi's office and drove home. He parked then walked to Kandelaki Street, following a circuit which would eventually return him to his apartment, thinking of what he'd say to Tamuna.

He had his thoughts in order as she met him at their front door. 'Ramaz, are you okay?' she demanded, throwing her arms around him and pulling him close.

Donadze held her tight, his eyes prickling. 'I'm fine, I just had some thinking to do.'

She broke off their embrace, holding him at arm's length to scrutinise his face. 'Lela called me. She told me she'd spoken to you about Germany. She shouldn't have done that, Ramaz. I told her that. But there's nothing for you to worry about—because I'm not going.'

'Let's go inside,' Donadze said.

She nodded and took his hand to lead him into their living room.

'Have you had anything to eat?' she asked.

'No, but I'm not hungry.'

'Some wine?'

'Wine would be good.'

Donadze sat on the couch as Tamuna retrieved a bottle of *Tsinandali* from the fridge, placing the wine, two glasses and a bottle opener on the table in front of him.

He took his time cutting the foil and pulling the cork, pouring generous measures into their glasses. He lifted his glass and clinked it against hers. 'Here's to you, Tamuna.'

'And to you, Ramaz.'

He took a sip, letting the cold liquid trickle down his throat. 'I think you should go to Germany,' he said, at last.

'What? No, I told you, I won't break up the family. It's different for Lela, she and Paata aren't married, they don't have children.'

'That just makes her logistics easier. But the principle's the same. I think you need to go, Tamuna.'

'Why? You'd hate it. Hate not seeing Eka.'

'And hate not seeing you as well. But Lela's right, this is your opportunity to do something for yourself. You'll regret it if you don't go.'

Tamuna shook her head. 'It might have been different if we didn't have Eka.'

'She'll be okay. She'll have her mother with her.'

'But not her father…'

'No, that's not true. I might not be in Germany with you, but Eka will always have me.'

Tamuna took a sip of her wine, appraising him over her glass. 'I don't know what to say, Ramaz. I really wasn't expecting this.' She hesitated. 'Do you think I'm being selfish?'

Donadze forced a smile. 'A little, but no more than me. It's not like I'm volunteering to leave Georgia or give up the police.'

Tamuna hesitated a moment. 'So, you're sure? I'm going to Germany?'

'Yes, we'll make it work,' he said, echoing Lela's words. 'Just make sure you come back.'

'Never doubt it.'

'I won't,' he said, although that dark thought was already in his head. 'When do you think you'll be going?'

'Well,' she said, 'I'll have to apply for the job first, of course. Then—assuming I'm successful—I'd hand in my notice. Stuttgart would arrange a work permit, accommodation, a place for Eka in their creche. It happened quite quickly for Lela. Say about two months.'

'So we still have a couple of months together,' Donadze said.

'We have a lifetime together, Ramaz.' She stood and held out her hand. 'Come on.'

He smiled. 'My reward?'

'Come on.'

Later, lying in bed, Tamuna breathing quietly beside him, Donadze couldn't sleep, already dreading the day—possibly only two months away—when his wife and daughter would leave, the life he'd known and taken for granted, over.

SIXTEEN

Time together as a family was even more precious now, Donadze realised. Being apart from his wife and daughter for at least a year would be bad enough but he thought Germany would change Tamuna. That she wouldn't be content to return to Tbilisi and a relatively junior position at the Medifirst Clinic, her career once again subordinate to her role as wife and mother.

She topped up his coffee and dropped a few grape halves onto Eka's plate.

'*Madloba*,' he said, generously estimating how much sugar he would need to re-sweeten his coffee. 'How do you go about applying for the Stuttgart job?'

'By email. I just have to update my resumé and send it off with a covering note. I can do that today. There's a recruitment team in Tbilisi and they'll probably want to see me at some point.'

'Sounds very efficient…'

Tamuna must have picked up something in his tone. 'I

don't have to do this, Ramaz. Not if it's going to be too difficult for us.'

Donadze forced a smile. 'No, we discussed it yesterday, you need to go to Germany.'

'Okay, I hope you mean that.'

'I do.'

'Good.' She paused a moment. 'I think you were right about Eliso. I'm going to speak to her this morning.'

'So something *is* bothering her?'

'Yes, I think so.'

'You're not worried about Eka?'

'No, of course not. Whatever's bothering Eliso won't affect how she cares for Eka.'

'Okay, if you're sure.' He gulped some coffee and stood. 'Better get going.'

'Busy day ahead?'

'Most days are but I've had an idea and I need Irina's help to make it work. The thing is, I don't think she's going to like it.'

Tamuna laughed. 'Is it *unconventional*?' Donadze had told her how Colonel Meskhi had described his new role.

'I suppose it is.' He kissed her then crouched to kiss Eka in her high chair, her sticky fingers on his face and in his hair. He placed his hands on either side of her beautiful face and kissed her again. 'See you later, *chemo gogona*,' he said then stood, walking quickly to the door.

He phoned Jaqeli on the stairs to the underground parking. 'Are you still in your apartment?' he asked.

'Yes, we're just about to leave.'

'Stay put. I'll be with you in twenty minutes.'

'Are we going somewhere?'

'Maybe. Has Dea gone to Scotland yet?'

'Dea? No, her flight's tomorrow, I think. Do you want to see her before she goes?'

Donadze unlocked his car and pulled himself into the driver's seat. 'Possibly. Twenty minutes,' he said, ending the call.

❖

Arziani was waiting with Jaqeli as Donadze pulled up outside their apartment block.

He wound down his window. 'Hey, Misha. Need a lift?' he asked.

'No, Ramaz. But I am interested in this scheme you're concocting with Irina.'

'It's got nothing to do with me,' Jaqeli said. 'This will be one of Ramaz's genius ideas.'

Donadze glanced at his dash clock and reluctantly got out of the car to join his friends on the pavement. 'Connor MacLeod,' he summarised for Arziani's benefit. 'Killed, we think because he was about to break a story on his website. The story would have been written on his laptop, ready to post when he was happy with it. But the laptop was stolen from his apartment and—as it stands—we don't know if he had any backup. It'd be surprising if he didn't, but no memory device was found and our tech people couldn't find anything on the cloud.'

Donadze paused, looking at Arziani expectantly.

'Go on,' he said. 'I'm following you, so far.'

'It's possible,' Donadze continued, 'that Connor did have cloud backup but that his killers deleted it. Our tech people don't have the capability to determine if that's the case or not.'

'But someone else does have that capability?' Arziani guessed.

'Yes, England's MI5,' Jaqeli said. She turned to Donadze. 'This goes back to Roman's suggestion about getting MI5 involved, doesn't it, Ramaz? But what's changed? You were certain Rory MacLeod wouldn't order MI5 to investigate the London Met just because we asked him.'

'Wait,' Arziani said. 'Irina, you just mentioned the British Home Secretary, the British Security Service and investigating the London Metropolitan Police—all in the same breath. Have I missed a briefing somewhere along the way?'

'No, Misha,' Donadze said. 'You haven't missed anything. This is just an idea I had and I wanted to run it by Irina before deciding what to do with it.'

'Well, run it by me first.'

'Okay, no problem, I wasn't trying to sideline you.' Donadze paused. 'It's possible that Connor had found new evidence for his Met story. We know he was working on something new and was excited about it. If it was the Met story, then we've identified a possible motive for his murder.'

'Okay. So if MI5 determines that there had been a cloud backup, could they also retrieve the deleted data?'

'Maybe,' Donadze said.

Jaqeli shook her head. 'I know where this is going, Misha. Rory MacLeod has the authority to instruct MI5 but it's too difficult for him politically. He won't do it, not if the request comes from us...'

Arziani frowned. 'But he might if someone else made the request? Who are we talking about here?'

'Connor's girlfriend, Dea Lapachi—my cousin.'

'Is Irina right, Ramaz?' Arziani asked. 'You want Dea to ask MacLeod?'

Donadze shrugged. 'That's why I wanted to run it passed you first, Irina.'

'Because you want *me* to ask Dea.'

'She's more likely to help if the request comes from you.'

'That's pretty cold, Ramaz,' Arziani said.

'Maybe, but we've got a killer to catch. This could be our best chance of doing that.'

'But why would MacLeod go along with it just because Dea asks him?'

'Because they got on well together.'

Jaqeli laughed. 'It's a bit more than that, Misha. MacLeod knows his son was going to propose to her. He took a lot of comfort from the meeting that Ramaz set up for them—to the extent that he asked Dea to meet his wife in Scotland. He thinks of her as family now.'

'Okay. But assuming we could get MI5 involved and Connor *did* have a cloud backup which they *could* retrieve—why would they give it to us?'

'They would be giving it to MacLeod, hopefully he would forward it to us. But if nothing else, we'd have established a motive for Connor's murder and evidence that the British authorities could use.'

'What does Colonel Meskhi say about this?' Arziani asked.

'He doesn't know about it yet. As I said, it's just an idea I had.'

'And how do you think he'll feel when he *does* find out?'

'I don't know, the politics could get a bit messy. But he

shouldn't rule it out. We're not breaking any laws, just doing something that's a little *unconventional.*'

'As he instructed,' Arziani agreed. 'What do you think, Irina?'

'I don't like it. Dea will know we're manipulating her. It's not right, she should be given space to grieve in peace.'

'I don't think Ramaz wants to manipulate her, Irina. Dea wants Connor's killer found even more than we do. This would be her chance to help make that happen.'

'*You* want me to ask her?'

Arziani nodded. 'I think so…'

'Okay, Misha, you're the boss,' Jaqeli said, folding her arms across her chest.

'Yes, I know that.'

'Thanks, Misha,' Donadze said, thinking again that his friends would have to change their working relationship soon.

'What about Meskhi?' Arziani asked.

'I'll brief him.'

'*After* Irina has spoken to Dea and *after* she's spoken to MacLeod?'

'Probably.'

Arziani smiled. 'Thought so,' he said.

❖

Janice Patterson kept Donadze waiting just long enough to be irritating. She eventually strode into the embassy's modernistic atrium, her hand outstretched to take his. 'Lieutenant,' she said in a booming voice. 'Good morning! How kind of you to come and see us.'

The Deputy Head of Mission was about forty, tall and slim with the broad shoulders of a swimmer. Her hair was cut into a blond bob and she wore a black knee length dress with a pearl necklace, gold studs in her ears. Her handshake was more than firm.

'Good morning, Ms Patterson,' Donadze replied in English.

It was Colonel Meskhi's instruction rather than kindness that had obliged him to meet Patterson, a foreign civilian with no link to his investigation. Her call had felt like a summons, especially as she'd politely but firmly insisted on them meeting at the British Embassy, her home territory.

Patterson made a dismissive gesture. 'Oh, please call me *Janice.*'

'Good morning, Janice,' Donadze said, declining to reciprocate by inviting her to call him *Ramaz.*

She turned to the receptionist. 'Do you have Lieutenant Donadze's pass, Keti?' she asked sweetly in accented Georgian.

'Yes, of course,' the receptionist said. She pushed a clipboard forward on her desk. 'Sign here, please, sir.'

Donadze signed the form, nodding his thanks and hanging the security pass around his neck.

'Well, this way, *Ramaz,*' Patterson said, her smile bright and toothy but failing to reach her eyes.

She led the way along a short corridor and pushed open the door of a meeting room, following Donadze inside. 'Please take a seat. Tea, coffee, water?' she asked, her hand hovering over a conference phone's keypad.

'Nothing, thank you.'

'If you're sure.' She smiled again. 'May we continue in English? My Georgian is just about good enough to order a meal or a glass of wine but your English is so much better.'

Donadze suspected that Patterson's Georgian was as

good as his English and that she was attempting to unsettle him by having him speak in his second language. But he was already tired of her games. 'That's fine, Janice,' he said, declining to give the polite response she probably expected: by insisting that her Georgian was, in fact, excellent.

She frowned slightly then got down to business. 'Poor Connor…'

'Did you know him well?'

'Not *very* well. We were aware that he was in Tbilisi, of course. The Home Secretary's son, you understand…'

'I understand. So, what can I do for you, Janice?'

'I'm sorry, of course, you're busy.' She shuddered theatrically. 'A murder to investigate…'

'Actually, two murders.'

'Ah, yes, the young law student. I read the reports. How awful,' she said, her face conveying contrived horror.

'Yes, awful. So what can I do for you?' he repeated.

'Politicians,' Patterson said, shaking her head ruefully. 'Our lords and masters. The Home Secretary requested,' she glanced around the room as if checking for eavesdroppers, 'or should I say, *instructed* the Ambassador to liaise with you over this dreadful business and to offer you our full support. And, of course, to receive and forward any updates you may have,' she added, as though an afterthought.

'As reported by the BBC?'

'Ah, you saw that?'

'Wasn't I supposed to?' Donadze took out his wallet and retrieved the business card Rory MacLeod had given to him. He passed it to Patterson. 'This is the Home Secretary's personal number,' he said. He pointed to the conference phone. 'Please call him.'

'You want me to call the Home Secretary?'

'Yes, Connor's father.'

'May I ask why?'

'To provide the update you both require. It'll be more efficient that way. And it's likely that Mr MacLeod will have questions which only I can answer.'

'I see,' Patterson said, rubbing the card between her fingers. 'Of course, the Home Secretary's a very busy man, he may not be immediately available…'

'Well, let's see, shall we,' Donadze said, pointing again to the conference phone.

Patterson fixed her smile. 'Certainly,' she said, leaning across the table to read from the card whilst quickly punching numbers on the keypad with slim fingers.

The phone buzzed several times. Patterson shook her head and was reaching for the keypad to hang up when the call was answered.

'MacLeod.'

'Home Secretary,' Paterson said. 'It's Janice, calling from Tbilisi.'

There was a pause as MacLeod seemingly attempted to recall the woman he was speaking to. 'Ah, Janice,' he said, at last, a note of forced joviality in his voice. 'How are things in Georgia?'

'Excellent, sir.' She paused. 'I have Lieutenant Donadze with me.'

'Really?' MacLeod said, surprised. '*Gamarjoba*, Lieutenant,' he added in mangled greeting. 'Did I get that right?'

'*Gamarjoba,* sir. Yes, that was perfect.'

'Have there been any new developments?'

'It's early days, but yes, there's one significant development I want you to know about. We now believe that Connor wasn't killed by chance. He may have been targeted to stop him disclosing certain information.'

'Information? But that doesn't make sense. What information could Connor have that would have cost him his life?'

'You invited Dea to visit you in Scotland…'

'Yes, of course. She's arriving tomorrow. What's Dea got to do with this?'

'I'd rather not go into detail over the phone, sir.'

'This is a secure line, Lieutenant, you may say anything you wish.'

'Yes, sir, but I'd rather you hear it from Dea tomorrow. We'll speak again after that.'

'Are you sure?'

'Yes, I'll call you after you've spoken to her.'

MacLeod sighed. 'Very well, Lieutenant, we'll do it your way.'

'Thank you, sir. If there's nothing else then—'

'Wait, Lieutenant.'

Donadze guessed what MacLeod was about to say. 'Yes, sir?'

'You said Connor's killer *targeted* him?'

'Yes, we believe so.'

'And the first victim, the young female student?'

'We continue to believe her killer chose her at random.'

'But why would anyone kill this student at random but target Connor?' MacLeod was getting angry. 'This doesn't make any sense, Lieutenant.' He paused. 'Wait, you talked about the student's killer *and* Connor's killer—not *their* killer. They're different people, aren't they, Detective. It wasn't this *Fenrir* character who murdered my son.'

Donadze glanced at Patterson, listening to the exchange, her eyes wide. He'd decided to call MacLeod from the embassy on a whim, a reaction to Patterson's summons and her attempt to manipulate him. But he regretted doing that now. He'd been instructed by Colonel Meskhi not to disclose that there was a second killer in order to provoke Fenrir. Donadze had disagreed with that tactic but understood its logic. 'It's early days, sir,' he said. 'Let's speak again after you've met Dea.'

SEVENTEEN

Sergo Kokoevi felt the policeman's eyes on his back. He shuffled from the doorway, his sleeping bag stuffed into its cover and tied with bootlaces to the rucksack holding every other item he possessed. This cop had been okay: young, softly spoken, apologetic even, giving him a ten *lari* note along with an instruction to buy food. *Food*, he'd stressed. *Food, nothing else.*

It was different last night. That cop had kicked him awake, threatening, disgust and contempt washing off him in waves. But Sergo recognised him for what he was, reading fear in the man's narrow eyes and tight mouth. *Yes, you should be scared*, he'd thought. *How many pay checks would you have to miss before you're out here with me, on these streets?* But he'd said nothing of course, submissive, hoping to avoid a sly kick to his belly or ribs, accepting—as if he had a choice—the finger in his face, the sour breath, *I don't want to see you on this street again. Find yourself somewhere else to sleep, do you understand?*

It was June now, ten months since the injury which had cost him his job at the car wash and disqualified him for any other physical work. Eight months since his landlord had thrown him out, delighted to rent the tiny bedsit to Russians dodging the war in Ukraine. Six months since he'd exhausted his only friend's charity and slept rough for the first time—cold and terrified—on a park bench.

Sergo could barely remember life in South Ossetia, the home and family he'd lost when Georgia and Russia went to war—a tragically unequal struggle. A Russian shell had destroyed their home, killing his father. His mother should have fled with him but wouldn't, and now she too was dead, her grave tended by Ossetian neighbours—friends who'd become enemies then friends again in death. And his sister, Kristy, eight when he'd last seen her, separated during the fighting, a fading picture his last and only connection to her.

Life had been hard even before his injury. Refugees from the conflict zones had created a pool of cheap labour for unscrupulous employers to exploit. Sergo had taken whatever work was available for whatever money he was offered, earning just enough to get by. He'd bustle to or from building sites, hotels, bars, wherever he'd found work, hurrying passed the homeless men and women he'd encounter, some from South Ossetia—a blight on the city. Or so he'd thought. He'd walk past their sad, grubby blankets, their broken paper cups held in grimy, outstretched hands, their hard luck stories penned onto cardboard placards, fingers at their throats making the universal sign for hunger. He'd keep his distance, avoiding eye contact, telling himself they were lazy, alcoholics, junkies, mentally ill, fakers.

But their life was *his* life now: exhausted, hungry,

lonely, too cold or too hot, always scared. A continuous mission to find food and a safe place to get through the night.

The killer known as Fenrir watched the exchange, unobserved in the shadows blanketing the far side of the wide road. A patrolman had moved a vagrant on from the store's entrance. A few words had been spoken and he was on his feet, his gait stiff and sore, his cardboard bedding abandoned. The patrolman hesitated a moment then returned to his car where his partner waited. The car drove off, its siren blipping a perfunctory farewell.

Fenrir hated cops. He wished he could kill one tonight. He wished it could be Ramaz Donadze, the cop trying to find him, the cop who'd ignored his message about the Scotsman's murder. But he wasn't ready for Donadze—not yet. His first message had been ignored but he would send another. He wondered if the vagrant, a hunched, shuffling excuse for a human being was worthy. He shrugged then crossed the road, unsheathing his knife. *Probably not,* he thought. *But someone would die tonight and it might as well be him.*

EIGHTEEN

'Lieutenant! Lieutenant!' the TV reporter shouted, frantically attempting to attract Donadze's attention. 'Has Fenrir killed again? Can you confirm the victim was a homeless man this time? Do you have a name, yet?'

Donadze locked his car, ignoring the rapid-fire questions.

The reporter turned her attention to Jaqeli. 'What reassurance can you offer our viewers, Detective? Are the police any closer to finding Fenrir?'

'Excuse me,' Jaqeli said.

The journalist muttered something then snapped an instruction to her cameraman. She took a moment to pat her lacquered hair and compose her face into a picture of compassion and concern before a bright light snapped on and she addressed her television audience.

'Let's go, Irina,' Donadze said, walking to the police barrier.

'Sorry, Lieutenant,' one of the officers said. 'They got here just after we did. Someone must have tipped them off.'

'It looks that way, doesn't it? Any idea who that could have been?' he said, watching the officer colour.

'No, how could we know that?'

'No way at all,' Donadze said, ducking under the barrier.

'Did you just accuse these cops of tipping off the media?' Jaqeli asked as they walked towards the forensic tent.

'They got the message then? I wasn't too subtle?'

'Oh, they got the message alright, subtlety's not your thing.'

'Good, they might think twice next time.'

Roman Ketsbaia was standing outside the tent, wearing a protective suit and boots. He took a deep draw on his e-cigarette, exhaling a cloud of scented vapour into the warm, still air.

'Hey, Roman,' Jaqeli said. 'I didn't know you smoked.'

Ketsbaia smiled. 'Used to. Vaping doesn't count.'

Donadze nodded his greeting. 'Have you been inside yet?'

'Yes, sir. I arrived about the same time as Natia.'

'Okay, so what have we got?'

'Sergo Kokoevi, thirty three, homeless.' Ketsbaia paused. 'His throat's been cut…'

'Another stealth killing?'

Ketsbaia nodded. 'Just like the other two.'

'So, Fenrir then.'

'I don't know, Lieutenant, possibly. But we got it wrong before…'

'Not this time. It's Fenrir, I'm certain of it.' Donadze

forced a smile. 'Keep your eyes on me. Don't make any sudden movements,' he murmured. He waited until certain that Ketsbaia and Jaqeli had understood his instructions. 'Fenrir could be here, watching us.'

'He might be…' Ketsbaia agreed.

'Let's try something. I'm going to take out my phone as if I'm receiving a call.' Donadze patted his pocket, removing his phone and turning away from Ketsbaia and Jaqeli. 'Yes, Colonel?' he said, frowning as he used peripheral vision to survey the small gathering which had formed behind the police barrier. 'Okay, Roman,' he said, still speaking into his phone. 'Back of the group, to your left. About forty, dark hair, denims, black leather jacket.'

'Got him.'

'Good. I'm going to hang up now and give you my car keys and ask you to bring me something. Walk slowly to the barrier, keep your head down, avoid eye contact. Go through the barrier to the back of the group as if you're walking towards my car. Get behind Black Jacket then move in. Make it quick.'

'Sir.'

'Be careful, if that is Fenrir, we know he can use a knife.'

'Understood.'

Donadze shook his head. 'But, Colonel,' he said then stopped talking as if being reprimanded. 'Yes, sir,' he added, then made a show of hanging up and returning his phone to his pocket.

'Colonel Meskhi?' Jaqeli asked, going along with the ruse.

'Who else?' Donadze fished in his pocket to retrieve his car keys. 'There's a folder on the back seat, Roman. Could you bring it over while Irina and I talk to Natia.'

'Okay, Lieutenant,' Ketsbaia said, walking towards the barrier, swinging the keys casually on his finger before dropping them into his pocket.

Donadze turned to face Jaqeli, his back to the gathering. 'Tell me what's happening, Irina.'

'Black Jacket's still there. But what makes you think he's Fenrir?'

'I don't know, just a feeling. What's happening now?'

'Roman's talking to the cop at the barrier, pointing at us. Right, he's through the barrier now, pushing through the crowd. Black Jacket hasn't moved yet.'

'Okay, pretend you're arguing with me about something.'

Jaqeli shook her head, 'That doesn't sound right to me, Ramaz,' she said, her voice rising.

'Well, you might not be happy with it, Irina, but that's the way we're doing it.'

Jaqeli dropped her voice. 'Roman's just about there.'

'Let me know when—'

'They're fighting, Ramaz! Black Jacket has—'

'Let's go!' Donadze said, turning and sprinting towards the barrier.

The group scattered, some screamed, panicked by the sudden outbreak of violence and the sight of the two detectives running towards them. By the time Donadze reached him, the man they'd called Black Jacket had been subdued, his arm twisted hard behind his back, a trickle of blood flowing down his face from a cut over his right eye.

'Okay, good work,' Donadze said, catching his breath. 'Check him for weapons.'

Ketsbaia cuffed the man's hands behind his back then

searched him, passing his wallet, mobile phone, keys and a small pocket knife to Jaqeli.

'What have I done?' he demanded, his voice tight and unsteady.

Donadze appraised the man, blood dripping off his chin onto a grubby shirt, clearly upset and frightened. Not how he'd imagined Fenrir the god killer would behave when arrested. 'What's your name?' he asked.

'David. David Kokhia. Why do you want to know? I've done nothing wrong.'

'Check his ID,' Donadze told Jaqeli.

She found the man's ID card in his wallet and showed it to Donadze. 'It checks, David Kokhia…'

'Okay,' Donadze sighed. 'Listen, David, we're going to—'

'Ramaz, behind you,' Jaqeli interrupted, her voice low and urgent.

He turned, startled as a bright light snapped on.

'Lieutenant Ramaz Donadze, have you finally caught your killer?' the reporter demanded. 'Is this man Fenrir?'

Donadze turned away from the camera and lights.

'What happened to his face, Lieutenant? Why is he bleeding?'

Donadze took the pocket knife from Jaqeli and opened it. The blade was spotted with rust, its edge blunt. He closed the knife and handed it to the frightened man. 'It's not him. Fix that cut and let him go,' he said.

❖

Natia Gagua's technician couldn't hide his smirk as Donadze and Jaqeli returned to the forensic tent. 'Parasites, right, Lieutenant?' he said, nodding in the direction of the retreating television crew.

He and Donadze had clashed during an earlier murder investigation. Donadze had thought him callous and disrespectful of the dead who were placed in his care. 'No, I don't think that. They're just doing their job.'

The technician shrugged. 'If you say so.'

'I do. Can we go in?'

The technician's mouth twisted as he tried and failed to find a clever response. 'I suppose you'd better,' he said, reaching for his cigarettes.

Gagua was packing her instruments away as Donadze followed Jaqeli into the tent. 'Irina, Ramaz,' she greeted them.

'Hey, Natia,' Donadze said. 'Sorry we kept you waiting.'

'No apology required.' Gagua smiled. 'I saw your encounter with the television people—you're going to be famous, Ramaz!'

'Can't wait.' He pointed to the corpse lying near the centre of the tent. 'So this is Sergo. What can you tell us about him?'

'Yes, this is the unfortunate Sergo Kokoevi. Probably not much *to* tell. Thirty three, according to his ID. Clearly living on the streets. Met his end in much the same way as your other victims.'

'Single deep cut, sharp blade, slicing rather than sawing across the neck,' Donadze recited.

'I'm glad you were paying attention, Ramaz,' Gagua said. 'At least your killer's been consistent.'

'Anything in the holdall, Natia?' Jaqeli asked.

'All of Sergo's worldly possessions, I would say—which

don't amount to much. Mainly the essentials for sleeping rough. However,' Gagua reached into her instrument case and retrieved two clear plastic evidence bags, each containing a photograph, 'you may be interested in these…'

Jaqeli took the bags from Gagua, examined them and passed them to Donadze. 'A young girl and a grave…' she said.

'*Kristy,*' Donadze read from the back of the first photo. 'Short for *Kristina,* probably. His daughter?'

'No, the picture's a bit beat-up but, judging by its resolution and how much it's faded, it looks to me like it was taken some time ago. How old would you say the girl is?'

'It's difficult to be sure, about seven or eight?'

'That's what I would guess. So even if the picture was taken say, ten years ago, that would make her at least seventeen or eighteen now. Sergo wasn't old enough to have a daughter that age.'

'So another relative, a sister?'

'Maybe.'

Donadze examined the second photograph. Its paper was creased, its image faded but still clear enough to capture a simple, well-kept grave with a small headstone, a vase of fresh flowers placed in its shade. 'The inscription's in Cyrillic. Russian?' he asked.

'No,' Gagua said. 'It's not Russian. Did you notice the letter *AE*? Only one language uses that letter in its Cyrillic alphabet.'

'Ossetian…' Jaqeli said.

'Yes. Sergo would have been seventeen when the Russians invaded South Ossetia and we went to war.'

'An IDP then…' Donadze said.

Jaqeli shook her head. 'And this is how we looked after him.'

'We could have done better,' Donadze said, remembering how his own family, classed as internally displaced persons—IDPs—had been forced to flee Abkhazia and how his mother had somehow kept the family fed and housed in ways he still didn't understand. Without her, what would his own fate have been? He crossed to Sergo Kokoevi's corpse—a dishevelled mound lying in a pool of congealing blood—and silently promised him he'd catch his killer.

Donadze and Jaqeli left the forensics tent and returned to his car. 'That was stupid,' he said. 'In front of the TV cameras as well.'

'There was nothing stupid about it, Ramaz. We just made the wrong call this time.'

He shook his head. 'There was something about that man that made me think he could be Fenrir. Probably just wishful thinking. Or desperation, maybe...'

'No, it wasn't either of these things. On another day we'd have been heroes. Anyway, nothing's changed, we've still got a killer to catch.'

'Yes, ma'am, you're right.' Donadze threw her a casual salute. 'And—try to keep up—it's two killers to catch.'

'I think I knew that, Ramaz,' she said as her phone buzzed. She looked at the screen and swiped to answer it. 'Koka?'

'Hey, Irina. Are you with the Lieutenant?'

'We're in his car,' she said, switching to speaker mode. 'What is it?'

'Have you checked your Insta?'

'Instagram,' she translated for Donadze. 'No, something interesting?'

'Definitely. Fenrir's posted again. Let me send you a link.'

Jaqeli's screen flashed a notification and she tapped it to bring up the post, reading it quickly. 'Well, we wanted to make Fenrir angry,' she said, handing her phone to Donadze. 'But is *this* what we wanted?'

There were two images: one of David Kokhia being arrested, his arm twisted behind his back, blood on his face, the TV crew lighting up the scene to capture the moment for posterity; the other taken outside the forensic tent hiding Sergo Kokoevi's body from public gaze. The accompanying caption read, *THIS IS 1 SHEEP THAT DIDN'T HAVE TO DIE! ASK RAMAZ DONADZE WHO KILLED CONNOR MACLEOD*!

Donadze returned the phone to Jaqeli. 'He's punishing me for letting the public think he killed MacLeod…'

Jaqeli ended her call with Patarava and turned to Donadze. 'That wasn't your decision, Ramaz. Colonel Meskhi gave you an order.'

Donadze shook his head. 'I don't always follow orders, Irina. Maybe I shouldn't have this time.'

'Do you think that would have stopped Fenrir killing again?'

'No, but it might not have been this soon. Sergo Kokoevi might still be alive and we might have stopped Fenrir before anyone else died.'

'Maybe that's all true, but we were a long way from catching him. We're much closer now. I didn't think so at the time but Colonel Meskhi was right, we've provoked him into making mistakes.' She paused, staring at Donadze expectantly. 'Didn't we?'

Donadze looked along the street. 'He chose the wrong location…'

'Yes. Some of these stores have CCTV, they might have recorded him in the area. I'll ask Misha to send uniforms to visit when they're open. What else?'

'Fenrir *did* return to the crime scene, he must have been here when we arrested Kokhia. His photos prove that.'

'You were right, Ramaz, he was in the crowd all along. We just guessed the wrong man.'

Donadze shut his eyes, trying and failing to recollect the other faces he'd seen behind the police barrier. 'No, I didn't register anyone else.'

'That might not matter…'

'The TV crew?'

'Yes. It wasn't just us they were filming.'

Donadze started his engine. 'Okay, Irina,' he said. 'Let's see what the GPB has got for us.'

NINETEEN

Donadze pulled up outside the Georgia Public Broadcaster's studios on Kostava Street. His phone had been buzzing incessantly on the drive over. 'Reporters,' he said, scanning his call history.

'How did they get your number?' Jaqeli asked.

'Our colleagues provide them—for a price. Haven't they got yours yet?'

'No, I'm obviously not important enough.' Jaqeli unclipped her seat belt. 'You know you're going to be asked about the Fenrir post, don't you?'

'I'd be amazed if I'm not.'

'What are you going to say?'

'I don't know, I'm still thinking about it.'

'Well, don't take too long.'

Their names were on the receptionist's visitors list. 'Take a seat,' he said, pointing to a waiting area. 'I'll let Nugzar know you're here.'

'Nugzar?' Donadze asked.

'Nugzar Janashia, *Moambe News* Editor.'

'Who did you speak to when you called?' Donadze asked, taking his seat.

'The station manager,' Jaqeli said. 'He must have asked Janashia to meet us.'

Donadze pointed to two large wall-mounted screens. 'That looks like his programme running now…'

The screens were displaying GPB's two channels live. TV1 was broadcasting its latest news bulletin, headlining the murder of a homeless man, Sergo Kokoevi. The sound was muted but closed captions followed the dialogue between a well-known studio presenter and the reporter who'd filed the story, the woman who'd tried to question Donadze. Her report included video of the detectives' arrival at the crime scene, a forlorn shot of the forensics tent where Kokoevi's body lay and the crowd panicking as David Kokhia was apprehended, only to be almost immediately released, his bloodied face featuring in closeup as the report ended.

The coverage returned to the newsroom where the presenter commented on the dramatic footage. She asked about the latest development in the police investigation, the Instagram post thought to have been made by the man known as Fenrir.

The reporter replied that, in an amazing twist, the killer, Fenrir—although claiming to have murdered student, Rusiko Darsalia—appeared to have denied killing Connor MacLeod, the British Home Secretary's son. She was sombre as she concluded that this latest development would do little to restore faith in the police investigation being led by Lieutenant Ramaz Donadze.

'That doesn't make our job any easier,' Jaqeli said.

'No, but then again, it wasn't meant to.'

The news programme finished and a middle aged man bustled up to them a few minutes later. 'Lieutenant, Detective,' he said, his hand extended. 'I'm Nugzar Janashia, News Editor. 'Sorry to have kept you waiting, I like to be in the control room when we're on air.'

'We'd guessed that's where you were,' Donadze said, pointing to the TV screens.

'Ah, yes. What a marvellous story.' He smiled, his hands moving excitedly. 'Fenrir, wolf and god killer, no one safe as he stalks a terrified city...'

'And brutally murders innocent people. That's not a *story* for us, Mr Janashia, *marvellous* or otherwise.'

'No, of course not, sorry,' Janashia said, his broad smile contradicting any contrition he may have felt. 'Well, let's talk in my office.'

He led the way to a compact, modern room with glass walls, his name and job title displayed on the door. 'Please sit down,' he said pointing to a small conference table and taking his own seat. He smiled at Jaqeli. 'You spoke to my manager, I believe?'

'Yes, that's correct, sir. As I mentioned to him, we'd like a copy of all the video your crew took at the crime scene, not just the edits that were broadcast.'

'So I understand. And the reason for that is?'

'Police business, Mr Janashia,' Donadze said. 'We need your footage to assist our investigation.'

Janashia smiled again. 'I'd realised that much, Lieutenant.' He dropped his voice and leaned forward. 'Tell me, the man you arrested, why did you think he was your killer?'

'Again, sir, that's police business, not something we can discuss with members of the public.'

'But there's legitimate public interest in your investigation, surely? This Instagram post, what did Fenrir mean when he said to ask you who killed Connor MacLeod? Have you been looking for the wrong man?'

'I'll ask Fenrir what he meant when I see him, *Nugzar*. Now, are you going to give us that video or do we have to come back with a warrant? And wouldn't that be a *marvellous* story, how Georgia's national broadcaster refused to cooperate with a murder investigation?'

Janashia hesitated a moment then opened a drawer to retrieve a memory stick, tossing it onto the table. 'It's usually better to keep the media onside, *Ramaz*,' he said.

Donadze lifted the stick. 'Good advice, sir,' he said, standing. 'I'll bear it in mind.'

❖

Patarava jumped to his feet as Donadze and Jaqeli entered the MIR.

'Relax, Koka,' Donadze said, nodding to Ketsbaia.

'Good timing, Lieutenant,' he said. 'Colonel Meskhi's on his way in.'

Donadze inwardly groaned. 'Did you find anything on the stores' CCTV?'

'We're still looking,' Patarava said. 'But we've only got video of Sergo so far.'

'Let's see it then.'

'Shouldn't we wait for the Colonel?' Jaqeli asked.

'No, he can catch up.'

'The resolution isn't great,' Patarava said, as fuzzy video

displayed on the screen. 'But this is the best we have so far.' The video followed a homeless man shuffling into a store entrance, stiff and clearly in pain as he pulled a cardboard box apart to lay it on the concrete.

'Making a bed for the night,' Jaqeli said. 'What a way to live.'

Patarava clicked on the progress bar. 'He's got some food here; that's a McDonald's carton. We wondered if someone had bought it for him.'

'Anything significant in that?' Donadze asked.

Jaqeli shook her head. 'Probably not, he might also have found it lying in the street or even pulled it from a bin.'

The door opened and Colonel Meskhi walked in ahead of Misha Arziani. '*Gamarjoba*,' he said, looking around the room and nodding in apparent approval.

'The Colonel would like to know more about Fenrir's latest victim, Ramaz,' Arziani said.

'Sergo Kokoevi, sir. We're reviewing the CCTV footage now.'

'Well let's do that together. Tell me about Kokoevi first.'

Donadze summarised what they knew of the victim, a thirty three year old homeless man, probably displaced from South Ossetia during the war with Russia, his throat cut using the same *technique*—a term Meskhi had disapproved of—that was used to kill Rusiko Darsalia and Connor MacLeod.

'And the Instagram post?'

'Fenrir's angry, Colonel. You got the result you wanted.'

'The result I wanted? I want two killers caught, Lieutenant. Do you think we're any closer to that now?'

'We may be,' Donadze conceded. 'Closer to catching Fenrir, at least. It looks like he miscalculated; there are several CCTV cameras on the street where Sergo was killed, he may be on one or more of them.' He held up the memory stick he'd taken from the GPB studios. 'And he may also be on this news footage.'

'That was careless of him, wasn't it, Lieutenant? But anger can do that to a person, I suppose.' Meskhi pointed to the screen. 'Carry on.'

'Sir,' Patarava said, nervously fumbling his mouse and keyboard. 'Should I go back to the beginning?'

'No,' Meskhi said. 'Keep going.'

Patarava clicked on the progress bar, the video now showing Kokoevi removing two photographs from his holdall and looking between them before returning them to the bag.

'We have these photos,' Donadze told Meskhi. 'A grave and a young girl. We think the girl is a relative, a sister maybe. The grave's in South Ossetia.'

'Which is why you believe Kokoevi was an IDP, I assume. And the grave?'

'Someone close to him, his mother, possibly. The photo's damaged and the inscription's in Ossetian Cyrillic but we should be able to identify it.'

Patarava advanced the video again. 'This is the last footage we have of Sergo—being moved on from the store by a patrolman.'

'You've spoken to him?' Donadze asked.

'Yes, but he didn't see anything out of the ordinary.'

'How far is it from the store to where the body was found?' Arziani asked.

'Not far,' Donadze said. 'What do you think, Irina? Less than a hundred metres?'

'Yes, about that.'

Arziani nodded. 'It wouldn't have taken Sergo long to cover that distance, even at the pace he was walking. Fenrir must have been watching him while he was in the store entrance. He must have been close.'

'Probably just across the road,' Jaqeli said. 'It's darker there, more places to hide, fewer cameras.'

'What do we do about the Instagram post, Colonel?' Donadze asked.

'We release a press statement and inform the public that we're looking for two killers now.'

'What do we say when we're asked how long we've had that information?'

Meskhi unfolded his long body out of his chair. He stepped close to the screen, the video paused—fuzzy and dark—as Sergo Kokoevi shuffled out of the camera's field of view, a dead man walking. 'I'm sure you'll think of something, Lieutenant,' he said.

❖

Patarava finished writing on his pad, thanking the caller and hanging up.

'Anything useful?' Ketsbaia asked.

'That was Kristina Kokoevi, her friends call her *Kristy*…'

'The girl in the picture? Sergo's sister?'

Patarava nodded. 'She saw the news reports.'

'It's definitely her?' Donadze asked.

'Yes, definitely. Her account matches what we know of

Sergo. She said they were separated during the war and she hasn't seen him since. Didn't even know he was in Tbilisi.'

'Did you ask her about the grave?'

'Yes, I did. She hasn't been able to visit it and didn't know there was a photo. But she confirmed the name on the headstone, it's her mother's.'

'Does she have any other relatives?'

'Some cousins, an aunt, all still in South Ossetia as far as she knows. But with the border closed…'

'I know, it's nearly impossible to get in touch. Is she in Tbilisi now?'

'No, she's living in the Shavshvebi settlement.'

'That settlement was supposed to be temporary,' Ketsbaia said. 'It's been there more than fifteen years now—and counting.' Seven thousand homes had been rapidly constructed to house the estimated 26,000 people displaced by the war with Russia, three hundred being built near the village of Shavshvebi, an hour's drive from Tbilisi. Government policy was to return all displaced people to their homes in South Ossetia but that had proved unrealistic as the border hardened under Russian influence.

'She wants to see her brother,' Patarava said.

'That's understandable. Do you think we need to interview her, Ramaz?' Jaqeli asked.

'We should do, although I doubt she'll have anything useful for us after all this time.' Donadze thought for a moment. 'Koka, call her back and tell her I'll pick her up tomorrow. I'll take her to see Sergo and we can talk in the car.'

'Are you sure you need to go, Ramaz?' Jaqeli asked. 'It'll take up a good part of your day. Why not let me go instead?'

'No, that's okay, it's something I should do.' He looked

at the wall clock. 'It's getting late, do you want to stop now and make a fresh start tomorrow?'

Jaqeli shook her head. 'No, I'm okay. I'll stay and work on the video.'

'I'll stay a bit longer as well, Lieutenant,' Patarava said.

Ketsbaia reached for the GPB memory stick. 'And me….'

Donadze hesitated, knowing he would miss eating with Tamuna, miss giving Eka her bath and putting her to bed, their time together as a family fast running out. 'Okay, thanks,' he said, reaching for his keyboard. 'In that case, I'd better stay and keep you company.'

Donadze had a call to make. He left his team working in the MIR and went outside. He took a deep breath, getting his thoughts in order, knowing the conversation would be difficult.

Rory MacLeod picked up almost immediately. 'Ah, the scheming Lieutenant Donadze,' he said. 'One minute.' The line went quiet, Donadze imagining the Home Secretary requesting privacy in his office. 'Tell me why I should even take this call, Lieutenant,' MacLeod said a moment later.

'With respect, sir, you already know that or you wouldn't have taken it.'

'Oh, very good, the kind of clever response I should have expected,' MacLeod said, his tone sarcastic but mild, his words measured but somehow more threatening because of that. 'Have you any idea how angry I am, Donadze?'

'I can guess, sir. But it wasn't my intention to upset you.'

'I'm not upset, Lieutenant. I'm angry, very angry. I have your Minister of Internal Affairs' number on my desk. Tell me why I shouldn't call him.'

It was late in the evening in Tbilisi. Donadze was tired and becoming angry himself. 'If you think that would help catch your son's killer, Mr MacLeod, then go right ahead.'

There was a moment's pause. 'No, I don't imagine that would help at all,' MacLeod said, suddenly deflated. 'You're a rather unconventional police officer, aren't you, Donadze. Are they all like that in your country?'

'Thankfully not, sir.'

MacLeod made a sound that could have been a short laugh. 'Well, Lieutenant, despite your unusual methods, I do believe you sincerely want to catch Connor's killer. And that's why I took your call.'

'Have you spoken to Dea, sir?'

'Of course I have. She delivered your message. I don't know who you put in the worst position, her or me.'

Donadze didn't want to reopen their argument. 'In that case, you know everything I know. We think Connor was targeted to stop a post going out on his website. His laptop was stolen but it would be unusual not to have a backup. That could have been deleted from the cloud but still retrievable with the right expertise.'

'Which MI5 has.'

'Yes, if it's there, MI5 could find it.'

'I understand, but this wouldn't be the first time the United Kingdom has supported an ally. Why not make a formal request? I'd make sure it was approved.'

'Again, with respect, sir, I think you know why we shouldn't do that.'

'Because the Metropolitan Police may have killed my son?'

'It's one line of enquiry, but it's credible. Any support would have to be discreet.'

'You understand how dangerous this could be for me—politically?'

'I don't have much time for politics, sir.'

'Or politicians, I imagine.'

'Will you help us find your son's killer, Mr MacLeod?'

'You're good at this, aren't you, Lieutenant? Using words to manipulate the outcome you want, emotional blackmail.'

Donadze didn't respond, knowing the Home Secretary had made his decision.

'Of course I'll help you find Connor's killer,' MacLeod snapped, abruptly ending the call.

TWENTY

Donadze returned to the MIR where Ketsbaia was waiting for him. 'How did it go, Lieutenant?' he asked.

'He's going to help. Are you ready?'

Ketsbaia lifted his laptop. 'Yes, I've got it on here.'

'Good. It's late, take your own car and we'll call it a night after this.'

Ketsbaia arrived at Kurdiani Street first, Donadze pulling up behind him. He nodded towards the neglected building. 'You said you haven't been here before?'

'It's not my kind of place, Lieutenant.'

'Nor mine.'

The Squad was as busy as it ever got, nine or ten men, but no women, sitting around four or five tables, solemnly and determinedly drinking to get drunk. What little conversation there might have been stopped as the two detectives entered.

'Who's this?' Beka Gabelia asked as they approached the bar.

'I'm Sergeant Roman Ketsbaia. Who are *you*?'

'You know who I am.' Gabelia straightened, appraising him. 'Army?'

'Once upon a time.'

Gabelia turned to Donadze. 'And that's why you brought him?'

Donadze shrugged. 'That's right.'

'What do you want, Ramaz?'

'You should have got back to me by now.'

Gabelia gestured and the man whom Donadze remembered was called Sasha ambled over. 'Everything okay, Beka?' he asked, sizing up the detectives.

'Yes, there's no problem. Keep an eye on things for me.' He pointed to a table where two men were hunched motionless over an empty bottle and shot glasses. 'They've had enough. They don't have to leave if they behave themselves but don't give them any more to drink.' He removed a grubby towel from his shoulder and dropped it onto the bar top. 'I'll be in the backroom,' he said, wincing as he limped from behind the bar.

The backroom was as dishevelled as Donadze remembered from his previous visit, the bed unmade, the room unventilated after Gabelia had last cooked, a frying pan and dishes dropped into the sink unwashed.

'What a rat hole,' Ketsbaia said. 'I thought you said he was Army, Lieutenant?'

Gabelia froze, his face dropping all expression. Then he laughed. 'What did you say your name was?'

'Roman Ketsbaia, Sergeant Roman Ketsbaia.'

'Okay, Sergeant Ketsbaia. Do you want a drink?'

'I'll take a beer. Don't bother with the glass,' he added pointedly.

Gabelia smiled. 'Don't blame you. What about you, Ramaz? You look like you need a drink.'

'Just coffee.'

Gabelia crossed to the kitchen area and flicked a switch on an electric kettle. He picked up a mug, examined it then spooned in a mound of instant coffee and sugar. He opened a small fridge and retrieved a bottle, opening and slamming drawers as he searched for an opener. He eventually gave up and flipped the top on the edge of the worktop, beer foaming out of the neck and dripping onto the already sticky vinyl floor.

Ketsbaia nodded his thanks and took a swig from the bottle.

'Where did you say you served?' Gabelia asked.

'I didn't.'

'Thought so, you've got that look about you.' He lowered himself onto a chair, grimacing as he straightened his prosthetic leg. 'So, what can I do for you, Ramaz?'

'We're still looking for Rusiko Darsalia's killer. And now he's killed again, a homeless man this time. His name was Sergo Kokoevi, a refugee from the war. Both murders look like military stealth killings.' Donadze paused. 'You said you'd let me know if there's anyone we should be looking at.'

Gabelia grinned. 'So, it's my fault this homeless guy was killed?'

'I didn't say that.'

'You didn't have to. I said I'd ask around and that's what I did. There wasn't anyone.'

'Well this might help.' Donadze turned to Ketsbaia. 'Show him the video.'

Ketsbaia took his laptop from his bag, opened the lid and passed it to Gabelia.

'It's short,' Donadze said. 'Watch carefully.'

Gabelia pressed play. 'Fenrir?' he asked, his mouth tightening.

The video ended.

'Play it again.'

Gabelia shook his head as the clip played once more. 'Fenrir?' he asked again.

'Yes, do you recognise him?'

Gabelia gazed at the screen, the store CCTV and GPB news video compilation ending on the clearest shot of Fenrir that Donadze and his team had found: a man walking the street where Kokoevi had died, the same man watching from behind the police barrier, hooded, his face in shadow.

'No,' Gabelia said, his voice flat. 'I can't help you.'

'Take another look.'

'There's no need.' He returned the laptop to Ketsbaia. 'I've got to get back to the bar. Finish your drinks.'

'You never gave me mine.'

'No, but you didn't want it anyway,' Gabelia said, standing and limping out of the room.

Ketsbaia poured his beer down the sink, turning to Donadze. 'Did you believe him?'

'Did *you*?'

'No.'

'Neither did I.'

❖

Ketsbaia turned to Donadze. 'So what do we do now?'

'It's late, we go home.'

'But what about Gabelia?'

'What about him?'

'He recognised the man in the video, we both saw that. He can tell us who Fenrir is.'

'But he also denied knowing him. What should we do, arrest him? Lock him up and sweat him till he tells us what he knows? That wouldn't work on Gabelia, just as it wouldn't work on you.'

'So we do nothing?'

'I didn't say that. You don't know him like I do. The Army was everything to him. It still is. If Fenrir is—or was—a soldier then he's brought dishonour on himself and the Army. At least, that's the way Gabelia will see it. I'll speak to him again tomorrow, maybe he'll be more open if I'm on my own. Anyway, I know he'll do the right thing, he just needs time to think about it.'

'And while he's doing that, Fenrir is still out on the streets.'

'Yes, but he's only just killed. It'll be a while till he wants—or needs—to do it again.'

'Are you sure about that, Lieutenant?'

'No, but I *am* sure we won't get anything out of Gabelia until he's ready to give it to us. Go home, Roman, I'll see you tomorrow.'

Donadze checked the time as Ketsbaia's car pulled away. It was after eleven, Tamuna would be sleeping. Once again, he'd prioritised his work over time with his family. He told himself he'd had no choice, that he was closing in on a killer and couldn't let up, it was the nature of policing. And he was making progress, he now knew what Fenrir looked like and was confident he'd soon have his name.

He got into his car and drove home, windows open and music playing, trying to stay alert as the exhilaration of the hunt gave way to bone-weary exhaustion. He parked and took the elevator to the fourth level, opening and closing his apartment door as quietly as its steel-on-steel construction allowed.

'Ramaz?' he heard Tamuna say.

He walked to their bedroom. 'Did I wake you?'

'No.' She sat up. 'Are you okay?'

'I'm fine. We had a breakthrough on the investigation, that's all. There was someone I had to speak to.'

'Do you want to talk about it?'

'Yes, but it can wait until morning.'

'Come to bed then.'

'I will, just let me check on Eka first.'

'Don't wake her,' Tamuna said, lying back on the bed and pulling the duvet up.

Donadze walked to his daughter's room, using his phone's flashlight to gaze down on the little girl as she slept. There was not much time remaining until she and Tamuna would leave him to go to Germany. He reached into the cot and placed his hand on her chest, feeling its slow rise and fall. 'Don't forget me, *chemo patara*,' he whispered.

TWENTY-ONE

It took Donadze a while to realise his phone was buzzing him awake. He groped for the hateful device and silenced it, resisting the snooze button and a delicious ten minutes longer in bed. He swung his legs from under the duvet and sat for a moment, his eyes closed and gritty.

Tamuna groaned. 'What time is it?'

'Five thirty, go back to sleep.'

'It's okay, I'll get up. I need to speak to you before you leave.'

'Something you want to tell me now?'

'No, it's nothing to worry about.'

Revitalised after a hot shower, Donadze dressed and walked to the living room.

Tamuna had made them coffee. He nodded his thanks, took a sip then spooned extra sugar into the cup when her back was turned.

'Does your early start have something to do with the breakthrough you mentioned?' she asked.

'No, I'm letting that sit for a while. Sergo Kokoevi's

sister got in touch. She asked to see his body and I said I'd take her. She's an IDP, living in the Shavshvebi settlement and I want to get clear of the town and onto the Expressway before the traffic gets too bad.'

'That's probably a good idea. So what *was* your breakthrough?'

'We've found someone who can identify Fenrir.'

'Wow, that really is a breakthrough.'

'I just need to handle him the right way. He's ex-Army, which means he has some loyalty issues to process before he'll speak to me. What did you want to talk about?'

'Eliso. You were right, something *has* been on her mind, that's why she'd been crying when you saw her. She's been charged with shoplifting.'

'Really? Did she admit it?'

'Yes, it was stupid really, less than a hundred *lari's* worth of groceries. She doesn't know why she did it and swears she's never done anything like it before.'

'She hasn't, at least she's never been *caught* before. I know because I checked to see if she had a police record before you hired her. Where does that leave us?'

'As far as Eka is concerned, nothing's changed. But she'll be out of a job if I go to Germany and she'd find it difficult to get another one with this on her record. Is there any way you could help?'

'How? You want me to get the charges dropped?'

'Is that something you could do?'

Donadze shook his head. 'No, Tamuna, I couldn't. It's not like the movies where you speak to a friendly cop and he gets your speeding tickets ripped up. There has to be a reason for the police to drop charges once they're made.'

'What sort of reason?'

'If it's not in the public interest, a first offence maybe. Or the victim could decide to withdraw the complaint.'

'Well, it *is* a first offence. And how could charging Eliso over less than a hundred *lari* be in the public interest?'

'It probably isn't, but she needs to make a case through her lawyer.'

'She doesn't have one. So you won't help her?'

'You shouldn't put it that way, Tamuna. I *can't* help her, it wouldn't be right if I tried.'

Tamuna smiled. 'Okay. You'd better get going,' she said. 'Forget I asked.'

❖

Donadze had planned to leave his apartment sooner, but it was still early enough to avoid the worst of the city traffic and he reached the S1 Expressway heading west in good time. It was a beautiful morning and, for once, a pleasure to be on the road, the three-lane highway fast, uncongested and relatively safe.

He replayed the conversation with Tamuna over in his mind, realising that he could have been more supportive in helping her get the charges against their nanny dropped. She wouldn't have asked for his help if she hadn't thought it important and he felt he'd let her down.

Donadze forced his thoughts back to his investigation. He almost regretted insisting on picking up Sergo Kokoevi's sister, knowing the round trip would take at least half the day. His best lead now was Beka Gabelia and he was keen to talk to him again, confident that, with a little persuasion, he would give up Fenrir's name.

A young woman was standing in the shade of the Shavshvebi settlement's community centre as Donadze drove in on the approach road. He stopped his car and wound down the window. 'Kristy?' he asked.

A warm, dusty breeze was blowing over the surrounding fields, whipping her long, dark hair across her face. She pushed it behind her ears as she approached the car. 'Lieutenant Donadze?'

'Ramaz will do.' He showed her his badge and leaned across the car to push the passenger door open. 'If you're ready…'

'Yes, I'm ready.' She walked around the car and got in. '*Madloba*,' she said, pulling the door closed.

Donadze turned the car and drove back to the Expressway.

He glanced at the young woman as he accelerated into the traffic flow heading towards the city. 'I'm sorry about Sergo,' he said.

She shook her head. 'I can't stop thinking about him. It's just so sad, my own brother living like that. Out on the streets, vulnerable. I suppose that makes me the lucky one.'

'Because you have a home in Shavshvebi?'

'At least I had people to care for me when I left South Ossetia. I could have looked out for Sergo if we'd stayed together—but it's too late to do anything for him now.'

Donadze paused, reluctant to talk about himself. 'I know how you feel,' he said at last. 'My family was displaced during the Abkhazian War. But I was luckier than you or Sergo, I still had my parents to watch out for me.'

'Is that what took you to Tbilisi?'

'Yes, but it's home now.'

'Do *you* have any siblings?'

Donadze hesitated. 'I used to. My sister, Ana,' he said. 'But she was killed before we could get out of Abkhazia. There was nothing I could do for her either,' he added.

'I'm sorry, Ramaz.'

'It was a long time ago. You would have helped Sergo if you could. Maybe you'd have helped each other...'

'That's what I tell myself. I did try to find him, a few years ago. I asked around, people who might know him, places he might go. But I didn't even know he was in Tbilisi, didn't even know he was still alive.'

'People can get lost in the city, Kristy. It's easy to live under the radar, if that's what you want to do.'

'I suppose so. Where is he now?'

'He's in the National Forensics building.'

'The morgue?'

'Yes, the morgue. You'll see him there.'

'Okay,' she said. 'That's good.'

Donadze picked up something in her tone. 'You don't have to go—if you'd rather not.'

'No, I want to. I'm just dreading what I'll see, what he'll look like.'

'He'll look like your brother, Kristy.'

A tear slid down her cheek. 'I don't even remember how Sergo does look. I've only got faint memories of South Ossetia, nothing of his, not even a photo. It's been sixteen years since I last saw him...'

'Well he had *your* photo, you must have meant a lot to him.'

'Maybe that used to be true.' She paused. 'Why Sergo, Ramaz? He couldn't have been a threat to anyone.'

'He wasn't. It was just bad luck. He wasn't targeted for any real reason.'

'And the man who killed him, was he the man who killed that young student, *Fenrir*?'

'Yes, it was Fenrir.'

'Do you think you'll find him?'

'I'm certain of it.'

'Do you always catch your killers, Ramaz?'

'No, not always,' he admitted.

Traffic was slowing and bunching as they approached the city's outskirts. Donadze guessed it would be another thirty minutes before they reached the morgue. He glanced at his passenger; she was sleeping now, her breathing slow and easy. *It really wasn't your fault, Kristy*, he told her silently. But he hadn't been able to save Ana and he knew that her guilt, like his own, would always be with her.

❖

Kristy Kokoevi asked to be dropped off at the community centre. Donadze watched in his rear view mirror as she waved goodbye, his wheels spinning clouds of dust and gravel as he accelerated away from the Shavshvebi settlement and the people who lived there; displaced by a war they hadn't wanted, housed in a region they hadn't known, abandoned with little opportunity or hope of escape.

Donadze glanced at his dash clock. He was glad that he'd taken Kristy to visit her dead brother, believing that seeing him one last time would help her accept his death. But it was mid-afternoon now and he was anxious to get back to work. He'd also spent too long in his car; what had begun as a pleasant experience had now become a chore. He eased the car over the Expressway's speed limit, hoping to shorten his journey time to Mtatsminda Station.

He needn't have bothered; the traffic was again dense around the city's outskirts and he reconciled himself to completing the journey at snails' pace.

'Hey, Ramaz,' the Desk Sergeant greeted him as he eventually entered the station. 'Did you know that Major Gloveli was coming in?'

Gloveli had messaged Donadze that he had business in Tbilisi and would visit friends and colleagues while there. Despite being retired, Gloveli had maintained his professional networks, being given information that often allowed impressive insights into current police investigations. But Donadze was busy and the old policeman's visit would, on this occasion, be a distraction. 'Yes, it's always great to see him,' he said.

'Definitely one of the best.'

Yes, he is, Donadze acknowledged to himself as he walked towards the detectives' bureau, confident that he'd find his friend there.

He was right. Gloveli was at the centre of a small group of police officers and admin staff, happily sharing jokes and retelling war stories, pleased to be reunited with their former commander. Donadze was reminded once again that his friend and mentor remained a natural and charismatic leader.

He held up his hand in greeting as he walked past the group to Misha Arziani's office. 'Hey, Misha,' he said. 'Busy?'

Arziani closed the lid on his laptop, pointing to the gathering outside. 'Trying to be.'

'Do you want me to arrest him?'

'No, that's okay,' Arziani said, laughing. 'He won't outstay his welcome. How was Sergo's sister?'

'Upset, but I think she'll be okay.'

'Did she have anything new for you?'

'No, but I wasn't really expecting anything.'

'Well, I'm sure she appreciated the ride to the morgue, if nothing else.' He paused. 'You're letting your Army buddy stew a bit longer?'

'He's not really my buddy, Misha. But no, his time's up. I'm going to his bar this evening.'

'You're convinced he can tell you who Fenrir is?'

'I'm sure of it. He knows what Fenrir did and he's not happy about it. It's just some kind of Army-loyalty nonsense that's holding him back. Brothers-in-arms, you know what that's like.'

'Yes, I do. But it's not entirely nonsense, is it?'

'No,' Donadze conceded. 'It's not.'

He watched through the office window as Gloveli got unsteadily to his feet, shaking hands with the men, exchanging kisses with the women, promising to keep in touch as his entourage broke up and returned to work. He steadied himself then crossed to Arziani's office. '*Madloba*, Captain,' he said, offering his hand and nodding to Donadze. 'I'm going now, I hope I haven't been too disruptive.'

'Not at all, Major, we're always pleased to see you.'

'That's good of you to say so. Do you mind if I borrow Donadze for a minute?'

'You can have him for as long as you want.'

'Come on, Major,' Donadze said. 'I'll walk you to the door.'

Gloveli's gait was slow and painful and Donadze walked beside him, ready to provide a steadying hand if required. 'How long are you in Tbilisi for?' he asked.

'Not long, I've got some business at the bank then I'm heading back to Shindisi.'

'That's a pity, Tamuna and Eka would have liked to have seen you.'

'Yes, I'd like to have seen them as well. But you're working this evening anyway, aren't you?'

'Someone's been talking?'

'Someone always talks. It's a human condition.' Gloveli hesitated. 'How *are* Tamuna and my goddaughter?'

'You've heard they're going to Germany?'

'Yes, I'd heard. How do you feel about it?'

'Is that really why you're in Tbilisi, Levan? To give me advice about my family?'

'No, I told you, I have to go to the bank. I'm lending Lasha some money to invest in the crypto scheme I told you about.'

They reached the station entrance. Gloveli exchanged a few words and shook hands with the Desk Sergeant as Donadze impatiently waited.

'Which bank are you going to?' he asked as he held the door open.

'The First National on Marjanishvili Square. Don't worry, I've booked a taxi,' Gloveli said, anticipating the offer of a lift.

'Okay.' Donadze paused. 'Crypto: you do know it's more of a gamble than an investment, don't you, Major?'

'Yes, but I'm not clearing out my accounts. Just lending Lasha enough cash to get him started.'

'And if it crashes?'

Gloveli's taxi pulled up. 'It doesn't matter,' he said. 'It's only money. So, how *do* you feel about Tamuna and Eka going to Stuttgart?'

'About as bad as you could imagine. But I have to let them go.'

Gloveli offered his hand. 'Yes, you do. It'll be better for you all in the long term.'

Donadze held the taxi door open as Gloveli lowered himself in. He held up his hand in farewell as it pulled away. 'So I've been told,' he said.

TWENTY-TWO

The Squad's door was locked, its lights off. A couple of frustrated customers, former soldiers Donadze guessed, stood outside, rattling the door, unable to accept that their favourite bar hadn't opened yet.

'You're the cop that Beka knows,' one said, his tone suggesting it was Donadze's fault they couldn't get in.

'That's right,' Donadze said. 'Do you two come here every night?'

The men exchanged a look. 'Not *every* night.'

'Most nights then. Have you ever known Beka not to open.'

'No, never. Six o'clock, every evening, regular.' One of the men rattled the door again, cupping his mouth and shouting, 'Beka' at the unlit building.

'Better try somewhere else,' Donadze advised.

'Why, do you think something's happened to him?'

'Try somewhere else,' Donadze repeated. He ran his phone's flashlight along the door's edges and locks, seeing no obvious damage. He pressed his face against the window, his hands blocking out what little streetlight there was, observing the unattended bar and stacked chairs, unmoved since the seating area had last been cleaned.

The two customers had retreated a few steps but were watching him closely, one talking into his phone. He ended his call as Donadze strode towards him. 'Who were you speaking to?' he demanded.

The man, definitely a former soldier, Donadze realised, dropped his phone into his jacket pocket and took up a fighting stance, his hands raised, knees softened. 'If that were any of your business,' he said, his nostrils flaring, 'I'd tell you.'

'Leave it, Dima,' his friend advised.

The first man took a couple of breaths then dropped his hands. 'It's still none of your business, cop.'

The confrontation had been an unnecessary distraction, Donadze thought. He looked up and down the street, calculating how to get to the alleyway which ran along the back of the bar and adjacent buildings.

A side road took him there. The alleyway was unlit but he moved quickly over the broken cobbles, avoiding discarded bags of garbage, empty bottles and cans, his eyes adjusting to the poor light. He reached the bar's rear entrance, an insubstantial door leading to Beka Gabelia's back room. A dim light was flickering through the single window, the murmur of what Donadze took to be a television advert, the only sound from inside. He used his phone's flashlight to illuminate the immediate area, observing wood splinters by his feet and the damaged door they'd come from. He moved clear of the line of fire, removed his pistol from its holster, sliding its safety off and cocking its hammer before calling for backup.

Weapon in hand, Donadze moved the door—its hinges dry and squealing—a couple of centimetres with his foot. He guessed it would take ten minutes or more for his backup to arrive and Gabelia might not have that long. Taking three deep breaths, he kicked the door fully open, pausing before stepping into the room, arms extended to hold and support his weapon, its sights aligned with his dominant right arm as he swept the area, seeking targets.

Gabelia had died in his squalid backroom. His tattooed arms and only leg had been lashed to the chair with wire, his prosthetic limb lying on the floor by his bed. His throat had been cut. The chair had either been pushed over by the killer or had fallen in the struggle and his blood had pooled around it, spilling across the grimy vinyl flooring.

Donadze took a deep breath then moved again, his weapon extended, following the route to the bar until, satisfied there was no one else in the building, he returned his pistol to its holder, his heart racing, his hands shaking.

He returned to the back room, found a switch and turned the lights on. He looked down on the body, remembering his service in the Army and Georgia's war with Russia. Gabelia had promised his terrified conscripts that he would keep them safe. And although they knew that warfare was indiscriminate and that Gabelia might not be able to deliver on his promise, they had still found comfort in his words. Donadze looked into his squad leader's lifeless eyes. 'I'm sorry I couldn't do the same for you, Sergeant,' he said, standing to salute his fallen comrade.

A patrol car had arrived, its blue and red roof lights strobing against The Squad's faded, grimy exterior.

Donadze left the bar and instructed the uniformed officers to call in Beka Gabelia's murder then secure the crime scene.

He returned to his car and called Roman Ketsbaia. 'Gabelia's dead,' he said.

Ketsbaia took a moment to respond. 'Fenrir?' he asked.

'Had to be. It was a knife to the throat, his favourite way to kill. He must have broken in when Gabelia was asleep, probably used a gun to subdue him and force him onto a chair, tied him to it then killed him. Or slaughtered him, more like.'

'I'm sorry, Lieutenant. I know you were close.'

'I wouldn't say we were close. We weren't even friends, as such. It was more like a shared history, some kind of *connection*.'

'Yes, but these connections can sometimes be stronger than friendship. You're assuming Gabelia was killed to stop him speaking to us?'

'What else could it have been?'

'But how did Fenrir find out?'

'I've been thinking about that. We know Gabelia recognised Fenrir from the video we showed him. But maybe he wanted to check out our story for himself, some kind of Army brotherhood thing. Maybe he didn't want to believe a soldier could do such a thing and decided to challenge him on it. And maybe it was that challenge that made Fenrir realise Gabelia had to die.'

'That's a lot of *maybes*, Lieutenant.'

'I know, too many. But it doesn't really matter *how*

Fenrir found out. Just that he *did* and decided to stop Gabelia speaking.'

'So, bottom line, we've lost our best lead,' Ketsbaia said.

'Bottom line, a man is dead who shouldn't be. I gave Fenrir too much time.'

'Don't put that on yourself, Lieutenant. You knew Gabelia wasn't going to talk to us right away.'

'Don't worry, Roman, this isn't the first bad decision I've had to live with. And anyway, none of this is about me. Gabelia's gone now and we'll have to think what to do next.'

'Yes, but that's obvious, isn't it?'

Donadze paused a moment. 'Not to me it isn't.'

'*The Squad* isn't a typical bar, Lieutenant. It's more like an Army social club than anything else. If Gabelia knew Fenrir then the chances are that some of his regulars know him as well.'

Donadze thought for a moment. 'There were a couple of military types hanging around outside when I turned up. Regulars, there most nights, they said. They were watching me and it was more than just curiosity. One of them was on his phone. There was something about him, the way he was observing me. It was almost like he was reporting in to somebody.'

'You don't know who that was?'

'No, I asked but nearly got into a fight over it.'

'And you didn't get any other names?'

'It didn't seem important and I didn't want to waste time getting to Gabelia. Wait, I remember, one was called *Dima*.'

'Dima, a regular at *The Squad*. He shouldn't be too difficult to find.'

'We'll have to move quickly. I want Fenrir caught before he kills again.' Donadze paused, thinking. 'These two wanted a drink. If they couldn't get one at Gabelia's place, they'd go somewhere else.'

'There are a lot of bars in Tbilisi, Lieutenant.'

'Yes, but these guys wouldn't care about ambiance. They'd want somewhere close by, on or around Kurdiani Street, somewhere that the drink is cheap and where they'd feel at home.' Donadze looked out his window at the patrolmen who were stringing crime scene tape. 'Call you back,' he said, hanging up.

❖

The patrolmen gave Donadze two possible places to try, both about five minutes' walk from Beka Gabelia's bar. One of the patrolmen thought the man Donadze knew as Dima was Dima Tugushi, a regular at The Squad and a known troublemaker. He couldn't identify the other man.

Donadze called Ketsbaia and told him to bring his laptop to *The Dragon*, the closer of the two bars. He considered walking there but decided he would be less conspicuous in his car. He arrived within a couple of minutes and parked where he had a clear view of the bar's entrance. He could see why the patrolmen had identified *The Dragon* as a likely place to look. Its frontage was as faded and grimy as *The Squad's*, with what had once probably been a glorious depiction of Saint George, his horse rearing as he speared the dragon, now in desperate need of a rub down and fresh paint.

Donadze settled into his seat, observing the bar as he waited for Ketsbaia.

A few minutes passed and Dima Tugushi came out of the bar, striding to Donadze's car and slamming his fist on its roof. 'Are you following me, cop?' he shouted.

Donadze pushed his door open, hard and fast, forcing the other man back on the pavement. He sprang out of the car. 'Yes, you're right, I've been looking for you, Tugushi,' he said.

Tugushi had made up for lost drinking time, his breath sour as he stepped closer to Donadze, his fists balled. 'Congratulations,' he slurred. 'So you know my name.'

'I know everything about you, Dima,' Donadze bluffed. He stepped even closer. 'How would you like another six months in Gldani?' he asked, guessing that the former soldier had served prison time there.

Tugushi attempted to laugh. 'For what?'

'For assaulting a police officer.'

'I didn't lay a *fucking* hand on you,' Tugushi said, less confident now.

'What if I say you did?'

Ketsbaia's car pulled up behind Donadze's. 'Everything okay, Lieutenant?' he asked, getting out.

'No problem, Sergeant. Dima was just telling me he doesn't want to go back to Gldani.'

Ketsbaia shuddered theatrically. 'Can't say I blame him, sir.'

'Bastards,' Tugushi mumbled, his fists unclenching. 'What do you want?'

'Where's your drinking buddy?'

'Vaso? He's gone home, why?'

'We might want to speak to him. Where does he live?'

'How would I know? I see him at Beka's place. We drink together, that's all.'

Donadze decided not to push it. 'You know what happened to Beka?'

Tugushi blinked several times. 'Some bastard killed him.'

'Yes, and you're going to give us his name.'

Donadze watched a sly look come over the other man's face. 'Look, Beka was a friend. Don't you think I'd tell you if I knew who killed him?'

'You don't have any friends, Dima. Get your laptop, Sergeant.'

'Sir,' Ketsbaia said, returning to his car. 'The video?' he asked, carrying the device back.

'Yes. Watch carefully, Dima.'

Ketsbaia opened the laptop's lid and faced the screen towards Tugushi.

Donadze observed the man closely as the video played. 'His name, Dima?' he demanded as the short clip ended.

Sweat had beaded on Tugushi's forehead. 'No, I don't know who that is.'

'Pity.' Donadze turned to Ketsbaia. 'Read Dima his rights then take him to the station. Charge him with that punch he threw at me and for resisting arrest.'

'Yes, sir. Turn around, Mr Tugushi,' Ketsbaia said, reaching for his cuffs.

'I'll meet you back at the station, Sergeant,' Donadze said, turning away.

'Okay, okay!' Tugushi snapped. 'I remember now. He comes to Beka's place now and again. Strange guy, always on his own, doesn't speak to anyone, sits all night with one beer. Anyone other than Beka would have thrown him out…'

'Army?'

Tugushi shrugged. 'Yeah, logistics or something like that. Not infantry, nothing front line.'

'Name?'

'I don't know.'

'Sergeant, take Dima—'

'For fuck's sake, do you want me to make something up? I told you, he never speaks to anyone. I don't know his *fucking* name.'

Donadze appraised Tugushi for a moment. 'Who were you speaking to on your phone?'

'My phone?'

'Outside Beka's place. You hung up when I came over.'

'Just someone who drinks at *The Squad*. I was letting him know it hadn't—'

'Don't lie to me, Dima. Who were you speaking to?'

Tugushi sighed. 'I called the Captain.'

'Captain who?'

'Captain Tatishvili. Sasha. You must have seen him at *The Squad*.'

Donadze nodded. 'He covers the bar for Beka?'

'Sometimes. Beka watches out for him, keeps him straight.'

'What does that mean?'

Tugushi shook his head.

'Does he have a habit?' Ketsbaia asked.

'How would I know?'

'Why did you call him?'

'I don't know. It was obvious something had happened to Beka, it just seemed the right thing to do…'

'They were friends?'

'No, not friends.'

'They served together?'

'Yes.'

'Where does he live?'

Tugushi shook his head again. 'Do what you want, that's all I'm saying.'

Donadze paused a moment. 'Okay,' he said. 'Let me see your phone.'

Tugushi sighed then patted his pockets, handing his phone over to Donadze.

He scrolled its call history, the last call made was to a contact listed as *captain s.*'

He took a photo of the contact with his own phone and returned Tugushi's. 'Call him. Tell him the police want to talk to him.'

'He'll know I've been speaking to you.'

'He'll know that anyway. Call him. Put him on speaker.'

Tugushi hesitated a moment then angrily jabbed the contact name. Tatishvili's phone rang, unanswered.

'Okay,' Donadze said. 'If he rings back, tell him we'll be in touch.'

❖

'The nocturnal Ramaz Donadze,' Jaqeli said, her voice croaky as she answered her phone.

'I know. Sorry.' He heard Misha Arziani stir and say something he couldn't make out. 'Apologise to Misha for me as well, would you?'

'Ramaz says he's sorry,' he heard her say. There was a mumbled response and Jaqeli laughed. 'He says not to worry, he was only sleeping anyway.'

'Tell him sleep's overrated.' Donadze paused. 'Listen,

Irina, I need you to check something for me. The Ministry of Defence file, do you have it with you?'

'Yes, it's on my laptop.'

'Could you get it?'

Jaqeli sighed. 'Misha wants a word.'

'Where are you, Ramaz?' Arziani asked a moment later.

'In my car, outside a bar called *The Dragon*.'

'That sounds like fun.'

'It's not.'

'What's up?'

'Fenrir, we've almost got him, Misha. Beka Gabelia knew him and so do some of the regulars at his bar. We haven't been able to get his name or address yet but there's a retired Army captain—Sasha Tatishvili—who should have it. I'm trying to track him down now.'

'Which is why you and I are talking at two o'clock in the morning?'

'Sorry, but it couldn't wait. I have Tatishvili's number but he isn't picking up and the phone's not registered. I'm worried he'll disappear without telling us how to find Fenrir.'

'And Irina's file?'

'If Tatishvili left the Army in, say the last ten years, his address should be on it.'

'Wow, Ramaz. The things you get up to when the rest of the world's asleep. What can I do to help?'

'Nothing for now, I'll let you know if I need anything.'

'Okay, Irina's here,' he said, yawning.

Jaqeli took her phone back. 'Ready when you are, Ramaz.'

'I'm looking for a Captain Sasha Tatishvili. Search for

Alexander Tatishvili and if that's not there try the Russian version, *Aleksandr*.'

'Okay,' Jaqeli said after a moment. 'This looks good. There are about twenty Tatishvilis and two *Alexanders* but only one with the rank of captain on his discharge date.'

'When was that?'

'The 4th of September 2018.'

'Is there an address?'

'Yes, but you're not going to like it. It's on Kurdiani Street…'

'Don't tell me. *The Squad*, Beka Gabelia's bar. Tatishvili doesn't live there, though, I would have noticed if he did…'

'Well, maybe he lived there after he left the Army but moved later. Or maybe he uses it as a forwarding address or somewhere to register with his bank.'

'Any of that could be true, Irina but it doesn't help me find him now.'

Jaqeli didn't respond, a silent reprimand for being abrupt, he realised. 'Sorry, Irina, it's been a long, frustrating night.'

'That's okay, you're tired.' She paused. 'You could try tracking his phone.'

'I could but everyone knows how that works these days. He'll just turn it off or dump it if he doesn't want to be found.'

'You need to get some sleep, Ramaz.'

'I know, I'll pick up on it again in the morning.'

'It is the morning…'

'You know what I mean. Say goodnight to Misha for me,' he said, ending the call.

Donadze dropped his phone onto the passenger's seat

and closed his eyes, thinking. He felt himself slipping into delectable sleep and forced himself awake again. *One more try*, he thought. The phone rang several times before the call connected. No one spoke.

'Captain Tatishvili?' Donadze asked eventually.

'Lieutenant Donadze.'

'I've been trying to contact you.'

'I know.'

'I need your help to find someone.'

'So I was informed.'

'You know who I'm talking about?'

'You want to find the man who killed Beka Gabelia, the man you call Fenrir.'

'I need his name and address.'

'Well then, you're in luck, I have both. You and Beka served together, didn't you? Come to *The Squad*, any time after twelve. We'll be having a drink in his memory, you should join us.'

'Sasha, I need that information now, we—'

'Twelve o'clock at *The Squad*. See you there, Lieutenant,' Tatishvili said, ending the call.

TWENTY-THREE

'Come for a drink and I'll tell you who killed Beka Gabelia,' Jaqeli said. 'It's crazy, Ramaz.'

'I know it's crazy but what else can we do?'

'How can you even be sure that Tatishvili will give Fenrir up?'

'I'm not *sure*. I don't know why he's doing this—but I don't think he's playing games with me.'

'It looks like a game to me.'

'Maybe to you it does, but I don't think Tatishvili sees it that way.'

'I don't think so either, Irina,' Ketsbaia said. 'He and Gabelia served together, that means a lot to him.'

'Crazy or not, we'll follow the plan,' Donadze said. 'I'm going to *The Squad* to see Tatishvili. He's going to give me Fenrir's name and address. I'll pass that on to you and you'll arrest him and bring him back here. It's simple enough.'

'Okay,' Jaqeli said. 'But are you sure you don't want to be there for the arrest?'

'I do want to be there but I'm staying with Tatishvili until you have Fenrir in cuffs.' He turned to Patarava. 'Koka, you go with Roman and Irina.'

Patarava straightened in his chair. 'Really, Lieutenant?'

'Yes, this is what we've worked for, you deserve to be part of it.'

'Thank you, sir.'

Donadze turned to Ketsbaia. 'What about tactical support?'

'In place, Lieutenant,' Ketsbaia said. 'My old team.'

Donadze shook his head. 'Led by George Losava, another good reason for me not being there.'

'We'll pass on your regards,' Jaqeli said, smiling.

'Thanks, I'm sure he'll appreciate that,' Donadze said, his tone flat. He stood and reached for his jacket. 'Fenrir's about to discover he's no god killer. Let's take this lunatic off the streets.'

'You're going to the bar now?'

'No, Misha wants to see me, then I'll go.' He showed them his radio. 'Be ready for my call.'

Arziani was in his office, tapping rapidly on his keyboard, a detective turned bureaucrat, Donadze thought.

He stood and stretched. 'Big day, Ramaz.'

'I'm hoping so, there's still plenty that could go wrong, though.'

'No, you've got everything covered.' He hesitated. 'I hear you're not going to be there for the arrest.'

'I can't be. Roman, Irina and Koka are on standby with George Losava's team. I want them moving as soon as I get Fenrir's whereabouts. They can't wait for me.'

'Losava will be in charge then?'

Donadze shrugged. 'He would be anyway, at least for

the arrest. That's his job, Misha. Fenrir's dangerous, that's why I requested his support.'

'Yes, I know. It was the right thing to do.'

'But?'

Arziani shook his head. 'George is all about George, all about making himself look good. He doesn't care about his men.'

'Or the detectives who are with him?'

'That's what worries me. Do you think I should go along and keep an eye on things—if you're not going to be there?'

'No, Misha, you really shouldn't.'

Arziani held Donadze's gaze for a moment then sighed. 'I know, you're right. Don't worry, I'll monitor things from here. She'll be okay.'

'They'll all be okay.'

'Yes, that's what I meant.' He grinned. 'Getting this far has been a great result, Ramaz. I hope you get the recognition for it.'

'I might but I'm not holding my breath.'

'Well, let's see.' Arziani hesitated. 'I wouldn't want Irina to know we've had this conversation.'

'Yes, okay, Misha,' Donadze said, losing patience. 'That's another one that never happened.'

❖

Donadze parked on Kurdiani Street, a short distance from The Squad. It was just after eleven but the gathering in Beka Gabelia's memory was already underway. Jaqeli had described him attending the event as *crazy* and he wondered if Tatishvili really was playing some kind of game with him, a game he couldn't understand.

He slumped in his seat, watching the entrance. A squat, tough looking man in leather jacket, denims and boots was guarding the door, ensuring the event stayed private.

Fifteen minutes passed and Donadze had seen enough. He radioed George Losava, requesting confirmation that he and his team were ready and standing by.

'Confirmed standing by,' Losava replied. 'Confirm your entry twelve hundred.'

'Negative twelve hundred. Entering bar now.'

The doorman watched him approach, moving to block the entrance. 'Private function,' he said curtly. 'Try somewhere else.'

Donadze took a step forward. 'Police. Get out of my way.'

The man smiled, unperturbed and moved to the side, pushing the door open. 'Lieutenant Donadze, you should have said. Sasha's expecting you.'

Donadze entered the bar, pausing as his eyes adjusted to the dim light. He scanned the room. Most of the tables were occupied; scruffy, taciturn men hunched over bottles and glasses, their sparse conversation fading as they turned to scrutinise the intruder. He sniffed the air, the sharp tang of stale male bodies and cigarettes transporting him back to the time when men like these were his friends, his comrades, his family.

A group was huddled at the bar, flanking a framed photograph of Beka Gabelia; young and smiling, the soldier he'd been before the driving accident had taken his leg and the life he'd been born for.

The man whom Donadze remembered was called *Sasha* was serving drinks from the bar. He said something to the group and they slowly dispersed, eyeing Donadze suspiciously as they drifted away.

Tatishvili offered his hand. '*Gamarjoba*, Ramaz. Glad you could make it.'

Donadze nodded, surprised by the other man's friendly greeting. 'You didn't give me much choice.'

Tatishvili poured vodka into two shot glasses. He lifted his own. 'To Sergeant Beka Gabelia. *Gaumarjos.*'

Donadze eyed his glass for a moment then lifted it. 'Beka Gabelia, my squad leader, the best soldier I ever knew. *Gaumarjos.*'

Tatishvili nodded his approval. 'He was the best I knew as well,' he said, refilling their glasses.

Donadze pushed his glass away. 'I'm here for a name.'

Tatishvili smiled and took an envelope from under the bar. He placed it on the counter top, keeping it covered with his hand. He gestured towards his fellow drinkers. 'Look at these men, Ramaz. All soldiers once; some served with Beka, some served with me. Looked after by the Army but unable to adjust to life on the outside. It's called becoming *institutionalised.* That didn't happen to you but it did happen to Beka.' He emptied his glass. 'And it also happened to me.' He patted the counter top. 'This bar, it's not much but it gave us somewhere to belong. Beka gave it to us. Some of us wouldn't be here today without him.' He reached for the vodka bottle. 'And now he's dead.'

'Why are you telling me this?'

'Because I know what you did for him.' He took his hand off the envelope. 'And so you'll understand.'

'Understand what?'

Tatishvili held his shot glass in salute and tipped the

vodka into his mouth. He pushed the envelope forward. 'You'll find what you need in there.'

Donadze lifted the envelope, sliding his thumb under the flap to open it. He extracted a single sheet of paper, printed with a name and address. 'How do I know this is the right man?'

Tatishvili shrugged. 'It is. Beka told me. He recognised him from that video you showed him. Aleksi Nachkebia, you'll find him at that address,' he said, refilling his glass once more.

Donadze stepped out of the bar and out of earshot of the doorman then radioed the information to Losava, noting the excitement in his voice as he acknowledged and mobilised his team, giving an ETA at that address of twenty minutes.

His phone buzzed an incoming message from Misha Arziani. *Got that, checking records.*

Donadze's instinct was to return to his car, to be there when Nachkebia—whom he would never again call *Fenrir*—was arrested. To look him in the eye as he came to understand that he had never been a wolf or a god killer, that he had lost and that he—Donadze—had won. But he'd told Jaqeli that they would follow their plan and he returned to the bar, the doorman throwing him a mock salute as he entered.

Tatishvili's entourage had regrouped, a fresh bottle of vodka on the counter top in front of them. They made way as Donadze approached, one patting his back. 'I was just telling these guys that you and Beka served together during the Russian war,' he said, filling a shot glass and pushing it towards him.

Donadze ignored the vodka and the invitation to

reminisce about his wartime experiences. 'I need you to come outside with me, Sasha.'

He sensed the men tensing, shuffling into position, ready to protect one of their own.

Tatishvili lifted his glass, looked at it wistfully for a moment then returned it to the counter top. 'It's okay,' he told the men. 'Ramaz is just doing his job.'

Donadze turned and walked for the door, pushing through a group of drinkers who jostled him as he passed.

'Everything okay, Captain?' the doorman asked, no longer friendly.

'All good, Erekle,' Tatishvili said, patting his arm reassuringly.

Donadze unlocked his car. 'Let's sit in there,' he said.

Tatishvili got in and he took his own seat, placing the radio on the dash between them.

'How long?' Tatishvili asked, nodding at the radio.

'Ten minutes maybe.'

'Okay,' he said, settling into his seat.

Donadze turned to observe him. 'What's your story, Sasha?'

'Story?'

'You were a career officer, a captain. What happened?'

'Why am I drinking myself to death in a miserable, rundown excuse for a bar in Kurdiani Street?' Tatishvili smiled. 'Because that's all I've got.'

'You left the Army in 2018…'

'Yes, that's when I *resigned my commission*. Why does that even interest you?'

'I just wondered how you and Gabelia—'

'You're not going to give up, are you, Ramaz? Okay, I'll make it easier for you. There was a training exercise, live ordnance, I was in charge. Something went wrong and someone died. A boy, eighteen years old. There was an investigation. No proof but I was *invited* to resign. And I did—because it *was* my fault. I was high on cocaine when it happened. So I left the Army and realised I had nothing. No one wanted to know me. No one except Beka, that is. He took me in, got me off the coke. I'd be dead by now without him.'

'And Aleksi Nachkebia?'

'A nobody and a coward. He could never have taken Beka without a gun.'

The radio squawked as Losava reported his team had arrived and were taking up position.

'It's happening now,' Donadze said.

Tatishvili shrugged. 'Sounds like it.'

A few moments passed before Losava gave the command, 'Go! Go! Go!'

Donadze sat back in his seat, imagining black-clad men in snake formation, adrenaline pumping and as deadly as *ninjas*, a door battered down, blinding smoke, ear shattering noise and shouted commands.

The operation lasted less than two minutes before Losava gave the order to stand down.

Donadze's phone buzzed. Losava.

'Your suspect's here, waiting for you, Donadze.'

'Is everyone okay?'

Losava laughed. 'Well, your suspect isn't. He's dead, tied to a chair with his throat cut.'

Donadze turned to Tatishvili.

'Sorry, Ramaz,' he said. 'But what did you think would happen?'

'I should have known,' Donadze said.

Tatishvili smiled. 'Known what?'

'That you were going to kill Nachkebia.'

'*I* didn't kill him.'

'Killed on your orders then?' He gestured towards the doorman. 'By him? Or maybe by one of your private army misfits?'

'You shouldn't speak about your former comrades that way, Ramaz. Some might call *you* a misfit. But, just to be clear, I don't have an army, private or otherwise.'

'But you did have Nachkebia killed,' Donadze stated. 'You had him killed for what he did to Gabelia.'

Tatishvili sat back in his seat. 'Well, that's something you're going to have to prove.'

'It must have been you. You knew he was dead before I did.'

'*Live by the sword, die by the sword.* It was just a lucky guess that that's how someone like him would end up.'

'We both know that's not true.'

'Tell me, Ramaz, how many people did Nachkebia kill?'

'Three, as far as we know.'

'Three, as far as you know. And one of these three was Beka Gabelia, your squad leader, the man you fought alongside. Doesn't that mean anything to you?'

'Of course it does but I wanted Nachkebia to go to trial.'

'Are you sure about that?'

Donadze hesitated, uncertain for a moment of what he *had* wanted. 'Yes, I'm sure,' he said eventually.

'You took a touch too long before answering, Ramaz,' Tatishvili said. 'But that's good. It tells me something about you—you're still Army.'

'I stopped being *Army* years ago—if I ever was. I'm police and you're going to prison.'

Tatishvili shrugged. 'Well, let's see.'

Six or seven former soldiers had left the bar and were gathering around Donadze's car, their expressions hard, their faces flushed with alcohol and grievance, eager to fight. A fist slammed on the roof.

'I'd get out of here if I were you,' Tatishvili said.

Donadze started his engine but the men closed in, stopping him moving.

Tatishvili shook his head and wound down his window. 'It's okay, men,' he said. 'I know the Lieutenant, he's one of us.'

'He doesn't look like one of us, Sasha,' one of the group argued.

'No, he's okay. He just asked me to go with him to sort out a few things. Go back inside and have a drink, I'll see you in a couple of hours.'

'Have you been arrested, Captain?' another asked.

'No, nothing like that,' Tatishvili said. 'Have a drink. I'll see you soon.'

Donadze's roof was struck again but the group shuffled away, mumbling dire warnings as they returned to their free vodka.

'Thanks,' Donadze said, pulling onto the road. 'But just so we're clear, I know you had Nachkebia killed and you *are* under arrest.'

TWENTY-FOUR

'Waiting for me, Roman?' Donadze asked. He'd left Sasha Tatishvili at Mtatsminda Station in the care of the Desk Sergeant and driven to the address he'd been given, the address where Aleksi Nachkebia had lived and died.

'I thought I'd give you a guided tour, Lieutenant,' Ketsbaia said.

'I hope I'm not disappointed.' Donadze stood on the pavement, looking down a short flight of steps into a basement apartment, the area at the bottom littered with empty food cartons, cans and broken glass. 'You'd have thought a top wolf would have found somewhere better to live than this.'

'I don't know, it looks a bit like a cave to me. Somewhere a wolf would feel at home.'

'I suppose so. How was your old boss?'

Ketsbaia shrugged. 'Lieutenant Losava? We didn't speak. I knew he wasn't happy that I'd left his unit and even less happy that I'm working for you. But it was good seeing the team again.'

'Did you miss being part of the action?'

'Kind of, but it's out of my system now. There's more to policing than that.'

'I hope so.'

A uniformed officer was guarding the stairs. Donadze nodded to him and he moved aside to let them pass.

He led the way down the worn, mossy steps, not touching the rusty handrails in case there were finger prints or other recoverable evidence still intact after Losava's men had stormed the apartment.

The door had been insubstantial and easily smashed open. 'Don't you guys ever knock?' he asked.

'We always knock, Lieutenant. Just that we do it with a ram instead of our knuckles,' Ketsbaia said.

Donadze stepped through the broken door and into a short, dimly lit corridor, the air damp and musty with green and grey patches of mould colonising the walls and ceiling. 'I'm surprised this place didn't kill him first.'

'Yes, it's grim. It looks like some kind of cellar conversion. Probably okay for storing wine or keeping family junk in—but no place for anyone to live. It makes you wonder where other ex-servicemen end up.'

'Don't feel sorry for Nachkebia. There may be other ex-servicemen living in places like this but they don't murder innocent people.'

'Some are luckier than others, though, Lieutenant. Like you and me for example.'

Donadze used his foot to push open the bathroom door. The tiny room was windowless, dark and dank. 'Anything to see in there?'

'Nothing of interest.' Ketsbaia pointed to another door a few metres along the corridor. 'The body's in there. Natia's still working on it but she should be finished soon.'

Donadze walked to the doorway. Natia Gagua was directing her technician as he took pictures of a body strapped to a chair with green canvas belts, the neck wound which had killed him, wide and gaping.

'We're keeping you busy, Natia,' he said.

Gagua pushed her protective hood off her head. 'You certainly are, Ramaz.' She winked and threw him a pouty kiss. 'But you know I'd do anything for you. Anything at all.'

'Don't encourage her,' Donadze said as Ketsbaia tried and failed to suppress his laughter.

'Not that I need much encouragement when it comes to you, Ramaz.' She smiled, teasing over for now. 'So this is Fenrir?' she asked.

'Yes, but we've stopped calling him that. His name was Aleksi Nachkebia, an inadequate man who thought he was something special.'

Gagua nodded. 'That sounds about right.'

Donadze took a moment to appraise the scene. 'Messy.'

'That's exactly what it is—which, in my profession is a good thing. The men who did this are amateurs; they've left their boot prints in the blood pool, fingerprints on one of these belts. And Nachkebia put up a fight—there's a good chance we've got useable DNA.'

'Solid evidence to take to the Prosecutor then. How many were involved?'

'Two to get him on that chair, tie him and cut his throat.' She pointed to a faint, rust-red mark on the greasy carpet. 'That's a different footprint from the other two. Someone standing back and watching…'

'Giving orders?'

'Could have been. It tells me there was a third man here but the print itself is too scuffed and indistinct to match it to a specific shoe or boot.'

Donadze thought for a moment. 'Maybe we won't have to,' he said. 'What about the neck wound?'

'Different from the others. Ragged, not clean…'

'A serrated blade?'

'Yes, a kitchen knife, I think. Same method, just a different type of blade.'

'That's no coincidence. They would have wanted Nachkebia to know what was going to happen to him.'

'That's pretty cruel…'

'It was meant to be. Anything else?'

Ketsbaia pointed to a sleek looking device standing on the floor beside the television. 'His games console, Lieutenant. A PlayStation—he was a gamer, as we thought. Some disgusting sadomasochistic porn magazines under his bed as well. There's also an iPad, password protected but we should be able to get in and see what sites he's been on, including, hopefully, his Instagram account.' Ketsbaia paused. 'There was something else. Something you probably remember.' He turned to Gagua. 'Natia?'

Gagua retrieved an evidence bag from her case and handed it to Donadze.

'Familiar?' Ketsbaia asked.

Donadze weighed the knife in the palm of his hand, rubbing the handle's stacked leather rings—designed for comfort and grip—through the bag's clear plastic. He remembered his Army instructor saying the blade was 18 centimetres long. He held it to the dim light; its steel: coated black, its purpose: evil. He felt a chill, knowing this weapon had taken three lives. 'Yes,' he said. 'It's a KA-BAR 1217 combat knife. I used to have one.'

'Me too,' Ketsbaia said. Nachkebia had good taste in blades if nothing else.'

Donadze returned the knife to Gagua. 'I think we're done here, Roman,' he said.

'Don't you want to take a closer look?' Gagua asked.

Donadze turned to Nachkebia's body: bound, butchered and left in his miserable cave of a home, his brief reign as god killer and terror of the city over. No one would mourn him, many would be glad he was dead. 'No,' he said, turning away. 'I don't think so.'

❖

'So, Lieutenant,' Ketsbaia said. 'Boot prints, fingerprints and DNA, solid evidence and plenty of it.'

'Solid evidence, plenty of it, but it's incomplete. You heard what Natia said about the third man's footprint. Scuffed and indistinct, not possible to match it to a specific shoe or boot.'

'So we find the other two and make them tell us who he is.'

'We already know that.'

'Sasha Tatishvili?'

'It must be. These men think of him as their commanding officer. And that's the way he sees himself. He would have wanted to have been there.'

Donadze continued driving to Mtatsminda Station, his mood gloomy. Aleksi Nachkebia had been found and had received justice of sorts. But Donadze thought death for the self-styled god killer was an easier outcome than being taken through the courts. He wondered if Rusiko Darsalia's parents and Sergo Kokoevi's sister would feel the same.

'Great result, Lieutenant!' the Desk Sergeant said as they entered the station.

'Thanks, Dato. We all played a part, you as well. Has Tatishvili asked for a lawyer yet?'

'No. I offered him his phone call but he turned it down. He seems very relaxed.'

'Well, maybe that'll change. Take him to an interview room, would you?' He looked at the wall clock, it was after six. 'Roman and I will be there in about twenty minutes.'

'Okay, Lieutenant, will do.'

Donadze turned to Ketsbaia. 'I need coffee.'

'Me too, I'll get them.'

Donadze walked to the detectives' bureau. Soso Chichua was hunched over his desk, jabbing his keyboard with two fingers, hating the technology.

'Don't take it personally, Soso,' Donadze said.

Chichua pulled himself out of his chair. He held out his hand to Donadze then thought better of it and pulled him into a warm, odorous embrace.

Donadze reluctantly returned his hug and pulled away as soon as he could do so without causing offence.

'I told you you'd get him, Ramaz.'

'Yes, and you were right.'

'Well, congratulations.'

'We all played a part,' Donadze said for the second time.

'Do you want one of these, Soso?' Ketsbaia said, carrying two mugs into the bureau.

Chichua shook his head. 'I need to cut back a bit—high blood pressure apparently.'

'Well, you've got more willpower than me,' Donadze said, taking a welcome sip of the strong, sweet coffee. He carried his drink to his desk and sat down, closing his eyes to think.

Fifteen minutes later and, boosted by the caffeine, he stood and walked to Ketsbaia's desk. 'Let's go, Roman.'

Tatishvili was in the interview room, slouched on one of its uncomfortable metal chairs. He straightened as Donadze and Ketsbaia entered. 'How was Aleksi?' he asked, smiling.

Donadze didn't respond. He and Ketsbaia took their seats on the opposite side of the table. He dismissed the uniformed officer and waited until the door was closed before starting the recording equipment.

'Were Dima and Vaso the best you could find?' Donadze began, referring to the two former soldiers he'd spoken to outside Beka Gabelia's bar.

'Nice try, Ramaz,' Tatishvili said.

'That was one of the sloppiest crime scenes Sergeant Ketsbaia and I have ever worked. Footprints everywhere. Even yours. We've got DNA. And what happened with that belt? Did one of your men take his gloves off to tie it?' Donadze stopped the recording equipment and leaned forward. 'We don't have much time, Sasha.'

Tatishvili's smile was less confident now. 'Time to do what?'

'The right thing.' Donadze placed his phone on the table. 'Call your men and tell them to come in. We'll find them anyway but coming in voluntarily will go better for them when they go to trial. The judge will take it into account during sentencing.'

'Again, nice try. But *if* I knew who killed Nachkebia and I called them, I'd be implicating myself as well as them. Why would I do that? You may or may not have enough evidence to bring charges. But even if you do *and* it turns out that soldiers were involved, the soldiers I know understand loyalty. They'd never inform on one of their own.'

'They would eventually, believe me. But by then it would be too late. For them and for you. You'd get no leniency from the court.' He paused. 'I'm trying to help you, Sasha. Call your men now. Get them to make a statement. I'll let the Prosecutor know you all cooperated.'

'No, you're bluffing, Ramaz…'

'Tell me, Sasha. The boy who died during that training exercise, when you were high on cocaine. Do you ever think about him?'

Tatishvili shook his head, his eyes closed. 'Every day,' he said.

'I thought so.' He turned to Ketsbaia. 'What does that tell you about Captain Tatishvili, Sergeant?'

'That he's still an officer, Lieutenant. That he puts his men's interests ahead of his own.'

'Is Sergeant Ketsbaia right, Sasha? Are you still an officer?'

Tatishvili's shoulders slumped. He put his hand on the phone, keeping it there for a long moment as he appraised Donadze. He straightened, seeming to come to a decision and stood, dialling a number. The call was answered after several rings. 'It's Sasha,' he said in a strong voice. 'I'm with Lieutenant Donadze at Mtatsminda Station. It's no good, you and Vaso need to come in.'

TWENTY-FIVE

Donadze's phone buzzed a message from Jaqeli, *Col Meskhi here.*

'Great,' he mumbled.

'Something wrong, Lieutenant?' Ketsbaia asked.

'No, nothing. Just that we're wanted in the MIR.'

Meskhi stood as he and Ketsbaia entered. 'Congratulations, Lieutenant,' he said, offering his hand.

'Thank you, sir, it was a team effort, we all had a part to play,' Donadze recited again.

'Yes, of course, that's always the case. *The whole is greater than the sum of its parts*. Do you know who said that?'

Donadze wasn't in the mood for a general knowledge quiz. 'I've no idea, Colonel.'

'Surprising,' Meskhi said. 'But you'll look it up, I imagine.'

'Yes, sir, first chance I get.'

Arziani threw Donadze a look of warning. 'We're going for a celebratory drink,' he said. 'Are you coming?'

'Sorry, Misha, I think I need to go home.'

'Well, okay, I suppose that's more important. Colonel, will you join us?'

'No, thank you, Captain.' Meskhi appraised Donadze for a moment. 'I'd like to speak to the Lieutenant privately if I may,' he said.

'Okay, everybody,' Donadze said. 'We've done enough for today. Tomorrow, we'll speak to the next of kin. Irina, you and Roman go to Rusiko's parents. I'll get on the road early and visit Kristy Kokoevi.'

Meskhi waited until he and Donadze were alone then crossed the room and closed the door. 'Sit down, Lieutenant,' he instructed, taking his own seat. 'You're not in the mood to celebrate?'

'No, sir, I'm not.'

'Are you prepared to say why?'

Donadze considered spinning a tale: that he was tired; that he'd spent little time with his family recently. He decided to be honest. 'I misled Tatishvili,' he said. 'I tricked him, told him I would speak to the Prosecutor to secure a lighter sentence for him and his men. But only if he confessed and told them to come in. It wasn't in his interest to do that but I shamed him into it, made him realise it was something an Army captain should do for the men under his command.'

'Well, you were successful. Tatishvili and his men did kill Aleksi Nachkebia and should face justice for that. And you're still free to speak to the Prosecutor if you wish. I won't stop you.'

'With respect, sir, I hadn't intended requesting permission.'

Meskhi frowned. 'We'll talk about *requesting permission* in a minute. But let's finish this conversation first.' He paused. 'I know why you're upset. You did mislead Tatishvili. You promised him something you won't be able to deliver. The Prosecutor will take a view that the crime was both premeditated and brutal and will offer limited or no leniency. And that was something you knew when you made your promise. Tatishvili trusted you and you used that trust against him.'

'Yes, he trusted me because we're both ex-Army. But the Army never meant much to me. It was just a year out of my life, something I had to do.'

'I don't believe that, Lieutenant. If the Army really meant so little to you then you wouldn't be so upset now. But you have nothing to feel sorry about. Loyalty is a noble human quality but *misplaced* loyalty certainly isn't.'

'Thank you, sir,' Donadze said, surprised that speaking to Meskhi had made him feel better.

'Good. Now, let me get to the other reason for my visit. You asked the British Home Secretary to bring MI5 into your investigation—without consulting me first.'

'Yes, sir.'

'Why?'

'Because MacLeod has responsibility for—'

'Why was I not consulted, Lieutenant?'

'Time pressure. There was a lot—'

'Don't insult me, Donadze.'

Donadze nodded. 'I *should* have consulted you, Colonel but I thought the politics might have been too difficult and you'd have stopped me.'

'Thank you for your truthful response. MacLeod contacted me earlier today. He assumed I was aware of and had approved your request. I didn't correct him—that would have made us both look unprofessional. But your approach did make me question whether I could still have confidence in your judgement.'

'I'm sorry, sir.'

Meskhi shook his head. 'I don't know how I would have reacted if you *had* consulted me. The politics could have been difficult and I may well have stopped you.' He paused a long moment. 'But I would have been wrong.'

Donadze didn't respond, knowing Meskhi had more to say.

'The Home Secretary told me he's grateful for our efforts,' he said at last. 'He believes that your actions, although questionable were well intentioned. He also believes that his son's killers are more likely to be caught if you continue to lead this investigation.' Meskhi hesitated. 'And that's also *my* belief.'

'Thank you, Colonel.'

'You're tired, Donadze, go home to your family.' He stood. 'Take your win, don't over analyse how you got there.'

'Thank you, sir,' Donadze repeated.

'And that quote about team working? Don't bother looking it up—it was Aristotle.'

'Yes, sir,' Donadze said to Meskhi's back.

❖

Donadze heard female laughter as he opened his apartment door.

Tamuna and her friend, Lela Tabagari were in the living room enjoying a glass of wine together.

It had been several days since he'd last seen Lela, when she'd advised him that Tamuna should be encouraged to go to Germany. That message hadn't landed well and he thought she looked nervous as she stood to kiss his cheek.

Tamuna was sitting on the couch with Eka sleeping on her knee. She looked up to return his kiss.

'The conquering hero,' Lela said.

Donadze touched his sleeping daughter's cheek. 'You mean finding Aleksi Nachkebia?'

'Yes, of course. Congratulations, Ramaz!'

'Thanks, it's a pity the relatives won't see him face justice. But at least he can't hurt anyone now.'

'Do you have any idea why he killed these people—complete strangers—in that horrible way?'

'I don't know and, to be honest, I don't care. I just wanted to find him and take him off the streets.'

'Irina's a psychologist, does she have a theory?' Tamuna asked.

Donadze shrugged. 'Last time we discussed it she told me Nachkebia had the characteristics of a psychopath: notions of self-importance and a lack of empathy. So maybe that's what he was. He was certainly arrogant though and that's what helped bring him down.'

'Well, I'm glad you caught him, Ramaz,' Lela said. 'Let me pour you a glass of wine, then I'll go.'

'Pour the wine but there's no need to go. You can update me on Stuttgart.'

He noticed Lela glancing at her friend.

'My application's gone through,' Tamuna said. 'I've been accepted.'

Donadze had guessed that was the reason for Lela's visit. 'It was never in doubt,' he said.

Lela handed him a glass and he raised it to them. 'Here's to you. Tbilisi's loss is Stuttgart's gain and the Germans are lucky to have you both. *Gaumarjos*!'

'*Madloba*, Ramaz,' Tamuna said, smiling and taking a sip of her wine.

Lela put her glass down. 'I *will* get away now, you've got things to talk about,' she said, crossing to kiss her friend and the little girl.

'We'll chat some more tomorrow,' Tamuna told her.

Donadze put his own glass down. 'I'll see you to the door.'

He walked ahead of her out of the apartment, pressing the elevator call button.

'It was nice to see you, Lela,' he said.

The elevator door opened and she leaned forward to give him a hug and kiss him on the cheek. 'You're a good man, Ramaz,' she said. 'Tamuna's lucky to have you.'

She stepped into the elevator and Donadze watched as the door closed and it started its descent. 'Just make sure you keep them safe,' he said softly.

He took a deep breath and returned to the apartment. Tamuna had carried Eka to her cot and was sitting on the couch with two full glasses of wine in front of her.

'The conquering hero,' she repeated her friend's salute.

Donadze sat beside her and lifted his glass. 'To mending German bones,' he said, taking a sip of the wine.

'Seriously, well done, Ramaz. Now it's on to the British boy?'

'Connor MacLeod? Yes, there's always someone. Did Lela come over to help you celebrate?'

'Kind of, but we had a few things to talk about as well.' She paused. 'Like how much notice I should give.'

'The Germans are being flexible?'

'Up to a point. I could give the clinic a month's notice but Stuttgart will keep the job open for up to three months, if that's what I want.'

'What *do* you want?'

'Well, Lela has offered to share an apartment with Eka and me and I wouldn't want to keep her waiting too long. There's also the creche start date to consider...'

'It sounds like you're thinking of going soon?'

'I thought maybe six weeks. What do you think?'

'I just want what works best for you and Eka. If that's six weeks then I think that's when you should go.'

'I haven't signed anything yet. Are you sure you're still okay with all of this?'

'Yes, it's definitely the right thing to do.'

Tamuna looked at him closely. 'We'll make it work, Ramaz. I promise.'

'Yes, I know we will.' He drained his glass. 'I need to make a call,' he said.

'Will you be long?'

'Ten minutes.'

She leaned over and kissed him. 'Don't be any longer, she said, standing to lift their glasses.

Donadze stepped onto the apartment's balcony, taking deep breaths of the warm, humid air as the incessant traffic rumbled and hummed through the streets below. Six weeks would quickly pass and his wife and daughter would leave to travel to a strange city in a strange land, separated by four thousand kilometres, her ambition and his intransigence, telling themselves they would make it work. But Lela had been right, they had to go. He put his unhappy thoughts aside and took out his phone.

Levan Gloveli answered almost immediately.

'Major,' Donadze said. 'I need a favour.'

TWENTY-SIX

Donadze had set his alarm to be up early.

Tamuna was sitting up in bed when he came out of the shower, a towel wrapped around his waist. 'I'll not get up yet, if you don't mind,' she said.

He leaned over to kiss her. 'No reason why you should. Eka will have you up soon enough.'

'That's true. Oh, I meant to tell you, your colleagues have dropped the charge against Eliso.'

He sat on the edge of the bed. 'That's good. Did she say why?'

'The complaint's been dropped apparently.'

'Apparently?'

'No, it *has* been dropped. The supermarket manager seems quite a decent man.'

'How do you know that?'

Tamuna laughed. 'We talked, *Detective.* Eliso apologised. I gave her a character reference. He was happy to let it go at that.'

Donadze took her hand. 'That's great, Tamuna. I'm sorry I didn't do more to help.'

She squeezed his hand back. 'I know you couldn't and I'm sorry I asked you to.'

He kept hold of her hand, rubbing it with his thumb.

'I know that look,' she said.

He dropped the towel and slipped back under the duvet. 'Now who's the detective,' he said.

The traffic was building as Donadze left the apartment but he reached the Expressway in good time and took up position in the middle lane, setting his cruise control to slightly exceed the speed limit.

He took a sip of coffee from his travel mug and turned on the radio. The news cycle hadn't moved on, the identification and poetic murder of Aleksi Nachkebia still headlining. The commentary expressed sympathy for Sasha Tatishvili and the other two men charged with taking Nachkebia's life; Army veterans who, if guilty had reacted almost understandably to one of their comrades being murdered. Donadze was also sympathetic but knew the Prosecutor would take a hard line, given that Nachkebia's murder had been both premeditated and cruel.

The reporting moved to an interview Lieutenant George Losava had engineered for himself, describing with false modesty how he and his team had stormed Nachkebia's apartment, whilst skipping over the detail that the man inside was already dead. Donadze found the interview comical, reinforcing his view that Losava's need for recognition reflected his inherent insecurity.

There was limited and grudging praise for the police. Nachkebia had been found but not before three innocent people had died. And the police appeared no closer to solving the murder of the British Home Secretary's son, an embarrassment for the entire country. Lieutenant Ramaz Donadze, the detective leading the investigation was reported as being unavailable for comment.

The broadcaster was clearly struggling to manufacture a new slant on the same story and Donadze switched to a music channel, easing his speed still higher to eat up the remaining kilometres to the Shavshvebi settlement.

Kristy Kokoevi was again waiting for him at the community centre.

He leaned over and pushed the passenger door open. 'Hey, Kristy. Is there somewhere we can talk.'

She got in the car. 'I thought we could go to my house, there's no one home at the moment.'

She guided Donadze to her home, the car bouncing and lurching over the potholed roads. The settlement had been laid out in a strict grid pattern, each identical home allocated a plot of land, most of which had been cultivated to grow fruit and vegetables for their residents. Donadze was again reminded how a temporary housing problem had resulted in a permanent but unsatisfactory solution.

Kristy told him to stop near the end of a long, straight road. They got out of the car and she led the way through an unlocked door and into a small living room. A table had been set with food and drink and she invited him to sit.

Donadze took a sip of water before speaking. 'How have you been, Kristy?'

She shrugged. 'Okay,' she said. 'Just frustrated, I suppose. I keep thinking I could have helped Sergo if I'd tried harder to find him.'

'You did try to find him. You couldn't have done any more.'

'I wish that were true.'

Donadze knew there was little point arguing with her. 'Is there anything you want to ask me about Sergo's death or the investigation?'

She sniffed and held a handkerchief to her eyes. 'The man who was killed by these soldiers, Ramaz. Was he definitely Fenrir?'

'Aleksi Nachkebia. Yes, no doubt at all.'

'And you still think he picked Sergo at random?'

'Yes. He was looking for a victim that night. Maybe there was something about Sergo that attracted him, a vulnerability perhaps. But that's all there was, there was no other connection.'

'Poor Sergo,' she said.

Donadze gave her a moment. 'You might want these.' He reached for a folder and took out an envelope, laying it on the table. 'We have to keep the originals for now.'

She lifted the envelope and pulled out copies of the photos which had been found on Kokoevi's body: herself as a young girl and her mother's grave.

She gazed at the photo of the grave for a long moment, her eyes misting once more. '*Madloba*, Ramaz,' she said in a small voice.

'Kristy.' Donadze waited until he had her attention. 'Would you like to go there, to visit your mother's grave?'

She frowned. 'How could I?' She tapped the photo. 'That's my village, isn't it? It's in South Ossetia, there's no way in or out.'

'What if there *is* a way in and out? I know someone, a

friend, a former police officer. Someone you could trust. I spoke to him, he knows people on both sides of the border. They could take you to your mother. You could spend time with her, pray for her at her grave.'

'But crossing into South Ossetia is illegal. You and your friend could get into trouble.'

'Yes, it's illegal, but it shouldn't be. Not for something like this. My friend and I both want to help. What should I tell him?'

She reached across the table to take his hands in hers, searching his face. 'Tell him, *yes*,' she said.

Donadze left Shavshvebi, stopping for coffee and arriving on time at the British Embassy.

Janice Patterson was waiting for him in the atrium. 'Ramaz, *gamarjoba*! How nice to see you again,' she gushed, her toothy smile on full view as she strode towards him.

He braced for her vice-like handshake. '*Gamarjoba*, Janice.'

Patterson's smile was quickly replaced by a look of admiration and awe. 'Many congratulations on capturing that dreadful man, Ramaz. You must be terribly proud.'

'Thank you. I'm glad we found him but he wasn't exactly *captured*.'

'Yes, quite so. Well, we have your pass ready if you'd be kind enough to sign Keti's form.'

Donadze scribbled his signature and took his security pass from the receptionist, hanging it around his neck.

'Excellent!' Patterson said. 'We'll be in the SR this morning, I'm afraid.'

'SR?'

'Shielded Room. All our embassies have them. Just in case anyone tries to eavesdrop on our *sensitive* conversations.' She gave him another wide smile. 'Very cloak and dagger but the spooks insisted.'

'MI5?'

'Well yes, although these days they prefer to be known as the *Security Service*. Ah, here's Richard...'

A man approached. 'Good afternoon, sir,' he said, opening a clear plastic bag. 'Your phone please.'

Donadze dropped his phone into the bag.

The man sealed it then lifted a hand-held scanner. 'Are you carrying a sidearm, sir?'

'It's in my car.'

'Thank you. Would you please stand with your legs apart and your arms raised.'

'Sorry, Ramaz,' Patterson said as the scanner was run over his body. 'Checking for recording devices mainly. Standard procedure, you understand.'

Patterson walked Donadze passed the meeting room they'd used previously to a door at the end of the same corridor. She used her pass to open the door and led the way into a stark, windowless chamber containing a shiny metal, box-like enclosure.

She unlocked the enclosure's door and held it open for Donadze to enter, gesturing at the tile-clad walls and ceiling. 'It works on a Faraday cage principle apparently.' Her voice dropped to a conspiratorial whisper. 'Although, to be honest, I have absolutely no idea what that means.' She picked up a remote control and waved it at the table and chairs located in front of a wall-mounted screen. 'Take a seat while I grapple with this frightful technology.'

Patterson defeated the technology quickly enough and the screen woke to display a coat of arms above the legend, *Foreign & Commonwealth Office.* She hit buttons on a keyboard and the screen changed, advising attendees that their meeting would start soon.

Patterson took her own seat, glancing at her watch. 'Shouldn't be long, the Home Secretary's a stickler for punctuality.'

A few moments passed and the screen changed again to display video of two men sitting together in a conference room.

'Janice?' one asked as communications were established.

Patterson flashed her smile. 'Good afternoon. How are things in London, Roger?'

'It's still morning here, Janice,' the man said distractedly. 'And this is Lieutenant Donadze I assume? I'm Roger Donnelly, the Security Service's Intel Manager. I have Bob Aitken with me. Bob's been doing the geeky work for us.'

Aitken held his hand up in greeting. 'I'm going to link in the Home Secretary now,' he said.

Another window opened on the screen: Rory MacLeod sitting on a burgundy leather office chair. He coughed to clear his throat. 'Good morning.' He peered at his screen then put on his glasses. 'I see I have Thames House and the Tbilisi embassy with me.'

'Yes, sir,' Donnelly said. 'I think we can start now.'

'Thanks Roger but let me first summarise why we're here.' MacLeod paused, gathering his thoughts. 'I visited Tbilisi soon after my son was murdered. It was there that I met Lieutenant Donadze, the lead detective on this case. The

Lieutenant asked for the UK's help in resolving an IT issue which may have been pertinent to his investigation. Specifically that Connor may have been killed because of something he was about to disclose on his blog. His laptop was stolen and no cloud backup found. However, it's possible he had a cloud account which was wiped and that's where 5's expertise was requested. Is that fair, Lieutenant?'

'Yes, sir, very fair,' Donadze said, conscious that MacLeod had made no reference to the Metropolitan Police or Connor's allegations against them. 'I was advised that your Security Service would have the expertise to tell us if Connor had a cloud account and if so, could it be recovered? It was fortunate that we met in Tbilisi and I was able to make the request to you directly. Time is always important in cases like this.'

'Quite so,' MacLeod said, clearly pleased with Donadze's response. 'Although I did of course insist on obtaining the correct approvals to allow 5 to look at this equipment as it's located outside the UK. Isn't that so, Roger?'

'Yes, of course, Home Secretary.'

'Janice?'

'Absolutely, sir.'

Donadze knew that MacLeod was making sure his version of events had been established but he was becoming irritated by the politician's back-covering. 'So what *did* you find, Mr Donnelly?' he asked.

Donnelly smiled. 'Yes, you did say that time was of the essence, didn't you?' He turned to Aitken. 'Bob?'

Aitken hesitated a moment. 'Well, you didn't make it easy for me. The *Cloud's* a vague term; there are any number of storage and file-sharing services which Connor could have subscribed to. However, his banking records indicated he used a lesser known service called *iDriveSecure*. And knowing that at least gave me somewhere to look. Bottom line, Connor did back up his work but it was nearly all deleted—by an expert. There wasn't a lot I could recover, a few words or part words, a couple of partial sentences here and there. Nothing that made any sense, not to me at least. Sorry.'

There was a moment's silence as Aitken's report was absorbed.

'Well that's unfortunate,' MacLeod said. 'However, at—'

'What does deleted by an *expert* mean?' Donadze interrupted.

'Someone who knew what he or she was doing, a professional. Not just some hack using over-the-counter software.'

'Could it have been a government agency?'

Aitken shrugged. 'Yes, some security and intelligence services would have that capability.'

'Police services?'

'Possibly.'

'Do you know when the account was deleted?'

'I do. It was the same day that Connor was killed.'

There was another long moment of silence.

'Could you send me what you have?' Donadze asked.

'I could, technically at least…'

'There are protocols about sharing information,' Donnelly said. 'But I think our warrant covers sharing with the Georgian police. Just let me check with Legal first.'

'Thank you,' Donadze said. 'There's no other way to retrieve Connor's data?'

'Not from his cloud account, no,' Aitken said. 'Your only other source would be his laptop or his external drive—if he used one.'

'It sounds like this hasn't been particularly useful, Lieutenant?' MacLeod suggested.

'No, sir,' Donadze said. 'I disagree. It's been extremely useful.'

Donadze had instructed his team to regroup in the MIR. 'How were Rusiko's parents, Irina?' he asked, hanging his jacket on the back of a chair.

Jaqeli shrugged. 'Still trying to make sense of why their daughter died. Still angry, still sad, relieved it's over but disappointed that Nachkebia won't face trial.'

'Her friend Nini was there when we called,' Ketsbaia said. 'It looks like she's been stepping up to support them.'

'Good for her, she didn't strike me as the type.'

'Nor me, but maybe she's changed as well.'

'Do you think I should visit them?' Donadze asked.

'Probably, but you might want to leave it for a while. They've had a lot to think about but could have some questions for you later.'

'How did you get on at the embassy, Ramaz?' Jaqeli asked. 'Did the Home Secretary join the call?'

'Of course he did, he wouldn't have missed it. His main priority was to make sure there wouldn't be any political embarrassment.'

'For himself?'

'He's a politician, who else would he care about?'

Donadze summarised the video call with the British Home Secretary and the two men from MI5.

'So Connor did have cloud backup but there wasn't much that could be recovered,' Jaqeli said. 'Are they going to give it to us?'

'Yes, through Janice Patterson, after they've cleared it with their lawyers. A day or two probably.'

'But if MI5 couldn't make any sense of it then we're not much further forward,' Ketsbaia said.

'I don't agree. Recovering Connor's data was always a long shot but without MI5 we wouldn't even have known he'd made a backup. We've only been able to speculate up to now but this confirms a clear motive: the suppression of information.' Donadze held up his thumb. 'Connor's laptop was stolen from his apartment because it contained information that couldn't be allowed to come out.' He held up a second finger. 'We now know for sure he had a cloud account which someone wiped—because it contained the same information.' He held up a third finger. 'The only other source of that information was Connor himself. It was in his head and that's why he had to be killed.'

Ketsbaia nodded. 'Yes, you're right,' Lieutenant. 'Suppression of information, nothing else would make sense. So, our focus stays with the Metropolitan Police?'

'For now at least.'

Patarava coughed to clear his throat. 'I may be off the mark here…'

'Go ahead, Koka,' Donadze said.

'Well, we agree that Connor was killed to stop certain information being disclosed.' His face had reddened. 'Connor's dead but someone else has that information now…'

'You mean the killer?' Ketsbaia asked.

'Yes.'

'And?' Donadze prompted.

'We know it was a professional hit. The hitman is probably smart, he's sure to have figured out why he'd been told to break into Connor's apartment and take the laptop. But now he's—'

'Now he's become a loose end himself?' Donadze interrupted.

'Yes.'

'And maybe he needs insurance in case *he's* become a target. You think he kept the laptop?'

'It's possible but unlikely. He'd probably been told to hand it over once he'd stolen it. But there'd be nothing to stop him making his own backup first.'

Donadze nodded. 'So the information we're looking for might not be totally lost. That's very good, Koka.'

'That *is* very good,' Jaqeli agreed. 'But here's another way of looking at it; as you said, the hitman is smart, he would know why he had to take the laptop. He *might* be worried that he's become a loose end *or* he might have realised that he's acquired something of value, something that could be used to extort cash from his employer.'

'Yes, Irina. You're right, either scenario is possible.'

'I'm not sure it helps us much...'

'Everything helps,' Donadze said. 'It's just not always clear how.'

TWENTY-SEVEN

'You should have brought your family,' Gloveli complained, pouring wine into Donadze's glass.

Donadze raised the glass in salute and took a sip. 'Tamuna wanted to come but it would have been too late for Eka.'

'She could have stayed over, Veronika would have looked after her.'

'Maybe next time…'

'I hope I'll see them before they leave for Germany.'

'You will, Major. There's no way Tamuna would go without saying goodbye.' Donadze closed his eyes and took a deep breath of cool, clean air. Shindisi was only forty minutes from Tbilisi but Gloveli's quiet, fragrant garden felt like a continent away from the chaos of a million people jostling for space in the city below.

Gloveli had been watching him. 'You look tired, Ramaz.'

Donadze stifled a yawn. 'No, I'm okay. It's the fresh air and the wine, they always have that effect on me.'

'Of course they do.' Gloveli drained his glass and reached for the bottle. 'That girl who wants to cross into South Ossetia, Kristy Kokoevi? I've set it up for next week.'

'Next week? You're slipping, Major. I thought you would have had her on the first bus.'

'Except there aren't any. The only way I'm slipping is by agreeing to help you.'

'Are your friends from the *old days* taking her over?'

'You don't need to know, Donadze. But let me tell you, the *old days* weren't all bad. Some of the best police officers I know were KGB.' He tore off a piece of *lavash* bread and dropped it onto his plate. 'Although, there aren't that many of us left now…'

'Well, thankfully we still have you,' Donadze said, raising his glass again. 'To the best police officer *I* know, Major Levan Gloveli. *Gaumarjos*!'

Gloveli looked at his friend closely.

'I mean it,' Donadze said.

Gloveli dipped his head. '*Madloba*, Ramaz, I appreciate you saying that.' He half emptied his wineglass. 'But don't be getting all sentimental on me,' he added.

Donadze speared a piece of *sulguni* cheese and put it in his mouth, sitting with his friend and mentor in companionable silence, a candle flickering in a jar the only light in the garden. 'Where are Veronika and Lasha this evening?' he asked eventually.

'At his parents. Lasha is feeling very pleased with himself. His *Bitcoin* is already up five percent.'

'*Bitcoin*? I thought he was buying something new?'

'He was, something called *Newmmus*. But he checked it out and didn't like what he saw so went with *Bitcoin* instead.'

'And it's up five percent?'

Gloveli shrugged. 'It's up now but could be down again next week. Who knows? Lasha's happy with it and that's good enough for me.' He topped up their glasses. 'How's your investigation going?'

Donadze shook his head. 'We had good news and bad news. Connor did backup his work to the cloud but someone attempted to delete it. And they were quite successful apparently, there's not much of it left.'

'Have you seen what *is* left.'

'Tomorrow, I've got to go to the British Embassy and sign some forms before they'll hand it over.'

'Well, that's the trouble when you're dealing with a country that respects its laws. Life was much simpler in the Soviet.' Gloveli sighed. 'It doesn't sound like you've got a lot to work with.'

'We don't. Our best hope is that the hitman kept the original data. Either Connor's laptop or maybe the laptop backed up to an external device.'

'But you don't know who the hitman is or even if he's still in Georgia...'

'I didn't say it was going to be easy.'

'How about the political angle? With MacLeod being the Home Secretary's son?'

'That doesn't help, although it's one thing Meskhi is good at, keeping the politicians off our backs.'

'Meskhi's good at more than that, Ramaz.'

'I know, he's got his qualities. But working for him isn't always easy.'

'Maybe you're not that easy either?'

Donadze smiled. 'No, that can't be true.'

'Maybe I just spoiled you then?'

'It didn't feel that way at the time.'

Gloveli looked at his friend for a long moment. 'Meskhi is who he is, Ramaz. It's his personality. *You* know you're doing a good job and so does your team. And if you thought about it, you would realise Meskhi does as well. That should be enough for you.' He paused. 'So how are you going to find this hitman?'

'No idea, Major. That's why I'm here, I was hoping *you'd* tell me,' he said.

Janice Patterson had already kept him waiting more than twenty minutes. She had something he wanted—Connor MacLeod's recovered cloud data—and she'd make him jump through hoops to get it. At least that's what Donadze told himself as he sat, fuming in the British Embassy's atrium.

The receptionist left her desk and crossed to the waiting area. 'Janice sends her apologies and asked me to say she'll be with you soon, Lieutenant.'

Donadze nodded his thanks and took several deep, calming breaths.

A few more minutes passed before Patterson breezed in, her hand extended in bone crunching greeting. 'Ramaz! *Gamarjoba*! I'm so *sorry*, my London call overran, I'm afraid. They just *would not* let me go.'

Donadze fixed his smile and resisted an impulse to return her steely grip. 'Not at all, Janice, it's good of you to see me.'

She waved her hand in dismissal. 'Oh, *tosh*, you know you're always welcome. We're all so terribly grateful for everything you're doing to find poor Connor's killer.' Her face took on a look of grave concern. 'Have you *at least* been offered coffee?'

'Yes, of course,' he lied, catching the receptionist's conspiratorial smile. 'Keti's been looking after me.'

Patterson turned and beamed at the receptionist. 'Excellent! Well, let's get these dreadful forms signed, shall we?' She led Donadze to the meeting room they'd used previously. 'Please sit down,' she said, taking her own seat and pulling a folder towards her.

'No SR today?' Donadze asked.

'SR?'

'Shielded Room.'

'Ah, of course. Sorry, I'm a bit slow on the uptake this morning.' Her voice dropped to a whisper. 'I probably shouldn't have had that second glass of *Saperavi* yesterday evening.'

'I usually find it's the second bottle that gives me problems.'

Patterson's braying cackle was forced and short lived. She placed her hand on the folder. 'Before we begin the formalities, perhaps you could tell me if there have been any developments I should be made aware of.'

There was nothing of significance to pass on but Donadze was tired of being manipulated. 'There's nothing I can discuss with you today, Janice. Sorry.'

Patterson blinked in theatrical surprise. 'Oh, I thought we had an understanding, Ramaz?' She kept her hand on the folder.

Donadze smiled. 'Police business, Janice. There's only so much I can tell you. I'm sure you understand.'

Patterson now looked hurt, her hand still on the folder. 'I promised the Home Secretary I'd keep him appraised…'

'And I know he's grateful.'

'You've spoken to him?'

'Yesterday evening,' Donadze lied again. He gestured towards the folder. 'I called to thank him for recovering what's left of his son's cloud data. We talked for some time and he asked me to keep in touch, to let him know if there's anything he could do to help.'

Patterson held Donadze's gaze for a long moment then showed him her toothy smile, her eyes cold. 'We're *all* here to help, Ramaz,' she said in a bright, brittle voice. She opened the folder. 'Now let's get this beastly paperwork out of the way, shall we?'

◈

Donadze kissed the small, brown envelope containing the memory stick given to him by Janice Patterson and slipped it into his jacket pocket. She'd eventually surrendered it after he'd signed the disclaimers and dire warnings required by MI5 protocols and UK law, the embassy woman achieving a face-saving victory by dragging the process out longer than was necessary.

Donadze was worried that the small device, containing only a limited quantity of recovered data was now the investigation's best lead. Or possibly its only lead, he thought. He told himself that the MI5 man who'd found and partially restored Connor MacLeod's online account was an IT geek, not a detective and he hoped his team would have a better chance of extracting something of value from it. But it still didn't feel like they had much to work with.

He knew their investigation would be in trouble if he couldn't bring charges soon and Colonel Meskhi might then bow to political pressure and replace him. He put these troubling thoughts to the back of his mind as he drove to Mtatsminda Station.

His team were in the MIR and, with nothing new to work on, were awaiting his arrival.

'Okay, got it,' he said giving the memory stick to Patarava. 'Let's see what the Brits have found for us.'

Patarava viewed the stick with suspicion. 'Have you scanned it for malware, Lieutenant?'

Donadze sighed. 'No, but I suppose we should, given that MI5 is essentially a spy organisation.'

Patarava inserted the stick into a USB port. 'There's not much on it,' he said. The scan lasted less than a minute. 'It's clean, okay to use.'

'Good, then let's see what we've got.'

Patarava activated the MIR's overhead projector to display a column of folders, numbered 1 to 8.

'Something tells me this isn't going to be easy,' Jaqeli said.

'That's why we need you here, Irina,' Ketsbaia told her, smiling.

'What's in folder number one, Koka?' Donadze asked.

Patarava clicked the icon. 'Images. But only six of them,' he said, opening and closing each file in turn.

'There's nothing of interest there,' Donadze said.

'I've got about eight thousand photos on my phone,' Jaqeli said. 'How about you, Ramaz?'

'Less than eight thousand but more than six. MI5 did say they couldn't recover much. Let's try folder number two.'

Donadze felt his spirits slump as each folder was opened to reveal only limited numbers of salvaged files, some of which were corrupted and unreadable. 'Last folder then,' he instructed Patarava.

That folder contained several PDF files and a Word document titled, *Read this first.* The document had been written by the MI5 analyst and explained that the PDF files contained what he described as *fragmented* text. He'd utilised AI software to organise the fragments and fill in some of the gaps, saving the text onto a single file titled, *Collated.*

The analyst warned that the AI based technique wasn't foolproof and that even the collated file did not read in any kind of meaningful way. *At least to me!!!* he'd added.

'Okay, Koka,' Donadze said. 'Let's take a look at the collated version.'

Patarava opened the PDF file to reveal about twenty pages of seemingly random words, part words, letters and symbols.

'This *isn't* going to be easy…' Jaqeli repeated.

'Scroll to the top, Koka,' Donadze instructed. He stared at the projected image for a long moment. 'These top, left hand letters. If you filled in the gaps, they could be a heading for something.'

Patarava picked up the laser pointer and ran its beam under the letters and spaces, *ou o ru s.*

Donadze stood and crossed to the screen. 'There's something there, he said. 'I'm just not quite seeing it yet.' He continued staring at the screen.

'Maybe we should come back to—'

'Irina, what did Connor call his blog?'

She searched her memory. 'It began with something like Journal. Give me a minute to find it.'

'It's JournoTruths,' Ketsbaia said.

Donadze took the laser pointer from Patarava. 'Spell it,' he instructed.

Ketsbaia spelt the website's name whilst Donadze followed his progress with the pointer. He turned to face his team, squinting into the projector's bright light. 'We've found it,' he said. 'That's Connor's blog.'

❖

'We've only got two words,' Ketsbaia said. 'JournoTruths. The rest is just a jumble.'

Jaqeli stood and stared at the projection. 'Maybe not, Roman,' she said, her tone tentative. 'You've heard of the Rosetta Stone?'

'I've heard of it but don't know much about it. Something that came from Egypt…'

'That's right. It was a stone slab that Napoleon's army found when they were fighting over there. The stone was chiselled with a decree made by a king about two thousand years previously. I can't remember who the king was or what the decree said, but neither of these things matter. What was significant about the Rosetta Stone was that the decree was in three languages, only one of which was still understood. But—and this is what made the Stone important—because the decree said the same thing in all three languages, scholars at the time were able to use the language they already knew to learn the other two. And once they'd learned these languages, they could read and understand other things that had been written.' She smiled and tapped the screen. 'We have our own Rosetta Stone here. This *jumble* is the language we don't know. The language we do know is—'

'The stories Connor posted on his website. All in understandable English,' Ketsbaia said. 'But we've already seen them, they're still on his website. Sorting out this jumble won't give us anything new, even if we can find a way to make sense of it.'

'It might, though, Roman. You're right, we've seen and read what Connor's already posted. But what about any work in progress? Partial stories he'd written but hadn't put online yet? There may even be something new on his Met allegations.'

'Yes, I see that, Irina,' Ketsbaia conceded. 'His girlfriend told us he was working on something new for his blog, it'd be good to know what that was.'

'So,' Donadze said. 'We use *our* Rosetta Stone to see if there's anything new to look at. But how do we do that?'

Patarava coughed. 'This might work, Lieutenant.' He was colouring from the neck up. 'I might be able to superimpose what we've already seen on top of the scrambled data, the *jumble* as Sergeant Ketsbaia described it.' He waved the laser pointer at the screen. 'It'll take me a while to duplicate the font sizes, spacing and margins. But if I can do that then anything we haven't seen before should stand out from the rest.'

'And that's what we'd focus on,' Donadze said. 'Is that what you had in mind, Irina?'

'Yes, definitely, if Koka can find a way to make it work.'

'Do you need any help, Koka?'

'No, I should be okay, sir. I just need some time.'

Donadze took a breath, disappointed that, for now at least, nothing of value had been found on the recovered data. He sensed the same disappointment in his team. 'All right,' he said, forcing optimism into his voice. 'Great work everyone, this is promising. Let's give Koka some space and we'll meet back here when he's done.'

TWENTY-EIGHT

Donadze returned to his desk to catch up with his admin, leaving Patarava in the MIR trying to decipher Connor MacLeod's blog.

Misha Arziani was in his office. He raised his hand in greeting and came over. 'Your turn to buy the coffee,' he said.

'Again?' Donadze asked, looking at his watch.

'Come on, Ramaz. You can spare half an hour, can't you?'

'Sorry, Misha. You're right, no one should ever turn down a decent cup of coffee. Let's get some fresh air.'

They walked to the coffee shop on Mtatsminda Street where Donadze and Ketsbaia had confronted the drunken Russians. The same waitress was on duty. She gave Donadze a wide smile, smiling still wider for Arziani. He gave her a dazzling version of his own, bending to read her name tag. 'We'll sit here, Nino, if that's okay?'

'Of course it is. Nice to see you again, Ramaz,' she said, patting his arm. 'Coffee?'

'Yes, make it strong please,' Donadze said, taking a chair.

Arziani pulled out his own chair and sat, removing his designer sunglasses and laying them on the table. 'Pretty girl,' he said.

'Is she? I hadn't noticed.'

Arziani grinned. 'If you say so.' He leaned back, shut his eyes and raised his face to the hot sun. 'Did MI5 give you anything worthwhile?' he asked.

Donadze brought him up to date, saying he hoped the data recovered by MI5 would provide a new lead.

'Sounds like a bit of a long shot to me,' Arziani said. 'Pity.'

'It *is* a long shot but why's that a pity?'

Arziani sat up. 'I'm moving on, Ramaz. Meskhi will announce it in a couple of weeks but I wanted to give you a heads up first.'

'That's great, Misha. Promotion?'

'More of a sideways move, I'd say. There's a vacancy coming up at Vake-Saburtalo.'

'Well, we'll be sorry to see you go.'

'It's not something I want, to be honest, but Irina and I can't keep working together. At least we'll be able to plan the wedding now.'

Nino returned with their coffee and water, again offering Arziani her best smile.

'*Madloba*,' he smiled back. He waited until she'd left. 'Of course, you realise that with me going there'll be a vacancy at Mtatsminda.'

'Yes, I had realised that. But you still haven't told me why you said, *pity*.'

'Would you want the job?'

Donadze shrugged. 'I don't know. I watch you in your office, head down over your keyboard and I wonder if that's right for me.'

'It's certainly not right for everyone. It even gets *me* down sometimes. But it would be a promotion so I suggest you get your head around whether you want it or not—because you'll need to know the answer if Meskhi offers it to you.'

'Do you think he will?'

Arziani pushed the plunger on the cafetière and poured their coffee. 'Solve Connor's murder and I think he'd have to give you something.'

'And that's why you said, *pity*?' Donadze asked once more.

Arziani nodded. 'Yes, it's a pity you have this case at the same time a promotion's coming up. It's bad enough Connor being British but being the Home Secretary's son raises its profile even more. Solve it and you'll get the recognition you deserve. But if you don't…'

'They'll hang me out to dry. Levan Gloveli told me the same thing recently.'

Arziani took a sip of his coffee. 'And he was right,' he said.

❖

Koka's almost done, Jaqeli's message read.

On my way, Donadze replied, logging out of his police account.

'Success?' he asked as he entered the MIR.

Patarava was smiling broadly. 'It's not quite as good as I'd hoped, Lieutenant.'

'Ignore him, Ramaz, he's just being modest,' Jaqeli said.

'Okay.' Donadze took a seat. 'Show me.'

'Just a minute…' Patarava clicked his key board several times then activated the overhead projector.

'So, what do we have here?' Donadze asked. He kept the disappointment out of his voice, the projection was still a jumble of partial words, letters, symbols and spaces.

'That's just the data MI5 gave you, sir. And this,' he clicked his mouse and a section of text scrolled three quarters of the way up the screen, stopping with a digital shudder, 'is Connor's blog superimposed on top.'

'Show-off,' Ketsbaia said, winking at Patarava.

Patarava smiled. 'Ignore the animation, Lieutenant.'

Donadze stood. 'The lower section is Connor's posts, the stuff he'd already put online?' He pointed to the screen. 'And everything up here is his work in progress, what he hadn't got round to posting before he died?'

'Yes, that's what we think,' Patarava said.

Donadze looked at the muddle on the screen, still disappointed. 'Great work,' he said, trying to sound positive. 'We can focus on his work in progress now and try to make sense of it.'

'Put him out of his misery, Koka,' Jaqeli said.

'Okay,' Patarava said grinning. 'There's something more for you to see, Lieutenant—but I'd better explain what I've done first.' He paused, gathering his thoughts. 'As Irina told us, the stone found in Egypt—the Rosetta Stone—was used by scholars to learn two forgotten languages. I don't know how long that took them, probably months or even years. But we're not scholars and we don't have the luxury of time. That led me to think about how MI5 had used AI software to recover Connor's cloud account. AI is all about computers doing tasks much faster and more reliably than people, and I wondered if we could use it here. So, I downloaded an open source AI app.' He paused and looked at Donadze expectantly.

'Keep going, Koka, I'm following you so far: *Rosetta Stone, AI, faster, reliable, open source...*'

'Okay, that's great, Lieutenant. Just checking. So,' he continued, 'I assumed that Connor's work in progress included his Met story. And based on that, I instructed the app to generate relevant words from his recovered data. Basically, filling in the gaps and rearranging some letters and text. I told it to look for key words like *police, Metropolitan, children, conspiracy, cover up, senior, politician, abuse* and *paedophile.* It's something we could have done ourselves but it would have taken days or maybe even weeks. And we'd probably have missed a lot of it. Anyway, this is what I got.'

The projected image dissolved and was replaced by text spinning in from the top, right hand corner.

'Sorry,' Patarava said. He waited a moment. 'So, as you can see, it looks like Connor was working on—'

'Two blogs, not one,' Donadze interrupted. 'But the app has only filled in the gaps for one of them?'

'Yes, it could only work on the key words I gave it. We'd have to know the theme of the other blog to identify key words for it.'

'But Connor *did* have something new on the Met. Can you hide everything else?'

'Here we are,' Patarava said a moment later. 'It looks like he wrote about eight hundred words. There are still some gaps, some words which are obviously in the wrong place—but you can understand the gist of his story now...'

'Make it bigger, Koka,' Donadze instructed. He sat back in his chair to read how a group of at least five, named officers in the Metropolitan Police had been running a paedophile ring for a period of three years or more. Four of the officers were still serving. Girls and boys from vulnerable backgrounds, some as young as eight had been abused by the officers, with the children then being passed onto other abusers. *JournoTruths* had already brought this criminal activity to the attention of two of the Met's most senior officers, who were named, but its allegations had been largely ignored, supposedly because they lacked corroborating evidence.

'Amazing,' Donadze mumbled as he read on. *JournoTruths* had also brought its allegations to the Home Secretary, Mr Rory MacLeod, but they were not acted upon, again supposedly because of lack of corroborating evidence. However, regardless of whether that explanation was justifiable or not, *JournoTruths* had now come into possession of images and video of children being raped or being forced to commit sex acts. Three of the police officers were recognisable from the video—incontrovertible evidence of wrong doing. The video had been sent to the Commissioner of Police, Sir John Aitken. No response had been received to date. The blog stated that the Met was more concerned with protecting its own reputation than safeguarding children at risk. It went on to say that Rory MacLeod was negligent in his duty as a senior government minister, the government's first responsibility being to keep British citizens safe.

There was a long moment of silence.

'And there's your motive,' Ketsbaia said, eventually.

Jaqeli shook her head. 'But there's still no evidence. Where do you think Connor kept these images and videos?'

'His laptop and the cloud,' Donadze said. 'The cloud's gone and his laptop's missing.'

'This might sound crazy, Lieutenant, but Connor was pretty scathing about his father's part in all of this. Do you think it's possible that—'

'That MacLeod had his own son killed?' Donadze remembered how upset the Home Secretary had been on seeing Connor's body in the morgue. 'It's not crazy, but I really don't think so.'

'So, what do we do now, Ramaz?' Jaqeli asked. 'Hand the file over to the UK authorities?'

'No. Connor was murdered here, in Tbilisi. It's still our responsibility to find his killer. Besides, who would we hand it over to? The Met clearly doesn't want to know…'

'In that case, what *do* we do now?'

'It's obvious,' Donadze said. 'We find the laptop.'

❖

It was after eight before Donadze returned to his apartment, the aroma of warm food welcoming him as he opened the door.

'I waited for you,' Tamuna said as she stood to kiss him. 'Are you hungry?'

He realised he hadn't eaten since breakfast. 'I am now.'

'Good, you can have your shower while I finish up. Fifteen minutes.'

'Okay, fifteen minutes it is.'

'Red or white?' she asked.

'Both?'

She laughed. 'Has it been that kind of day?'

'Not really, just the usual frustrations...'

Donadze diverted to look in on Eka as she slept in her cot, then crossed to his bedroom to take a long, hot shower, playing the steaming, pressurised jets on his face and head until his skin tingled and flushed pink, his fatigue draining away with the soapy water.

He dried himself and pulled on shorts and a T-shirt, returning bare footed to the living room.

Tamuna had set a table on the balcony; cutlery and glasses sparkling in flickering candle light.

'Don't tell me I've forgotten our anniversary,' he said.

'You'd be eating in the station canteen if you had. Red or white?' she asked again, her hand poised over both bottles.

'Let's start with the white.'

She poured two generous measures of *Tsinandali* and raised her glass in salute. 'To you, Ramaz.'

'And to you, Tamuna,' he said, taking a sip of the wine.

She slid an earthenware pot of *lobio* towards him. 'Your mother's recipe,' she said.

'That was brave of you.' He spooned a generous helping of the bean stew onto his plate and ripped off a chunk of bread to dip in its sauce. He nodded his approval. '*Deda* would have been proud.'

'Tell me about your investigation,' she said.

Donadze shrugged. 'What do you want to know?'

'Nothing in particular. Just how you feel it's going. Are you confident you'll get the result you want? Anything about it that's worrying you? You hardly ever talk about your work and I usually don't ask. It makes me sound like I don't care—and I really do.'

‘I’ve never thought you didn’t care, Tamuna,’ Donadze said. He described how the initial euphoria on finding Aleksi Nachkebia had dissipated after he’d been killed by Sasha Tatishvili and his men, the victims’ next of kin being denied a trial. He went on to describe how he now had motive for Connor MacLeod’s murder, but no evidence to corroborate his hypothesis.

‘Does that put you under more pressure?’ she asked.

‘Yes, I need a result. Meskhi will have to do something if we don’t get one.’

‘He’d take you off the case?’

‘Possibly. I might already be off it if Connor’s father hadn’t intervened.’ He smiled at her. ‘Anyway, that’s where I am. What about you?’

Tamuna refilled their glasses. ‘I’ve been given a date to go to Germany. It’s four weeks tomorrow.’

Donadze sipped his wine. ‘A bit sooner than we’d thought…’

‘A few days. I could have held out for longer but…’

‘No, that’s okay, if that date works for you and Eka.’

‘It does.’ Tamuna hesitated. ‘Come with us.’

‘What do you mean?’

‘I had a video call with our HR Manager today, going through some of the contract details. He mentioned there’s a scheme for helping employees’ partners find work. He thought that wouldn’t be an issue for you—if you were interested.’

Donadze tore off another chunk of bread. ‘It’s not that I’m not interested, Tamuna. It’s just difficult for me to imagine what I’d do if I weren’t in the police. What did your HR man have in mind?’

'He mentioned private security, consultancy perhaps.'

'For a year? Then what? I wouldn't get my job back here.'

'We don't know that, you might. But you could find something else in Tbilisi. Didn't Levan offer you a hotel job recently?'

'Yes, but it wasn't for me. Why do the Germans want to find jobs for partners?'

'Probably to make their employees feel more settled.'

'And to encourage them to extend their contracts?'

'That might be part of it. But it's not something I would do unless we both wanted it.' She put her hand over his. 'But I do want us to be together. Will you think about it?'

Donadze understood enough about his own psychology to know why he needed the police: his quest to find and punish killers a proxy for finding and punishing the men who'd killed his sister. But he had a new family now and losing them would be unbearable. He looked at his wife across the table, her beautiful face shadowed in soft candlelight. 'Yes,' he said. 'I'll think about it.'

TWENTY-NINE

Koka Patarava was already in the MIR and began getting to his feet as Donadze entered.

'Don't,' Donadze said, signalling for him to stay seated.

Patarava paused halfway to standing, hesitated then dropped back onto his chair.

'You're in early.'

'Yes, I couldn't sleep.'

'Guilty conscience?'

'No, it's nothing like—'

'I'm joking, Koka.'

'Ah, right…'

Donadze sighed. 'What are you doing?'

'Working on these blogs again.' He powered up the projector, waited for it to warm up then clicked his mouse. 'This is what you saw yesterday, Lieutenant—Connor's Met post. We got the gist of his story but there were still gaps in the text and I wondered if we could find a way to fill some of them in by using AI differently.'

'And could we?'

Patarava grinned. 'We could and we did. It occurred to me that everyone has their own writing style; things like the words and phrases they use, how they structure paragraphs, their grammar. So I instructed the app to analyse all of Connor's published posts and then apply the analysis to his two works in progress, the story about the Met *and* the story we couldn't make any sense of. I got it to run ten thousand iterations, something that would have taken us months, even if we could have seen the patterns.' He clicked his mouse again. 'This is the Met story now. You can see that there are fewer gaps, more complete words.'

Donadze nodded. 'That's great, Koka. It's clearer now but we still need evidence to back up the allegations.'

'I know, it doesn't give us that. But what it does give us is a clearer understanding of his other work in progress.' He clicked his mouse again. 'This is how it looks now. Still not perfect but you can see what he was writing about.'

Donadze sat back to read the screen. 'That's incredible, Koka,' he said, after a long moment.

'Thank you, sir, but it wasn't really—'

'Call Irina and Roman, tell them to meet us here,' he said, standing.

Donadze left the MIR and walked to the station exit, finding a quiet area away from the personnel who were arriving to start their shifts.

Levan Gloveli's phone rang interminably before cutting off.

Donadze called back immediately.

'I hope this is important,' Gloveli grumbled.

'Is Lasha with you, Major?'

'He's in his room, I imagine. Why?'

'I need to speak to him.'

'Now?'

'Yes, now.'

Gloveli sighed. 'I'll get him for you.'

Donadze heard a door being knocked and Lasha's name being called. 'Ramaz wants to speak to you,' Gloveli said.

There was a muffled response.

'Are you still there, Donadze?' Gloveli asked after a moment.

'Yes, I'm still here.'

'He's on his way.'

'Thank you, Major. I'll…' Donadze stopped talking when he realised Gloveli had put his phone down.

A minute passed before it was lifted again. 'Is something wrong, Ramaz?'

'No, there's nothing wrong. Levan told me you bought some *Bitcoin* recently.'

'Yes, but I didn't buy it for myself. It's an investment for Levan and it's already—'

'Gone up in value. Yes, I know. What was the name of the crypto you were originally going to buy?'

'It's called *Newmmus*, it's just been issued, had its ICO a few days ago.'

'What's an ICO?'

'Initial Coin Offering. It's a crowd funding thing. Investors can buy in early before the crypto goes onto a wider market. *Newmmus* seems to be doing okay though. Fifteen million dollars raised at the ICO. Maybe I should have bought into it after all.'

'Why didn't you?'

'There was something in the white paper I didn't like. If it had been my own money, I might have taken a chance but—'

'Lasha,' Donadze interrupted.

'Yes, Ramaz?'

'What's a white paper?'

'It's a kind of marketing tool, a document written to persuade investors to part with their money. In this case, to buy *Newmmus* coins.'

'And there was something about it you didn't like?'

'Yes, I had some doubts about the company behind the issue...'

'You mean the company that created *Newmmus*?'

'Is there a problem with them?'

Donadze ignored the question. 'What was it you didn't like?'

Lasha hesitated. 'I probably shouldn't say this...'

'Say what, Lasha?'

'The company's Georgian, *Newmmus Investments*. But it's owned by a Russian, someone called Anatoly Bazarov.'

'There was something about him that made you suspicious?'

'It's probably just me being prejudiced because he's Russian and because of what happened to Veronika and her family in Ukraine. His promotional video makes the right kind of noises, saying he'd come to Georgia to run his business because he opposes the war in—'

'He's in Georgia?'

'Well, he says he is. But who knows, he could be—'

'Thanks, Lasha,' Donadze said, ending the call.

❖

Roman Ketsbaia had joined Koka Patarava in the MIR when Donadze returned.

'Did you speak to Irina?' he asked.

'She's on her way, sir,' Patarava said. He looked at the wall clock. 'About five minutes.'

'Something going on?' Ketsbaia asked.

'Yes, there is. Thanks to Koka. But let's wait for Irina before we get into it.'

Jaqeli arrived with Misha Arziani a few minutes later. 'You don't mind if I join you, Ramaz?' he asked.

'No problem at all, Misha. And good timing, Koka's about to bring us all up to speed.'

With everyone's attention on him, Patarava blushed as he summarised how he'd used AI to progressively restore the text received from MI5 into something that could be read and understood. 'This is what Connor's Met post looks like now,' he said, projecting it onto the screen.

'And your AI app did that, Koka? That's amazing,' Jaqeli said as she finished reading. 'The future of policing…'

'AI will put us all out of work,' Donadze agreed. 'But not today. You can bring up the second post now, Koka.' He waited until everyone had finished reading. 'What do you think?' he asked.

'It's certainly clear enough,' Arziani said. 'Connor was working on another exposé. But a crypto scam this time. Is that something we know enough about?'

'What do you mean?' Donadze asked.

'Remember the financial analyst who helped us with the First National Bank investigation, Tina Ninua?'

'How could we forget?' Jaqeli asked, straight faced. Ninua was one of Arziani's former girlfriends.

'Yes, okay, Irina,' he said. 'But seriously, if this is a financial crime, we should think about bringing her in.'

'I don't think we have to do that, Misha. Connor explained how the scam works in his blog, we don't need Tina's help to understand it. It's simple enough. Draw in money by promising unrealistic returns on an investment then run off with the cash before anyone catches on. It might be based on crypto this time, but the fraud itself is as old as the hills.'

'This type of fraud is also pretty common now, Captain,' Patarava said. 'It seems that about $100 million a year is stolen through ICO exit scams.'

'The scam's got a name and people still fall for it,' Arziani said. 'Do we know how much was raised at this ICO?'

'Lasha told me fifteen million dollars. But who knows? That number could be fictitious, just another part of the scam.'

'Sounds like it could be substantial though.' Arziani shrugged. 'Okay, Ramaz, we'll leave Tina out of it for now.'

Donadze nodded his thanks. 'I'll call her if we get out of our depth.'

'So,' Jaqeli said. 'Great work by Koka. But we still have the same issue that we have with the Met story—no evidence, only allegations.'

'We'll find the evidence when we find Connor's laptop,' Donadze said.

Arziani shook his head. 'But now you have two suspects: the Metropolitan Police and a Russian scammer. Both with strong motivation to stop Connor's posts going public. Who would you put your money on, Ramaz?'

'I really don't know. But there's only one candidate we can look at for now…'

'The Russian?'

'Yes, the Met are untouchable without evidence.'

'What do we know about Anatoly Bazarov?' Ketsbaia asked.

Jaqeli picked up the laser pointer and played the beam across the screen, highlighting text. 'We know this: Connor gave Bazarov a right to reply to his allegations—and then he died.'

'But that might be a coincidence,' Donadze said. 'We'll find out everything about Bazarov that there is to know. But he's got a Russian passport and possibly fifteen million dollars in his pocket. He might run if we spook him.' He paused a moment. 'I've got an idea…'

Donadze left the MIR and returned to the same quiet spot outside the station entrance.

Meskhi answered his phone almost immediately. 'Lieutenant?'

'Colonel,' Donadze said. 'I need your help.'

THIRTY

The surveillance vehicle was parked on Grishashvili Street, near the Old Town's Sulphur Baths. It was a prestigious and consequently expensive area for any business to rent office space in. Donadze however understood that Newmmus Investments' façade of success and wealth was designed to hook the gullible, their doubt and sound judgement swept aside by the promise of easy money, smug in the knowledge that they'd identified a smart way to get rich.

Donadze realised that he'd not given Lasha credit for recognising the ICO for the scam it was and he made a mental note to congratulate him on his financial acumen, also assuring Levan Gloveli that his money was in—relatively—safe hands.

The surveillance vehicle had been repainted since Donadze had last been inside it and was now branded in the colours of a company providing digital network services. He tapped the rear door and was let in by the comms technician.

Jaqeli was already inside, having agreed to arrive separately. 'Badri's lined up a camera on the office entrance,' she told him.

Donadze observed the screen. He'd walked past the historic building many times but hadn't previously noticed how effectively it'd been converted to a modern office by sympathetically merging its traditional red brick construction with smoked glass, galvanised steel and other modern materials. 'Thanks for your help, Badri,' he said. 'How's our audio feed working?' Meskhi had approved the planting of listening devices in Bazarov's office and these, along with a tap on his land line, were now in place, covertly installed by a police technician who'd temporarily joined the contract cleaning team.

'Nice and clear, Lieutenant. I'll hook you up when the Colonel arrives.'

'It's a pity there's no video.'

'Yes, but that's more difficult to install at short notice, especially if you want a live stream.'

'I know, power for the transmitter's an issue...'

Donadze fidgeted as he drank coffee from the technician's flask and waited for Meskhi's car to arrive. 'At last,' he said as the black SUV pulled up outside Newmmus Investments' door, its flashing grille lights proclaiming its occupant's importance.

The technician pulled on a headset and turned to his control panel. He adjusted the settings then gave Donadze and Jaqeli a thumbs up, signalling for them to put on their own headsets.

Donadze listened as Bazarov spoke, passing on instructions to a member of staff, pausing before speaking again.

'He's on a mobile phone,' the technician said, his voice coming through Donadze's headphones.

Donadze watched the driver get out of the car and hold Meskhi's door open. They exchanged a few words then Meskhi walked briskly to the entrance.

A few minutes passed before Donadze heard a female voice, 'Colonel Meskhi, sir.'

He sat back on his swivel chair and closed his eyes, trying to picture the scene as Meskhi entered Bazarov's office, the Colonel adopting an uncharacteristically deferential tone as he thanked the Russian for seeing him.

Donadze would have liked to have been at the meeting himself, to have talked with Bazarov, to have looked him in the eye and judged if he was responsible for having Connor MacLeod killed. But the Russian would have been suspicious, identifying him as the detective leading MacLeod's murder investigation. In any event, Donadze admitted to himself, Meshki's instincts were as good as his own and they had agreed to confer later.

'I must admit, I'm intrigued, Colonel,' Bazarov said, his Georgian only slightly accented. 'Your office said you needed to talk with me urgently.'

'That's correct, sir.' There was a pause. 'Not many people realise the extent to which police work is intelligence led. A lot of information comes in from different sources and it has to be sifted and assessed for credibility.' Meskhi paused again, before taking on a sombre tone. 'And I'm sorry to advise you, sir, that we have received information which suggests there may be an attempt on your life.'

'I see,' Bazarov said after a long moment. 'That *does* sound urgent,' he tried to joke. 'You said there *may* be an attempt on my life. Does that fall into your *credible* information category?'

'Unfortunately, yes.'

'Do you know who might be involved?'

'We don't have a name yet. And we haven't identified a clear motive either. That's partly why I'm here, to try to understand why an assassin would target you.'

'An *assassin*?'

Meskhi seemed to hesitate. 'I probably shouldn't have used that term…'

'But you did, Colonel. So, you think I'm being targeted by a professional hitman?'

Meskhi changed tack. 'You've been critical of your country's role in Ukraine…'

'And Putin's hired an *assassin* to kill me? I don't think so, Colonel. I'm really not that important.'

'I understand.' Meskhi paused as though thinking. 'You also launched a new crypto currency recently?'

'*Newmmus*, named after my investment house. We've just had its ICO. A great success, I might add.'

'An Initial Coin Offering? That's an early investment opportunity, isn't it?'

'Yes, but what's that got to do with someone wanting me dead?'

'That's what we're trying to determine, sir. Tell me, was there a reason you chose to launch your currency in Georgia?'

'Well, there are always sound financial reasons, of course. All crypto uses a lot of energy, and electricity in Georgia is relatively cheap. But Georgia isn't the only option for cheap power. There are Kuwait and Kazakhstan for example. No, Colonel, the main reason I chose to invest in

Georgia is because Georgia took me in and made me welcome when I needed a home. I wanted to give something back to this country.'

'I see, that's very commendable, sir. You said your ICO was successful. Does that mean you'll be making a wider offering soon?'

'Of course, Colonel. In fact, this coming Wednesday.' Bazarov laughed. 'Are you thinking about investing?'

Meskhi also laughed. 'I might if I understood your business a little better. But what would happen if you weren't able to launch on the wider market?'

'If I were dead, you mean? My company would still go ahead.'

'But without you fronting it?'

'I see what you're getting at. You're right, it might not be as successful,' Bazarov conceded. 'You think that's why I've been targeted? Somebody wants the launch to fail?'

'I don't know, it's one possibility.' Meskhi paused. 'Can *you* think of another?'

'No, of course not.'

There was a moment of silence. 'Well, I don't want you to be too concerned, Mr Bazarov. These things often come to nothing. And, as you said, there's no obvious reason why anyone would want to harm you. But just to be sure, I'll have a patrol car stationed outside your home overnight, at least until we can determine if there really is anything to be worried about.'

'That won't be necessary, Colonel. My company has its own security people.'

Meskhi paused, as though reluctant to agree. 'As you wish. But you will take sensible precautions, I hope?'

'I will. Although you'll understand that I can't live my life based on police *intelligence,* credible or not.'

'Yes, I understand that, sir. Well, I've taken up enough of your time.' Donadze heard a chair being scraped back. 'My card,' Meskhi said. 'Call me if you have any concerns.'

'Thank you for coming, Colonel.'

Donadze kept listening as Meskhi left Bazarov's office. There was a long silence and he looked at the technician. The technician raised his thumb, the audio feed was still working.

'Fuck!' Bazarov exploded, hitting something hard—his desk, Donadze guessed.

Donadze heard a door opening a moment later. 'Is everything okay, Anatoly?' the same female asked.

He pictured the Russian struggling to regain his composure. 'Yes, there's no problem, Megi. Would you bring me a coffee, please?'

'Of course, sir,' the woman replied sweetly, closing the door.

A few minutes passed before Bazarov spoke again. 'I need to see you,' he said in Russian. 'Yes, another job… This evening, eleven o'clock… Somewhere public… Rose Revolution Square, the Giant Bicycle sculpture.'

The conversation ended and a few more minutes passed before Donadze heard Bazarov again. 'We have a problem, sir,' he said, again in Russian, his tone respectful. 'The police were here, a colonel. He thinks someone will try to kill me, an *assassin,* he called him… Yes, it must be the Syrian… I think he's probably made a connection, knows why we had to protect the launch and realised he's also at risk… I know, I remember you said that… Yes, I agree, we should have done something before now… No, he doesn't know the police are looking for him. Not yet, anyway… I've already made arrangements... Tonight, in Rose Revolution Square... I told him to be there at eleven… I understand, there won't be… Yes, sir, I understand.'

There was silence for a long moment. 'Fuck,' Bazarov said again, his voice now soft and despairing.

The technician looked at Donadze expectantly and he nodded, removing his headset.

His phone rang a moment later. 'Yes, Colonel?'

'Bazarov's investing in Georgia because he's grateful to our country? What nonsense. He's in Georgia because he doesn't want to fight in Putin's war.'

'One of many, sir.'

'What did he say after I'd left his office?'

Donadze relayed the conversations he'd heard over his headset.

'So, Bazarov called the hitman *the Syrian* during a phone conversation, that was rather careless, don't you think?'

'I'd say so, Colonel.'

'And the second call, that sounds to me like he was speaking to a superior, someone higher up the chain?'

'That's how it sounded to me as well.'

'So our conspiracy extends beyond Anatoly Bazarov.' Meskhi paused. 'Well, we can't think about that now, Mr Bazarov is our immediate problem. You're confident that he hired this *Syrian* to murder Connor MacLeod?'

'Yes, sir. He said it himself, his ICO was successful. He's made millions and stands to make millions more. Connor would have stopped that happening and that's why he had to die. It was Bazarov who had him killed, I'm certain of that now.'

'And he's meeting the Syrian tonight. What do you think will happen?'

'That was the reason for the second call, Colonel. Bazarov is bringing someone along with him tonight and the Syrian won't be going home afterwards.'

'I agree,' Meskhi said. 'Eleven o'clock then. Better make sure you get there first.'

❖

Donadze was excited, his investigation would soon be over. He didn't have proof yet but knew that Anatoly Bazarov had ordered Connor MacLeod's murder. Meskhi had played his part well, convincing the Russian that his own hitman, whom he'd called The Syrian, would attempt to kill him. The two would meet this evening in Rose Revolution Square where Donadze would be waiting. Much could still go wrong, but the plan he'd proposed to Meskhi had worked—so far. 'Could you ask Captain Arziani and Soso to join us, Koka?' he asked.

'Sir,' Patarava said, reaching for his desk phone. 'Lieutenant Losava's already here,' he added.

'Wonderful,' Donadze said. 'Anyone like a coffee while we're waiting?'

Ketsbaia took the hint. 'I'll get one for you, Lieutenant. Four sugars, right?'

'Only if that's your recommendation, Roman.'

'It is.'

'Thanks, it's always best to consult an expert.'

Patarava put his phone down. 'Ten minutes, Lieutenant.'

Donadze took a seat, allowing his mind to drift. Should he leave the police to be with his wife and daughter in

Germany? Tamuna was patient but she'd expect his decision soon. Solving Connor MacLeod's murder and charging his killers could provide a natural break with police work—if that's what he wanted. *One thing at a time*, he told himself, pushing the dilemma to the back of his mind as Ketsbaia placed a mug in front of him.

Soso Chichua and Misha Arziani entered the room together, followed a moment later by George Losava, commander of the tactical unit which would support the operation that evening.

Donadze stood, offering his hand. 'Thanks for coming over, George,' he said.

Losava was dressed in black fatigues, his black combat boots laced high up his calves, an empty shoulder holster strapped to his broad chest. *Every bit the swaggering warrior*, Donadze thought.

'No problem, Ramaz. Always happy to help.' He gifted Jaqeli a roguish grin. 'Did you miss me, Irina?'

'George,' she replied, unsmiling.

'*Gamarjoba*, Lieutenant,' Ketsbaia greeted his former commander.

'Ketsbaia,' Losava nodded a curt response.

'So, Ramaz,' Arziani said after an awkward pause. 'You've found your man?'

'We think so, Misha.' He turned to Patarava. 'Koka?'

Patarava activated the overhead projector. 'This is the man we're looking for, Captain, a contract killer known as the *Syrian*.' The screen filled with an image of a fit looking man of about forty, his white, even smile contrasting with his black, gelled hair, neatly trimmed beard and thick monobrow, his curly chest hair escaping the confines of a white T-shirt. 'His name's Kinan al-Hadid, a former operative in Syria's Military Intelligence Directorate—the MID. Now selling his services in Georgia and beyond, resident here since 2020. We have a file on him. He's suspected of several high profile assassinations but there's never been enough to bring charges. He's—'

'You've got an address?' Losava interrupted.

'No, Lieutenant,' Patarava said, colouring. 'It's not in his file. Sorry.'

Donadze bit back a reprimand to Losava. 'No need to be sorry, Koka, it's not your fault. And anyway, we don't need an address, George—Hadid's coming to us.'

'Are you sure about that?' Losava demanded.

'As sure as we can be about anything.' He turned to Jaqeli before Losava could respond. 'Tell George about Meskhi's meeting with Bazarov.'

Jaqeli relayed how Colonel Meskhi had told Bazarov that he'd been targeted by an *assassin*. 'He used that term as though by accident,' she said. 'Hoping Bazarov would pick up on it.'

'And he did,' Donadze said. 'He made the connection and understood why the Syrian—Hadid—would want him dead. But of course—'

'Yes, I get it, Donadze. No need to spell it out. Your hitman's a loose end, Bazarov needs him dead but the Syrian's going to get him first—it's not that complicated.'

'Okay, let's keep this civil,' Arziani said. 'Ramaz, why wouldn't Bazarov just take the ICO money and run?'

Donadze took a breath, conscious his fists had clenched. 'He can't do that if we're watching him, Misha—and we are. But I don't think he'll try to get away, not yet anyway. His scam's not run its course yet, there's a lot more money to be made at the full launch.'

'I agree,' Chichua said. 'It'd be difficult for Bazarov to walk away this close to payday. Your plan's good, Lieutenant, there's no reason why it shouldn't work.'

'It's our best chance to flush out Hadid, Misha,' Jaqeli said. 'Colonel Meskhi thinks the same, he wouldn't have given us permission to go ahead otherwise.'

'Okay, I'm convinced,' Arziani said. 'Where do you want us?'

THIRTY-ONE

Colonel Meskhi had joined Donadze in the surveillance van which was parked about fifty metres from the Giant Bicycle sculpture on the opposite side of Rose Revolution Square. Its location had been chosen to provide a clear line of sight to the unlikely artwork and to allow a camera to be lined up on the sculpture and the area immediately around it.

It was almost ten thirty in the evening and the takedown team had been in position since nine. It felt longer. The van was warm and muggy and Donadze tried and failed to stifle a yawn.

'Coffee, Lieutenant?' the technician asked.

'I thought you'd never ask,' he said. He watched the technician unscrew his vacuum flask and pour dark, oily liquid into a plastic cup, a welcome aroma of roasted beans filling the confined space. Donadze reached to take the cup. 'How many is that I owe you now, Badri?' he asked.

The technician smiled, passing Donadze several paper

sachets. 'I don't mind supplying you with coffee, Lieutenant, it's the sugar I can't afford.' He showed the flask to Meskhi.

'*Madloba*, no.' Meskhi shook his head, his eyes fixed on the screen. 'Too many people...'

'That's why Bazarov chose this spot, Colonel.'

'Yes, Lieutenant, I'd realised that.'

Donadze took a sip of the coffee and bit back a response, keeping company with Meskhi was always difficult.

His phone buzzed an incoming message from Roman Ketsbaia: Bazarov was still eating a solitary meal in a restaurant on Rustaveli Avenue. It was a ten minute walk from the restaurant to the sculpture and Donadze thought the Russian would judge his departure to arrive there by eleven, the time he'd specified to Kinan al-Hadid—the Syrian.

'Comms check, Lieutenant?' the technician suggested.

Donadze nodded, reaching for the stalk-mounted microphone. 'Mobile 1, copy?'

'Control, copy,' George Losava replied after a brief delay, sounding bored but—more likely—posturing for his men, Donadze thought.

He completed the comms check and glanced at the CCTV screen. The bicycle sculpture was popular with tourists as a well-known city landmark and with local people as a conspicuous place to meet. There were more civilians in the area than he was happy with, but the square itself was wide and flat with no way to approach unseen; Bazarov's choice of location would work in favour of the police.

Donadze felt uneasy not knowing how Hadid was to be killed. He believed that Bazarov was essentially a conman, with neither the skills nor the courage to take on Hadid himself. It would take a hitman to kill another hitman and the police would have to deal with him when he showed. *Shouldn't over-think it,* he told himself.

His phone buzzed again, *Subject 1 finished meal and asked for check.*

Donadze reached for the microphone. 'All stations, be aware, Subject 1 preparing to move.'

He instructed Jaqeli and Arziani to leave their car and take a table on the patio of a late night cafe, located about forty metres from the sculpture.

He turned to Meskhi.

'Go ahead, Lieutenant. Be careful.'

'Sir,' Donadze said, pulling his sweatshirt hood over his head. He nodded to the technician and slipped out the door as it was opened for him, taking a moment to allow his eyes to adjust to the bright street lights. He waited for a gap in the traffic then crossed the square, swaying as he walked, a vodka bottle swinging from his hand. He reached his designated position, a raised shrub bed and slumped heavily onto its walled enclosure, his back to the sculpture. He placed the bottle by his side and adjusted his hood, his face deep in shadow as he took out his phone to simulate browsing social media and video clips.

A few more minutes passed before Donadze's phone buzzed again. *Subject 1 now left restaurant, walking your direction, following.*

Meskhi spoke over Donadze's earpiece, 'All stations, Subject 1 on the move. ETA this location, ten minutes. Stand by.'

Donadze glanced to his right. A group of about eight young people—students, he guessed—had bunched in front of the sculpture, grinning and displaying two-fingered peace signs as they arranged themselves for their inevitable selfies. Another minute or two passed and—images captured for posterity and social media posts—they drifted away, unaware of the photo-opportunity they were about to miss.

Ketsbaia reported that Bazarov had now passed the Biltmore Hotel, three or four minutes from the sculpture.

Hadid hadn't been spotted yet but Donadze's instinct told him he was close, hiding in shadows as he observed his surroundings, checking it was safe before revealing himself.

The net was being tightened as planned: Soso Chichua taking up position on the far side of the sculpture, supposedly enjoying views over the city as he mumbled into his phone; Losava and his men on standby, ready to secure the perimeter and block possible escape routes; Ketsbaia, Jaqeli and Arziani positioned to follow Bazarov as he entered the square.

Ketsbaia reported Bazarov crossing Inashvili Street. Donadze glanced to his left, easily picking out the Russian in his light-grey suit. He'd stopped walking about one hundred metres out, checking the location for possible threats, Donadze thought. He reached for his vodka bottle and took a slug of water, grimacing theatrically before returning to his phone.

Bazarov must have been reassured by what he saw and continued walking into the square. He reached the sculpture and stopped, looking around, his eyes briefly resting on Chichua who was still conducting a fake conversation over his phone.

'All stations, hold,' Meskhi instructed.

Donadze saw a figure rapidly cross the square towards

the bicycle sculpture where Anatoly Bazarov stood, looking as helpless as a goat in a tiger trap. Hadid had shaved his beard and let his hair grow out but was still recognisable from the photograph Patarava had found. His hand was hanging loosely by his side.

This is it, Donadze thought, his pulse racing. 'Subject 2 confirmed on scene,' he spoke into his microphone.

'All stations, Subject 2 on scene, standby,' Meskhi instructed.

'Gun!' Donadze shouted, observing Hadid's hand rising, his pistol pointing at Bazarov. He ran towards the two men, his own weapon out of its holster and aimed at Hadid. 'Armed police!' he shouted. 'Weapon on the ground! Do it now!'

'Go! Go! Go!' Meskhi ordered.

A mother grabbed her young son and civilians screamed and scattered as the takedown team ran towards the two men, their weapons drawn, bawling the same urgent command, 'Weapon on the ground! Weapon on the ground! Do it now!'

Hadid looked at his pistol as if surprised to see it in his hand. He crouched and placed it on the cobbled road, taking a step back and lacing his hands behind his head, a half-smile playing on his lips. He appeared to recognise Donadze and nodded a greeting. He had started to say something as a bullet hit him in the side of the head and he collapsed onto the road like a puppet whose strings had been cut.

'Shot fired! Shot fired!' Chichua shouted.

Donadze and Ketsbaia instinctively turned back-to-back, their weapons raised, as they tried to determine where the shot had come from.

'Mobile 1, shot fired. Secure area,' Meskhi ordered.

'Sniper,' Ketsbaia said. 'The Radisson.'

'Mobile 1. Sniper location, Radisson Hotel. Secure exits. No one to enter or leave the building.'

Donadze turned to Bazarov. He was crouching, his hands raised as a second bullet blew out his skull, red and grey mist spraying the ground where he fell.

❖

'Weren't these guys supposed to be taken alive?' George Losava asked, looking down on the two bodies. He turned to Roman Ketsbaia. 'Still glad you joined the B team, *Detective*?'

'Every day, Lieutenant.' Ketsbaia winked at his former commander. 'Although, some days more than others.'

Losava's mouth twitched as he tried and failed to find a retort.

'Drop me a text when you get there, Lieutenant,' Ketsbaia said.

Donadze nodded towards the uniformed officers getting out of their patrol car. 'Tell them we'll need most of the square blocked off, Roman. No one gets within fifty metres of these bodies.'

'Sir,' Ketsbaia said, brushing passed Losava.

'What do you want, George?' Donadze asked.

Losava shook his head in mock disappointment. 'Just taking a look, *Ramaz*. Unlike you, my team knows what it's doing. The hotel's contained, we'll find your sniper for you.'

'I hope you do.' Donadze stepped closer to the bigger man. 'But just so we're clear. Insult my detectives again and you and I will no longer be friends.'

Losava's eyes darted left and right, his mouth tightening as he realised his men weren't there to back him up.

Donadze jabbed a finger in his chest. 'On your way, George.'

Losava hesitated a moment then took a backward step, striding passed Donadze towards the Radisson Hotel, a hard man doing tough, dangerous work.

'What was that about, Lieutenant?' Colonel Meskhi asked. He'd left the surveillance van to cross Rose Revolution Square.

Donadze pointed to the Radisson Hotel, about one hundred and fifty metres away, the Giant Bicycle sculpture well within a marksman's range. 'Losava wanted me to know his men have all the exits covered, Colonel.'

'Is that what that was?' Meskhi said dryly. 'What else did he tell you?'

'He thinks the sniper will still be inside the hotel.'

'Is that what *you* think?'

'No, I think he'll be gone. He wouldn't have taken too high a position in the building, the third or fourth level, perhaps. He'd have planned his way out and it wouldn't have been through the main door. Possibly down the fire exit and out through the kitchen. I doubt if Losava's men got to all the exits in time, even if we'd identified them all—and that's something we should have done.'

'No, I don't want to hear that, Donadze. There was always a risk the Syrian would be killed. The only sure way to have prevented that was to have flooded the area with police, but he would have noticed and just stayed clear.'

'Yes, sir, I know. But we lost Bazarov as well…'

Meskhi glanced at the two bodies, blood and brains draining onto the cobbled road. 'Bazarov?' He shrugged his indifference. 'A despicable man, preying on the gullible, ready to kill to cover his tracks and protect his embezzled cash. I have no sympathy for that man—and neither should you.'

Donadze hesitated. 'Thank you, sir.'

Meskhi frowned. 'For what?'

'Your support. This didn't go the way I'd planned.'

'Who says it didn't?'

Donadze gestured towards a GPB news van which was pulling up at the police perimeter. 'They'll say it, Colonel.'

'Oh, you shared your plan with the media?'

'No, of course not.'

'Then how would they know this wasn't what you'd planned.'

'Yes, but—'

'I'm getting tired of this, Donadze. Here's my understanding of what happened. You presented me with a plan to flush out Connor MacLeod's killer. You explained that your suspect was a professional hit man and that you couldn't guarantee he and Bazarov, his employer, would be taken alive—although that was your clear intention.' He looked at Donadze. 'True?'

Donadze nodded. 'True, Colonel.'

'Good. Now, Bazarov and Hadid's murders today confirmed our suspicion that there is a deeper conspiracy behind Connor MacLeod's murder. That will, of course, be investigated. However, thanks to exemplary work by you and your team, Bazarov and Hadid are no longer a threat to the public and the British Home Secretary has seen justice for his son. Furthermore, a massive fraud involving fake cryptocurrency was stopped before more innocent investors could be duped.'

Meskhi looked at Donadze expectantly.

'That's also my understanding, Colonel,' he said at last.

'Then that's what we'll tell GPB News. Now, let's think about Anatoly Bazarov—who wanted him dead?'

'It's obvious, he was another loose end. We were looking at him and he had information he could have given up.'

'I agree. But what if Bazarov wasn't a draft dodger after all?'

'It wasn't just a coincidence that he left Russia before being conscripted, Colonel.'

'Not a coincidence but convincing cover perhaps. What if Bazarov was *sent* to Georgia with a specific mission? Putin's game plan includes destabilising countries he has an interest in. One way of doing that is to disrupt their economies and discredit their financial institutions. And that's nothing new of course; Germany tried to weaken the British economy by flooding the country with fake bank notes during the war. It could be that Bazarov's fake crypto scheme was a modern approach to achieving that same objective.' Meskhi paused. 'Or maybe that's fanciful, it could just have easily been simple criminality. Perhaps involving the *Bratva*,' he added, using the collective term for the Russian mafia.

More patrol cars were arriving and civilians were bunching behind the police tape and barriers, an excited buzz building across Rose Revolution Square.

Meshki's mouth turned down in apparent disapproval. 'Anyway,' he said. 'That's for the future, I seem to remember you're looking for a laptop?'

'Yes, sir.'

'In that case, Lieutenant,' he said, pointing to the dead Syrian. 'I suggest you start looking over there.'

THIRTY-TWO

Tamuna was giving Eka her breakfast when Donadze returned to their apartment. She jumped to her feet to hug him then took a step back, holding his hands as she scrutinised his face. 'Are you alright?' she demanded.

'Yes, fine, just a bit tired.'

'Just a bit tired! Why didn't you call me, Ramaz?'

Donadze frowned. 'About what? The shooting?'

'Yes, the shooting. What else would I be talking about?'

'You saw it on the news?'

'Well, I certainly didn't hear it from *you*, did I? Someone shoots at you and you don't think to call me to say you're okay?'

Tamuna was still gripping his hands, waiting for his answer.

'Nobody shot at *me*, Tamuna.'

'Don't split hairs! You couldn't have known that. And in any case—'

'No, you're right, I didn't think.' He paused. 'I should have called. I don't know why I didn't.'

Her eyes blazed into his for a moment longer then she pulled him into a tight embrace. 'Don't ever do that to us again.'

'No,' he said. 'I won't.'

Eka was watching her parents, a troubled look on her beautiful, innocent face. Donadze lifted her from her high chair and put her on his knee, kissing the top of her head and inhaling the scent of her shampooed hair. 'Don't worry, *chemo gogona.* It's just Daddy being silly.' He blew a raspberry on her neck. 'Again!' he added, as the little girl shrieked with laughter.

'*Silly's* certainly one word to describe you,' Tamuna said pouring him coffee. 'You look tired, Ramaz. When do you have to go back to work?'

Donadze looked at his watch. 'Soon. I just need a shower and change of clothes.'

'What's happening with your investigation? Will it be closed now?'

Donadze shrugged. 'There's still a bit of tidying up to do, then it'll depend on how Meskhi wants to play it. What we need most is the evidence Connor used to corroborate his posts. We've been looking for his laptop but I think that's probably been destroyed by now. Hadid was smart though and would have realised the evidence was too valuable to give up. We searched his hotel room last night and found an external drive and I hope that's where we'll find it. If we get it then the loose ends will be tied up and Meskhi can shut down the investigation, if that's what he wants to do. I'm sure it's what the politicians will want, considering who Connor's father is.'

'So why would Colonel Meskhi do anything different?'

'Because there's something bigger going on. Meskhi thinks it could be the Russian state playing games but it could also be a scam dreamt up by the *Bratva*. We might never know. Anyway, I think we'll probably claim a victory and move on.

'It's a bit more than *claiming* a victory, isn't it?'

'No one gives the police much credit, Tamuna. Victory or not.'

'Well, at least give *yourself* some credit.' She paused a moment. 'Have you thought any more about Stuttgart?'

'I think about it all the time. I want us to be together but it's a big change to leave Georgia and give up the police...'

'I'm not trying to force you into anything, Ramaz. There's no point in going to Germany if you think you'd be miserable there.'

'Or I could be miserable here, on my own,' Donadze said. 'Two more days. Give me two more days to decide.'

❖

Donadze appraised himself in the shower room mirror; he hadn't slept and his face was pale and puffy, his eyes red and gritty. He told himself there was no need to shave then sighed, extracted his electric shaver and ran its heads over his greying stubble, the heat from the foils burning and reddening his neck. Already starting to feel more awake, he took a long, hot shower, playing needles of near-scalding water over his face and head, trying to convince himself that fatigue is only a state of mind. He reluctantly finished showering and towelled himself dry, getting dressed whilst ignoring the temptress in the room: his soft, warm, welcoming bed.

Tamuna had filled his travel cup with coffee. 'Your usual dose of sugar—against my better judgement,' she said.

Donadze was in a hurry to get back to work now. He kissed Tamuna and Eka and left the apartment, hurrying down the stairs to collect his car.

Jaqeli and Patarava had arrived in the MIR before him.

'Irina, Koka,' Donadze greeted them. 'Couldn't sleep or just trying to make me look bad?'

'No, not at all, Lieutenant,' Patarava began before Jaqeli shook her head to stop him. 'Okay, I get it, you're joking.'

'About time. What are you doing?'

'The drive you recovered from Hadid's hotel? I asked Gia to do me a favour and prioritise it.'

'Gia?'

'The analyst the drive was assigned to. He's a gamer, like me. I've never met him in person but he's kind of a friend. We sometimes play PvP together, Fortnite Battle Royale's our favourite.'

Donadze looked at Jaqeli for help.

'Gia's a digital forensic analyst in Tech,' she translated. 'He was asked to crack the password on Kinan al-Hadid's external drive. Koka knows Gia, they play video games together online, player versus player, as opposed to individually against the computer. Fortnite Battle Royale's a game they both like playing.'

Donadze sighed. 'Sometimes I feel the world is passing me by.'

'Don't worry, it's not just you. I knew nothing about gaming until I went out with Misha.'

'I thought he'd given up video games. Didn't he say something about his priorities changing?'

Jaqeli smiled. 'Yes, that's what he said.'

'Okay Koka, that all sounds great. How's Gia getting on with the drive?'

'He's cracked it already, Lieutenant. Simple, he just attacked it with *John the Ripper*, no problem at all.'

Donadze looked at Jaqeli again.

'I'll tell you later,' she said.

Donadze shook his head. 'Don't bother. So, where's the drive now?'

'Still in Gia's lab, he'll send it over soon,' Patarava said. 'But to speed things up a bit, I asked him to extract any Word docs, images and voice memo files first and email them over as soon as he has them—they're the files we're most likely to need'

'Any idea how long that'll take?'

Patarava swung round on his chair and moved his mouse to activate his screen. 'It looks like they're coming in now.'

THIRTY-THREE

'*Gamarjoba*, Lieutenant,' Rory MacLeod answered his phone. 'I had a feeling you'd call.'

'*Gamarjoba*, sir. Is this a good time to talk?'

'It's as good as any. Lesley's here, let me put you on speaker.'

'Good evening, Lieutenant,' MacLeod's wife greeted him a moment later.

'Are you calling about Connor?' MacLeod asked.

'Yes, sir. We're closing our investigation soon and I wanted to make sure you have all the information you need first.'

'Well, Janice Patterson called earlier, I think we have—'

'I'd like to hear the Lieutenant's account first hand if that's alright, Rory,' his wife interrupted, her tone gentle but firm. She paused a moment. 'I'm sorry, Lieutenant, I'm not very good with formalities, may I call you *Ramaz*?'

'Yes, of course.'

'And please call me *Lesley*...'

MacLeod didn't invite Donadze to call him *Rory*. 'Please go ahead, Lieutenant,' he said.

Donadze took a moment to gather his thoughts. 'I should say that this was a complex investigation,' he began. 'We initially believed that Connor had been targeted at random. But that's what his killers wanted us to think. They disguised his murder to look like the work of a would-be serial killer. Someone the media had dubbed *Fenrir* but who was just a sad and disenchanted man whose real name was Aleksi Nachkebia.'

He paused, giving the couple an opportunity to ask questions.

'Yes,' Lesley MacLeod said, her voice now small and tight. 'Quite a notorious case, I believe. I remember watching a report on BBC News. There was some kind of wolf connection. But that was before poor Connor was…'

Donadze gave the woman a moment to compose herself. 'I know this is very difficult for you both,' he said. 'Should I continue?'

'Yes, please carry on,' MacLeod instructed.

'It was Nachkebia himself who told us—who told me—that he wasn't responsible for Connor's murder,' Donadze continued. 'We believed him and that led us to consider alternative motives. We thought that only a professional hitman would have been able to copy Nachkebia so convincingly. And when we searched Connor's apartment, we saw that his laptop had been taken. That led to our hypothesis, which proved accurate, that Connor had been killed because he was about to reveal certain information on his *JournoTruths* website. As it—'

'But that wasn't information about the Met, was it, Lieutenant?' MacLeod interrupted.

'Please, Rory, let Ramaz finish,' Lesley MacLeod said.

'I'll come back to the Metropolitan Police in a moment, if you'll allow me, sir.'

MacLeod grunted reluctant agreement.

'Connor was killed,' Donadze continued, 'because he'd uncovered a scam involving a fake cryptocurrency launch. The mistake he'd made was to give the man behind the scam, a Russian called Anatoly Bazarov, the right to respond before he posted the story. As a credible journalist, that was the professional thing to do—but doing so left him exposed. There was a lot of money in play and Bazarov couldn't allow the truth to come out. So he hired an assassin, a Syrian national called Kinan al-Hadid to silence your son.'

'And now both these men are dead,' MacLeod said.

'Yes, they had information that could have been incriminating to someone above them.'

'But you're closing your investigation down even though you know there *was* someone above them, presumably giving them orders.'

'That's a fair point, Mr MacLeod. We think Bazarov was working for either Russia's security service, the FSB or the Bratva, the Russian mafia. It's even possible the FSB contracted the Bratva to run the scam to destabilise our country. But we have no evidence that anyone other than Bazarov ordered Connor's murder.'

'But you can't be sure of that?'

'No, sir, we can't be sure.'

'But you're still happy to close down—'

'Thank you, Ramaz,' Lesley MacLeod interrupted her husband again. 'That was very helpful and it was kind of you to take the time to speak to us. I'm sure this hasn't been easy for you either.' She hesitated a moment. 'You said you'd come back to us about the Metropolitan Police?'

'Yes, Lesley, I did,' Donadze said. 'The crypto scam wasn't the only story Connor was working on. He'd also reopened his investigation into the Met: serving police officers operating a paedophile ring; senior officers choosing to cover it up.' He paused. 'And a Home Secretary who'd been informed that children were being abused but took no action to—'

'No, Donadze,' MacLeod said, his voice rising. 'That's not what happened. None of this is new. These were all just wild allegations that Connor threw out, none of his claims were ever corroborated. That's why he had to leave the UK and go to Georgia.'

'Well, I must tell you, Mr MacLeod, Connor did corroborate his story in the end. I've read his post and seen the evidence and it's all credible.'

There was a long moment of silence before Lesley MacLeod spoke. 'I'm glad Connor was able to do that, Ramaz. It's vindication for him and it shows that Rory and I should have done more to support him. He shouldn't have had to leave the UK.'

'I'll send you Connor's files, Mr MacLeod. It's up to you what you do with them.'

'You know I won't survive this, don't you, Donadze?' MacLeod said eventually, his voice flat.

'I suspect you'll find a way, sir.'

'We both loved our son, Ramaz,' Lesley MacLeod said. 'Rory will do the right thing.'

'Good. I think Connor deserves that. Is there anything you want to ask me, Lesley?'

'Yes, there is. I want to visit Georgia soon, with Rory if possible. I'd like to meet you and your colleagues, to see the city where our son lived, to talk to his friends. And Dea, I don't want to lose touch with her, she's family now. Do you think that would be okay?'

'I think that's a very good idea, Lesley.'

'Thank you, Ramaz, you've been very kind. But, if I may, there's one last thing I'd ask you to do.'

❖

'So, are you going to tell me?' Jaqeli asked.

'Tell you what?' Donadze said, manoeuvring into the traffic.

'What's on your mind.'

'What makes you think anything's on my mind?'

'You're not your usual chatty self.'

Donadze glanced across to see Jaqeli wink at him.

'Funny,' he said.

'So you're not going to tell me?'

Donadze sighed. 'Tamuna wants me to go to Germany with her.'

'Ah, now that's big. You've told her no?'

'Why do you say that?'

'I just can't imagine you doing anything other than policing. Did you say you *will* go?'

'No, but I need to give her an answer soon. What do *you* think?'

'You want my opinion?'

'Yes.'

'I don't know, Ramaz. Our situations are totally different. Misha and I aren't married yet, we don't have children. But not seeing him for weeks on end would kill me. And as for work, I love this job but there are other things I could try. I don't think you'd find it that easy.'

'So you think I shouldn't go?'

'I didn't say that. But it would be difficult for you to just walk away. Your victims are always on your mind, no murder forgotten.'

'No, never,' he agreed.

'And that's not all…'

'What's not all?' Donadze asked after a moment.

'Nothing. I just realised how much I'd miss you.'

'Don't you start, I'm finding this difficult enough as it is. Anyway, now you know what's on my mind.' He decided to change topics. 'What did you tell Dea?'

'Just that we'd like to chat about the investigation.'

'How is she?'

'She's okay. She has a lot of friends and they're keeping an eye on her.'

'That's good. She's young, she'll find someone new, eventually.'

'Probably, but that's not what she wants to hear right now.'

'I know. Anyway, she's your cousin, you can do the talking.'

'Your delegation skills, that's what I'd miss most if you leave.'

Donadze found a parking space within walking distance of the coffee shop. Dea was waiting for them inside, the building cool and dark, a tantalising aroma of roasted beans and frothed milk competing with the dank stench of mud drying on the riverbanks nearby.

Dea stood and stepped clear of the small, rickety table to kiss her cousin. She looked at Donadze for a moment then pulled him into a long, tight hug. '*Madloba*,' she whispered.

'For what?'

'For Connor.'

'There's no need—' he began but was stopped by Jaqeli putting her hand on his arm.

They sat on tired wooden chairs. A middle aged man left his counter to amble over to their table, his mouth turning down in disapproval when they only ordered coffee.

Jaqeli and Dea exchanged small talk and chatted about family members until their drinks arrived.

'Irina's been keeping you up to date?' Donadze asked, spooning sugar into his cup.

Dea smiled at her cousin and reached to take her hand. 'Yes, she's been great.'

'You know most of what's happened,' Jaqeli said, 'but there have been a couple of recent developments I need to pass on.'

Donadze tuned out as she summarised their investigation to date.

'Poor Rory,' Dea said when Jaqeli had finished. 'He'll never forgive himself…'

Donadze suspected that the Home Secretary would already have justified—to himself at least—his failure to act against the Metropolitan Police. 'Lesley MacLeod is going to visit Tbilisi,' he said. 'She wants to keep in touch.'

'Does she? Good, I want that as well.'

'There's one more thing.' Donadze reached into his jacket pocket. 'She asked me to give you this.'

'Oh, God,' Dea said, her hand going to her mouth. She

took the small jeweller's box from Donadze, stared at it for a moment then opened its lid.

'Should I have changed the box?' Donadze asked.

'No, definitely not,' Dea said, rubbing the ring's mud-stained satin mount. 'It's beautiful.' She looked at Jaqeli. 'Should I put it on?'

Jaqeli nodded. 'Yes, I think you should.'

Dea took the ring from its box and slipped it onto her wedding finger, a single tear running down her cheek. She gazed at the ring for a long moment then raised her hand to kiss it. 'What do I do now?' she pleaded.

Jaqeli took Dea's hands in her own. 'Do what Connor would have wanted you to do,' she said. 'Remember him, but get on with your life, live it the best way you can.'

THIRTY-FOUR

Donadze's phone buzzed an incoming message, *Report to my office this morning. Advise arrival time.*

'Meskhi wants to see me,' he told Tamuna.

She finished buckling Eka into her highchair. 'That's okay, I'll take a taxi into work.'

'No, I said I'd take you. I'll drop you off first then drive over to his office.'

'If you're sure.' She clipped a plastic bib around Eka's neck and placed a bowl of milky oatmeal on the highchair's tray. 'What does he want to see you about?' she asked.

Donadze scooped oatmeal onto a plastic spoon and held it to his daughter's lips. 'I don't know. Maybe some kind of debrief. Or it could be another case he wants me to take on, something that needs an *unconventional* approach.'

'You don't sound very happy about it?'

'It's not that I'm *unhappy*. Just that, whatever I do, it's never quite enough for him.'

'He must have been pleased that you solved Connor MacLeod's murder?'

'It's difficult to tell. He was supportive at least, especially as no one is going to trial.'

'Well, at least you have an option now.'

'Yes, I know, Germany. Let's talk about it this evening.' He picked up his phone. 'I need to get back to him, what time do you want to leave?'

'Eliso will be here by eight, can we go after that?'

'Yes, that'll be fine,' he said, typing a reply, *ETA 0930.*

Tamuna finished drinking her coffee and stood. 'I can get ready in peace now that you're not rushing away.'

'Take your time,' he told her, recovering spilt oatmeal from the bib's food catcher and reoffering it to his daughter whilst singing about cheeky baby birds being fed wriggly worms by their mothers who trilled *tweet, tweet, tweet.*

Times like this, when he was alone with his daughter were rare and to be treasured. He thought about the letter of resignation he was drafting in his head, imagining how satisfying it would be to commit it to paper, to sign it and hand it over to Meskhi, to know that he wouldn't be separated from his family for the next year or more. But he also knew that being a detective defined him in some way, that it might not be enough for him to live in a city he didn't know, unable to do the job he was born for.

'What should I do, *chemo patara*?' he asked his daughter.

She responded by blowing an oatmeal thickened raspberry in his face.

'Good advice,' he told her, smiling as he wiped the cereal away.

Eliso arrived on time and he and Tamuna left the apartment a few minutes later, Eka already turning her attention to the games she wanted to play with her nanny.

They took the elevator to the underground car park and set off to the Medifirst Clinic.

'They're going to miss you here,' Donadze said as he pulled into the drop off area.

'Not for long, Ramaz. The graveyards are full of indispensable people.'

'Who said that?'

'My father. And it's true. Something you should think about.'

'Well, I will now…'

'Ramaz...' She waited until she had his full attention. 'Make your decision for the right reasons. Don't decide because you're scared you'll lose Eka and me or because you're angry with Colonel Meskhi. You *won't* lose your family and Meskhi won't always be your boss. You don't have to do anything rash.'

Donadze leaned over and kissed her. 'Thanks, I won't.'

She held his gaze for a moment then kissed him back and got out of the car.

He watched as she walked to the entrance, turning to wave before going through the clinic's double doors.

Don't do anything rash, he told himself as he signalled to pull out of the drop off area. He arrived at the MIA building, collected his pass and took the elevator to the fourth level. He walked to Meshki's office and knocked on the door, pushing it open.

Meskhi looked up from his desk. 'Donadze,' he said in greeting. 'You're early.'

'Yes, sir. Should I come back?'

Meskhi closed his eyes and sighed. 'That won't be necessary.' He pointed to his conference table. 'Take a seat while I finish this email.'

Donadze crossed the office and sat down, watching Meshki's back as he tapped rapidly on his keyboard. He finished typing, then read from his screen before clicking his mouse to send the mail. 'Sorry,' he said, standing. 'I promised the Deputy Minister he'd have that by ten.'

Donadze couldn't remember Meskhi apologising for anything. 'That's no problem, sir,' he said.

Meskhi joined Donadze at the conference table. 'I'm sure you've heard that Captain Arziani is taking on a new role?'

Donadze had been asked by Arziani not to speak to anyone about his move. 'Yes, sir, I'd heard,' he said.

'And you'll have realised that leaves a vacancy for commanding officer at Mtatsminda Station?'

'Yes, sir. Of course.'

'Well, I'm afraid that can't be you,' Meskhi stated. He paused a moment. 'I realise you may find that disappointing, but I don't think you're suited to *any* command role. I don't think you'd like it and I don't think it's where you would be most effective. Do you agree?'

'Would it make a difference if I did or didn't, Colonel?'

Meskhi drummed his fingers on the table top. 'Not to a decision I've already made,' he conceded. 'You have many talents, but management isn't one of them.' He paused, his gaze on Donadze. 'That said, none of my detectives could have handled these investigations the way you did—and I don't want to lose you. Not in the long term anyway.'

'Sir?'

'You're considering resigning from the police and following your family to Germany.'

Donadze leaned forward on his seat. 'How could you know that, Colonel?'

'An acquaintance, not somebody you know, told me your wife is going to Stuttgart,' Meskhi said. 'I assumed that's what's been bothering you lately.'

'It's true. My family are going to Germany but I haven't decided what I'll do yet.'

'Good. There may be another way. You're aware that Georgia has an operational and strategic cooperation agreement with Europol?'

'Yes, of course. I've requested Europol's support in previous investigations.'

'I know you have. Well, it appears the Minister has identified a need to strengthen these ties. Especially in areas such as money laundering and human trafficking, aspects of international criminality that you're already familiar with.'

'The *Minister* identified a need?'

'He's open to advice. Regardless, a position has become available. A one-year secondment to The Hague as liaison officer. Are you interested?'

'The Hague, sir?'

'Europol's HQ. You'd be based in The Netherlands but would travel to all member states—especially the largest and most influential. A country whose support Georgia will eventually need to achieve EU accession.'

'Germany…'

'Yes.'

Donadze held Meskhi's gaze for a long moment. 'Why are you doing this, Colonel?'

'Doing what? The Minister tasked me to find a suitable candidate for the role. That candidate is you, Donadze—but I have other officers in mind should you not be interested.'

Donadze felt a wave of relief wash over him. 'Thank you, sir. I accept.'

'Do you want to think about it? I could give you two days.'

'No, sir. That won't be necessary.'

'Good.' Meskhi slid an envelope across the table. 'Your letter of appointment. Read it outside, Captain.'

'Captain?'

'Yes, Donadze, Captain. Read it outside.'

The End

ACKNOWLEDGEMENTS

Writing and publishing a book is a collaborative exercise and I'm incredibly grateful to the people who gave me their time and encouragement to help develop No Murder Forgotten into—what I hope—is an enjoyable and informative read.

My wife, Jacqui Liddle reads everything I write first and last, telling me what does and doesn't work and holding her ground when I argue the point.

My 'beta readers' were Annette Rose; Tom Stewart; Fiona Russell; Mary Puttock; Douglas King; David Main; Brian McKinstry; Josh McIntyre; my daughter, Kirsty McMillan and my son, Ross Liddle who generously read and critiqued my draft manuscript. Feedback can sometimes be difficult to hear but the finished product is so much better for it.

Although I worked and lived in Georgia for many years, getting cultural aspects right is important to me and I was again advised by my Georgian friends, Sandro Chitadze and Nino Meladze on the quality and authenticity of my writing.

Ruth Sherpa is an incredible proofreader. I thought I'd nailed every annoying typo but, inevitably, I hadn't and Ruth flushed out the survivors.

Georgia is a wonderful country with a unique language and culture and I sprinkle Georgian words and phrases throughout my books to add flavour and a sense of place. If I've done my job properly the meaning of these words and phrases should be obvious, given the context in which they are used. If you would like more information, please visit my website—ajliddlebooks.com—where you will see and hear them spoken and explained (a kind of online glossary) in conversation with my good friend, Maka Gogia.

I am indebted to my author friends, busy people who nevertheless found time to read and provide their assessment of my completed book: G.R. Halliday; Marion Todd; Mark Wightman; Craig Robertson; Marsali Taylor; Lydia Travers; Gordon Brown (aka Morgan Cry); Andrew James Greig; Adam Oyebanji; Mac Logan; Jonathan Whitelaw; Allan Martin and Emma Christie. It was a real buzz to receive positive feedback from writers of such quality.

ABOUT THE AUTHOR

Alistair Liddle is a former ships' captain, business advisor and operations manager in the oil and gas industry. No Murder Forgotten is the fourth novel in his series featuring Lieutenant Ramaz Donadze.

Alistair is married with two grown children, a granddaughter and a grandson. His interests, when not writing, include travel, walking, cooking, supporting Heart of Midlothian FC, swimming in Scotland's beautiful lochs and playing guitar badly with his old-boy band, The Grumps.

After a lifetime of travel, Alistair has settled in Stirling, Scotland.

Visit Alistair at ajliddlebooks.com

AUTHOR'S NOTE

I lived and worked in the Republic of Georgia for fifteen years and the country has been a big part of my life. Covid restricted travel for several years but Jacqui and I returned in 2024 and this book is set in the summer of that year.

Much of what we saw during our visit was familiar and the welcome we received from our Georgian friends as warm as ever. However, the war between Russia and Ukraine continued to grind on, with memories of Georgia's own war with Russia on people's minds. That and the perception that the ruling parliamentary party was turning the country unwillingly away from its western-leaning trajectory provided the background for much of this book.

Printed in Dunstable, United Kingdom

66324592R00194